FOR ALL OF EV

She's a modern woman in love with a medieval knight. He imagines her ghostly image. Will love be enough to bring them together?
Sometimes to find your future, you must look to the past…

Katherine Wakefield has dreamed of her knight in shining armor all her life. Never finding a man to measure up to her imagination, she and her three closest friends take a trip to England. But she never could have anticipated the strange turn of events when visiting Bamburgh Castle and she's thrown back in time.

Riorden de Deveraux knows his past life is about to catch up. But nothing prepares him for the beautiful vision of a strangely clad ghost who first appears in his chamber. And when they strike up an otherworldly conversation, he never could have predicted that she would capture his heart.

With centuries that should keep Katherine from her love, she holds tight to a fragile hope of staying. But when his past could consume their joint future, Riorden will do whatever it takes to keep them together. Will time tear apart the ultimate love affair?

FOR ALL OF EVER

THE KNIGHTS OF BERWYK, A QUEST THROUGH TIME NOVEL (BOOK ONE)

SHERRY EWING

Copyright © 2014 by Sherry Ewing

All rights reserved. No part of this book may be reproduced in any form or by any electronic or mechanical means, including information storage and retrieval systems, without written permission from the publisher, except for the use of brief quotations in a book review.

Kingsburg Press
P.O. Box 475146
San Francisco, CA 94147
www.kingsburgpress.com

Publisher's Note: This is a work of fiction. Names, characters, places, and incidents are a product of the author's imagination. Locales and public names are sometimes used for atmospheric purposes. Any resemblance to actual people, living or dead, or to businesses, companies, events, institutions, or locales is completely coincidental.

Editor: Barbara Millman Cole
Front Cover by SelfPubBookCover.com/Tigerlily

For All of Ever/Sherry Ewing -- 1st ed.
ISBN 13 978-0-9905462-3-8
ISBN eBook 978-0-9905462-2-1
Library of Congress Control Number: 2014919577

OTHER BOOKS BY SHERRY EWING

Medieval & Time Travel Series

Knight of Darkness: The Knights of the Anarchy (Book One)

Knight of Chaos: The Knights of the Anarchy (Book Two)

Knight of Havoc: The Knights of the Anarchy (Book Three)

To Love A Scottish Laird: De Wolfe Pack

Connected World

To Love An English Knight: De Wolfe Pack

Connected World

If My Heart Could See You: The MacLarens (Book One)

For All of Ever: The Knights of Berwyck,

A Quest Through Time (Book One)

Only For You: The Knights of Berwyck,

A Quest Through Time (Book Two)

Hearts Across Time: The Knights of Berwyck,

A Quest Through Time (Books One & Two)

A special box set of For All of Ever & Only For You

A Knight To Call My Own: The MacLarens (Book Two)

To Follow My Heart: The Knights of Berwyck,

A Quest Through Time (Book Three)

The Piper's Lady: The MacLarens (Book Three)

Love Will Find You: The Knights of Berwyck,

A Quest Through Time (Book Four)

One Last Kiss: The Knights of Berwyck,

A Quest Through Time (Book Five)

Promises Made At Midnight: The Knights of Berwyck,

A Quest Through Time (Book Six)

It Began With A Kiss: The MacLarens (Book Four)

Regency

A Kiss for Charity: A de Courtenay Novella (Book One)

The Earl Takes A Wife: A de Courtenay Novella (Book Two)

Before I Found You: A de Courtenay Novella (Book Three)

Nothing But Time: A Family of Worth (Book One)

One Moment In Time: A Family of Worth (Book Two)

A Love Beyond Time: A Family of Worth (Book Three) in the Bluestocking Belles boxset *Under the Harvest Moon (2023)*

Under the Mistletoe

A Mistletoe Kiss in the Bluestocking Belles boxset *Belles & Beaux* (2022)

A Second Chance At Love

A Countess to Remember

To Claim A Lyon's Heart: Lyon's Den Connected World

The Lyon and His Promise: Lyon's Den Connected World

Learn more about Sherry's books on her website at www.SherryEwing.com/books

Join Sherry's newsletter at http://bit.ly/2vGrqQM

DEDICATION

For my beautiful daughter Jessica Ann

*The little girl who grew up to become someone
I call my best friend.
Her gift of song always fills my heart
with immeasurable joy. I'm so proud of you, Jessie.
Mom loves you!*

PROLOGUE

Once, there were four young women who were such good friends, they considered themselves to be genuine sisters of the heart. Together they dreamed that each would find true love and her very own knight in shining armor.

But, as women of the twenty-first century, they found themselves hard pressed to find gentlemen who had the knightly virtues dreams are made of — genuine men who knew the real meaning of chivalry and protecting one's lady from all manner of harm.

For many years, they had unrelentingly searched for true chivalrous men. Now their resolve had begun to waver, and all were on the verge of giving up hope of ever finding such men worthy of their love until...well...

This is their story...

CHAPTER 1

San Francisco, California
Present Day, Spring

Katherine Wakefield looked up from her laptop, noticed the time, and quickly saved her work. Running toward the bathroom, she looked in the mirror and saw her disheveled appearance. Taking off her computer eyeglasses, she grabbed a towel to rub the smudges from the lenses, and then hooked the glasses in the neckline of her shirt. She looked tired, with dark circles under her bluish-green eyes...not that anyone would care or bother to notice. These days, more often than not, she just felt plain invisible.

Knowing she was running late, she grabbed her brush and a tiny barrette to clasp her blondish-brown hair in a small ponytail atop her head. Forgoing makeup, she went to her bedroom and searched for her purse, which had somehow found its way beneath her bed.

She was half way through the living room before realizing she was still wearing her slippers. With an exasperated sigh, she went back to her bedroom, found her sneakers, and then rushed to her desk to search for her keys. With a quick glance at her small apartment, it was clear she would need to do something soon about all the research scattered from one end to the other. She continually put off the inevitable job of cleaning by justifying to herself that it was organized chaos. At the very least, she could say the kitchen was clean.

Placing a pen behind her ear, she picked up the small spiral notebook she always carried with her then locked her apartment door. She hated when she forgot it, which wasn't often. Those rare times when she did was usually when she inevitably came up with some brilliant idea for a plot twist in her latest work-in-progress. Her friends tried to remind her that her smartphone could perform the same function, but she was a bit old fashioned.

Nothing like a good pad of paper and a pen, Katherine thought, as she hurried down the block. *For some things, technology is highly overrated. Give me a good book with pages to turn. Surely, that's better than anything electronic.*

She quickened her pace and was thankful the coffee shop, where she was to meet her girlfriends, was at least downhill. Though her return would not be as fast moving since she knew she would huff and puff her way back up the mountainside. She loved living in the San Francisco area, but really...who thought of the ridiculous notion of building a city into and on top of a mountain?

The coffee shop loomed up ahead on the corner, and Katherine waited for the light to turn red before crossing the busy street. She had almost reached her destination when she was shoved, causing the contents of her purse to go spilling onto the sidewalk as she tried to catch herself from falling. Without even the slightest show of an apology, the gentleman, and she thought that word loosely, went inside the café. *Perfect*, she thought, as she stooped to gather her meager possessions. Then, quickly composing herself, she entered the busy establishment.

She let her eyes adjust to the dimly lit room after being out in the bright sunshine, while she breathed deeply the heavenly aroma of fresh brewed coffee that filled the air. Seeing the line was to the door with almost every table filled to capacity, she sighed. Such was usually the case on a Saturday morning. Conversations in multiple languages hummed in the room, filling her senses while she looked for her friends.

"Katie!" She heard her name called and saw the three women she had searched for seated in a corner booth. Brianna waved a coffee cup in her hand and beckoned Katherine with a welcoming smile. At least her friends were thoughtful enough to have already ordered for her.

She began to weave her way through the crowd and sat down with a huff, pulling out her notebook and searching her purse for her pen.

"Umm, Katie..." Juliana said, trying to get her attention.

Katherine looked up and observed her friend pointing to her ear. She felt behind her own until her hand came in contact with her errant pen, which had all but been forgotten in her haste to see her friends.

"Sorry," Katherine said sheepishly, "it's been one of those mornings."

"You've been writing," Juliana and Brianna replied at the same time, and both broke out into girlish giggles.

"Drink your coffee and chillax for a while, sis," Emily chimed in, without looking up from her laptop while the keys clicked and clacked as she typed. She, too, was apparently on a writing roll.

Katherine sat back, took a sip of her drink, and almost moaned in pleasure as the hot coffee slipped down her throat to warm her. It was the small things in life that made life worth living, even if it was only her daily caffeine fix to make her smile. Her friends all went back to their respective writing projects. This was their normal weekend routine, when they got together each Saturday to write before they gave way to sharing what their week had brought them. Katherine took this time to contemplate each of her dearest friends, while she drank her coffee.

They called themselves members of the Hopeless Romantic's Unite ~ *Carpe Diem* Club. *Carpe Diem*...Latin for seize the day. Katherine couldn't remember the last time she had seized the day, let alone anything else for that matter. Still, she was thankful for the friendship she had found with the three women who sat opposite her at the table. They were as dear to her as any sister could ever be.

Juliana was the oldest of their group, at twenty-six, although Katherine herself was only a few days shy of her. Tall, with a dark complexion, her long wavy black hair hung down past her waist and was the envy of many. Juliana, or Jewels to her friends, had eyes the color of light green that, to Katherine's thinking, were her biggest asset. She was strikingly beautiful, in a classical sense of the word, and tended to be the mother of their little group, always ensuring everyone was well taken care of. Jewels was their rock foundation.

Brianna, or Brie, was the prankster of the bunch and had a vitality for life that was sometimes hard to keep up with, but such is the case of the young at heart. She was olive skinned with short, dark black hair, brown eyes, and had recently taken up self-defense classes. It was hard to imagine teeny, tiny, little Brianna in such a class. Then again, she was a smidgen rebellious at times, so maybe it shouldn't have come as any surprise. Not only could this amazing, twenty-three year old woman write, she also created her own compositions and played guitar. With her gift of language, Katherine considered Brianna the Queen of Rhyme.

Last, but certainly not least, was Emily, who just turned twenty-three, as well. She was tall, with wavy, long, sandy colored hair and green eyes the color of the tropical sea. Emily always complained she would never find a man who was taller than her, and she was tired of trying. She hated her height. Though, in Katherine's opinion, Emily was elegantly statuesque. She had at one point in her life wanted to pursue a career in acting, but the call to write took precedence. She was currently working on four books, all at the same time. It was a shame, though, that she would not at least give more effort to performing on the stage. Granted, acting was a rough field to excel in. But what really was sad, was that Emily could sing like no other vocalist Katherine had ever heard. Emily could make the angels above weep from the purity of her voice, and her friends had counted themselves blessed on numerous occasions to hear her songs lifted to the heavens, even if it was only while driving in the car.

The four had become true sisters in every sense of the word and, at one time or another, had wept alongside whichever friend currently had her heart broken. Oh, they had their arguments, like any siblings who had been raised together would have shared, but for the most part, they all had a common bond...to find true love and, with its finding, know such a thing could really exist. At this point in their lives, they all doubted that it did.

"We're a fine group," Katherine sulked. "What we need is a bit of an adventure."

The women looked up and began saving their work or, in Katherine's case, setting aside pen and paper.

"Be careful what you wish for," Juliana cautioned, the voice of reason in their group. "You never know what karma will throw your way."

"I hate the bar scene," Emily said with conviction. "I won't go looking to pick up some random guy that way."

They all nodded their heads in agreement.

Brianna couldn't wait to chime in. "I heard, if you're looking to meet men, you should go where they hang out."

"Well, we can spend all our hard earned money from working our modest jobs and go to all the baseball and football games we like, but in the end, we'd still be without dates," Juliana replied quickly.

"Been there, done that," Katherine retorted with a shrug. "Besides, we've been saving up all our money to go on a vacation somewhere together. Maybe we should decide on where we'd like to travel?"

"The tropics," Juliana offered hopefully. "We should go to Hawaii."

"Too humid, and most of you have already been there before," Emily said. "Besides, I'd burn to a crisp in all that sun."

"Well, I'm not going any place where it rains twenty-four-seven just to make you happy, Emily," retorted Brianna, crossing her arms in an obvious display of feeling put out. Everyone knew that Emily just loved the rain, but it was hardly what the rest of them would want on a daily occurrence for their dream vacations.

Katherine closed her eyes. A vision of a castle came to her mind. "England," she whispered breathlessly.

Juliana gave a merry laugh. "I suppose, if we're to ever get any rest from your endless desire to set foot on the battlements of a castle wall, we should at the very least consider a trip over the pond."

"You all must think I'm just acting like some naïve school kid," Katherine declared sadly. "Forget it. We can find another place everyone would be happy with."

"I never said I wouldn't be happy going to England," Juliana replied and patted Katherine's hand in comfort.

"Katie's idea does have some appeal," Emily said and looked to Brianna, whose eyes had begun to twinkle in happiness. "We could travel up to Scotland, too, or maybe over to Ireland. I always wanted to see where my great-grandparents came from."

Katherine watched in delight as the conversation took flight and ideas of where to travel once they were abroad went round and round with her friends. She fingered her notebook and thought of the handsome knight she had written about in her latest manuscript. He was the stuff dreams were made of and occupied her mind, day and night. The funny thing about this particular character was she had been dreaming of him for as long as she could remember. She didn't want her friends to think she was crazy, however, so she'd never said anything about her dreams. Instead, she wrote about him and he lived on paper as a figment of her imagination.

"Don't be too disappointed if you don't find him in England, Katie," murmured Juliana.

"Who's that?" Katherine asked softly.

"Your knight in shining armor, that's who, my friend."

The conversation came to a screeching halt as one woman looked to the other. It was a topic they all had on their minds of late.

"You'd think they'd know where to find us," Brianna said, looking around the coffee shop. From the grimace plastered on her face, she obviously didn't see any men worthy of consideration.

"All mine have been left out in the rain too long and, I'm afraid, have rusted solid," Juliana added. "Maybe if we head to England, we can find a castle pit and throw all the men who ever broke our hearts into it together."

"I can cast a spell on them while they're down there awaiting their impending doom," Brianna chimed in happily.

Emily laughed. "That won't work. Between the four of us, there'll be so many of them, they'll just climb, one on top of the other, to their freedom."

They all seemed to get the same vision in their heads, of their ex-boyfriends trying to scramble to reach the top of some slimy pit without success, and burst out laughing. When their amusement subsided, Katherine's mind wandered, not even seeing the crowded coffee shop anymore.

"Maybe we shouldn't be so picky," Katherine said quietly.

"Well, I, for one, won't settle for anything less than what I want out of a relationship," Emily replied, then took a sip of her hot chocolate. "If he's not up to my standards, he's history!"

Katherine nodded her head in agreement but continued staring out into space at nothing in particular.

"It's Bamburgh again, isn't it?" Juliana guessed.

Katherine looked up at her friend and gave her a small smile. "You know me only too well, Jewels," she proclaimed. "I just can't seem to help myself from thinking of the place, no matter where I might be."

"What's so special about Bamburgh, more than any other castle you've dreamed about over the years?" asked Emily curiously.

Katherine gazed sheepishly around the table at her friends and gave them a slow smile. She had only told Juliana of what had happened to her one day while she was surfing the internet.

"I was typing away on my story when my fingers stiffened above the keys. A writer's worst nightmare hit me as though I was being slammed up against the wall. Writers block. Nothing would come to me, no matter how hard I tried to concentrate. Having figured there was no sense trying to force my character to talk to me, I had spent some time looking at images of various castles on the internet, trying to get inspired to write again. And then…there it was…a link for a virtual tour of Bamburgh Castle. I had felt drawn to the place, sensing the many souls who had walked the castle passageways over the centuries, and as if one of those souls was calling out to me."

She glanced at her friends to determine if they thought she was crazy. Seeing the look of interest on their faces, she continued. "I was scrolling with the mouse on the site's virtual tour page, moving the mouse in such a way I had felt as though I had been actually walking across a battlement wall. A strange sensation came over me. My hand froze, refusing to move, and goose bumps raised up on my arms, as if my fate had walked across my soul. It was as though a scene from another time was playing before my very eyes. I actually felt as if I was standing on the castle wall itself, feeling the wind upon my face. I could taste the saltiness of the ocean mist on my lips and could see several knights standing vigilantly at their posts."

"No way," Brianna shouted out.

"Hush up, Brie," Emily interjected giving the girl a poke in the arm.

"Ouch! Cut it out, Em" Brianna grumbled with a none-too gentle shove of her own.

Juliana held up her hand to silence the two women. "Both of you behave. Go on, Katie."

"One knight, in particular, came toward me with a confident stride, his dark blue cloak billowing behind him in the ocean breeze. As he came closer, I saw the imprint of a black lion's head on his tabard, and I wondered at its meaning. With his helmet held under one arm, he reached up with his free hand and removed the chainmail helm from his head. It was at that precise moment that I knew him. He was so very tall that when he came to stand in front of me, I had to lean my head back just to look at him. His black hair fell in a wave to his broad shoulders, but it was his piercing blue eyes, as he gazed at me, that left me feeling completely stunned. He took my breath away with just one look, especially when he held out his hand for me to take. I remember reaching out to feel its warmth.

"Then a car horn sounded out on the street and brought me back to my senses. I know this may seem odd, but I never felt at such a loss as when I found myself sitting back at my desk," Katherine said with a trace of sadness to her voice. She finished in a hushed whisper. "I still can almost feel the heat of his touch."

Brianna and Emily could only stare at her, their mouths open yet silent. Juliana gave a small smile and drank her coffee, having already heard the story more than once.

Before anyone could speak, Katherine continued. "I suppose it explains much of why I can't fall in love with a modern man, when none of them can even begin to measure up to what I experienced then, if only for an instant."

"It's almost too much to believe," Emily said, the first to recover from Katherine's story. "I know you would never lie to us. I just wish something like that would happen to me."

"No wonder you're always saying you were born in the wrong

century, Katie, if you have these kinds of visions," sighed Brianna. "I mean, you should have seen your face while you were talking about him. It completely transformed to show so much longing while your words poured out from your heart. If only time travel were possible. You could go back and find him."

"Wouldn't that be somewhat messing with the whole fabric-of-time issue?" Emily replied sarcastically.

"Not if she was really meant to go back, it wouldn't!" Brianna retaliated.

"Ladies, let's get a grip on the conversation shall we? Since we can't obviously go back in time, and our knights have all turned a little rusty, I say there is only one conclusion for our vacation together," Juliana said, as if the decision, in all their minds, had already been made.

"Bamburgh!" The four women replied in unison and raised their cups in a unified salute of agreement.

Katherine looked at her best friends with hopeful eyes. To Bamburgh they would go, and at long last, she would have a stamp in her otherwise empty passport. She could at the very least then say she had been somewhere in her life where medieval English history had once been made. It was more than she could ever hope for, and a slow smile lit Katherine's face. For what her friends didn't know, since she had kept the secret to herself, was that the handsome knight she had envisioned at Bamburgh...well...he was the very same knight from her dreams.

CHAPTER 2

The Year of Our Lord's Grace 1179
Berwyck Castle

*R*iorden de Deveraux strode sure-footed in his steps along the narrow parapet walkway. He nodded to the guards he passed, who stood at their posts as lookout for any who approached the castle grounds. Yet, no enemy came near, and none had for several years. Berwyck's people had known only peace and prosperity while under the careful watch of the first Earl of Berwyck. One with any sense would think twice afore attempting to take any lands claimed by the Devil's Dragon.

Riorden chuckled at the thought of his lifelong friend. At the prime of his career as champion for King Henry II, he had been called the Devil's Dragon of Blackmore and had quite the reputation of instilling fear into those around him. Dristan still held such a reputation in some of those same circles, but if the truth were to be told, his lord had become a bit domesticated of late. *Such is the fate of a married man*, Riorden supposed. Aye, the cause could almost certainly be laid at the feet of Dristan's beautiful wife, Amiria, or mayhap, even fatherhood. Still, Riorden would never underestimate Dristan in the lists, for that is when one ended up on one's backside in the dirt. Dristan radiated sheer power and a fierceness with which few could contend. 'Twas considered a privilege to train with the man, and more so to call him a friend, although not many could claim such a kinship.

With a shake of his head, he turned his gaze south and watched as the ocean waves crashed loudly onto the sandy beach below. 'Twas a favorite location of the Lady Amiria, and he would often catch her unaware in this very place. Riorden laughed aloud, thinking of the few times he was actually able to take said lady off guard. 'Twas a rare occasion to be sure, and usually included having a sword or dirk to one's throat, if one was not too careful.

The woman was a bit of a spitfire, which seemed somewhat fitting, given the length of her glorious red hair. She was the perfect companion for his lord. However, he was glad he was not tied to a woman of such determination to always have her way or give aid when the need arose. Dristan had told him, on numerous occasions, he would never change a thing about his lovely wife, and he loved her just as she was. Amiria could wield a sword as no other woman of Riorden's acquaintance. When it became time, he had no issue pledging his life in her service just as fully as he served Dristan as captain of his guard.

Riorden leaned his gloved hands on the battlement wall and sighed. There was not much of a chance of him finding a lady of his own here at Berwyck, and the village whores only offered satisfaction to his baser needs. Not that he was truly looking for a wife since years afore he had been soured by a lying, deceitful lady. He did not feel love truly existed for him.

Life was what one made of it although serving another lord with no castle walls of one's own to call home was not much of a life in which to raise one's family. It did not hold much merit for most women he had ever encountered. Each had wanted to be the lady of her own hall, with servants aplenty. Love had seemingly passed him by, and good riddance! At the age of a score and thirteen, he decided a solitary life was how the remainder of his days would be spent. Some days, he cared not that he would have no lady by his side, and yet there were times he felt the bitter stab of jealousy. When he heard the childish laughter of Dristan's son, sadness would overcome him, knowing he would never have a child to follow in his footsteps.

He heard his name called and stood upright, trying to shake off his sudden melancholy mood. Women! They either drove one mad from wanting them or with their demands for one's attention. Either was just as bad as the other and a distraction Riorden did not need wreaking havoc with his mind.

Turning, he saw Fletcher making his way up the stairs to stand beside him on the parapet. Fletcher bore the same uncanny resemblance to all of the other men personally chosen over the years for Dristan's personal guard. He, too, had black hair as dark as night, but where Riorden's eyes were a deep blue, Fletcher's were an amber colored brown with golden flecks residing in their irises. 'Twas a striking combination that only enhanced his good looks and had many a maid beckoning to him over the years. Fletcher felt 'twas his duty in life to never leave a maid saying he did not pleasure her to her fullest potential. So far, he bragged, he had succeeded in his quest.

"Is there aught amiss?" Riorden questioned, as they both now stared out to the sea's distant horizon.

"Depends on how you look at it, I suppose, Riorden," Fletcher answered. "A messenger has arrived from the king. Dristan requests we join him in his solar, posthaste."

They began to carefully make their way off the narrow walkway and down the steps heading to one of the towers housing a set of circular stairways leading to the lower floors, one of which housed the keep's family. The sound of their armor clanking against the stones echoed and ricocheted off the walls as they made their way below. When they reached the third floor landing, they turned left and continued on down the passageway 'til they reached Dristan's solar door. Riorden knocked and heard the call to enter.

Opening the door, Riorden was not surprised to witness the entire family gathered within the chamber. There was only one exception, for one of the daughters, Sabina, had desired a life at a nearby abbey. Dristan sat at his desk, perusing various parchments demanding his attention. Berwyck Castle was but one of his many estates, both in England and abroad in France. If he was not in the lists, keeping his form fit and pursuing the continual training of his knights, Dristan would be found here in this room, attending to business with his steward; ensuring the rents were collected, petitions were addressed, and justice was dispensed.

Amiria sat comfortably in a chair close to the warmth of the fire. She continued to fidget and reposition herself. Perhaps, given she was heavy with child, she was not as comfortable as she wished to be. Riorden watched in amusement as the lady continually reached to finger the hilt of the sword her husband had gifted to her afore their marriage. 'Twas kept at her side, although Dristan had forbidden her to lift it lest she wished to endure his wrath. Her son Royce, who was aged three summers, was toddling around his father's desk 'til his sire made a grab for the lad and threw him up in the air, much to the delight of the boy. He squealed with laughter as Dristan began to tickle him.

Amiria's twin brother Aiden sat on the floor at his sister's feet, sharpening a dirk. Their resemblance was a bit uncanny although whereas Amiria's form was petite, given her womanly stature, the same could not be said of her brother. At a score and four, 'twas clear Aiden had been spending much of his time in the lists, training with Dristan. 'Twas the only place he ever wanted to be, since he felt 'twas his irresponsibility the castle had fallen to the English.

Still, after four years, he felt no ill will towards Dristan. Anyone could see for themselves, Amiria's marriage was a happy one, and Aiden had made it known he was pleased for his sister and her husband. Unfortunately, since Aiden had one day hoped to be lord of Berwyck, he felt restless with the need to prove himself in the world and make a name for himself. Riorden did not think Aiden would remain much longer at Berwyck.

The youngest daughter of the old laird Douglas MacLaren was Lynet, who sat on a stool on the other side of her sister with a bit of stitchery in her nimble fingers. She was a rare beauty with hair the color of golden honey and eyes as blue as a clear sky above. In the past five years, Lynet had become a bit defiant, much like her sister had been at the same age of ten and nine. She was not as yet wed as most girls her age. Unfortunate for those lads brave enough to enter the

Devil's Dragon's lair, she refused all offers brought forward and made clear to all who cared to listen, she would wed only for love. Amiria had sworn to ensure this would come to pass. Riorden could only begin to imagine the pains Dristan must bear, dealing with two headstrong women under his care. Many a night had Dristan and Riorden shared a drink or two to ponder the fools who only sought the gold a union with Lynet would bring. The true treasure that would be brought to a marriage with the Lady Lynet was the lady herself.

The last family member present was young Patrick, who stood behind Dristan staring out the small window, looking towards the inner and outer baileys. Black hair with brown eyes, he was now aged ten and three summers and had taken his previous duties as Dristan's page most seriously, along with his studies. For reasons only Dristan knew for certain, the boy had not been sent off to foster with another lord so he could begin the proper duties of squire. 'Twas the next logical step in order to one day earn his spurs and claim a knighthood.

"My lord," Riorden said as he came to stand before Dristan with a bow. "You called for me?"

Dristan tossed Royce up into the air one last time before placing him on the floor and rumpling his hair. Amiria called to the boy, and he went to sit on the floor next to his Uncle and began to play with a bit of wool, which was left near Lynet's feet. He seemed content to sit there, but for how long was anyone's guess. He was a most curious boy and not one to sit for any length of time in one place.

Dristan came and leaned against the edge of his desk, leisurely perusing Riorden. As Dristan's captain, he waited patiently for his orders and tucked his gloves into the belt at his waist. Although Riorden thought of Dristan as his liege lord, they were, in truth, more than that. They were even more than just friends and comrades-in-arms.

They had grown up together since Riorden had come to Dristan's father's estate to serve as a page, and they had gotten into more mischief than two lads should at such a young age. At least, that was the tale Dristan's mother had proclaimed on numerous occasions in their youth. So alike, they could have been brothers. Same black hair down to their shoulders; same broad shoulders with chiseled features on their visage; same physical form of rippling, lean muscle from years of training or fighting to stay alive; same ability to train, no matter the weather conditions, and preferring a challenge rather than an easy win in the lists; same ability to kill when the need arose; and same sense of honor and chivalry, despite their perceived reputations of severing heads of any left in their wake.

The only difference between the two men was the color of their eyes. Whereas Dristan's eyes were the hue of cold grey steel, Riorden's were an unusual shade of the deepest blue. Amiria had often mentioned that perchance the angels rejoiced when they saw the extent of color God had graced in his eyes. Surely, many a maid could easily fall under his spell and never want to leave if he were to but gaze upon them, she had teased. Though he had never met one to go so far as to ask her to be his lady wife.

Their apparent silence at an end, Dristan reached back onto his desk, retrieved a piece of parchment, and handed the document to his lifelong friend. Riorden read the missive, but he had to read it a second time in order for the words to take meaning inside his head. Even a third reading did not, unfortunately, change its wording.

Dristan raked his hands through his hair, although regret remained on his features. "You are to leave us, it appears. You have been summoned to Bamburgh Castle where the king will soon be in residence."

"Why would King Henry wish to have me at hand at Bamburgh?" Riorden asked as he too ran his hand through his hair in frustration.

"You would refuse his command?" Dristan queried, raising a brow at his friend.

"I may question his motives and reasoning, but I would never be so foolish as to decline such a request," Riorden declared as he began to pace to and fro within the chamber. He bumped into Fletcher, who grumbled about the state of his toes, afore he once more stood in one place.

"You will be missed, Riorden," Amiria and Aiden said together, exchanging a silent look, which only twins could possibly share or interpret.

Riorden stared silently at those souls within the chamber who, for the most part, were the closest thing he could call his family. They all began to stand, although they, too, were seemingly at a loss of words.

Dristan came to him and clasped his hand on his shoulder. "It appears there is not much else for me to say after the two of us have traveled and fought beside one another for as long as I can remember. So...since you do not care to have ownership to the title and lands that are rightfully yours from your sire, which I will never understand, you leave me no choice than to see to matters myself. I will have no knight of mine and from my household going to the king lacking," Dristan announced, breaking the silence of the room. "Patrick," he called and watched as the boy turned his gaze as if seeing the room for the first time.

"Aye, my Lord Dristan," Patrick answered when he came to stand before his liege with a bow.

"You have served me well these many years, Patrick, but it seems fate has other plans for us, for she is a fickle mistress," Dristan proclaimed and turned the boy to face Riorden. "As you have served me, now go and serve your new master as his squire. He will need you more than I during his days at court, I think."

"Dristan, really, I cannot–" Riorden began.

"As you wish, my lord," Patrick answered promptly, ignoring Riorden's protests.

Patrick knelt, bowing his head and holding out his hands towards his new liege as if in prayer and complete submission. He patiently waited 'til Riorden at last came to his senses and clasped the boy's outstretched hands in his own.

It seemed as if Patrick's oath of fealty to Riorden came easily to his lips, almost as though he had waited a lifetime to make such a commitment and sacrifice. "I, Patrick of Berwyck and of Clan MacLaren, do so swear on my faith in God the Almighty, to serve thee as my liege lord, Riorden de Deveraux. I promise in the future to be faithful to my lord, never causing you harm, and will observe my homage to you completely; against all persons, in good faith, and without deceit."

"I accept thee as my vassal," Riorden whispered and watched as Patrick stood afore him with pride.

"Watch over my brother, Riorden, and do not fail me in his care. I know you will do right by him in continuing his training so that he, too, may be a great knight someday," Dristan replied, and the two men clasped each other's shoulders once more.

"Of course, I will ensure his training and care, Dristan."

Dristan nodded and gave a bit of a smirk. "He can be a bit mischievous, our young Patrick here, which is not much of a surprise, given who his sister is."

"Dristan...really!" Amiria said, aghast, as she managed to remove a dirk from her boot and point it at her husband.

"You see what I must contend with?" Dristan laughed with an amused quirk of his brow towards his wife. He came to her and rested his hand upon her shoulder, which had a calming effect. "Now I have another, who seems hell bent to avoid wedded bliss no matter how many worthy lads I lay at her feet."

Lynet could be heard muttering a very unladylike reply and took up a stance at the now vacated window. Everyone in the room knew the reason behind her continued rejections, for Lynet had fallen in love with Amiria's captain, who had not graced the walls of the castle for nigh unto five years. 'Twas doubtful Ian would return anytime soon.

When the family began to leave the chamber in preparation of Riorden and Patrick's departure, Riorden went to the young girl. As he drew near, he saw upon her face one lone tear running slowly down her cheek. Before she could brush it away, he reached out to cup her face. Ever so slowly, he brushed his thumb across the smoothness of her face to dry her tears.

He gave her a brief embrace, this young girl who had been like a little sister to him, and took her chin so she would stare up into his eyes.

"If Ian does not come to his senses soon, Lynet, he never will. Do not shed one more of your precious tears on his behalf since he will not be worthy of them," he whispered. "Promise me you will not spend your life pining away for someone who could not see the prize that was right afore his very eyes. You deserve much better than that."

Lynet only stood there, trying to find the words to ease his mind.

"Your promise to me, Lynet," Riorden urged.

Lynet gave a heavy sigh of resignation. "Aye, I promise, Riorden. Safe travels and God speed to you."

"Good lass. I shall endeavor to return soon to ensure you have kept your word, for I am sure our paths shall cross again." Giving her a quick kiss on the forehead, he left her standing there and made his way to collect his belongings.

The courtyard was filled with familiar faces, people who had come to wish him well as he traveled to serve the king. Riorden's goodbyes were brief and to the point, for there was no sense dwelling on what this place had come to mean to him. Dristan lifted his hand in farewell, and he returned the gesture. Gathering the reins of his mount, he turned his mighty war horse and proceeded through the inner and outer baileys.

He looked back only once to see Berwyck off in the distance, afore he turned his attention to the road ahead of him. At least, he was not alone with only Patrick for a traveling companion. Aiden had joined his company.

CHAPTER 3

Bamburgh, England
Present Day, Spring

Katherine pulled into the car park of the inn. With a heavy sigh of relief, she turned off the rental car. Leaning her head back, she gratefully closed her eyes amid kudos from her friends for her driving skill. Skill...that word was almost a joke, considering her hands felt as if they were still clenched in a steely grip on the wheel. Driving on the wrong side of the road with everything she knew about driving being backwards was no small feat, and she was glad to have this last leg of their journey at an end.

The four women unloaded their luggage and started making their way to check in. The hotel was small, cozy looking, and fashioned in a lovely Tudor style. Upon entering, Katherine could almost envision the dark paneled room from days of old, filled with locals as they drank their mead or lounged near the fireplace that took the chill from the room. Although exhausted, she took a moment to look with longing out the window at a small portion of Bamburgh Castle in the distance. As much as she wanted to rush there to see its sights, it would have to wait until the morning. With the coming sunset, visiting hours would soon be over for the day.

"Katie," Juliana called as she waited on the stairs with Emily. "Are you coming?"

Brianna came up next to Katherine and gently took her bag. "It's been standing there for centuries waiting for you, sis." Katherine's face must have shown her desire for where her heart really wanted to take her. "It will still be there for you tomorrow."

Turning her gaze from the window, she slowly made her way up the stairs, feeling as if the weight of the world rested on her shoulders. Brianna opened the bedroom door, since it was their turn to share a room. It was quaint with tiny lavender floral wallpaper on the walls, rich mahogany bedposts, and easy-on-the-eye, pale blue quilts for bedspreads. Katherine went to one of the beds and lay down as visions of their trip flashed in her memory.

To say this had been a dream vacation would be an understatement. Between the four of them, they had spent a small fortune, but it had been worth every penny. Traveling throughout Scotland and England, they had hit as many sights as they could cram into one day and gotten a good taste of what life here was all about. Emily had looked as though she felt she had tasted heaven itself, Brianna had been busy composing a song, Juliana's pen never seemed to stop its writing unless she was to take her turn at the wheel, and as for herself...well...Katherine felt that if she were to die tomorrow, she would be content.

There had only been one time that had marred an otherwise perfect vacation for Katherine. The ruins of Warkworth Castle, where they had stopped on their way to Bamburgh, had brought her to her knees in grief. She had no clue as to why such was the case. It wasn't as though she hadn't seen other similar ruins that had also saddened her in their travels within the past week. But for some unknown reason, she couldn't find any comfort in the hollow shell of the keep, which the ravages of time had been rather unkind to over the centuries. She had almost felt as if a piece of her, inside, had died that day, especially when her friends had to help her from the ground.

Was that really only yesterday? she wondered, not for the first time this day. What was it about those ruins that could have affected her so? She would have thought such a reaction would occur at Bamburgh. It had taken everything within her not to rush to the castle, if only to lay her hands on its outer walls and feel the cold rough stones beneath her fingertips. She only had to wait until tomorrow for it to become a reality.

Brianna came over to place a light blanket over her. "Get some rest, sis. I'll take care of putting our stuff away."

"You sure you don't want some help," Katherine said, even as she felt her eyelids become heavy.

"Nah, I got it."

Katherine rolled over on the bed and watched Brianna begin to busily put away their clothes. She smiled as she heard her friend humming the tune she had been working on for most of the day. With no motivation to do anything else this afternoon, she closed her eyes and dreamed…

∽

He stood before her with his hand outstretched for her to take, a bit of arrogance and impatience clearly etched across his features.

"Is it you?" she heard herself ask, even though she would have known this man before her no matter where in time he had found her.

"I only mean to keep you safe," he declared, not answering her question as he shifted uneasily on his feet. His eyes were ever watchful on the knights standing guard nearby.

"Yes, I know. Have you seen me before?" she asked quietly, hoping that he, too, had dreamed of her.

He gazed down upon her, searching her face until the ocean winds whipped the hood on her cloak from her head then watched with interest as her hair became tossed about. Finally, he reached out to catch one of her errant curls. The tendril wrapped itself around his hand, almost as if laying some kind of claim to him. He began rubbing the tresses between his fingers as if memorizing the silkiness of her locks. She watched as he came back to his senses, and he frowned, she assumed, at her words. "You're speech is most strange, **mademoiselle.**"

"I'm not from...the area."

"You travel with King Henry? Mayhap, you are one of the ladies in waiting at court?" he inquired. One look at her humble cloak would have told him this wasn't the case.

"No," she replied simply, for what explanation of where she came from would make sense to him.

"You're sire is here then. Perchance, I may return you to his side so I can ensure your safety," he concluded. Once more, he held out his hand for her to take.

She acknowledged his gesture with only a sad smile. "I suppose I'll one day see my parents again, but I think it's impossible for now."

"Then let me, at the very least, see you inside the keep so I may rest, knowing you are not in danger."

She looked up into his blue eyes and began to wonder if she'd ever seen their color on another. To say they were blue, didn't do them justice. She had dreamed of him for so many years, she could only stare in wonder that he really stood before her. There was no doubt she trusted him, so she did the most natural thing she could do. Smiling, she looked into his eyes as she reached out to take his hand.

Neither was prepared for the reaction of their hands touching, nay, going through one another. For in truth, they did not stand there in the flesh. They were but memories of what could have been, if only they had been born in the same century. Their heartrending loss brought tears of sorrow to her eyes. With only one look at his face, she knew he felt it, too.

"I do know of you..." he whispered, his voice like a silken caress across her soul.

"You're name!" she cried out. "Tell me your name!"

He began to fade from her vision, yet still, she heard his voice clearly inside her head. "Katherine...come back to me, my love—"

"I will find you," she promised him as a mist appeared, surrounding his body until he was at last taken from her sight. Emptiness consumed her entire being with the knowledge he might be lost to her forevermore. She could do only one thing, now that he had been torn from her side. She wept.

CHAPTER 4

⌘

Bamburgh Castle
The Year of Our Lord's Grace 1179

"*I will find you...*" Riorden awoke with a start, still hearing the haunting words and seeing the tears of the woman from his dreams. There had been such longing in her voice that, for some unknown reason, the sound seemed achingly familiar. Yet, he knew her not...or so he thought. So why did he know her name?

He threw the coverlets off and rose naked from his bed. Kneeling afore the hearth, he began to rekindle the few remaining embers into a small semblance of a blaze. It took but a few moments 'til most of the chill began to recede from the room as the fire grew brighter. As he went to grab his tunic, he noticed his hands were actually shaking. *God's wounds! What is wrong with me?* He continued to watch his hands as if they were not his own 'til, disgusted, he donned his remaining garments.

Despite the fact he had just warmed the room, he went to the shutter and flung it wide open, letting in the cool air to clear his confused head. He peered out into the early morning hours, but 'twas still too dark to see much of anything. Looking back into the chamber, his brow furrowed. It had all begun with this damn room.

After pouring a chalice of wine, Riorden sat upon a stool and ran his still trembling fingers through his mussed hair, recounting the events of the past hours. Upon his arrival yester eve, he had assumed he would be shown to the Garrison Hall. Instead, a servant had shown him to a richly appointed chamber. Afore the man had left, he had informed Riorden the table held instructions from His Majesty King Henry.

He had begun to walk across the room to retrieve the missive, when he had halted as he had felt a presence in the chamber with him. A shadow of a woman had appeared, dressed in the oddest blue hose he had ever seen. Her strange lavender tunic was cut shockingly low with some sort of odd fasteners running down the front of the garment. Tawny colored hair fell well past her shoulders in soft waves of long, loose curls, which flowed teasingly when she moved. She had been touching the frame of the bedpost, almost reverently, 'til she at last had turned to stare upon him, as if she had finally taken note that he, too, was there. Recognition had flashed across her face with a look of such yearning reflected in her aquamarine eyes, it had torn at his heart, for he had never in his life seen a sign of elation of this magnitude in another.

He remembered having rubbed his eyes to clear his vision of what surely must have been some kind of trickery, and she had been gone. At the time, he had shaken off what he knew was his imagination making a fool of him. He had begun to leave the room to find Aiden and had not gone but a few steps past his door into the passageway when, blinking his eyes in disbelief from what he was seeing, he had had no doubt that his mind was once more playing games with him. There she had stood, yet again, looking just as lovely as she had but moments afore inside his chamber.

This time, she had been walking down the corridor towards him whilst brushing her hand along the stones of the wall. His footsteps had faltered and he had felt unable to move by what he was witnessing. He had stared in wide eyed fascination at the strange lights hanging from the ceiling. 'Twas not any kind of candelabrum he had ever seen afore. Even the torches placed in the sconces on the wall had not been familiar to him.

The woman's tinkling, merry laughter had rung out, drawing his attention back to her. The sound of her unmistakable joy, which he had been privy to hear, had filled his head with a sense of contentment. He had wondered what she had found so entertaining to make her face radiate such happiness. Her smile had lit up her entire visage with so much delight that it almost seemed unfair that he had not been able to join her in the knowledge of whatever had pleased her so.

She had continued her steps toward him, but afore he could comprehend her actions, she had begun to vanish, passing right through him and causing his breath to catch in his throat. 'Twas as if they had been one, for the briefest of instances, as he had felt an icy shudder rush through his entire body. He had turned, scanning the passageway behind him, but there had been no sight of her. In truth, if he had not seen her for himself, he would have thought she had not been there at all. Yet, with her disappearance, he had felt a strange, unknown sense of regret, almost as if he had lost something most precious to him.

A shiver that had nothing to do with the breeze coming from the window began at the top of Riorden's head and made its way clear down to his feet whilst he was brought back to the present. 'Twas almost as if the dead were calling to him from the grave with these hallucinations of ghosts. But why, then, would he dream of her? Did she have some message to impart to him? Who was she and, more importantly, why did he feel as if he, in truth, knew who she was? She had appeared so real when she had come to him in his sleep, and even now, he could feel the bitter disappointment when he had lost her in his dream as the mist had all but consumed them.

Riorden stood, grabbed the wooden shutter, and closed it with a soft click as the latch fell into place. He turned and stared at the obnoxious, dark blue, velvet box he had all but forgotten the day afore. *No good will come of whatever it holds*, he thought, as he made his way to the table. Reaching out for the parchment, he broke the wax seal of the king and scanned the brief few words that seemed to blur as he read. *'Tis time to claim your birthright* swam afore his eyes, along with the king's signature. Opening the box, he swore, for inside was his father's signet ring. Set in heavy gold, a lion's head carved from black onyx looked back at him with mocking eyes. The fact that the ring was here could only mean one thing. His father was dead, and the title Riorden never wanted now belonged to him. Damn his father's soul to hell!

He shut the lid with a snap. 'Twas obvious King Henry had plans for him, and with this subtle message, he would be duty bound to return to Warkworth, despite his desire never to set foot upon that land ever again. But 'twould not be this day, and, 'til the king came into residence here at Bamburgh, Riorden would continue to put off the inevitable.

A short knock came at the side chamber where a sleepy eyed Patrick entered. "My lord, you dressed without me assisting," he cried out in disappointment.

"Not quite. Help me don this armor, Patrick. I must needs get out of this place, once the sun has risen. We shall find Aiden, break our fast, and head to the stables. Perhaps, a ride on the strand will clear my head."

"Does something ail you, Lord Riorden? I can seek out the castle's healer, if there is a need."

"Nay. 'Twas just a restless night, Patrick, not that I need to explain myself," Riorden declared briskly.

"My apologies, my lord. I forgot myself."

Riorden grumbled beneath his breath, hearing the words *my lord* one too many times to his liking. He did not care for this form of address when it was referring to him, and yet, he had the distinct feeling 'twas something he must needs get used to.

The ritual of donning one's armor took some time, but 'twas better to be prepared, since he did not have a guard to call his own watching his back. Riorden cursed, knowing this would be the next thing to irritate him if the king was to have his way. He quickly realized Patrick was chattering away, and he had no idea what the lad had been saying.

"...and I have heard tell the place is full of ghosties."

"What place?"

"Well, Bamburgh, of course. I hope we do not run into any that are restless with incomplete business. Do you think 'tis true, Lord Riorden?" Patrick said with a fearful, squeaky voice.

Riorden looked quickly about his chamber for the apparition that had appeared afore him and yet he saw nothing but the room.

"Come, Patrick, and let us be about this day," Riorden uttered, not answering his squires question.

They made their way to the tower stairs to the sound of Riorden's metal armor clanking then descended to the lower floor. He would put away his fanciful thoughts of the woman in his dreams, wanting nothing more than to enjoy what he could of the morn to its fullest. First, to find Aiden, and then some much needed food. Surely, everything would appear normal on a full stomach.

∽

Present Day

Katherine's footsteps faltered suddenly on the tower stairs. She felt dizzy, and it wasn't from the fact that these blasted circular stone steps were oddly laid. No! She was dizzy because she could have sworn she had caught a vague glimpse of her knight ahead of her in the turret!

"Come on, you pansy," Emily prompted with a laugh. "I told you I'd help you down."

"You and your silly fear of heights," Brianna said smugly as she hopped down two stairs at a time.

Katherine threw them both a look, silencing any further laughter. "It's not silly, and it's not the height that's the problem...well, maybe it is a little," she declared. "Don't you hear it?"

They all stood there in silence, waiting to hear something that, apparently, only Katherine could hear.

"I don't hear anything other than tourists," Juliana replied.

"Shh!" Katherine hissed as she held up her hand and listened intently. She noticed her friends continued to stand in place, patiently waiting for something to happen. "There it is again."

"What?" Brianna, Juliana, and Emily asked, all at the same time.

Katherine looked at her friends and could only whisper her answer.

"Armor." She noticed the shock on their faces. "Now let's hurry, and Emily, please help me."

"Well, you're the one who's taking so long and has to put both feet on one stair before you move on to the next. You're such a pan–"

"Don't you dare call me a pansy again, Emily... Just get me down these damn stairs!" Katherine shrieked.

It was slow going until Katherine was at last on a lower level floor. Looking for her knight, she observed only the busy hall, overflowing with tourists milling around. Their voices and accents annoyed her as their chatter filled the room.

"Well? Do you still hear it, Katie?" Juliana questioned awkwardly.

Katherine only shook her head. "No. It's all silent now. Dammit...you guys are going to think I'm nuts."

"We'd never think that, Katie," Emily replied.

"Please don't worry, sis. It'll be okay, so don't look so crestfallen," Juliana reassured her with a pat on her shoulder.

"Ooh! I like that word, *crestfallen*. Can I use it, Jewels, for my dialog I've been stuck on?" Brianna asked hopefully.

"Brie!" Juliana and Emily screeched together.

"It's okay, guys. I do feel rather crestfallen," Katherine croaked through a forced smile.

"It *is* a great word," Brianna declared brightly.

"Let's grab us some lunch and have a picnic on the beach," Emily suggested. "I know you love this place Katie, but to be honest, although Bamburgh is magnificent, it makes me a little uneasy. For some reason, it gives me the creeps...as though, I can almost feel the suffering that has gone on in its history."

"Of course it gives you the creeps, silly. The brochure says it's haunted," Brianna announced and pulled the pamphlet out of her purse.

"Not now, you two. Can't you see Katie is having a hard time?" Juliana said and began ushering the younger women through the throng of tourists.

"I'll catch up in a minute," Katherine called out.

Leaning her head back, she peered up to once more glance into the turret, straining to keep her sanity, yet at the same time, knowing she hadn't imagined things. She couldn't shake the intense feeling that something, or someone, was calling to her. Her nerves were stretched taut, almost to the point where she felt as if they were breaking. To steady herself, Katherine placed her hand on the stones in front of her, the wall of the stairs leading up into the tower. An electrical shock jolted up her arm, causing her to jerk her hand back, rubbing her numb fingertips. Now *that* was something real, and surely, not just her over active imagination. What the hell was going on with her and this place?

She needed fresh air…that's what she needed. Turning into the Great Hall to catch up with her friends, she found herself riveted to the floor. Even if she'd wanted to move, she couldn't have. Hardly believing what she was seeing, she became mesmerized when the tourists milling around the chamber slowly vanished before her eyes.

Only one man was left standing at the far end of the room, or rather, one knight. He had been reaching for something on a table when Katherine saw his shoulders flinch. His red cape swirled around his legs when he turned to face her. Their eyes locked and Katherine's breath left her at the intensity reflected in his face. Shock, intermingled with excitement, rushed through her. Her whole body began to tingle. *Good God, it's him!* Her mind screamed. He stood there with such a commanding presence about him that she had no recourse but to move in his direction.

Inch by inch, the distance between them lessened as he, too, moved swiftly across the floor. Her arm extended, she reached for him, and yet their meeting was not to be. He quickly vanished, passing right through her. Her body lurched from the contact when the wispy vapor that had been him disintegrated upon their meeting. A soft cry of distress escaped her lips. How could fate be so cruel as to take him from her before they could speak even one word together?

Modern surroundings returned, and Katherine became disorientated when she was rudely bumped by some jerk, who didn't even mutter an apology. She swiveled around, trying to see if her knight was maybe still lurking in the hall, but there was no trace of him.

She had taken no more than a few short steps, when a voice whispered inside her head. *Katherine…come back to me, my love.* Practically falling into a nearby chair, her hands began to tremble uncontrollably. Certainly, she couldn't mistake the words that had come upon her, for he had called out her name. Jesus Christ! It was just like in her dream. She ran from the room as if a burning fire were licking at her shoes.

Her friends gave her a what-the-hell-took-you-so-long look, but Katherine only shrugged. She decided, then and there, to keep what had just happened to herself for a change. The last thing she needed was her friends to think she should be admitted into the closest psych ward.

It was a beautiful day outside, but Katherine saw none of it, as their little group made its way down to the beach. She refused to go too far from the castle, so they plopped themselves down on the sand with Bamburgh's shadows surrounding them. They ate their sandwiches with their normal, easy conversation, but something was different. Not with her friends, but with herself. It wasn't too long before her friends decided to take a walk down the beach. Katherine assured them that she would be fine and just needed some time alone.

She watched them go to enjoy the afternoon, but Katherine could only feel a sense of loss surrounding her heart. She gazed back over her shoulder where the walls of the castle loomed high above her. Pulling her legs close to her chest, she rested her head on her arms and knees. Try as she might, she couldn't make sense of the confusion coursing through her. She gave a weary sigh and felt on the verge of crying.

A sound, almost like thunder, registered in her senses. But even knowing there wasn't a cloud in the sky, she looked up. Three riders were fast approaching. As they drew closer, she noticed how one raised his hand and stopped to stare in her direction. Startled, her mouth hung open in silence, and she could only surmise she must have fallen asleep. How else, but in a dream, could her knight be riding to her side?

CHAPTER 5

Riorden raised his hand and halted his group's progress along the beach. They had pushed their steeds hard this morn as they galloped along the strand, but that is not what had caused him to stop their return to Bamburgh. There, against the backdrop of the castle, was the woman who had appeared to him yester eve. The very same woman from his dream, and the one he had seen in both the passageway and the Great Hall. Her clothing was unchanged, but he could not, for the life of him, explain her odd garments.

Aiden came abreast of Riorden's horse with a question upon his visage. "Is something amiss?"

Riorden quirked his brow, letting out the breath he had been holding. "Do you see the woman there?" he asked, pointing in the direction of the sand dune ahead of them.

He watched as Aiden's gaze swept the sand, but apparently he saw nothing out of the ordinary; just the ocean, the beach, and the castle looming high above. "I see naught, Riorden, and certainly nary a woman."

"You will think I am mad when I tell you I see her, but I assure you, I am not."

"'Tis a ghostie," Patrick whispered as he began to cross himself to ward off any evil spirits.

"Hush, Patrick," Aiden told his brother.

Riorden watched as Aiden searched his face, as if to check to see if he were, in truth, a bit mad. He refused to feel ill at ease. So he showed the younger man as normal an appearance as he could muster, to prove he was, indeed, in control of his senses. He nodded to Aiden, who relaxed and leaned back into his saddle to await his orders.

"Stay here," Riorden commanded, and then kicked his horse forward 'til he came abreast of the woman sitting on the blanket in the sand. His horse reared as if spooked, and he watched the woman rapidly move in fear of being trampled beneath the heavy hooves. She tripped on the blanket she had been sitting on, but quickly regained her footing to stand afore him although 'twas done somewhat shakily. He got control over his steed and slid from the saddle, giving his mount's neck a calming pat. It seemed placated as it now stood still as stone.

Riorden removed his gauntlets and placed them on the saddle. To say that he was hesitant to come too close to this ghostly apparition, was an understatement. As he drew closer, Riorden tried to conceal his shock when he saw the woman had her oddly shaped hose rolled up, exposing her ankles. As he gazed at her feet peeking through the sand, he backed up, thinking perchance she was plagued with some sort of malady since her toes were oddly colored. Still, he could not take his eyes from her although, in truth, she was but a vague transparent vision and, mayhap, merely a figment of his imagination.

"I can't believe it's you," she exclaimed in a hushed, excited tone, more to herself, he thought, than for his ears. "But, you're dressed differently."

Riorden's brow drew together in confusion. Looking down at his attire, he saw nothing out of the ordinary of how he had garbed himself for the past ten years. They were Dristan's colors, true, but he saw no harm in wearing the garments 'til ordered otherwise by his king. His eyes widened in further disbelief. Although he had seen her mouth moving, her words were not spoken out loud. They came, instead, into his head. He scowled in frustration, thinking he appeared an imbecile. He understood nary of what was going on, but he cared naught for it at all!

"Who are you," he questioned irritably, "and what is it you want from me, ghost?"

"Ghost? What are you talking about?" she replied. There was just a touch of annoyance in her stance to show she was as affected as he by what was happening to them. "You're the ghost, not me."

A forced laugh burst from his lips, and Riorden placed his arms across his chest in an attempt to recover his senses. "'Tis just my luck, I come upon a spirit not of this world, and she does not know her place. Dristan would be most amused." He looked back towards Aiden and Patrick and heard their nervous laughter. He must look the fool to be standing here alone, talking and laughing to himself.

She cocked her head to one side as if assessing his worth. "Well, I don't know who this Dristan is, but I assure you, I know where I come from and where I belong."

"Do you?" he harrumphed. "I think you must be a witch, so be gone and leave me in peace."

Riorden watched her face fall in sorrow. She appeared as though she was about to cry, if a ghost could possibly shed tears, that is.

"You want me to go away?" she asked quietly, almost in disbelief he would ask such of her. Her lower lip quivered, surprising him that even a wraith could have tenderhearted feelings.

"I do not know why you have appeared to me, but you must return to the afterworld and leave me be. I can only surmise by your strange garments and the way you expose yourself that you were a loose woman. I have no time to assist you with your unfinished business to save your immortal soul. I am here on important matters for the king."

There was a short catch in her breath. Was his mind playing tricks with him yet again, or did it appear as if she was attempting to memorize his features.

"Even here, across the span of time, I finally find my knight, only to learn his armor has rusted solid, and he has no place for me in his heart."

"Do not upset yourself, damsel," Riorden said, offering what limited amount of comfort he could, for he saw the anguish in her eyes from his words. It mattered not he was still distressed that he was observing this specter in front of him, let alone having a conversation with her. He did not like to cause any lady harm, be she ghost or of this world. 'Twas against his knightly vows to protect, against the code of chivalry he had lived his life by.

She continued gazing upon his face 'til she reached out her hand to touch him. The gesture startled him, and instinctively, he jerked away. She gave him a sad sort of smile, afore she, too, stepped further back with an apparently irritated stomp of her foot. "Jesus Christ! I can't believe this," she swore.

"My lady, I—"

"Ugh!" She all but growled at him, and he was puzzled as to what had caused her outburst, let alone to take the Lord's name in vain. Turning her back to him, she began muttering beneath her breath. She ran her hand through her tawny colored hair, afore she finally returned her attention to him with a grim expression. Her aquamarine eyes leveled on his face, all but boring into his very soul. "I've dreamed of you my entire life, for God's sake, and now that you're here, you can barely stand the sight of me. I'm not some kind of freak, you know. You must be here for a reason, or didn't you think of that? It's not fair you can be right here in front of me and want nothing to do with me!"

Bitterness dripped from her words, along with a touch of helplessness. Her eyes pleaded with him for some kind of understanding. Something about her made Riorden pause. He wanted to know what troubled her, and why she was lashing out at him. What in her life had made her laugh? What made her cry? Was it just his imagination, or was there some twinge of a memory of her in the far recesses of his mind that was just out of his reach and recollection? He could feel 'twas of much import, so how could he have stupidly forgotten such a grave matter as to remember her possibly being a part of his life?

The odd sensation that she was significant to him lingered on the edges of what little he had left of his intelligence and the odd circumstances in which he found himself. The harder he tried to think of her and why he felt as if he should know her, the harder it became to keep a grasp on the reality that he was conversing with a ghost. *God's Wounds...get a grip, you fool!*

He shook his head at the fanciful notion that briefly crossed his mind. For a moment, he actually had thoughts of wanting to spend more time with her. He must put an end to such nonsense and any thoughts of what was not meant to be. Whatever was plaguing her, or even her reason for appearing to him, he was unable to do much for her other than to pray she would at last find comfort in her afterlife.

"I know not what you speak of, damsel. I wish you no ill will, but I cannot in all good conscience help you save your soul. Only God can forgive you of your sins whilst you were here on earth. You must atone for your sins to Him."

"You don't understand..." the ghost began, but Riorden held up his hand to halt any further words.

"Aye, you have that aright. I do not understand any of the past two days, nor do I wish to. I just want my life to return to the hellish circumstances put afore me of late that I must needs attend to. Those, I can comprehend and deal with, but not this this...absurdity with visions of ghosts, playing tricks inside my head. I say this to you again...be gone fair maiden, and may you rest in peace!"

She nodded her head, as if she finally understood his words to leave him be. But 'twas the tears coursing down her cheeks and the look of grief in her eyes that made him realize he had erred in not trying further to help her cause. He took a step forwards, but 'twas too late to offer her what solace he might afford her. He could already feel her slipping from his side.

She slowly backed away from him. "Oh God...I don't even know your name," she sobbed across his mind, and was gone.

"Katherine!" Riorden rasped out, for he felt an unfamiliar loneliness creep upon him as she vanished, yet again, afore his eyes. For one brief instant, when he had watched her crying, he had felt a connection to another he never thought would find him again. Her disappearance left him feeling bereft and out of sorts. Confused with his inner thoughts, he could only stand there in a daze. At least, he could tell himself he knew her name. *Merde...what had he done?*

∼

Katherine could only stare at the vacant space where, but a moment before, stood her knight; arrogant, suspicious knight that he was. She supposed she couldn't blame him, given the centuries separating them. She gave the briefest of glances down to the sand, hoping against hope she would see some evidence of his footprints, or that of his horse's. Of course, that wasn't to be. Although it saddened her, she had seen him with her waking eyes and knew, at some point in time, he existed. She smiled brightly. He had actually called her name, before disappearing from her view. Her heart filled with endless joy, knowing he knew who she was. They were connected. She had known it all along. All she wanted to do now was find out who he was and what part of history he belonged in!

She heard her friends calling out to her, their voices carried on the ocean wind. They hurried up the beach to her side as if something was wrong. Nothing could be further from the truth.

"Are you alright?" Juliana asked in concern. "We saw you stumble and fall."

"Was it a pesky bee?" pried Brianna with a grimace as she swatted at a fly. "I hate bugs; such nasty things."

"Ugh, and the germs they carry," Emily added as she reached inside her purse for her ever present bottle of hand sanitizer.

"Ladies, I must ask for your help with a bit of research," Katherine proposed with a smile. "I know this is our vacation and all, but it's important. If we could find the local library, I would appreciate anything you could dig up on the castle and its inhabitants over the centuries."

Katherine was amused as she watched her friends' facial expressions change from skepticism, to thinking her downright crazy, and then to hope while she told them of her knight. For if there was one thing the four of them were good at, it was research.

Katherine was determined to find out answers of who this man, who continued to haunt her dreams and now her waking hours, was. She must find out his name, right away, before her stay at Bamburgh was over. And time, unfortunately, was not on her side.

CHAPTER 6

The amount of history behind Bamburgh Castle, a fortification dating back to 547 AD, was staggering. It was no small wonder Katherine had a major migraine. Her friends had been relentless in their questions to somehow narrow down the time period her knight had lived. Since she could only give the description of the fire breathing dragon on his tabard, there wasn't much to go by. Even the lion's head from her dreams had given them no further clue as to who the man was. She was about to throw in the towel and call this a lost cause. Still...something nagged at her to keep on her quest to find her answers.

She stood, stretching her arms above her, and looked down at the bent heads of her sisters of her heart, while they continued perusing various books. She was surprised their pens still held any ink, since they had all been scribbling furiously across pads of paper for hours, or so it seemed. And yet, like the good troopers they were, they continued searching on her behalf. She couldn't ask for a better bunch of friends.

"You guys are the best, but I think I need a break," Katherine said quietly, so as not to disturb the other people sitting nearby. "Anyone want to come with me up to the castle?"

Emily rose. "I'll go. I'd hate for you to use your hands and knees to crawl up some turret just because you felt the need to get to the top. You'd never make it without me."

"Jewels? Brie? Do you want to come?" Katherine asked.

"You two go ahead. I'm on a roll here," Brianna said, returning to what she had been reading.

Juliana only mumbled something that sounded as if she'd stay put, too, so Katherine and Emily hopped in the car and drove the short distance up to the car park at Bamburgh. A bus load of tourists were disembarking from their vehicle at the same time they arrived, and Katherine got lost in the rush of mankind. Their conversations became a whirl as they busily talked and bumped into one another to get the best view. All the while, their cameras clicked and flashed. Katherine rolled her eyes. *Tourists!* Even though she was one of them herself, at least she wasn't obnoxious about it. She was getting tired of people rudely pushing her out of their way.

Emily saw her dilemma, since she could basically see over most people's heads, and took the lead, grabbing Katherine by the arm and ushering her through the throng of people. She gave Katherine a look that clearly had only one meaning.

"Thanks Em, but I'm afraid I'm not going to be growing taller anytime soon," Katherine laughed.

"You're such a short little pan–".

"Don't you dare finish that word," Katherine threatened, only causing Emily to roar aloud with elation.

"Come on, Katie. Let's see where you take us today."

To be honest, Katherine wasn't sure where she wanted to go and had no particular direction in mind. They'd been on the tour already and had seen the archaeological dig that was an ongoing project by the current owners of the castle. And they'd been in the courtyard of the keep where they'd seen several cheerful newlyweds getting married. That, of course, only caused them to mutter to themselves how they hated seeing happy couples everywhere they went.

"Let's go down to the armory. Maybe something there will pique our interest," Katherine suggested.

As they made their way to the lower floor, they were surprised to see that, for the most part, they were relatively alone. While they were looking at the detail of a glass encased suit of armor, most likely from the thirteenth century, a door at the far end of the room opened. They watched a man take off his glasses and proceed up the stairs, polishing something in a rag he held in his hand.

Katherine felt as if someone actually gave her a nudge. Her feet started moving in the direction of the partially open door. It was a welcoming invitation if she ever saw one. Looking to the left and then to her right, it appeared no one was bothering to pay much attention to her.

"Come on, Emily," Katherine whispered as she put her hand on the door knob.

"Are you crazy, Katie? We could get into so much trouble!"

"Shh, Em. I don't know why, but I've got to see what's inside this room."

"Geez Katie...we're going to end up in the gaol and thrown out of the country," Emily whispered emphatically, through clenched teeth.

Katherine opened the wooden door, expecting to hear an alarm sound off. But there were no bells or whistles ringing loudly to warn of intruders. Peeking inside the room only gave evidence of it being empty of other human beings. Quietly closing the door behind them, Katherine came rapidly to the conclusion the room was climate controlled when she heard the soft buzz of machines sucking the humidity from the air.

They made their way inside and admired the rare treasures before their eyes. It was a veritable goldmine of history at their fingertips. Armor, weaponry, arrowheads, period clothing, historic vases, and dinnerware were all within their reach, if they but cared to touch such rare artifacts, or at least those that were not enclosed in a protective case. They resisted the urge, knowing even one touch from the oil contained in their hands would deteriorate the fragile materials of such historic artifacts.

It was an ever so enticing invitation, but they put their hands in their pockets instead, just in case they couldn't help but give into the impulse. Temptation surrounded them with every turn they made. As they wandered around the room, they could only stare in speechless wonder at everything their eyes beheld. Katherine gave a sigh of pure pleasure to be able to view such a magnificent collection, most likely too fragile and valuable to be on display for the public.

Reaching the center of the room, she felt compelled to turn to her left. A painting of considerable size rested against a large easel, and Katherine had the notion that the gentleman who had left the chamber was in the process of restoring the artwork. Her feet moved without her even realizing she was walking as she made her way to see what was inside the golden frame. Once she stood before the canvas, she couldn't believe her eyes. Her breath left her. Her heart surely stopped beating. Her knees buckled beneath her, and she fell upon them onto the cold stone floor. Tears filled her eyes and ran down her cheeks in recognition of who was in the portrait.

It was him...standing there with Warkworth Castle in the backdrop. It was the same castle that had reduced her to tears only days ago. The artist, whoever he had been, had captured him to perfection, especially his incredible eyes. Katherine felt that she could drown in those eyes if she were allowed to gaze at him in the flesh. He was dressed as he had been in her dream, with the lion head on his surcoat. He held a sword in front of him, its tip gracing the earth. His hands rested one atop the other on the golden hilt, adorned by a large, sapphire stone that was obviously of some worth. His hair blew gently in the breeze, and one could tell by looking at his expression in this portrait that he had been none too pleased to have had to stand still for its painting. He portrayed enough pure, raw energy to knock her off her feet, and in essence he already had, given that she was kneeling on the floor.

As she continued staring at his portrait, she wondered what in the world he had been staring at, for the look on his face practically scorched her with passion. What had held his interest? Suddenly, the room became exceedingly hot. It seemed as if her knight was actually pulling her through time to be with him.

Katherine...come back to me, my love.

Her eyes widened to once again hear those haunting words inside her head. It was as if he was calling out to her and asking her to do the impossible. Her heart beat wildly in her chest. Her body began to shake all over. She sensed she was actually standing there next to him, even to the point of feeling the soft breeze ruffling her hair. She felt heat radiating from his body as desire coursed through her, knowing he was within reach. *Merciful heavens, he was close enough to touch.*

She watched in vivid fascination when his grin began to widen, and he held out his hand for her to take. Her own fingers began to tingle in anticipation of that very first touch. A gasp escaped her, and she knew a part of her dream was about to become a reality. She blinked, just to clear her vision from the tears threatening to fall down her checks. But that was a mistake, for she ruined everything by doing so.

Suddenly, she became disoriented, when she was unwillingly ripped back to the present as if she was being tossed about in the turbulent whitecaps of the sea. Wavering on her knees, air rushed back into her lungs while a feeling of desolation at what she had lost consumed her.

A high pitched whistle rent the air. "Wow!" Emily declared, just as stunned at what she, too, was witnessing. "Are you alright?"

"I'm fine, really."

"You don't look it. Your face is all pale."

She couldn't reply even if she wanted to. Instead, Katherine leaned forward, searching for a name plate, and discovered it was missing. Her legs wobbled when she finally managed to make it to her feet, and she reached out to turn the frame around.

"Don't touch that," a man's voice called sharply, halting her progress.

He came into full view of the room, and Katherine wondered if he had perhaps been watching them for some time. He must have noticed her tears, since he reached into his jacket and proceeded to hand her a handkerchief. She stared at it oddly, thinking to herself, *who carries a hankie with them anymore?*

"Thank you," she said softly, as Emily reached over to steady her.

"You shouldn't be in here," he stated matter-of-factly.

"Yes, I know. I really have no excuse why we're here. It's really not a habit of mine to go barging into rooms I shouldn't enter. This may sound really crazy, but I felt I just had to come inside, and now I know why," Katherine said as she returned her gaze to stare at her knight.

"Thought maybe you were out to steal something. That's generally the case when someone's caught *pilfering the coffers,* so to speak," he gave a brief laugh at his own joke. "Names Simon."

"I'm Katherine, and this is Emily."

"Pleasure. So...you're interested in my friend here?" he asked, apparently still leery that they were out to steal an object held in this room.

"Do you know him? You know his name?" Katherine asked, almost pleading with him to share what information he knew.

Simon watched her for a few moments before he gave her a smile. "Yes, of course, I know who he is." He proceeded to open the cloth he had been holding and went to work re-installing the missing name-plate into the frame.

Katherine stood there, fidgeting and willing Simon to finish his work quickly so she could at last know her knight's name. It seemed like an eternity before he was satisfied and finally stood. Katherine tried to look around him, but he stayed in front of the portrait, blocking her view.

"You know, I have to ask. What's so interesting about a twelfth century portrait of a man most people don't even remember or care about these days? Why would two young American women risk going to jail just to have a glimpse of my friend here?" Simon questioned as he pointed behind him to the painting.

Katherine and Emily both looked to the other, and Emily shrugged her shoulders. "You wouldn't believe it if we told you," Katherine said.

"Give me a try. I have a very active imagination."

"I'm not sure where to start," Katherine replied honestly.

Simon looked at them both again and shrugged before he turned his attention and stared directly at Katherine, who began to squirm under his intense stare.

"Maybe it will help if I tell you a bit of castle lore," he began, and, from their silence, he decided to continue. "It's said, the castle is haunted by several ghosts, who I'm sure you already know about, since it's pretty much common knowledge. What you may not know, however, is that it's said a particular knight has been haunting these walls for centuries, searching for a woman he lost," he explained, pausing in his story to look again at Katherine. Putting his hand to his chin, he continued his examination of her as his eyes raked her from head to toe. "You fit the description, especially given the many women who have come in contact with him over the years with similar looks. There is no proof, of course, they spoke the truth of what they saw. There never is in the case of a ghost."

Emily pulled the castle brochure out of her purse and scanned it quickly. "There's nothing here about a knight haunting Bamburgh."

Simon seemed suddenly ill at ease with Emily's observation. "Well, we tend to keep that story out of the press as much as possible. Some women have run screaming from the place when they've encountered him. He tends to be somewhat ornery that he can't find her, or so I've been told."

Katherine tried to look around the obnoxious man, but Simon still wouldn't move out of her way. She sighed and stared him directly in the face. "That can't be good for business."

"Precisely why we don't want to advertise it, not that that hasn't stopped all the ghost hunters from trying to get actual proof he exists. But still, he has been known to roam the passageways from time to time. It's obvious he hasn't as yet found whoever he is looking for."

"May I?" Katherine whispered. Simon at long last stood aside so she could view the name of the man from her dreams.

She had to admit she had a hard time focusing on the golden metal and had to wipe her eyes several times before it finally came into focus. But there, directly before her vision, were the words she had longed to know, etched lovingly in a beautiful Edwardian script: *Riorden de Deveraux, Earl of Warkworth*. She raised her head heaven bound in gratitude she now at last knew his identity. *Riorden*...his name caressed her mind as if he had touched her himself and in its knowing, she looked into those beautiful blue eyes once more, felt the world spin around her, and promptly passed out cold.

CHAPTER 7

◈

Riorden, Aiden, and Patrick entered the Great Hall in the midst of complete disorder. From the amount of cleaning and scurrying the servants were doing, 'twas clear King Henry would soon take up residence in the keep. He came here often since its construction several years prior, and it was generally where he preferred to reside. Furniture was in the process of being moved, and it appeared they would be in the way, unless they retired to their chambers. He was bumped into by a servant, who muttered a hasty apology, afore she began assisting with the rushes to be cleared out, along with the muck that had accumulated underneath the filthy straw.

The door to the keep burst open, and its sound echoed off the walls, drawing attention from the inhabitants within. Curses were shouted, followed by several grunts, afore a body was thrown in through the entrance. Several knights entered and grabbed at the now unconscious man, who lay sprawled upon the floor. As the knights hauled him to his feet, the servants turned back to their business of tidying the castle for the king's pleasure. 'Twas apparent they were used to such scenes as this.

The leader of the king's men strolled through the portal and looked upon his prisoner with a sneer. "Let us move this Irish scum down to the dungeon. Perhaps some time in his new quarters will remind this insolent pig to whom his allegiance is required and whom he must serve."

His words must have roused the man as he again began to attempt to fight his way to freedom. The prisoner's fists connected several times, amidst complaints from those trying to move him across the floor.

"Hail, Danior," Riorden called out as he made his way towards the ongoing scuffle.

"Damnation! What brings you here to Bamburgh?"

"Perhaps you are in need of assistance?" Riorden asked, with a smirk. He proceeded to cuff the outlaw on the chin and watched in satisfaction as the insensible man's head dropped back down to his chest.

"I was more than capable of handling the situation," Danior exclaimed, obviously annoyed at Riorden's interference. He placed his hand on the hilt of his sword to make his point.

Riorden laughed and put up his hands in mock surrender. "Do not take offense, *mon ami*. I but needed to release some pent up frustration. There are strange goings on here about the castle grounds."

The king's knights began making their way below the keep, and Riorden followed. They went down several flights of stairs still dragging the cumbersome outlaw, none too gently. Torches lit the tunnel they passed through with an eerie glow, and they came to an open chamber. The king's men took their prisoner to the far end of the room and began binding him with ropes attached high on the wall itself. The man fell to his knees, but did not rise. 'Twas evident he was in no condition to cause more trouble.

Riorden came to the man and pulled his head up by the hair. Hatred flashed in the man's eyes, but Riorden only gave a leer of satisfaction that another rebel against the king had been captured. He let go of the man's hair and returned his attention to those who still stood afore him.

"'Tis been some time since our paths have crossed, de Grey. I did not expect to see you here. Last I heard, you were still journeying in

France," Riorden commented dryly. "Did you tire of taking coins from the French as you won their tournaments?"

"'Twas time to come home, or so I thought. Nothing like good English soil beneath one's feet, eh?" Danior smiled. "But what of you, Riorden? Tired of following in the glory of the Devil's Dragon?"

"'Tis good you have been considered a friend for many years, or I would demand satisfaction in the lists."

"I may insult you again, just so I can get a good workout for a change," Danior guffawed. "I swear, I have not had a decent bit of training since last we met."

Riorden chuckled and introduced Aiden and Patrick. "Perchance, whilst we await the king, I can accommodate such a request."

Danior laughed at the thought of the challenge. "So good of you, old man."

"I am not much older than you, Danior."

"You still have a couple of years on me. Have you seen your brother?"

"Gavin? He is here?"

"Aye. I saw him but two days ago, when we split up to go in separate directions in search of our tricky scoundrel over there. He should be returning soon, for this is where we were to meet up again.

"Then I shall look forward to the reunion, as it has been many years since I last saw that troublemaking brother of mine."

"He has not changed much over the years, I am afraid," Danior replied, and slapped Riorden on the back. He then went to check the bonds to ensure a good solid knot had been tied about the criminal's arms and ankles. "But let us continue this later. I must admit, I am in need of food and ale after my chase through the countryside these many days. King Henry can deal out punishment and pass judgment on this rebel, now that we have achieved our goal. He's not going anywhere lest 'tis to have his neck stretched from a good solid English oak."

They left the man hanging from the wall. Yet, Riorden hung back, whilst everyone strode through the tunnel towards the stairs leading back above to the Great Hall. He had a strange feeling come over him, and he turned to look into the gloomy interior of the room. A doorway off to the side of the tunnel caught his eye, and he felt compelled to move towards it. Opening the wooden door, he grasped his sword hilt in his palm and peered into the room.

He was none too happy by what he was witnessing. His ghostly vision was again afore him, but she was not alone. And these ghosts were garbed in the same oddly fashioned garments as she had been the other times he had encountered her, he noticed with apprehension. When he observed her being held in the arms of another, his jaw clenched. There was yet one more wraithlike figure of a woman, but he dismissed her, even though she appeared concerned for Katherine's welfare. He came forward, pulling his sword from its scabbard. *How dare that swine touch a lady in such a manner?*

"Katherine," he called out, but 'twas obvious none could hear him. How was he to defend her honor, if drawing his sword did nothing more than to cause the man to swat at it as if shooing away a bug?

Jealousy swam afore his eyes when the male phantom began to lower Katherine to the ground. The other woman kept calling her Katie and took something out of the bag she carried. 'Twas some kind of parchment, although he had never seen the like afore. She began fanning it in front of Katherine's face, seemingly to revive her.

He knelt down beside her and saw she yet lived…well…lived being a figurative word, since she was naturally only a spirit. He was uneasy when the woman on the other side of Katherine looked up and gazed at him most intently. She gave him a broad smile and a bold wink. 'Twas such an unexpected gesture that it startled him. But then he returned his attention to the woman of his dreams, whose eyes began to flutter open.

He was so very close to her. As she turned to gaze upon him, he saw the beauty of her soul within the blue-green of her eyes. The smile she gave him lit up her whole face again when she recognized him. He could do nothing more than return her stare, for within the depths of those beautiful eyes, he beheld all the love one person could possibly hold for another. Her gaze pierced and entrapped his weary, ice cold heart. He stood and stumbled back from the intensity of what he had just witnessed, feeling as if he had just been burned. *God's blood…can this beautiful ghost be in love with me?*

She raised her outstretched hand towards him. "Riorden..." Her hushed tone was almost like a gentle caress.

He heard his name, this time as it reached his ears, and was pleasantly surprised to hear the loveliness of her voice out loud and not inside his head. Yet, he could not hide his shock to hear his name uttered by a specter, by a waif not of this world, no matter how seductive her tone. So, he did the only sensible thing he could do. He fled. Riorden knew that if he stayed, he would lose what little he had left of his mind, or else be consumed by the same burning passion that surely would lead him to want what, any sane person must realize, would be an unattainable situation throughout all time.

CHAPTER 8

"Katie... Katie... come on, sis. Wake up!" Katherine heard her name being called and felt a cool breeze. She swatted at whatever was annoying her so close to her face.

As she opened her eyes, she saw Emily hovering over her, along with Jewels, Brie, and Simon. Her gaze canvassed the room, but he was gone... again. "Oh God... Riorden," she whispered, and heard how her voice cracked in grief from his leaving.

She tried to rise and felt Emily's hands take a hold of her for support. She was sure she would never have been able to stand otherwise.

"Emily," she cried, turning her tear filled eyes toward her friend. "He was here. I swear it."

"I know," she replied with a faint smile. "I saw him, too."

"You did?"

"Yes, sis. I did. I called Juliana and Briana to come right away once you fainted."

"I thought I was losing it," Katherine said, once more using Simon's hankie.

"You actually saw a real ghost?" Brie exclaimed excitedly, as she jumped up and down. "What did he look like? Was he wearing a sword? Did he say anything? Do you think he saw you too?

"Do you think you frightened him?" Her tone changed to one of concern. "Were you scared? Is that why you passed out?"

Juliana came and put a comforting hand on Brie's shoulder. "Not now, Brianna," she said, trying to calm the enthusiastic girl.

"Really, Jewels? They just saw an actual ghost, and you want me to be quiet? This could so work in my storyline," Brianna replied sheepishly. "So spill the beans, sissy...what did your ghost look like?"

Katherine walked but a few steps until she stood again before the portrait and pointed wordlessly to the canvas.

"Oh my!" Juliana and Brianna gasped simultaneously as they stood next to Katherine.

"He's the one who has been haunting my dreams," Katherine said with a heavy sigh.

"You've got to me kidding me?" Juliana gave her a look that reminded her of a deer staring into a car's headlights.

Katherine only shrugged. "Really... that's him."

"Pretty spectacular, isn't he?" Emily suggested. "It's no small wonder she's fallen in love with him. He's so magnificently handsome, in a roguish kind of way, that is. I should probably tell you that I think I spooked the hell out of him when I winked at him."

"Emily, how could you?" Katherine yelled in frustration.

"Well... I just couldn't help myself. You should have seen the way he looked at you," she said to Katherine, before turning her eyes on Simon. "You, on the other hand, I think he wanted to run through with his sword. I don't believe he liked you touching her."

"I think I need a drink," Simon gasped with a wavering, animated voice as he took another handkerchief from his jacket and wiped the sweat from his face. "I can't believe I now have two witnesses who have actually seen the Earl. It's very exciting."

"Maybe we all need a drink and to also get Katie some fresh air," Juliana suggested.

Katherine continued to stare at the portrait. She felt so lost. "There's nothing I need right now, except the one someone I can never have."

Simon came forward and took Katherine's hand. "Well, maybe we can help each other out. There's a chamber upstairs we believe the Earl stayed in when he ventured to Bamburgh. Maybe, if he appears to you, you can give some credibility this is a fact. I must tell you, it's a chamber off limits to the public, not that this small detail stopped you earlier," Simon said with a smirk.

"I'm truly sorry," Katherine began.

Simon waved his hands, dismissing her words. "Would you like to see it?"

At Katherine's nod, they made their way back to the upper levels of the castle and through a doorway marked private. Confronted with another tower stairwell, Juliana this time assisted Katherine with the difficult ascent. They continued down several passageways until Simon came to a large oak door. Pulling out a pair of soft curator gloves from his jacket, he handed them to Katherine.

"If you wouldn't mind putting these on," he told her and put a key in the door's lock. "Since we limit the time in this room, I'm sure you'll understand if it's only Katherine who enters. We'll need to wait here."

Katherine turned back, only to stare in fascination at Simon. "Who are you anyway?"

Simon broadened his smile, knowingly. "Last names Armstrong."

Katherine faltered, only momentarily, with the realization that she was standing with a family member of the owner of Bamburgh. It explained much. With trembling hands, she opened the door and closed it behind her. As she stepped into the room, she could only wonder what fate had in store for her. It couldn't be any crazier than falling completely and hopelessly in love with a ghost.

∼

"Go sleep off the ale you have consumed, brother. I shall see you on the morrow," Gavin laughed boisterously and nudged his brother's shoulder with his own.

"I am not that deep into my cups that I cannot teach you a lesson or two in humility come the sunrise," Riorden grumbled, rumpling his brother's hair as he often had done in their youth.

Gavin laughed even louder. "I look forward then to the challenge.

'Tis truly good to see you, Riorden, and 'tis been too long a time in its coming."

Gavin turned to Aiden and put his arm around his shoulder as though they were long lost friends. "Come, Aiden. We shall continue to drink our fill, and you can tell me of the wilds of Scotland where your lineage lays. Is it really as fierce as the say?" Gavin questioned, and their voices dwindled down the passageway, away from Riorden's hearing.

He placed his hand upon the latch to his chamber to open the door, but halted. He knew with every fiber of his being she was inside. He could feel her presence, as if she were waiting for his arrival. He opened the door, closing it behind him, and went to the hearth to rekindle the embers into a low flame. He exhaled slowly, more to get his thoughts together than to appear as if he could not handle a situation such as this. Truly, what was there really to be afraid of?

He turned and looked towards his bed. She stood there, touching one of the posts admiringly, just as he had seen her the first time but days ago. He had the pleasure of idly watching her, since it appeared she as yet did not know he was here. In truth, to his way of thinking, he had never seen a woman as lovely as she. Her beauty did not come from an outside appearance that may have appealed to him with other women in his past. Nay...hers came from the depths of her soul and from being good at heart.

His contemplation of her only intensified whilst she closed her eyes and leaned her head back. It appeared as if she was looking towards the heavens and the guardian angels above to at last come and claim her soul. He did not want to admit it, even unto himself, but he did not wish for her to leave as yet to join God, for with her nearness, he felt a soothing comfort fill him as never afore.

Riorden reached for a nearby pitcher of wine and poured some into a chalice. His nervousness must have shown, for he almost tipped over the now filled cup. It rattled upon the table and at last drew Katherine's attention towards him. Her face transformed to one of pure radiance, and he felt he could stare into her glorious eyes for a lifetime, if the chance were given to them.

Riorden took a long drink of his wine before giving her a small bow. "Glad tidings to you this day, *mademoiselle*."

Katherine nodded her head. "And may I wish you the same, Sir Knight."

He watched her standing there, seeming to drink in the sheer sight of him, as he continued to take several deep sips from his chalice.

"You know, if you continue downing that in such a manner, you're going to have a nasty hangover in the morning."

He frowned at her strange words and took a deep breath. "I know not what you speak of, my lady," he declared, watching her every move.

She rolled her eyes and gave him an impish grin that surprised him. Apparently, she must have realized her words confused him, for she touched her finger to her forehead and tapped it. "You'll have a bad headache."

"Your speech is passing strange," Riorden commented. He put the cup back down on the table and placed his hands behind his back. Neither of them made any further comments whilst an awkward silence persisted between them. They only stared one unto the other. She, at last, came closer to stand afore him. He found that, for the life of him, he could not move away. Instead, he stood his ground, wondering what she would do next.

"You look so very real today," she declared softly.

"As do you, Lady Katherine," he said, giving her a small grin.

The smile she gave him in return was most serene. Even her eyes lit up at the reference to her name as it passed his lips. She reached up to touch him. Neither of them should have been surprised when her hand went right through him. She stepped back sadly and put her hands inside some odd fabric sewn into her hose.

Seeing her sorrow, he took a hesitant step towards her. Holding his hand palm up to her, he watched in fascination as she removed the white glove she had been wearing. She seemed uncertain, 'til she at last gave in to the impulse. Ever so slowly, she placed her hand but inches from his own. A tingling occurred in his palm, and from her expression, she must have felt it too, since she wrenched her hand back and rubbed her fingers together.

"What I would give to feel your heartbeat next to mine." She gasped when the words left his mouth, afore he realized he had said them aloud. Once suggested, the words hovered in the room, as if to give them some semblance of hope, even as both realized 'twas obvious they could never be together. 'Twas too late to recant his hastily spoken words, but he would have done so, if only to lessen the hurt flashing momentarily in her eyes.

"I would cross time itself, if it were possible, just to find you, Riorden de Deveraux."

"You know my name," he drawled the obvious.

"Yes."

"Who are you?" he asked solemnly.

Her face lit up again whilst she gazed upon his face. "I'm someone who loves you."

He kept his features expressionless. "I guessed as much, my lady, and yet you know nothing of me."

"That's true, and yet I've dreamed of you my entire life, enough to know you pretty well, I'm guessing."

He was taken aback. "How is this possible?"

"I feel we are connected somehow," Katherine began hesitantly. "I think perhaps our souls were meant to be together, but the centuries of time between us are keeping us apart."

"Centuries? Surely, you jest, *mademoiselle*," Riorden said with a raised brow of disbelief.

"I would never joke... err... jest about something as important as this. The fact we see each other as spirits speaks for itself, don't you think?" Katherine asked quietly.

"Are you attempting to tell me you are from the future?" he questioned aghast.

Katherine smiled slightly. "Yes, I suppose I am, from your perspective."

"Impossible," Riorden said gruffly.

She shrugged her shoulders. "Apparently, it's not as impossible as we may think, given we're both having a conversation with a ghost."

He took a step closer and stared at her for several moments, his face masking the inner emotions that were to the point of consuming him. "And if we are not losing our minds, then from whence do you hail?"

He watched Katherine take a deep breath and release it, afore quietly answering him. "For me, it's the year 2014, and I live in a country called America. It doesn't even exist in your day... um... well, that's not entirely true. It exists. It just hasn't been discovered yet."

He was not truly prepared for her answer. A low laugh escaped him, just as surely as his features cracked, whilst hoping he portrayed himself in control of the crazy situation he found himself in. It could not have been further from the truth.

"2014 you say? Ha! 'Tis the year of our Lord 1179. Now I know you but jest with me. Everyone knows the world shall not endure that long."

"I understand your doubt of me, but my clothing alone must have you a little mystified, at the very least."

"'Tis true, I cannot account for such strangely fashioned garments, and yet I hear some people dress differently abroad." Riorden folded his arms across his chest.

She smiled slightly at his words. "Aboard... yes, I'm afraid I've traveled a great distance just to reach Bamburgh Castle, even in my own time."

"You do not reside close by then?"

"No, I don't, and my time here won't last much longer, I'm afraid. I only have a few days left of my vacation until I have to go home."

"Then tell me where I can find you again," he demanded.

Katherine leaned back to look up into his face, and he wished he could cease the tears escaping her eyes. "Unless you know of some way to cheat time and bend it to our will, Riorden, then I feel our stolen moments together are almost at an end."

"'Tis an impossible request," he scoffed, none too happily.

"Yes, I know, but I will cherish for the rest of my life the gift I've been given to have at least seen you. Having you appear to me as a ghost is surely better than not at all. Once I return home, I can only hope I continue to dream of you."

Riorden pondered her words for a few moments until he had the only answer he could come up with to solve their dilemma. He gave her another formal bow then made his way towards the door. He turned back to take one last look at her before speaking. "I will go to the chapel and pray for you to be released from the torture of roaming the earth for all eternity. 'Tis the least I can do for such a charming ghost, who fancies herself in love with a mere mortal man."

"Riorden, I–"

He held up his hand to halt her words, knowing he could not bear to hear the declaration of love that would surely pass from her lips. 'Twould do neither of them any good to voice their hearts' desires. "I will pray you may at last rest in peace, Lady Katherine."

"Please Riorden... wait!"

He ignored her plea and quickened his step in his haste to have this madness at an end. Mayhap, when his prayers were answered on behalf of the lady, he would offer up a few more for his own poor, sorry soul. Only God above would be able to forgive him his thoughts of wanting to keep a ghost forever at his side.

CHAPTER 9

The evening had waned far into the early morning hours, and yet Riorden persisted in offering up prayers for Katherine's soul. Moonlight streamed in from one of the upper windows and shone upon the table in front of him, causing the jewel encrusted cross to gleam brightly. Nevertheless, he remained true to his vow and remained vigilantly on his knees. He did not know how long he had knelt afore the altar, but if the ache in his body was any indication, it must have been for the majority of the night.

Still... the pain he felt was nothing if 'twould but ease the burden Lady Katherine must be enduring to remain a spirit here on earth. Riorden reasoned, the more pain he himself felt, the more God would realize the sacrifice he made on his lady's behalf.

His lady... those thoughts were but a mockery. 'Twas as if some wily character used trickery to deceive them both into thinking they could have what was never meant to be. To have tasted love, if only for a moment, would have felt as if he had tasted heaven itself. He saw such a love shine down upon him whenever Lady Katherine gazed in his direction. Was it no small wonder that he had begun to wish he could have had such a treasure to call his own for all time. A low moan of anguish escaped him as he thought on his ghostly lady. He came to the conclusion that perchance he had not been praying as honestly as he should have and further reparation was in order.

Reorder humbled himself further by lowering himself down upon the floor. Stretching himself out, he extended his arms until his body formed a cross. His forehead touched the cool stones as he once more began his petition. He begged to let Katherine find peace and a place in heaven with God's angels whilst he also prayed for the forgiveness of his sins. His stray thoughts wandered, momentarily, with a vision of the woman of his dreams and the yearning for a lady who was not of his time. He sighed heavily and began from the beginning again. Surely, God would hear and answer his most fervent prayers...

Far into the morning hours did he continue his penitence, repeating his request with a submissive heart. Peacefulness began to fill his very soul, and Riorden at last found comfort surround his being. His prayers continued in earnest and, for the first time this night, he gave a small smile, knowing his faith in God would never fail him.

Unbeknownst to him, a stream of light unexpectedly came down from the windows high above and graced his motionless body in a soft golden glow. For with his deepest plea and sacrifice for another's soul, the heavens decided to smile down upon Riorden de Devereux and, in doing so, God above granted him his heart's truest desire.

~

Katherine flung open the door and looked both ways down the passageway, but Riorden was nowhere in sight. "Did you see which way he went?" she asked the startled group that had been waiting for her.

"Where who went, Katie?" Juliana inquired gently.

"Riorden, of course! Who else would I be asking about?"

She looked at Emily, who only shook her head no.

Brianna became excited again with the prospect of seeing a specter. "Was he really in there, Katie?"

Katherine ignored her and turned to Simon. "Where's the chapel?"

"Downstairs to the Great Hall and out the—"

"Thanks," Katherine proclaimed, cutting him off as she grabbed

Juliana's hand. Juliana, in turn, snatched on to Emily, who then clutched at Brianna. They began to run down the hall, hand in hand, at a rapid pace.

"Hey, wait for me!" Simon called out, as he attempted to lock the door quickly, but his voice was lost as their footsteps echoed off the walls.

They came to the tower stairs, and Katherine paused briefly with her foot in midair, feeling as if her heart had leapt up into her throat from the prospect of going down them again. She hated heights, and she hated these infernal spiral stairs even more. She looked up, asking for guidance. "Please God... grant me a miracle to help me find him," she whispered quietly "and perhaps, if you don't mind, and it's not too much trouble, a bit of assistance to assure my safety on these steps?"

Katherine tried to go as quickly as she could, but felt as though she wasn't making very good progress. She stopped suddenly. Looking up, she had the strangest sensation course through her body and began seeing minuscule lights before her eyes. They sparkled and twinkled before her like tiny little fireflies and felt, as they touched her cheeks, like the softest touch, like a butterfly's kiss.

She turned to look back up at Juliana, who was on the stair above her, and felt Jewels give her hand a reassuring squeeze. Emily and Brianna both tried to give her a comforting smile, but before she could say a word to them, the tunnel lit up in a flash of silvery-blue light. It was blinding, and a startled scream tore from Brianna's lips. The ground began to shake as Katherine heard Emily yell out, "Earthquake." The four women grabbed hands and held on as if their lives depended on keeping connected to each other.

Katherine was in no way prepared for the sudden force of unbelievable proportions that slammed into them, one by one, with the energy of being hit by a truck. They fell onto the steps still holding on to one another. The trembling ground continued it's shaking until it finally subsided, and the turret darkened with the exception of those tiny lights. Katherine gazed at her friends. They all had the same expression of wonder at what had just happened. To say they were scared, was putting it mildly.

"Is everyone okay?" Katherine asked with trembling limbs.

"I believe, Katie, your request has been answered," Juliana exclaimed with a shaky voice.

"What?" Katherine asked, confused, as they all began to stand on wobbly legs.

"Houston... we have a problem," Juliana replied, and she gave way to a nervous giggle.

"You're not making any sense, Jewels!" Katherine stated, looking back up the circular stairwell to Brianna and Emily high above her. Squinting, she tried to focus on what she saw as those little, tiny lights continued to fill the air, dancing above their heads. Fascinated, she rubbed at her eyes and noticed the flickering electrical light fixtures above on the wall. Was it just her imagination, or were they changing right before her very eyes?

"I don't think we're in Kansas anymore," Brianna croaked out in a fearful voice.

"And I think we've fallen into the rabbit hole, Alice," Emily said, just as terrified.

"Would you guys stop with the movie cliché's and tell me what you're talking about?" fumed Katherine. She saw them point again to the torches lighting the tower stairs. The smoke they let off made her eyes burn. She rubbed them again and coughed to clear her throat.

"What's the big deal about tor–" she began, until the reality of their situation sunk in very rapidly, and she felt herself sway before Juliana made a grab for her to help steady her footing. "What the hell?"

Katherine reached up, thinking this must be some kind of a trick, but pulled her hand back once she felt the heat from the flames.

"Perhaps, you should refrain from swearing, Katie, since God apparently seems to be listening intently to your prayers," Juliana suggested honestly as the women huddled together on the stairs.

"Where are we?" Brianna asked, panicking. "I'm really trying my best not to freak out here, but I'm afraid I'm about to fail miserably!"

"I think a better word is *when*, since we're obviously still at Bamburgh," Emily replied, more calmly than anyone thought possible, given the circumstances. "What were you thinking of, Katie?"

Katherine rubbed her eyes, thinking to clear her vision before she spoke. "Why are you asking me?" she snapped.

Emily wagged her finger in her direction. "Don't be getting all snarky with me. I just asked a question."

Juliana stepped forward on the stairs. "Everyone take a deep breath, and let's try to stay calm. Katie, were you thinking about your knight?"

"When am I not?" Katherine replied.

Brianna clapped her hands to her forehead. "I think I'm going to be sick," she moaned.

"Well, whatever time period we're in, doesn't matter at the moment. Although, seeing as how new these stairs appear, and given I was asking to find my very twelfth century knight, I can only assume we're back in...medieval times." Katherine rubbed at her temples while she tried to grasp the reality of the situation. She shook her head in disbelief and sat back down on one of the stairs, putting her head down between her knees. *Breathe, Katherine. Just breathe. In and out...in and out...*

"I think, now's as good a time as any for me to have a nervous breakdown," Emily cried out and sat down next to Katherine. "I think this all goes back to that Karma thing coming back to bite us in our as—"

"Emily, for goodness sake! Not now!" Juliana retorted hotly. "We have got to keep it together, ladies!"

Katherine tried to think clearly on what should be their first course of action, besides trying to find their sanity. "Let's try to think on this rationally, shall we?"

"Rationally? Really?" Briana cried out. "You've got to be kidding me, Katie. We just traveled through time, for God's sake!"

"Shh... Brie. We're all together, so that's what's most important. You can all blame me later for this mess I've somehow gotten us into," Katherine said with a slight catch to her voice.

"We should find Lord de Deveraux. I have a feeling, he'll know what to do," announced Emily.

Katherine gazed at her friends and then at their clothing. "Well, if he wasn't freaked out before when he saw me as a ghost, I'm sure he will be, if he sees us in the flesh dressed as we are. First things first, girls. We'd better find something to conceal ourselves with until we can find suitable clothing."

"Katie, you do remember what they do to thieves in this time period don't you?" Juliana asked. "Personally, if you don't mind, I'd like to keep my hands attached to my wrists."

"Clothes ladies... we need to find us some clothes, and until we do, we need to hide ourselves as much as possible. Losing our hands would be the lesser of two evils, if people instead believe we're heretics or witches because of how we're dressed. I, for one, don't want to be burned at the stake today, or any other day."

"And, for goodness sake, watch the way you speak," Emily added sharply. "Remember that whole messing-with-the-fabric-of-time issue we are always so intent on. We can't change history because we've introduced something that hasn't happened yet."

Katherine and the other women nodded as they silently made their way down the remainder of the tower stairs. Keeping to the shadows as much as possible, they observed servants rushing around in flurries of activity. She could only wonder why everyone seemed in a nervous frenzy, but knew she couldn't worry about that now. Truthfully, she was just itching to take a peek at Bamburgh's history-in-the-making right in front of her face, but needed to refrain for now.

It wasn't until much later in the evening, as they covered their clothes with their borrowed woolen cloaks, that Katherine realized she had practically ran down the tower stairs earlier when she had maneuvered them, sure-footed, on her own. God had granted her a miracle, and with such a blessing, she planned on taking full advantage of the opportunity he had given her. She only hoped she would stay alive long enough to enjoy it and find Riorden. And, if by chance this was just a dream... well... she prayed, she never woke up.

CHAPTER 10

~~~

*K*atherine awoke disoriented and confused, and swore even her hair was hurting. Focusing her vision, she saw the reason for her discomfort. Sleeping sitting up was certainly not good for one's back and the dampness couldn't have helped either. Looking around the room, she tried to determine whether it was morning yet. It was hard to tell, given the room they had found themselves in last night lacked any of the conveniences that a modern day Bamburgh held.

It was a familiar room, or would be several centuries from now when it would be used as a storage facility for antiques. Currently, it was filled with several large barrels and crates of various food stuffs.

Emily had figured, because it was so cold down here, it was like a cellar to keep their food from spoiling. They had done a thorough search of several crates and had found some apples, but not much else of what could be made edible without a fire and stove.

Stove! Guess she could forget that one. If it couldn't be cooked over a fire, it was pretty plain and simple, it wasn't going to get cooked at all. They had decided last night that starting a fire to try to roast something may not be in their best interest. Refrigeration? Not a chance, unless it was a cold stream somewhere nearby. But worst of all, at least to Juliana and Emily, who were never all that crazy about camping in the first place, was the fact they could kiss indoor plumbing goodbye! They had found and had made use of a garderobe out of sheer necessity, but they had thought Emily would pass out when she quickly came back out. She had looked positively green and had used a major dose of hand sanitizer. If she continued using up what she had with her in the short amount of time they'd been here, her little bottle would be out by the end of the day.

Still, it had been a productive night of finding several necessities for them to hopefully survive their time in the twelfth century. Cloaks, to cover their jeans and blouses, had been the easiest to procure. Juliana had found a large twill sack, and they had put their borrowed booty inside for safe keeping. There was a pot, a skillet, more apples, two knives, flint to start a fire, and a bow with several arrows. Katherine hadn't bothered to ask Juliana where she had gotten the latter, but it would come in handy, since Brianna, bless her soul, was an excellent archer.

Most of these small items, they had felt, would not be missed. They really hadn't taken all that much, or so they had reasoned. The only cause for alarm had been when Brianna had returned with a lute in her hands. Her eyes had looked radiant as she had caressed the strings of the instrument so lovingly. They had tried to protest that such an object would certainly be searched for, but she had refused to listen. It had been added to their stash of supplies.

While scouting the castle as secretly as possible, they had actually been surprised to see what Bamburgh looked like in this time period. When they had finally made their way outside, their mouths had opened silently in amazement. They had come out of the keep at ground level to find most of the remaining buildings that would one day make up modern Bamburgh hadn't as yet been built. Other buildings one would have expected to see in a castle were there, including the battlement walls that rose high above their heads, but most of what they were used to viewing in their own time wasn't even in the process of being built, or even started, for that matter.

Urging her friends onward, Katherine had found a hole in the outer wall big enough to fit through in the event they needed such a portal. Poking her head out to inspect where it led, she had been astonished to see trees relatively close to the castle wall. They had hidden their sack of borrowed booty outside of the hole, in the event they needed to grab it quickly. It was always a good plan to have an escape route and this one would be perfect since they would only have a short distance to run to the safety of the trees. Before returning to their refuge in the storage cellar, Katherine had spied hay bales nearby in the castle yard, and together the four women had managed to push one up against the hole, concealing its location.

Katherine handed an apple to each woman as she woke them. Brianna looked none too pleased to see that breakfast would be the same as her dinner, but she still began to munch on the juicy fruit. Gathering their cloaks around them and pulling up their hoods, they went to the door to head above and see if they could locate Riorden.

They hadn't gone far when Katherine noticed Emily was not with them. "Emily?" she called out softly. *Now where the devil had she gone?*

∼

Emily could hear Katie softly call out to her. She hadn't a clue what was drawing her down the darkened passageway, but she had to find out what felt so intriguing. She heard her friends' footsteps as they easily caught up with her, but she only motioned them to follow her.

They walked slowly and cautiously down the damp corridor while Emily continued leading the way, her curiosity giving way to whatever had piqued her interest. She traced the wall with her hand, not even cringing, despite her revulsion to germs. A light illuminated a room just ahead, and it was clear this was her destination.

"Emily, be careful," Katherine whispered harshly.

"Shh," Emily replied, not looking back.

Emily peered around the corner into the room, where a man slouched on the ground. His hands were bound above him to the wall. A plaid tartan sash lay across one shoulder, but was tattered and as filthy as he was. The loose strands of his reddish-brown hair fell over his dirty face. His eyes were closed. Emily walked to him slowly, but the faint sounds of her footsteps drew his attention as she got nearer. When he glanced up at her, she met his soft brown eyes and was lost.

A cup of water sat out of his reach, as if to remind him he was at someone's mercy to beg for a taste of what the cup offered. She knelt down beside him and pressed it to his lips for him to drink. He gulped the liquid as if it had been some time since his thirst had been satisfied.

She noticed there was only a small amount left, so she tore off a piece of her cloak and dipped the scratchy wool into the water. She shifted over to him and tried to move the loose strands of his hair. He moved back quickly, refusing her help. His well-built arms flexed, showing off his strong muscular form.

"Be careful, Emily," Juliana said, but Emily ignored her warning.

"I won't hurt you," Emily said to him.

"Why are ye helping me?" he croaked in a deep voice. She caught the Irish brogue and looked him in the eye.

"It's just a friendly gesture," she said.

His eyebrows drew together. "I dinnae recognize yer accent," he said gruffly.

"That's not important. May I, please?" she whispered as she held out the wet cloth. He looked down at it, back at her, and then to the women standing in the doorway. He nodded skeptically. Moving closer, she wiped the grime from his face. She took her ever present bottle of sanitizer out of her bag and put a dab on her finger. "This will hurt a mite," she said. As she put the gel on a cut above his eye, she heard him hiss from the sting.

"What's yer name?" he asked, as she continued her work on his face. His gaze focused on her smile.

"That's not important, either," she said softly.

"How can I thank ye, if I dinnae know yer name?" Their eyes met.

"It's Emily," she said breathlessly.

"Your name is beautiful," he gave her a handsome smile, "like ye are."

Emily blushed. "Thank you." She set the cloth down on the ground. "And yours?"

"Tiernan," he said simply, trying to catch her eye. "And, yer friends?"

Emily turned to her friends. The three women seemed to have tensed at his question. "Huh? Oh yeah. These are my friends, Katherine, Brianna, and Juliana," she pointed at each, and each, in turn, gave a small wave.

"Ladies," he nodded in greeting.

"Why are you here?" Juliana asked.

"'Tis not obvious to ye?" he stated as a matter-of-fact. Juliana shook her head, and he continued. "The English dinnae care fer Irishmen. I was captured and left here."

"Can we untie you?" Emily questioned hopefully.

"Not lest ye want to be imprisoned with me," he chuckled.

"We could help you escape," Emily suggested, showing her bravery.

"Emily? Are you crazy?" Katherine snapped.

"No, I just don't want to see him stuck here. The ropes are digging into his wrists."

"Not the worst thing, I assure ye." He smiled at her again, causing her heart to skip.

"We know where there's a hole in the bailey wall. We can sneak you out through there," Emily said excitedly.

"Emily, are you trying to get us killed?" Brianna said, trying to knock some sense into her friend. Emily looked back at Tiernan, who was watching them with amused attention.

"I don't want to leave him here," she said so softly that she knew her friends would barely hear her words. With a look of serious concentration, she began trying to untie the knots binding his hands. After several minutes, she realized it was an impossible task, and she gave up. Tiernan chuckled at her.

"That didn't work." Katherine said with a sigh.

"No, they're just too tight."

"I applaud ye for trying, Lady Emily," he declared honestly.

Voices down the hallway echoed up to them, and they all looked toward the door in a panic.

"Ye must leave," he pleaded, his gaze hurriedly sweeping over her as if he was memorizing her face.

"I–I don't want anything to happen to you," she whispered to him.

"I'll be alright," he said with a grin, "I have a plan."

"Emily, let's go," Katherine said sharply as she pulled Emily's arm and helped her up. They dragged her away quickly. She took one final glance at him before she was pulled back down the tunnel. They began making their way above, listening intently for any who may have been following them.

"Are you insane?" Brianna scolded Emily harshly, as they hastened down the hallway.

"He was so handsome," Emily smiled widely, as if in a daydream.

"Oh no..." Juliana said, looking over at Katherine, who rolled her eyes.

"You, dear, are nuts," Katherine said stunned. "He's obviously an outlaw, Em."

"What were you thinking, attempting to break him free? You, of all people and your love of history, should know the times and that the Irish are not favored here," Brianna retorted.

"I like him," Emily said slowly.

"Well, forget him. He's a prisoner." Katherine stated sternly.

Sunlight brightened the day as they exited the keep and Emily looked cautiously around the inner bailey to ensure they wouldn't be seen. Seeing that the way was clear, she leaned against the keep's stone wall in a daze.

"You're a crazy little girl with a crush on a man you just met. What are you thinking, Emily? He was tied to a wall, for God's sake," Juliana said, giving her a shake.

"Leave her be. She's always had a thing for redheads," Brianna laughed, winking back at Emily.

"Well, be that as it may, you probably won't even see him again." Katherine said.

Quick footsteps echoed in the tower where they had just come from, and they turned toward the opening.

"Tiernan?" Emily yelled excitedly. "How?"

"I told ye, I had a plan." He winked and flashed his smile.

"How did you escape?" Brianna asked with acute curiosity.

"'Twas only one guard," he shrugged and clapped his hands together. "Now, where's that hole ye spoke of?"

Emily laughed brightly. "This way," she said, leading the way, yet again.

They walked with caution to remain unseen through the bailey and began shadowing the wall. Tiernan followed Emily closely with everyone else bringing up the rear. A shout high above them sounded the changing of the guard causing Emily to hold her breath fearing discovery. When no further alarm sounded, they again began to move until they came to a hay bale. The women began to push at it until Tiernan took over to move it out of the way. Emily got down on her knees and reached out to feel the sack still concealed outside the wall. Wary of being seen, Tiernan looked around. Satisfied they were still undetected, he turned back to Emily. With a smile of satisfaction, she stood.

"You should be able to leave from here," Emily declared. "You'll be careful, won't you?"

"Of course, my lady," he said and took her hand, placing a soft kiss on its back. "I am in your debt."

Emily couldn't take her eyes from his and was sure hers were hazing over with affection for a man she hardly knew. With a final smile, he dropped to the ground, fit his way through the gap and was gone. She gave a weary sigh, knowing that with his leaving, he took a piece of her heart with him. She would never be the same again.

CHAPTER 11

Riorden had just risen to his hands and knees when he heard rapid footsteps entering the chapel. Aiden and Patrick came rushing to his side and grabbed him underneath his arms to assist him upright. He nodded his thanks as he felt the blood rush into his outer limbs after a night time of offering his devout prayers. He had no doubt they had been heard, and Katherine was now at peace. He had done his duty by her, so why did he feel so empty inside?

"You were here all night, Riorden?" Aiden asked in a hushed tone of reverence.

"Aye." He swayed, and they made a grab for him again. He held up his hand and turned, giving one last bow of respect towards the altar. Once more steady on his feet, now that he had feeling in them again, he began to make his way towards the Great Hall to break his fast. Knights running in every direction added to the normal hectic morning activities of the serfs as they prepared for the king's arrival.

"What is amiss?" Riorden demanded, becoming more aggravated at the disorder that surrounded him.

"'Tis why we were in search for you," Aiden answered. "The prisoner has escaped. The guard had left his post and, upon his return, it appears the rebel managed to obtain his freedom."

"Is the guard dead?" Riorden inquired.

"Nay, but he may wish he was, if Danior does not calm down. He said he will tear the castle apart, stone by stone, if he has to," Aiden smirked. "Most determined, I must say, not that I blame him."

"Neither do I...With the king's arrival any day, Danior most assuredly is not pleased the rebel is gone. The prisoner could have provided valuable information to King Henry's cause against the Irish."

"I agree," Aiden said. "What would you like to do?"

"Where are Danior and my brother now?"

"They search the castle and courtyard as we speak," Aiden declared.

"Find them and help in the search," Riorden ordered. "Patrick, you come with me."

Riorden watched as Aiden quickly disappeared from his view. He grabbed a loaf of bread off one of the trenchers placed on a table, broke off a piece, and handed the rest to Patrick, who followed in his wake. He strode confidently out the door into the courtyard to begin his own thorough search, when his steps faltered near an outer wall tower. He knew no reason why he suddenly began to make the climb up the narrow winding steps, but thought perhaps 'twas sheer intuition that led him forward.

He came upon the battlement wall with a feeling he had walked this path afore. The ocean air blew gently, leaving the taste of salt in the wind, and he saw several knights standing guard. All appeared as it should until he rounded the tower. His gaze swept the wall facing the ocean. His eyes must have deceived him, however, for there stood his lady ghost, as if she knew he would come this way and, once again, but awaited the pleasure of his return. As he began to stride in her direction, he felt an inner despair consume his heart, knowing that God had somehow failed him in his plea for Lady Katherine's eternal soul.

∽

Katherine and her friends stood quietly on the battlement wall and watched the procession along the beach make its way towards Bamburgh Castle. From the amount of retainers who traveled in this large entourage, it was clear someone of great importance was soon to be residing within the castle walls.

"It must be the king's standard," Katherine said in awe as she saw the pennants waving in the ocean breeze, "but which one, Emily?"

"Well, if I were to guess, I would say Henry II."

"You mean, father to Richard the Lionhearted?" Brianna said excitedly. "Oh, how awesome would that be to meet King Richard?"

"He's obviously not king yet, Brie, but I don't see how making the king's acquaintance will help us at the moment," Juliana proclaimed. "Besides, if I remember my history correctly, Richard takes the throne from his father, so that couldn't have been a pleasant time."

"Lower your voices, ladies," Katherine cautioned. "There are still listening ears close by, and we can't afford to draw attention to ourselves.

Katherine watched as each woman grabbed the edges of their cloaks to ensure their clothing underneath would remain obscured from the guards standing nearby. The knights, although vigilant, continued to glance at them from time to time, as if they were unsure why ladies would be walking along the battlements...that is...if they were ladies at all.

A movement suddenly caught Katherine's eye, and she lost her breath by who was coming into her line of vision. Her dreams were fast becoming true, and her heart beat rapidly in her chest, knowing she was about to encounter the very man who had stolen all sense of reality from her. "Give me a moment, would you?" Katherine whispered, and she felt, more than saw, as her friends stepped back to watch what was about to happen.

"Leave us," Riorden demanded, and the guards left their posts at his command.

He came ever nearer, his dark red cape billowing behind him in the ocean breeze. A fire breathing dragon was imprinted on his tabard. He held his helmet under one arm, and with his free hand, he reached up, pulling the chainmail helm from his head. His hair fell in a soft black wave down to his broad shoulders, even as his blue eyes showed an anger that stunned and surprised her. It wasn't the reaction she had expected.

Nor was it the reaction or reunion she had hoped for when he pulled his sword from his side and pointed it near her throat.

"Katie!" her friends screamed.

"Nay, my lord," Patrick yelled hysterically.

"Hold!" Riorden said to his squire as he threw his helmet to the ground. His blazing gaze settled on her and she was afraid to move. "How is it you haunt this earth still! Is this the work of the devil?"

"No! I'm not a ghost," Katherine answered. Her hands shook uncontrollably at her side. All she could see was the length of the silver steel of his blade and from the look of it, it was extremely sharp.

"I do not believe you. I prayed for your soul to be released. So be gone, and haunt me no more!" Riorden threatened, still holding his sword steadily in front of him.

"Katie, for God sake, tell him you're flesh and blood!" Brianna shrieked hysterically.

"Look at him! He doesn't believe me, Brie!"

"Then show him!" Emily cried out.

Katherine broke her gaze, momentarily, from her dilemma and quickly looked at her friends. Brianna and Emily clutched each other, clearly terrified of the unraveling situation they were in. Juliana, on the other hand, looked at her confidently.

"Katie, it's okay...show him," she said and nodded to the sword. "I can take care of things afterwards."

Katherine took a deep breath and returned her gaze to her knight. She gave him an ever so slight smile. "Riorden," she began in earnest, "I am...in truth...here with you."

Everything happened in slow motion, or so it seemed to her. Katherine held up her fingers and, before Riorden could stop her, she ran them against the edge of the blade. The sight almost made her gag. She held out her hand to show him her sliced fingers while crimson droplets of blood began falling to the ground.

"Nay!" Riorden yelled out. Dropping his sword, he grabbed her arm to assess the damage. His face contorted in surprise when he realized he was actually able to touch her.

"Katherine," he whispered. "*Merde*, what have you done?"

"Proved a point, I suppose," she whispered faintly. Her legs wobbled, and her fingers felt as though they were on fire. "Umm Jewels, some help please. I think I did far more damage beyond what I intended."

Juliana rushed to her side, followed closely by Emily and Brianna. Katherine also saw the young man Riorden had spoken to join their group as they lowered Katherine to the ground. Juliana worked quickly as she began tearing off strips of her shirt to staunch the flow of blood.

"Ugh, Katie, what have you done?" Brianna said queasily, and she held her hand to her mouth at the sight of Katie's blood running down her arm. "I think, I'm gonna hurl!"

"Emily, I need your hand sanitizer. Brianna, here's my Coach purse, and don't you dare throw up on it! You know how it cost me a small fortune. Find my small sewing kit and get the smallest needle, some thread, and the duct tape," Juliana ordered as she took command of the situation. The two women busily did as she had asked. Then Juliana's attention turned to look at the pale faced boy at Riorden's side. "Are you alright?"

Patrick looked at the woman, as if noticing her for the first time. "He held a blade to a lady. 'Tis against his knightly oath to do so and goes against his vow of chivalry."

Katherine surmised that Lord de Deveraux had fallen a few notches in the boy's eyes by his actions this morning, and, from Juliana's look, she had the same thoughts running through her head. "Yes, well, circumstances are a bit unusual. I am sure the lady will forgive his trespass," Jewels replied. Katherine held back a smile upon hearing Jewel's speech. You'd never know listening to her that she wasn't from the twelfth century.

"Do ye think so?" Patrick whispered.

"You will have to ask the lady herself, once she feels better," Juliana answered. "May I see her hand, my lord?"

Riorden shook his head, as if coming out of the trancelike state he had been in. Katherine realized he didn't even know he was holding her arm tightly against his chest. She stared up at him as he reluctantly let go of her arm.

Juliana examined her hand, and Katherine winced in pain. "You've broken through the second skin on your index finger. That one will need to be stitched. The other two should be fine, after I bandage them up," she said confidently. "I have to tell you, Katie, this is going to hurt like hell."

"You are a healer," Riorden stated the evident, but frowned at her curse.

Juliana looked up from her administrations to Katherine's hand. "Um, yes, a healer," Juliana replied slowly. "Perhaps, you could hold her steady, my lord, since this is going to cause her a great deal of pain."

Riorden brought Katherine's back up against his chest and circled his arms around her, holding her firm.

Juliana took the bottle of sanitizer that Emily held out to her, looked up at Riorden, and at his nod, looked down at Katherine and met her gaze. "Ready?" Katherine only nodded and squeezed her eyes shut.

Juliana began spreading the gel onto the injured fingers, and Katherine let out a small scream.

"Holy shit, Jewels," Katherine cried out.

Juliana ignored her outburst and worked quickly. "Only a couple of stitches, Katie, and you'll be good to go."

Katherine blanched, as Brianna handed Juliana needle and thread, and turned her head into Riorden's chest, knowing she couldn't watch any longer. The pain piercing her finger was beyond excruciating. She was in so much agony that it took her several minutes before she comprehended she was squeezing the hell out of Riorden's free hand.

She began to loosen her hold on his fingers, when she had to stop and listen to what she was actually hearing. She couldn't believe it. Every syllable Riorden murmured softly in her ear caused her to tremble. She supposed he was offering her some form of comfort, but she wouldn't know, since she couldn't for the life of her understand a word he was saying. *Good Lord above! Is he speaking Norman French?*

The breath she had unknowingly been holding came out of her in a loud whoosh when she heard Juliana say, "All done." She tried to rise, but Riorden continued to hold her within his arms.

"Not as yet, my lady. Let us ensure some color returns to your face, afore you attempt to stand," he said huskily. "Patrick, go to my chambers and turn down the covers. Lady Katherine must needs her rest."

Katherine watched in a daze as the young lad scurried off to do Riorden's bidding. Before his leaving, she could have sworn she heard him say, "The ghostie's come back from the dead." She gave a short laugh, knowing the boy would never believe even half the truth of their story. She could hardly believe it herself.

CHAPTER 12

It's been said that there is always one identifiable moment in one's life that shapes the course of where the rest of one's existence will lead one. For Katherine, this was that moment. Feeling Riorden's arms wrapped around her, keeping her safe, was the most glorious feeling she had ever experienced in all of her twenty-six years. Sure, she had been thrown back in time and was uncertain of her future and that of her friends'. Sure, the small links of his chainmail under his tabard were digging into her side a little, but she didn't care! She could stay in this moment for the rest of her life and be contently satisfied. Life was good.

Well...life was good until she felt her fingers begin to throb painfully. She winced as she carefully flexed them to ensure they were still in proper working order. Thankfully, despite the pain, she would still be able to type again...umm...write again. If she had her way, she would never ever leave Riorden's side, so there went technology, right out the window. It was a sacrifice she would willingly make.

Katherine turned slightly and reached up, placing her uninjured hand upon his shoulder, and prayed he didn't think her too brazen. A heavy sigh escaped her as she snuggled in as best she could and just held on to him. His arm tightened around her. She heard him again whispering against her ear words she didn't understand, but it was of no consequence. The deep baritone of his voice reached down to her very soul, filling it with a sense of belonging to someone who would care for her no matter her faults. If only someday he could love her as much as she loved him, life would be so very sweet.

She supposed it would take some time to get to know each other before the true blossom of love could fully flourish into something to last them a lifetime. To fall in love with someone from a dream, was one thing. To be given the chance to love that person in the flesh, was an entirely different matter. She only prayed they would be given such an opportunity. She could not imagine how her life could return back to any semblance of a normal routine, if she was unwillingly ripped back to her own time period. There wasn't a doubt in her mind that it would be like a knife to her heart.

Time passed, as time tends to do, and yet Katherine had no concept of how long she sat there, listening to the ocean waves crashing into the shore; listening to Riorden's even breathing in time with her own; and listening to her friends while they chattered up a storm, much like a bunch of clucking hens. Their conversation was what broke through her resolve to block out everything with the exception of Riorden.

Lifting her head, she looked into his eyes, and her breath left her. God Almighty, they were so very blue, and they looked down on her with a fair amount of fondness. Surely, this had to be a good sign of wonderful things to come their way.

Riorden stood and held out his hand to her with a bit of arrogance and uncertainty crossing his features. She reached up and placed her hand in his and felt a jolt travel up the extent of her arm. His expression told her he must have felt it too, since he gave her a small smile as he helped her to her feet. Katherine swayed, so he took hold of her elbow for additional support. Although she wished to be held closer, he made it clear by his stance that he'd only touch her as was appropriate. She frowned slightly. But she shouldn't be complaining about his chivalrous nature and a code he must have adhered to all his life. It was, after all, the twelfth century.

"'Tis you," Riorden said uneasily. She didn't miss that his voice shook when he spoke, or the fact that he appeared dumbfounded that she wasn't a ghost anymore.

"Yes," Katherine whispered softly. "I can't believe that I'm really standing here with you."

"I never meant for you to harm yourself and only mean to keep you safe."

"Yes, I know. You do know me then? You remember me?" she asked hopefully, as the wind whipped her hood from her head. Her hair became tossed in the breeze and began to have a life of its own.

He watched her ever so intently for several minutes until he at last grabbed one of her errant tresses and rubbed it between his fingers. Finally, as if he no longer trusted himself, he tucked the stray lock behind her ear. "Aye, Katherine, I do know you. I believe we have had this conversation in our dreams afore, have we not?" he inquired, for her ears alone.

"Yes, I know we have. I must remember to thank God for this unbelievable miracle we find ourselves in," she said quietly as her eyes closed in gratitude.

"I shall pray and thank Him, as well, when I can once more get myself to the chapel. I just do not understand how this is possible? Is it magic?" he asked with an insecure voice.

Katherine only shrugged her shoulders. "I believe we've been given the chance at a rare and special gift, don't you think?"

Riorden looked down upon her and she could tell he was quickly mulling over the probability of this unusual circumstance. "Aye, I suppose 'tis a gift, but also one that could just as easily be taken away."

"I hope not," she said warmly.

"I pray 'tis not so, but time will tell, Lady Katherine, what fate has in store for us," Riorden said affectionately. "I think there is much to discuss between us, *cherie*."

Katherine had to lean back just to look up at him, since he was so very tall. Their eyes met. Time itself stood still, as if no one else existed but the two of them, trapped forever in a gaze that spoke more than mere words could ever be whispered aloud. He gave her a roguish grin that just about knocked her legs out from under her as she tried to find something witty to say. Unfortunately, her tongue had become dry, as if a hundred cotton balls had found their way into her mouth. She was speechless...a rarity for sure, or so her mother would have told her.

"Did you see that look?" Briana said, louder than she probably intended. It broke the spell surrounding the couple. "I could die and go to heaven tomorrow if some guy would look at me like that."

"Shh, Brie," Juliana warned. "You're ruining the moment."

"Too late," Emily chimed in, as Riorden stepped back a pace or two. "Yup...it's gone."

Katherine turned to look at her friends with a sheepish smile. "These are my friends, Juliana, Brianna, and Emily...whom you may remember."

"Ladies," Riorden said with a bow.

He stood straight again and raised a brow towards Emily, although he said nothing. Katherine thought perhaps nothing needed to be said, since that look about said it all. It was obvious, he did indeed remember Emily and her bold wink at him. She could only imagine how a twelfth century man would interpret such a gesture.

Further conversations were halted as the sound of running footsteps came closer. Katherine saw Riorden's squire returning, completely out of breath.

"I told you to go and ready my chamber, Patrick. Why do you return?" Riorden demanded gruffly.

Patrick looked at the group of women in front of him, and Katherine saw how his eyes widened. She saw him noticing their cloaks exposing their modern clothing and cleared her throat to gain her friends' attention, and they all grabbed their errant wraps.

"I never got that far, my lord," Patrick wheezed. "'Tis the king. He asks you to join him in his private chambers, immediately. He has also called for Lord de Grey. The king did not look happy, my lord."

"I see," Riorden answered, turning back towards Katherine. "Generally, I would accompany you and the ladies so I could ensure you would rest. I must beg your forgiveness for such a lack of protocol. His Majesty, however, waits for no one, so I must answer his call, posthaste."

"Did you hear that? No one talks like that anymore," Brianna said with a heavy sigh.

"Shh!" Juliana and Emily scolded, together.

"Can you find my chamber?" he asked quietly.

"Yes, I can find it," Katherine answered, although curious of where this conversation was leading.

"Then gather whatever belongings you may have and meet me there."

"Really? In your chamber?" she asked, wondering if he was taking things a bit far, seeing as they had just truly met. "I'm not sure that's a wise decision."

"You have my word that no impropriety is intended. You shall only be held in the utmost respect and, as such, I would never take advantage of you, my lady."

"I'm still not sure, since, technically, we have just become acquainted. I don't think being shacked up...um...boldly ensconced in your chamber would be proper, even if it isn't such a big deal in my own time," she said, wondering what he must think of her to suggest such a thing.

"I assure you, I meant no offense. Besides, your lady friends are welcome to come with you, as well, and would be more than ample chaperones," he said reassuringly. "Truly, Lady Katherine, again you have my vow, no harm shall befall you whilst under my care."

There was such sincerity in his gaze that any doubt she may have had vanished. "Then, since I have your word as a gentleman, I'll be there," Katherine said with a shy smile, trusting him completely.

"I will come for you as soon as I am able," Riorden said, then he took her hand and gently placed his lips to the inside of her wrist. "I have your promise you will be there, do I not?"

"Nothing could keep me away, Riorden," she whispered breathlessly, and noticed some of the tension he may have been holding in check left him with her answer.

He gave her the briefest of nods. "I will do everything in my power to ensure you and the other ladies will be kept safe from harm. You have my word as a knight."

Katherine watched as he reluctantly turned from her and went to pick up his sword and helmet. He went to the tower door, opened it, and glanced back at her for another stolen moment of uncertainty. With the briefest wave of his hand, he waited until she returned the gesture, and then was gone.

She looked at her friends and was sure her dreamy expression must have been mirrored in their own faces. They spoke no words, for none truly were necessary. They made their way down the tower stairs from the battlement wall and carefully went to where they had hidden their stash of supplies. Once again, they pushed at the hay bale that hid their escape route.

Brianna made it to the sack first, and before any could stop her, she opened the bag and pulled out the lute, strumming a few chords just for good measure. There was a look of sheer happiness on her face as she handled the instrument, and soon a song began to form that was indeed very lovely. Katherine listened for a few minutes until she became suddenly aware of the commotion that was stirring at Brianna's playing.

"Thief! Thief! They stole my instrument!" someone yelled. "Guards! Come apprehend these thieves!

Katherine and her friends looked up to see a middle aged man pointing frantically in their direction, causing several of the castle guards to come running towards them.

"Damn it," Emily yelled, panicking. "Let's get the hell out of here!"

One by one, they squeezed through the opening in the wall and ran as fast as their feet would carry them. Katherine slung the sack over her shoulders, despite its weight, and kept on running. As they reached the forest, she glanced back, as if she could materialize Riorden before her eyes to protect her. But it was no use. The only person she saw was a knight attempting to crawl through the hole, but he was, fortunately, hindered by his armor.

They kept running deeper and deeper into the woods until, at last out of breath, they fell to the ground, side by side. No one knew what to say, particularly Brianna, who pulled herself into Katherine's arms as she told her over and over again how sorry she was. She cried her heart out, until only a hiccup or two was heard from the now sleeping girl. The beautiful lute with which she had performed such a pleasing, yet haunting, melody was now all but forgotten as it lay on the ground by her feet.

Katherine looked into Juliana and Emily's faces as tears of despair coursed down her own cheeks. Her thoughts were now focused on Riorden, and how he would feel when he did not find her in his room after her promise to him. She closed her eyes and willed the man to her side, hoping against hope he would somehow find her. She was unsure how many more chances at finding and keeping true love she would be allowed to have. She only needed one more.

CHAPTER 13

"I am displeased." King Henry was fuming whilst he looked down upon his two subjects. Riorden prayed they looked contrite enough, but it did not appear as if that alone would lessen their king's irritation.

"You," the king called out, pointing to Riorden. "Step forward."

Riorden advanced as the king began pacing back and forth across the raised dais. He knew where this discussion was heading, and he liked naught what the outcome was sure to be. He only gave the briefest of bows to show reverence.

"Sire..." he said quietly.

King Henry's eyes raked him in a silent command, afore Riorden finally knelt down on one knee.

"I did not think I must needs spell out my displeasure at finding you in the Earl of Berwyck's colors. Do you, perchance, have some other purpose in my directives than getting yourself to Warkworth? I would have thought my orders would be clear when I sent you your father's ring," King Henry roared, not waiting for Riorden's answer as he continued. "Well! Speak up Riorden de Deveraux!"

"I will, of course, do my duty, my liege," Riorden answered bitterly, "I but awaited your arrival to speak with you on such a grave matter as my returning to Warkworth. I prayed that I may serve you in some other capacity, other than returning to a place I despise."

"I care not if you loathe the place! You shall do as you are commanded," King Henry said angrily with a wave of his hand. "Good God man! Warkworth is in a prime location and must be secured in the name of the crown. Your father has been deceased these many months, and 'tis time to take your rightful place as the Earl of Warkworth. 'Tis your heritage, and you will return and administer the estate, as is fitting. I will not have the keep and its lands fall into the hands of the Scots or, worse yet, those filthy Irish rebels who continue to plague my realm."

"Surely, there are others who could see to such an important holding," Riorden countered. He watched King Henry's face turn purple with rage.

"Do not test my patience further, Riorden," the king said after several moments of silence. "For years, I have heard of your exploits whilst you have been captain of Dristan of Berwyck's garrison. Do you think I would have any other than the best settled at Warkworth?"

"Of course not, Your Majesty," Riorden agreed solemnly, knowing his fate had been sealed.

"Then this discussion is at an end. Get yourself to Warkworth as its Earl, and ensure your father's widow knows her place in your household," Henry declared with finality.

"I will go there, posthaste, sire," Riorden grimaced, keeping his temper under control. He was waved back to stand next to Danior.

"This brings me to you, Danior de Grey," Henry's voice boomed his fury and the sound echoed off the walls of the chamber. Danior now stepped forward, and he, too, only gave the slightest of bows.

"What insanity is happening to my knights to be so reckless that they cannot show their proper respect to their king? Has some witch perchance cursed you all?"

Those within the chamber all began to kneel, as if, mayhap, this show of submissiveness would appease their angry sovereign.

"I do not even know where to begin with you, Captain." Henry continued furiously. "You had Tiernan Cavanaugh, Irish rebel leader that he is, captured and held in my own castle, and yet you could not even keep him here long enough to be interrogated?"

"The guard I posted to watch the prisoner has been reprimanded, my liege, and shall not fail in his duty again," Danior promised.

"Mucking out my stables for the rest of his days is not good enough, in my opinion!"

"I will find the prisoner, sire, and bring him back to Bamburgh. He could not have gone far," Danior exclaimed.

"He should not have been allowed to escape in the first place!"

"Aye, Your Majesty. I take full responsibility for his escape, since the lapse occurred whist I was in charge. I swear, I shall find him."

"You had better, Danior, or I swear by all that is holy, I will have your head. Do not return without him, for if you do, you shall feel the entire extent of my wrath — at least until I summon the axe man. Once called, believe me, you won't feel a thing afterwards. Do I make myself perfectly clear?"

"Aye, Your Majesty," Danior said and rose.

"Do not fail me...either of you!" King Henry yelled angrily then called for wine. With a goblet in hand, he left the starkly silent room. Conversations quickly returned and grew in volume as those who traveled in King Henry's court began to whisper amongst themselves. 'Twas apparent to all within the chamber that Riorden de Deveraux and Danior de Grey had lost favor with the king, lest they could prove their worth once more.

∼

Riorden tentatively knocked on his chamber door. His brow furrowed in puzzlement when he heard no call to enter. He knocked again then looked towards Patrick, who only shrugged. Putting his hand upon the latch, he pulled it back and swung the door wide. He gazed into the chamber...the very empty chamber, and was filled with a bitter disappointment he had not felt in some many years. A quick look about the room gave evidence Katherine had not returned here. Everything appeared as he had left it.

Entering, he went to the trunk sitting at the foot of the bed and took a key from the pouch at his waist. Fitting the brass into the lock, he heard a sharp click. Opening the lid, he reached down towards the bottom and pulled out a dark blue tabard he had not thought to don ever in his lifetime. The embroidered black lion head symbolized his father's crest and title, a title that was now, apparently, his. He never wanted it, since it represented a life he had chosen to forget.

With a heavy sigh, he handed Patrick the tabard to hold then tore off Dristan's colors and neatly folded the garment. Taking one last glance at the fire breathing dragon that signified the majority of the life he had led, he placed it on the coverlet of the bed. It would do him no good to think on the past and what could have been.

"My lord?" Patrick urged as he held the lion's head garment out for Riorden to don.

Riorden took the tabard from his squire and pulled it over his head. A feeling of dread came over him as it fell onto his shoulders, like a dead and empty weight. Memories of the last time he had been at Warkworth assailed him from every direction. Love. Hate. Greed. Betrayal. They were all brought to the forefront of his mind, along with the vision of the most beautiful woman he had ever laid eyes upon. He had fallen in love with her the moment he had espied her, despite Dristan's words to tread carefully. All too late, he had learned that, although the lady was indeed fair of face, in her heart, she was naught but a callous and greedy woman.

For years, he would call himself a fool, more times than he cared to count, and had learned to close off any emotions concerning love by hardening his heart to such a troublesome emotion. Regrettably, he was now committed to the one place he never wanted to return and to face the one woman he despised more than any other he had ever known. She had chosen another over him. Normally, he would have learned to deal with the situation for what it was worth. Unfortunately, 'twas just not some unknown man she had professed to love. 'Twas unforgivably more devastating when the rival for her love was his own father. Riorden had not spoken a word to his sire, ever again.

Riorden went to the window and inhaled the fresh clean air, allowing it to have a calming effect on him. He closed his eyes, thinking of the one person who, until but a few hours ago, he thought he would never see in the flesh. *Katherine.* Her name whispered gently across his soul, and, although he felt a disappointment overcome him that she was not here, he had the distinct impression things were not as they appeared. The look in her eyes had spoken a thousand words. He could not believe she had lied to him. Something must have happened, preventing her and her lady friends from being here. If it was the last thing he did, he would find her again, even if it took until the end of his days.

"I will find you, Katherine," he vowed in a low murmur, hoping somehow she would feel his words.

As Patrick finished placing Riorden's belongings into a pack, Riorden placed the key to the trunk on the table. Reaching into his pouch once more, he pulled out his father's ring and put it on his finger. It felt heavy, almost as heavy as his heart. The eyes of the lion looked at him just as contemptuously as they did but days afore. 'Twas almost as if his father were having the last laugh.

He motioned to Patrick, who began following Riorden down the many passageways. He checked the battlement wall to ensure Katherine was still not atop. She was absent, but neither did he doubt that he had not imagined her. Droplets of her blood remained on the stones as a grim reminder, and he was determined to find out what had befallen her. They made quick work of the tower stairs until they at last stood in the courtyard where castle inhabitants were busily going about their everyday business. Riorden headed in the direction of the stables until he noticed a disturbance near one of the outer walls.

As he drew closer, he saw Danior, Gavin, and Aiden listening to a man's ramblings about his stolen lute. Riorden listened with only half an ear until the man's words piqued his interest at the mention of four women making their escape through a hole found in the castle's defenses. Riorden gazed in the direction of where he spoke and saw how workers were busily repairing the wall. 'Twas obvious, the ladies in question would not be returning by this ingress.

The minstrel continued to voice his displeasure that the castle guards would not be following the thieves who had run off with his most prized possession. Danior, it seemed, was at the end of his patience and was fingering the hilt of his sword in an irritated manner.

"I care not about some missing criminal you are looking for," cried the outraged man. "How am I to earn coin to feed myself, if I do not have my instrument to play upon?"

Riorden fingered a coin and flipped it to the musician. "Here...go purchase yourself another and speak no more of this."

"But someone must find those thieving wenches who stole what was rightfully mine," he yelled.

Riorden took umbrage at the disrespectful term the minstrel used for the ladies in question and grabbed the man by the front of his tunic. "You would be wise to listen to my words and let the matter rest, old man. The coin I gave you is enough to acquire another lute of better quality, no doubt."

Shoving the man away from him, he watched as the ungrateful oaf bit into the coin to test its worth and, once satisfied, left, continuing his grumbling about the injustice of life.

"Well...where to, Riorden?" Aiden inquired honestly.

"I have been ordered south to my home of Warkworth," Riorden answered with a bitter taste in his mouth as the words rushed from his lips. "I do, however, have a small detour of my own making; a most urgent mission to find the four errant ladies our erstwhile friend, who has just departed, mentioned."

"Ho, Riorden!" Danior laughed well-naturedly. "Now that is the man I used to know, always chasing after a willing skirt! Tell me...is she a good toss beneath the sheets, my friend?"

In the blink of an eye, Riorden had Danior in a hold with a knife to his throat. "Do not speak of her in such a manner," he warned and then quickly realized what he had done. Backing off, he sheathed his knife and placed it back within his boot. "My apologies, Danior. I do not know what just came over me."

"If I did not know you better, I would have thought you to be in love," Danior quipped wryly, "and that you had tasted the green-eyed monster of jealousy. She must be most beautiful, indeed."

"She is to me," Riorden announced, almost reverently.

"The lady means that much to you, then?" Gavin asked abruptly.

"She is all to me...or at least could be, given some time."

"Did you not just meet the fair damsel?" Aiden could not help but query.

Riorden only shrugged. "Aye, and yet, I do not understand it all myself, which I am sure makes no more sense to you than it does to me. But that is of no consequence. She is important to me and out there alone without someone to protect her. I will not rest until I find her, along with her lady friends."

Riorden donned his gloves and strode with his companions as they made their way to the stables.

"But, my lord, where will we begin to look for Lady Katherine? She could be anywhere," Patrick asked, keeping pace with his lord's long strides. He sounded as if he wanted Riorden to catch up with the ladies, if only to beg their pardon for Riorden's unchivalrous behavior toward Katherine.

Riorden got a far off look then grinned. He knew exactly where she would head, and he planned to meet her along the path he knew she was treading. "She goes to Warkworth," he said confidently.

"How can you be sure?" Aiden questioned in bewilderment.

Riorden gave a short laugh. "I just know." He looked at his comrades, who held serious looks of disbelief on their visages. "Do you doubt me? If this is so, mayhap we can place a small wager on the outcome."

"God's Blood, I have seen that look afore," Gavin smirked knowingly, "and my purse was all the lighter because I did not heed such a premonition of losing. Just believe me when I tell you to keep your coins, my lords, and do not wager against my brother."

Danior laughed loudly, closing his pouch and attaching it again to his belt. "Aye! I think I will decline on taking such a bet although, I must admit, I never thought to see the day when Riorden de Deveraux would be smitten by a pretty face."

"Nothing wrong with falling in love, not that I want such a thing to happen to me," Gavin chimed in. "I am too young to be saddled with a wife. Besides, there are plenty of willing wenches I must needs satisfy, afore I think on marriage."

Riorden only laughed, thinking to himself he had the same thoughts running through his head at his brother's age. They reached the stables and he noticed that none of King Henry's knights were joining Danior to find his missing prisoner. He raised a brow to his old friend. Although he spoke no words, the obvious question was felt in the air.

Danior swung himself into his saddle and took the reins of his horse. He did not look pleased. "I go alone. The king has refused me additional men for the search, although I have learned he sent out another party to scout the area for him. I believe King Henry feels I will fail in my quest and my head will soon be residing on a pike outside his gates. Gavin alone was willing to join me in my quest."

"Then let us ride together whilst we begin our search," Riorden proclaimed as he mounted his steed. Once he saw Patrick easily settled on his own horse and ready to ride, he said, "I will not put the women in danger, but I see no harm if we double our efforts and work together to find those who have gone astray."

Riorden gazed up momentarily at the battlement wall where he had touched Katherine for the very first time. He could almost feel the warm, silkiness of her arm and, more importantly, her rapid pulse as he laid a gentle kiss upon her wrist. He could only wonder at what magic could have possibly been strong enough to bring her to his side. Determination to find his errant lady coursed through his veins. He would not fail in his vow to find her. With one last look at Bamburgh, he turned his horse and began making his way through the courtyard.

Their party of five was indeed small as they went through the postern gate, but perhaps this could be beneficial. Without the additional support of extra men, they could travel swiftly and, if needed, sneak up on their missing prisoner in order to capture him once again. Finding both Katherine and Danior's rebel were equally important. At least once Cavanaugh was found, Danior could rest easy, knowing his head would remain where it belongs — firmly attached to his neck.

CHAPTER 14

Sunlight peeked through the branches of the tree limbs, stretching high above the heads of the four women, who slowly made their way across the forest floor. For two days, their pace had been steady as they followed closely behind Katherine, who seemingly knew the destination she had in mind. Several times during their flight from Bamburgh, they had heard horses and had hidden themselves in the brush in fear of being found by the king's guards or attacked by villains. So far, their luck had held out, and they had done a good job of hiding themselves.

Walking south, for what felt like miles, they were thankful for the sneakers they wore. That is, with the exception of one. They had scrounged shoes for Juliana to wear when they were looking for supplies at Bamburgh. Those designer, spiked, four-inch heels, no matter how pretty or comfortable she said they were, would have been a dead giveaway that there was something *different* about their group. Jewel's shoes would have been difficult to explain.

Ever onward, they trudged. Katherine turned back to look at her friends and noticed they appeared...well...for lack of a better word...wilted. Deciding they all needed to rest, she took the sack from her back and swung it onto the ground next to a fallen log. She happily plunked down beside it and crossed her legs in front of her to relax.

Not that she didn't enjoy a good stroll now and then, but how convenient would it be to be driving in her car right about now? That, obviously, wasn't about to happen. And she would have to wait more than another eight hundred years, if she ever wanted to sit behind the wheel of her own vehicle again. It was something she truly didn't want to think about, for if that were to occur, it would mean she had failed in her quest to keep Riorden forever at her side. She could only guess how long it would take to walk to a place that had only taken her a few hours to drive to in another time.

Looking up at the sun through a break in the trees, she estimated the time to be around noon and that they were still heading south. She could be wrong, though, since she seemed to be all turned around in her sense of direction. She was thankful for her love of camping, which had already helped them out several times this day, as well as Brianna's efficiency with a bow. Brie had been able to kill a small rabbit and after cleaning the meat, Katherine had proceeded to roast them a fine meal to start their morning.

A laugh escaped her as she remembered handing a small piece to Emily, who had looked at her with a horrified look. Katherine had reminded her that it could be some time before they had any form of food again, so she had better eat up, since she couldn't afford to be picky. Emily had mumbled something about eating poor little Thumper before she reluctantly put the juicy meat in her mouth and chewed. Katherine could just tell by looking at her that she was about to choke from the thought of eating the once furry little creature. She had looked positively green. At least, she had been able to keep the food down.

Katherine closed her eyes and thought of Riorden. Peacefulness washed over her like the refreshing smell of new fallen rain. With such a feeling of comfort, she was even more firmly resolved to head in the only direction she knew to go. She had the greatest faith in Riorden and knew with every beat of her heart, he would know where to find her. She smiled, thinking that it was only a matter of time before they would be reunited.

Opening her eyes, she saw Emily was peering into the forest as if trying to determine which would be the safest path to take in order to take care of some personal business.

"Take a knife, Em," Katherine ordered. "Remember, safety first."

"What the heck do I need a knife for?" Emily asked shortly.

Katherine rolled her eyes. "'Better to have it and not need it, than to need it and not have it. Isn't that how the saying goes?"

"Don't know what you think I'm going to do with the stupid thing. It's not as if I'm good at killing anything we can eat or protecting myself," Emily muttered.

Juliana laughed out loud. "You may not know how to use it, but I'd still hate to come up against you when you're feeling scrappy."

"And we've seen you when someone's ticked you off," Brianna added. "Not a good place to be."

"Fine, I'll take the dang thing," Emily finally relented. She went to the bag at Katherine's feet and began rummaging around, looking for one of the knives.

"Here Em, take this one," Juliana called out, smiling as she took the knife out of her waistband.

Emily looked at Jewels, who only gave her a sheepish smile and a shrug, as if it had been the most natural thing in the world to be keeping a weapon in such a place. Gazing at the knife, Emily looked at it as though she had never seen one before, and then she began muttering to herself about her ornery and cocky friends.

"Don't go too far, either," Katherine shouted in caution, when Emily trounced off into the woods, as she, too, pulled a knife from the back of her jeans.

Poor Emily, Katherine thought as her laughter resonated with the thought of her friend and the dilemma she was now facing. If Emily had her way, she'd be back sitting in the coffee shop in San Francisco with no further thoughts of having to go potty in the woods.

∽

Emily could have sworn she heard Katherine's laughter ringing out as she made her way deeper into the woods. The things she had been reduced to! Even a filthy, smelly, disgusting garderobe would be preferable than having to find a random place here in the woods to take care of her business. This was camping on a whole different level, and she wanted to go home! What the hell was she doing here out of her element anyway?

She continued making her way through the forest until she thought she was far enough from prying eyes. Stopping, her eyes began to adjust to the dimmer lighting found in the density of the trees. A branch snapped, and Emily quickly looked towards where the sound seemed to originate. She brandished her knife, hoping she looked menacing enough, while she continued peering into the darkness before her. She stood that way for several moments until she began to relax, feeling she had only imagined the noise.

Emily dropped her guard and lowered the knife, holding it loosely in her hand. It was a mistake. An arm snaked out from behind her, knocking the knife, which fell useless to the ground. A viselike grip wrapped itself around her waist and she was pulled up against a rock hard, muscular body. She tried to struggle, but it was no use. Captured in a steely grip, she cursed her stupidity.

"Ye shouldna' be out in the woods by yerself, milady," her assailant whispered huskily in her ear. "Ye never know who ye might meet that may wish ye harm."

Emily gave no thought to her own safety as she quickly ground her heel into the man's foot and brought back her elbow, landing it firmly in the man's ribs. His breath left him in a loud hiss as he loosened his hold. It was enough for her to break free and make a grab for her knife. She twirled around, not knowing what she planned to do next.

Seeing the man's body outlined in the darkness, her breathing came rapidly as her chest heaved in and out. Her panic surely shown in her eyes, but she refused to let this stranger drag her off and do whatever evil intent he had on his mind. Brandishing the knife in front of her, Emily hoped she appeared menacing enough to keep him at bay. Her eyes widened in surprise when the man, partially hidden in the shadows, held up his hands as if in surrender.

"Easy, lassie, 'tis just me."

His voice was like a gentle whisper on the wind. Her eyes

narrowed as she peered into the shadow until he at last stepped forward into the light. A pleasant gasp of surprise escaped her. "Tiernan!" she replied in excitement. Running towards him, she threw herself into his arms. He wrapped his arms tightly around her, and she listened to his amused chuckle, rumbling in his chest while he held her close.

"'Twas not exactly the welcome I was expecting, but I willna' complain," he said, with another soft laugh.

Emily disentangled herself from his arms and saw his eyes twinkle in amusement. He smiled broadly, and she just about lost her heart. She inspected him up and down for any further injuries. He was looking much better than when she had last seen him. She could only imagine he had found some river to take an icy bath in. Where he had come upon clean clothes, she didn't want to ask. Even his plaid tartan looked freshly laundered. He cut a most dashing figure.

"Sorry," she said blushing. "What must you think of me, throwing myself at you like that?"

His grin grew even larger, if that was at all possible. "Well, Lady Emily, I would think ye to be a most enchanting creature, coming to grace me with her presence."

She couldn't help the giggle that escaped her. "No one has ever called me enchanting before."

He reached out his finger towards her and ran it gently down her cheek. "They should have, but I am glad I am the first, if this is so," he said softly.

A shiver went through her at his touch, and she felt she was losing her grip on the reality of her situation. She did not know him, but, for whatever reason, she knew she would be safe with him. She seemed at a loss for words as she blushed again.

He laughed once more. "Aye, the shade of red becomes ye. Are ye perchance a woodland faerie coming to grant me a wish?"

She looked at him in surprise at his words. "And what would you wish for, if you were to ask?" she said so softly, he had to lean forward, straining to hear her words. When he stepped closer, she could feel the heat from his body radiate between them.

"If I were to wish for a kiss, would ye grant me such a request?"

His answer caused her to once more tremble in anticipation. A gasp escaped her, and she watched his face to see if he was mocking her. But no, she thought. There was nothing she could see within the depths of his soft brown eyes to show that he was anything but sincere. She traced the planes of his face with her eyes; from the reddish-brown hair, falling rakishly across his brow, to his square, firm jaw, to his chiseled cheek bones, and to a mouth she longed to taste. He had to be the most handsome man she had ever met, and he was gazing at her as if he could come to care for her too. She continued to watch his face and noticed a roughish grin appear.

"Perhaps the look ye just gave me said more than any words ye could speak," he said tenderly.

She gazed at him confused. "Did I look at you wrong?"

"Assuredly not, Lady Emily!" he replied honestly and chortled. "'Tis been some time since a beautiful woman has looked on me with something akin to affection. Not that this is the place or time for me to be dallying with a woman, no matter how much I would like things to be different at the moment."

Emily hung her head, feeling embarrassed that he could read her expressions so openly. "Yes, I suppose I should be returning to my friends."

"Where are yer guards and attendants?" Tiernan asked as he scanned the area, wary of being captured once more.

"Guards? We're not traveling with any guards. It's just me and my other three girlfriends...umm...lady friends," Emily replied, as if there was nothing wrong with four women traveling alone. In her time, it was never a problem. His look of concern overwhelmed her, and she could only wonder where his thoughts were running to. She did not have long to wait for his answer.

"Lady Emily, for the love of God, please dinnae tell me ye are alone with only three other women for protection," he said, running his hand through his hair in frustration.

"We're perfectly safe, I assure you," she replied confidently.

"Aye! I can see how safe ye are, and how well ye protect yerself, given as it took me all of two seconds to disarm ye," he yelled, taking her by the arms and giving her a small shake.

"Well...you caught me unaware," she retorted, just as hotly.

"And just what do ye think would have happened if it had been some other ruffian that had found ye? Ye wouldna' have fared as well, I guarantee ye! Damn it woman, what be ye thinking?"

Emily tilted her head and perused him at her leisure then gave him a slight smile. Clearly, he was very irritated with her. He let go of her arms and began pacing back and forth, cursing, she assumed, in Gaelic. *Geez...isn't he just an adorable sight, or what?* she thought, then out loud said, "Are we having our first argument?"

"What?" he asked breathily, as if he was trying to calm his racing heart.

"You know...are we having our first fight?"

He peered at her and softened his expression. "Aye, I suppose we are. But, anyone with enough common sense knows these are perilous times. Ye just do not go traipsing about in the woods without a proper escort, milady."

"I can tell you're upset, but I promise you, we are very independent women who are used to being on our own," she said calmly, trying to defuse his anger.

Tiernan stared at her as if she spoke another language, and Emily could only assume he had never heard of such an occurrence, especially for a woman. *Remember the times, Emily*, she wisely thought to herself. *It's unheard of for a lady to go about unescorted, unless she isn't a lady at all.*

"I have ne'er heard of such a thing," he said, through clenched teeth, "and I dinnae like it."

"I'm sorry, if I have angered you, Tiernan. What do you propose?"

He thought for several minutes before he finally shook his head, coming to a decision. "I wish I could accompany ye to yer destination, milady. But I fear, if I did so, I would bring down upon yer head the wrath of the king and his men, who are certainly searching for me. I wouldna' want ye caught with me, since I am still a wanted man. Instead, I shall send a small contingent of my men whom I trust, to watch over ye, and yer companions. They will be close at hand should ye have need of them and will be wearing a sash such as mine. Will ye be able to recognize it?"

"Yes, of course, Tiernan," she answered. Then she turned and began to make her way through the trees. She called back to him. "Thank you for the protection."

He caught up to her, took her arm, and turned her around when she apparently had headed in the wrong direction. Was it her imagination, or did everything in the world seem to right itself with his touch. She rethought her earlier exclamation of wondering what on earth she was doing in the twelfth century. They strolled for only a few minutes before he halted their progress and pointed through the trees.

"Yer lady friends are just on the other side of the tree's ahead. Ye shouldna' have a problem finding them now, milady," Tiernan said, dropping her arm. "Where is it you go?"

"Katherine seems to know the way to where we're going. I only know we're heading south to Warkworth."

He flinched at her words. "Warkworth?" he repeated.

"Yes. Katherine is trying to find Riorden de Deveraux," she replied curiously. "Do you know him?"

"Aye, I know him…more's the pity," he grumbled.

Tiernan's tense, faraway look captured Emily's full attention until he turned his gaze once more in her direction. His demeanor was now friendly again, so she gave no voice to the anger, seemingly simmering just below the surface, she saw in his stance but seconds before.

"What about you? Will I see you again?" she inquired, hoping this would not be the last time they would meet.

Tiernan began brushing the hair from her face. She held her breath in anticipation of…well…she didn't have a clue, but she hoped he didn't stop what he was doing. After several moments, during which she presumed he was trying to determine his next move, he reached out his hand and tipped up her chin. Looking into his eyes, she watched in fascination when he lowered his head, placing a soft kiss upon her lips. It was over all too soon. "Aye milady, ye shall see me again. Just remember to beware whilst ye travel these woods."

"We'll be careful, Tiernan."

She watched as he fumbled beneath his cloak and pulled something from within its depths. He took her hand and placed several coins in her hand. As she was about to protest, he closed her fingers around the metal.

"Take them, for 'tis all the aid I can offer ye now," he said, brooking no disobedience to his demands. "'Tis not much, but at least I shall know I have helped ye, however much I am able."

"Thank you Tiernan, but you've already helped by sending men to watch over us."

"I can offer you one more piece of advice, Lady Emily."

"Oh? What's that?"

"Ye stated ye and yer lady friends were headed south to Warkworth, but in truth yer going in the wrong direction."

"No way," she shouted out, thinking how her friends had prolonged her agony of being in the great outdoors. She stopped her tirade to look upon the confused medieval man before her. "Sorry," she muttered and changed her tone to hopefully sound more contrite. "And just which direction are we headed in, may I ask?"

"Yer far to the north, I am afraid."

"I'm not really sure what else to say to express my gratitude," she said. Then he smiled that smile of his again, making her melt.

"I'm sure ye'll think of something the next time we meet," he said in amusement. "In the meantime, if ye continue to head north, ye'll reach a village in a few days' time, depending on how fast ye walk. 'Twill be closer to anything else ye'll come upon, once yer headed in the right direction. Ye'll find lodging there, and food. The coin should be more than enough for yer stay, and for yer next stop along your travels."

She took her free hand and placed it upon his cheek, feeling the rough stubble of his beard gracing his face. He took her hand and placed a kiss upon its back then surprised her by leaning down again and kissing her forehead.

"We shall meet again," he whispered and quickly left her, disappearing into the forest.

It was with a glad heart that Emily returned to her friends without any further thoughts of her original purpose of going into the woods. For the first time since they had arrived in the past, she felt lighthearted. With such a joyous feeling filling her soul, there was only one thing she could do to express such happiness. Emily began to sing.

CHAPTER 15

Riorden kicked the ashes from a recent fire with his boot. Then he stood motionless as he watched particles of ash float into the air and examined the remnants on the ground. The remains of some small animal, most likely a rabbit, told him much, along with the odd looking tread from someone's footwear. He smiled. His lady was most resourceful. At least she was not starving.

Although she started out heading in the right direction, she was far off course of being anywhere near Warkworth. He had to admit, she was good at hiding and, mayhap, a little too good, considering he had lost her trail several times in the past two days. He had begun to doubt his tracking ability when they had come across the remnants of this fire. He only prayed she did not run into any miscreants or someone who would deal unfavorably with a poacher. He was determined to find her afore another day passed. He did not like to think of Katherine out in the woods alone, especially at night.

"Well?" Danior asked, clearly irritated.

"The women were here," Riorden replied, directing a smirk towards Aiden, who still looked as if he doubted Riorden knew where his missing lady was heading. He kicked at the dirt to disguise the impressions of his lady's futuristic footwear until they were completely erased from their campsite. "As for whom you seek, I cannot say."

"Bloody Hell! How the devil could he have just disappeared into the forest with no trace? He did not have that much of a head start on us," Danior complained loudly.

"Perchance, he had help. Mayhap, someone was waiting for him with horses," Patrick proposed honestly. Everyone turned to look at the lad who had spoken out of turn. Obviously embarrassed that he had declared what was on his mind, Patrick clamped his mouth shut.

Riorden reached out to give his squire a reassuring pat. "Have no fear, Patrick. You are only trying to help," he said firmly, trying to save face for the lad. "'Tis the very same assumption crossing everyone's thoughts since we began this chase."

"Considering the ladies are without horses, they seem to be making remarkable progress," Gavin said, impressed, "even if they are headed in the wrong direction. I never met a lady who did not travel with at least a dozen attendants and rode in some fancy coach, though. Where did you say they were from, Riorden?"

"I do not recall saying anything about their origins," Riorden proclaimed, evading the question posed by his brother.

"Why ever not, Riorden?" Danior asked as he continued his inspection of the ground, looking for clues.

"Aye, do not leave us guessing. Surely, where they hail is not such a big secret, or is it?" Aiden inquired offhandedly.

Patrick leaned over to his brother and tugged on his surcoat. "'Tis the ghostie come back from the dead, Aiden. I bet she brought her friends from the other side with her, too," he said frantically.

Aiden looked over at Patrick with a look of dismay upon his visage. "Surely, you jest?"

"Nay, I saw her with my own eyes, brother," Patrick whispered hoarsely whilst he crossed himself. "She is the ghostie he saw on the beach and on the battlements, I swear 'tis true!"

"How do you know of this?" Aiden questioned with furrowed brows.

"He sometimes talks when he sleeps," Patrick answered quietly.

"Patrick!" Riorden roared, aghast his squire would divulge such information. "That is enough. You speak far too freely, nor will you besmirch the Lady Katherine's good name."

"Aye, my Lord Riorden," Patrick said humbly. "My apologies."

"I never thought to hear you believe in ghosts, Riorden," Gavin laughed riotously then gave his companions a nod in his brother's direction. "I wonder what other secrets I can learn if I but listen closely enough whilst he slumbers." Gavin nearly came unbalanced, overtaken by his own raucous laughter.

Riorden rolled his eyes heavenward and threw his brother a scathing look. Gavin took the hint and closed his mouth although a shadow of a smirk lingered upon his lips. *Younger brothers can be such a pain in the arse!*

"If you do not mind, can we get back to the important matter of finding Cavanaugh?" Danior scoffed irritably. "I would so enjoy staying in the land of the living, if you would care to help me with such an insignificant endeavor."

Riorden approached his horse and adjusted the straps on the saddle. Placing his foot in the stirrup, he easily swung his leg over the large animal and began donning his gloves. The others mounted their steeds, as well, and they made their way once more into the forest at a slow trot.

"We will continue north," Riorden commented dryly. "Keep a close lookout for the ladies who, I assume, will be keeping close to the woods and not traveling on the open road. I hate the thought of them coming into contact with undesirables, or worse yet, a band of Irish rebels."

Forever onward did they travel, or so it seemed to Riorden who was becoming overly anxious to meet up with Katherine. It appeared as if 'twas already late afternoon, and night was fast approaching. Truly, would it have been asking too much to be allowed more time with the lady, afore she was taken from his side? His random thoughts began to turn to ones of every imaginable horror she could encounter. If they were actually from the future, and he still had his doubts about such a farfetched idea, then they were most likely in more danger out in the elements than they could imagine.

Did not women of her time know how dangerous life could be without a protector by their side? Did they not realize their dress could be construed as that of a witch? He did not relish the thought of someone attempting to burn his beautiful lady at the stake, along with her friends, because they were thought to be heretics. Aye, these were most perilous times and, as such, she needed him near her side to keep her safe.

Pushing his horse to a faster pace, he and his comrades continued on their path until they heard voices and began to slow their mounts. Leaning towards caution, they watched from the tree line and espied only a family of travelers in a small open glen. As their hearty laughter rang out, Riorden came to the obvious conclusion Katherine was not amongst those within the group. He was about to lead their group onward, staying his course to the trees, when the travelers' conversation halted his progress, and he listened intently to their words.

"I ne'er 'eard me such lovely singing in me life, John," the woman said happily. "I thought to meself, 'surely, the angels had come down to earth to hear such a beautiful melody.'"

The man called John came up to the woman and put his arms around her, kissing her cheek. "Ye could sing just as fine, Mabel, if'n ye wanted to."

The woman laughed loudly and slapped the man's shoulder playfully. "Bah! Ye know I canna carry a tune 'usband."

"Mama, can we follow the ladies so we's can 'ear more of their pretty ballads?" a young girl of perhaps ten and two asked sweetly.

"I wanna go's too!" a tiny tot of mayhap six chimed in as he jumped up and down excitedly.

"Now children, we canna be bothering them ladies more'n we already did. We should be thankful we were able to listen as long as we could," their father replied, much to the children's disappointment.

The young girl got a dreamy expression on her face whilst swaying back and forth, as if she still heard the women singing. "I ne'er 'eard such beautiful words, Papa. Lady Katherine called them love songs. She must be a great songstress to compose such nice melodies."

The boy puffed up full of himself as he corrected his sister. "Lady Katherine dinnae write them silly. She said so 'erself. Who's Barbara Celine, Mama?"

Mabel thought hard on her son's words and only shook her head. "I dinnae know for sure, Peter. I dinnae recall that was the name she used, though I may be wrong. Those sure were a different kind of ballad, weren't they John? I ne'er heard music such as their's afore."

"I wished they could have stayed longer," the youthful girl sighed. "I could 'ave listened to their voices all day long and ne'er tire of 'earing them."

"Ye 'eard the ladies, Mary," her father chimed in. "Lady Katherine said they mustna tarry as they 'ad to catch up with her lord. At least we sent them off with a fine meal. Ye did well by serving them, Mabel. Ye could tell they was most grateful for the victuals."

"Do ye think so, John?" Mabel asked hesitantly. "'Twas such a simple meal, I wasna sure it be to their liking."

"Aye they was 'appy to trade their gift of song for a bite or two of yer stew, although they ate most sparingly. I think they dinnae want to take food from the mouths of the children," John said praising his wife.

When Riorden had heard enough of their conversation, he made a clicking noise to urge his horse forward and made his way into the meadow. Upon seeing the group entering the glen, the father stood quickly and moved to protect his family. With a wave of Riorden's hand, the man relaxed his stance yet urged his family to drop to their knees upon espying a knight of the realm. Riorden took in the people who had last seen his lady and bid them rise then dismounted from his steed.

Taking a coin of some worth, he handed it to the older woman. "Accept this, with my thanks, for your care of my lady and her friends. Your kindness is most appreciated."

"'Tis very generous, milord," John replied on behalf of his wife.

"She was well?" Riorden asked.

"Aye, milord," Mabel replied. "Lady Katherine and her lady friends repaid us fer the meal by entertaining us with their love of song. 'Twas most beautiful to listen to them sing."

Riorden could only hope to have such a chance as to hear their voices lifted to the heavens in song. "I am sure she was most appreciative for the meal."

Mary stepped forward hesitantly. "Ye are Lord Riorden de Deveraux that Lady Katherine spoke of?"

Riorden gave the girl a small smile. "Indeed, I am."

Mary gave a dreamy sigh and broke into a radiant smile. "Lady Katherine spoke of ye most favorably, milord. It must be wonderful to have someone love ye as much as she loves ye."

"Mary, that's enough. Ye'll embarrass Lord de Deveraux," John chastised.

"Aye, father," Mary said softly then went to stand behind her mother.

"She means no offense, milord," Mabel answered quickly.

Riorden waved his hand, dismissing the matter. "When did you last see my lady?"

"Must be at least two hours passed, milord," John replied, pointing to the path at the other end of the glen. "They continued on in that direction."

"Again, my thanks," Riorden said gratefully. "If you are ever in need, I shall be heading to my home at Warkworth soon. Do you know of the place?"

"Nay, milord," John said.

"'Tis south on the seaside. If you and your family are in need of a location to live, I am sure I can find you space in the village for lodging. You have some kind of skill I presume?"

"I been a masonry most me life and would be most thankful to find a new 'ome for me and the family," John replied humbly.

Riorden nodded. "Then make your way to Warkworth, and I shall find accommodations for you in gratitude for your service to the Lady Katherine."

"Bless ye, milord, and our thanks," Mabel said, taking his hand as she knelt on her knees before him once more.

Riorden took his reins from Patrick, who had been holding his steed, and vaulted up into the saddle. They once more took up the trail of his lady. As they left the family, Riorden could still hear the daughter chattering on whilst she gushed over the handsome knight Lady Katherine had fallen in love with.

Thoughts of Katherine and how she would soon be within his reach caused his pulse to quicken, knowing she was close. Her words to the family had humbled him. Kicking his horse into a gallop, he began to lessen the distance between them. Katherine would have been most pleased to see the smile gracing his face, for it was filled with love and, if properly nurtured, would last them until the end of time.

CHAPTER 16

The flames before her feet burned bright orange as particles of grey ash rose high above her head, disappearing into the night sky. In the depths of the fire, the flames ignited in the deepest of blue, somehow reminding Katherine of Riorden's eyes. It was a large bonfire, larger than Katherine supposed she should have made. But Brianna and Emily had complained of being cold. Against her better judgment, she had built up the wood until it became a roaring blaze in the night. The women were warmer while they attempted to sleep on the hard, uncomfortable ground, but Katherine was more concerned the flames were a beacon, telling all and sundry where they were. They were alone...in the dark...with no one to protect them.

Well, perhaps that was not completely true. There were two that kept to the outskirts of their camp, keeping watch. Although she was grateful to have Tiernan's men keeping an eye on them, they were still strangers. She wasn't so sure Riorden would be pleased to know that rebel forces were in the area, no matter their good intentions for the women's safety. She was on edge, sensing something hovered in the darkness beyond her sight. It wasn't a good feeling.

No sound could be heard in the darkness surrounding them other than the snapping and popping of the dry, ignited wood. The eerie silence set Katherine's nerves on the brink of panic, causing her to keep a constant vigil on the shadows beyond her vision. She was definitely antsy and kept waiting for something to jump out at them from the night. Emily would have said to be on the lookout for a zombie invasion. It was about the last thing they needed right now.

Juliana stirred beside her and opened her eyes. She sat up and stretched, insuring her knife was still close at hand. "You've been up all this time?" she asked sleepily, seeing her friend nod. "Get some sleep. I'll keep watch for a while."

"No. It's okay. I'm wide awake anyway and couldn't sleep if I tried."

"You never did sleep well away from home, even when you were camping, did you?"

Katherine only shrugged in response. Taking up a stick next to her, she began poking the fire. "I'm sorry I got you into this mess, Jewels. I know you don't like the outdoors any more than Emily."

Juliana gave a small laugh. "As if you could have known what would happen to us. Besides, there must be some reason for the rest of us to be here. Aren't you always telling us that everything happens for a reason?"

Katherine gave a heavy sigh. "I suppose," she said, letting her words linger in the air.

"At least I'm not as big of a paranoid as Emily. She's such a germ-a-phobic."

"Oh, don't kid yourself, Jewels," Katherine smirked knowingly. "You're not too far behind her, not that I blame you, working with patients all day long."

"At least you and Brie seem to be in your element, Katie. You were both born for this time period." Juliana lifted her foot up, showing off her high heels. "I just love these shoes."

"I don't know how you can stand in those things, let alone walk in them."

"They're just so darn sexy. Besides...they're comfortable."

Katherine gave a muffled laugh. "I'll take your word for it, dear."

"You should get a pair when we get home," Juliana suggested, but Katherine's face fell at her words. "Sorry, sis."

"Don't worry about it." An awkward silence momentarily filled the space between them as Katherine continued prodding the red hot coals. "Who would have thought it would be possible we'd be thrown back in time? At the moment, I'm trying to remember why I'm even here," Katherine said, ever so softly.

Juliana reached out and grabbed Katherine's hand. "My dearest sister of my heart, you know why you're here. If you could have seen the way he looked at you from our perspective just a few days ago, you wouldn't even begin to question the reasoning behind this miracle."

"But he's not here," she whispered with a slight tremble in her voice.

"He will be," Juliana said confidently. "Don't lose your faith in him so readily, when you've not yet had the chance to really learn to love him fully. That, too, will come only with time."

"Next you'll be telling me to just have some patience," huffed Katherine.

Juliana quietly laughed. "Patience is a virtue, or so I've heard before."

"Ugh! That was never one of my strong points!"

"Yes, well, I have to admit, it's not mine either," Juliana said as she reached out once more and patted Katherine's arm.

Placing the stick next to her, Katherine leaned upon the log she had been using as a support for her aching back. It was a poor substitute for a cushioned chair, but it was all she had at the moment. She drew her legs up with her arms and put her forehead to her knees. She would just rest her eyes for a minute or two.

Katherine jerked awake with a start. Alarmed she had fallen asleep, she wondered what she had subconsciously heard that disturbed her slumber. She listened intently to the noise of the forest until a man's voice was harshly raised in an earsplitting roar of pain. It was followed closely by the distinct sound of steel sheering off steel and loud manly curses coming closer to their campsite.

Their small haven erupted into chaos as at least half a dozen men swarmed into the vicinity. Katherine yelled at her friends, who quickly got to their feet and prepared to defend themselves. She watched in horror as one of Tiernan's men was brutally slain right before her very eyes. His gaze met hers across the flames as a long saber protruding from the man's chest was removed from his back. His dead body tumbled to the ground in a heap.

Emily screamed, and the sound pierced the night as it echoed off into the distance. Katherine threw the knife she had held in her hands, tossing it towards her friend. It landed but inches from Emily's feet where it stuck into the dirt. Emily didn't hesitate as she quickly picked it up and, with a firm grip, brandished it in her hand. Now, the only weapon Katherine had available to her was a cast iron skillet. She reached down and picked up the heavy iron. She had no problem with whacking a few heads, if this was her only alternative.

The filthy men who advanced towards them grinned devilishly, showing their rotting and missing teeth. They came closer into the fire light, making obscene gestures and lewd remarks that caused Katherine to flinch, despite her knowledge and language of modern times. The women tried to keep themselves back to back, but it was soon apparent the men's objective was to split them up. They were clearly outmaneuvered before Katherine even realized what they had planned.

All hell broke loose as Brianna began her movements from her self-defense classes. It was obvious the two men, who had hoped to overtake the smallest of their group, had not planned on her putting up much of a fight. Since they were at such close range, Brie's bow and arrows were of no use, but at least she was holding her own.

Katherine struck one of the men in the head with the heavy skillet and was satisfied when he fell to the ground moaning. She turned to help Juliana. There was no need as it seemed that Jewels was doing her best by slashing out with her knife and inflicting cuts to her assailant's skin. She was fast as lightning and it was an impressive sight. Now if she would only quit her inappropriate laughter that seemed to be consuming her as this only appeared to egg on the goon bent on doing her harm. It was a terrible habit of hers whenever she was nervous.

A scream resounded in the air, and Katherine turned again to see where the newest threat to them lay. Her own shriek resonated when she yelled Emily's name and watched as two of their attackers were dragging her friend into the woods. Emily was cussing and kicking up a storm, but the two brutes that had her captured were the biggest of the lot. She watched in terror as her friend was backhanded and Emily became still. With her senseless, their burden had been lightened, and they had no difficulty disappearing into the night.

Katherine was about to run after Emily when suddenly her own ankle was grabbed, and she fell roughly to the ground. It was just her dumb luck to have underestimated the villain she had hit over the head. His gruff laughter rang out, giving her cold chills.

"My yer a pretty lil thing, aren't ye, me dear," he drawled. "I can 'ardly wait to 'ear ye a moaning beneath me."

"Dream on, buddy," Katherine cried out as she hurled the skillet at the man's arm in a downward plunge. A sickening snap, along with the man's cry of pain, was heard as she met her mark. She scooted her legs beneath her and stood staring at the bone piercing his limb in a gross display of oozing flesh and blood.

"Ye bloody bitch!" he bellowed in rage, making a grasp for her with his good arm.

"Go ahead and try it, you jerk, and I'll break the other one," she taunted menacingly.

Fury blazed in his eyes as he made a sweep for her, narrowly missing the skillet that was once again aiming for any part of him Katherine could reach. She watched in terror as he picked up a log of considerable width and now easily knocked the iron from her numb hands. He continued pursuing her until she unknowingly backed herself up against a large oak tree.

She felt his breath on her neck as she tried to kick and punch her way out of the predicament she now hopelessly found herself in. It was no use and, from the sounds she heard, Brianna and Juliana weren't fairing any better than she was. They were completely and totally outnumbered.

Her assailant was using his body to keep her pinned to the tree until she felt the man's uninjured hand on her. Dammit! She'd rather die than be raped by such a vile specimen of vermin who was already fumbling with his hose, knowing the prize had been won.

She was prepared for the worst, but instead began to pray for a miracle.

CHAPTER 17

*R*iorden urged his horse forward to leap over the low shrubbery. They landed into what could only be termed as mayhem. His stallion reared and pawed its front hooves wildly in the air. Quickly pulling his sword free from its scabbard, he made fast work of the menacing fool who came towards him. He gave no further thought to his adversary, who fell dead beneath his horse's hooves. He took quick note of the scene and the location of the women. One was missing and two were in the process of being dragged, most unwillingly, from the area. When he espied Katherine, he glared daggers at the buffoon who dared touch her thusly. Her eyes were tear filled as she caught his eye from across the flames of the fire, and he saw her wordlessly speak his name.

'Twas enough. Riorden's battle cry rang out, and the sound echoed harshly into the night. His comrades-in-arms began to fill the area, and the ruffians began to scatter, now that well-armed and mounted knights took the advantage of those on foot.

"Follow them!" Riorden ordered, and Danior, Gavin, and Aiden took flight through the trees. He jumped down from his horse, as Patrick grabbed the reins, and approached the man who had been assaulting Katherine. He watched as the man adjusted his hose. This only infuriated Riorden, all the more. But he was brought up sharply when a knife was skillfully lifted to Katherine's throat.

"Move, or I'll do 'er in." The man threatened, urging Riorden to distance himself.

"You will release the lady," Riorden ordered through clenched teeth.

The man laughed and only tightened his grip on Katherine, taunting Riorden, as if he was denying him a tasty treat. Riorden took a menacing step forward.

"Did you think I but jested?" the captor jeered.

Checking his advance and holding his stance, Riorden sheathed his sword when he saw the ne'er-do-well dig his dagger into the fair skin at Katherine's neck. A small trickle of blood appeared whilst Riorden clenched his fists. Not trusting himself to lessen the distance between them, he placed his hands behind his back and fingered the hilt of his own dirk, hidden beneath the folds of his garment. He stood silently, waiting for his opportunity to strike. He did not have to wait long.

A cocky grin appeared on the man's face as he lowered his hand holding the knife at Katherine's neck and made short work of fondling her breast. He gave it a hard squeeze, and a cry of pain wrenched from her lips.

"I always did like me more'n a 'andful." He laughed arrogantly.

They were his last words. At lightning speed, Riorden flicked his dirk to land squarely in the ruffian's forehead with a sickening smack. His eyes rolled back into his head. Riorden made a grab for Katherine before she too was yanked down to the ground. The man fell, landing in a heap at her feet. Her knees buckled as Riorden caught her. He pulled her close, his heart beating rapidly within his chest.

She squeezed her eyes shut, wrapped her arms around him in a death grip, and began shaking to her core. "Oh God, Riorden," she whispered numbly.

"'Tis all right, Katherine. I have you now," he whispered as he, too, felt himself trembling from having to watch the possibility of her life pass afore him.

Opening her eyes, she peeked around his head to stare at the man with a dagger protruding from his forehead. She made a strange sound of distress that he had never heard from a woman afore. "Is he dead?"

"I should think so, my lady."

"I think...I'm going to be sick."

"'Tis something one gets used to when one goes to war."

"Are we at war?" she questioned with a frightened look in her eyes.

"We are always at war with someone, Katherine. 'Tis dangerous times we live in."

She stood quickly and searched the glen. "My friends! You've got to find them, Riorden."

Before he could answer, two men jumped from the bushes and began to engage Patrick, who swung his blade to defend himself.

"My lord!" he yelled, obviously feeling he was in need of assistance.

Quickly pulling Katherine to a nearby tree, he cupped his hands in order for her to lift herself up to one of the lower branches.

"But I'm afraid of heights," she said fearfully.

"Do as I command, woman!"

As she placed her foot into his hands, Riorden deftly lifted her with ease until Katherine had her arms wrapped securely around the tree trunk, instead of his neck. He pulled his dagger free and again flicked it with amazing accuracy. It, too, hit its mark and one of the men fell dead.

He watched as Patrick stumbled on a low lying root. Thinking his prey was at a disadvantage, the assailant leaned forward to deliver the kill. Instead, he found Patrick's sword brought up at the last minute and the predator was all but skewered on the boy's blade. Afore he could fall on the youth, Riorden leapt to Patrick's aid and gave the dying man a swift kick, sending him sprawling to the ground. He heard Patrick gasp for air.

"You did well, Patrick," Riorden praised the boy as he helped him rise from the dirt. "Dristan would be most pleased with your display of sword work this night."

"Do you really think so, my lord?" Patrick said, as if the stars from heaven had come down to shine upon him.

"Aye! But you must still do me a favor and guard my lady whilst I go aid her friends," Riorden declared. "Do you think yourself up to the task?"

"But of course, my liege," Patrick puffed himself up that he should be given such an honor.

"Good lad." Riorden came to stare up into the tree limbs at his frightened lady. She appeared as though nothing would make her loosen her hold. "I shall return, Katherine. Patrick here will stand guard over you."

He watched her shake her head as if she dared not speak. But then, she surprised him with a request. "Before you leave, will you give me that iron skillet lying there on the ground?"

He handed it up to her, but how she maintained her position whilst holding the heavy iron was beyond his ken. She was like a frightened cat stuck up in a tree. If he had the time, he would have jested with her.

Riorden left his horse and set off on foot, running at a pace born from years of training. One did not get into the condition he was in by idly sitting afore a fire, eating and drinking one's fill day after day. He was used to his daily regime of training, and it felt good to feel as if he was of use again.

He had not gone far, when he heard strange laughter emanating close by. It sounded most odd, given the circumstances the women found themselves in. He came upon Danior, and he found his friend had his hands full with the woman called Juliana. She had been tossed face down across Danior's lap and saddle. Riorden watched in amusement as Danior landed a hearty slap upon her bottom. It had the desired effect Danior must have been looking for, since the woman at last quieted. Riorden raised his brow in question at such an action.

Danior only shrugged. "I could not get her to stop her uncontrollable laughter, and it seemed the only answer," he said with a satisfying smirk to Riorden's unasked question.

Another giggle erupted, along with a hiccup, from Juliana. "I couldn't help it," she gasped out between her mirth," that jerk broke my heel." She gave a little ladylike snort that turned back into laughter as she began mumbling about her shoes, which she waved in the air. Whatever further response she was attempting to make was lost to

Riorden, when Danior headed in the direction of Katherine's camp with his burden, who suddenly found her voice and began to curse most profusely.

Riorden stopped to listen to the sounds of the forest and to determine the direction he should now take. He saw two men on the ground and 'twas obvious Danior had dispatched them to a warmer clime. He saw another, barely visible underneath some brush, whose hand moved. Riorden proceeded cautiously. He pulled at the man's arm, but saw he barely lived. He should have been surprised by the colors the man wore to distinguish himself, but in truth he was not. Seeing his wound, Riorden knew there was not much he could do for the man. He began to rise, only to have his ankle taken in a surprisingly firm grip. He squatted down to hear the Irishman's dying words.

"Must save Lady Emily. I swore to protect her," he managed to say before his last breath left him.

Interesting information, to be pondered on later, Riorden noted. Once again, he did not progress very far when he came upon his brother and young Brianna. He watched in mild fascination as the youthful girl let out an ear splitting sound, much like her own attempt at a womanly battle cry. He had never heard the like. Her voice rang out with determination.

Yet, this is not what immobilized Riorden as he came to a skidding halt. His mouth hung open as he watched this tiny woman deftly twist his brother's arm until he somersaulted onto his back. Gavin must have been just as bemused as Riorden himself was, viewing her moves. He continued to scrutinize her in shocked bewilderment 'til Brianna smartly again twisted Gavin's arm, causing his brother to now lay face down eating dirt, to put it mildly. Everything happened so fast, he would not have believed it, if he had not seen it for himself.

Riorden called her name, but she continued to hold Gavin's arm with her knee positioned most firmly in his back. Riorden smiled at the vision of this tiny warrior. He laughed, thinking Gavin had at last met his match.

"'Tis my brother Gavin you have firmly pinned, Lady Brianna, and given the opportunity, I am sure he will explain he was only trying to help," he exclaimed.

"Oh dear," she said, clearly embarrassed. She took her foot off his back. Stretching out her hand, she politely stood, offering to assist Gavin from the ground. He, in turn, looked aghast that a woman would propose such aid, as if he needed it, or to think he would actually accept such a service.

Riorden gave his brother a satisfying smirk as Gavin rose of his own accord. Gavin glared at him, wiping at the open cut bleeding from his chin. Riorden watched in amusement as the now contrite Brianna began to coo at Gavin, like a little mother hen, as she tried to stem the bleeding.

"I cannot believe it," Riorden chuckled, "bested by a woman."

"Shut up, Riorden," Gavin shouted as he began to lead Brianna back to the camp.

Three down, one to go, Riorden thought, and if he were to have his guess, Lady Emily would be the toughest one of them all. He was not far off the mark, for he began to hear shouting up ahead. He quickened his pace and drew his sword in front of him 'til he once again came to a standstill, watching a most baffling scene unfold afore him.

There, afore his eyes, stood Lady Emily. Her tunic was torn. She held the fabric together with one hand whilst she prodded, for lack of a better term, a stick at Aiden, who tried to take it from her. 'Twas not too often that Aiden stood almost eye to eye with someone, especially a female. Yet, there she stood, holding her ground with one of the best knights he had ever known.

"I told you, buster, to keep your hands off me or you'll regret it!" she shouted and poked him again in his midsection.

"Stop that!" Aiden commanded. His words held no worth, for she smacked him again, this time on his upper arm.

"I won't, unless you leave me be. I appreciate your help with those two idiots over there, but I don't know you. I'm certainly not about to go anywhere with you, mister!"

Aiden held up his hands, as if to surrender. "Has anyone ever said you talk too much?" He made a grab for her and was rewarded with a stinging smack of her stick. "Give me that, wench!"

"Ha! Wench, am I? A few minutes ago you were thinking me more than some low bred wench, I'm thinking," she yelled, and brought down her stick upon his head.

Aiden had had enough and grabbed her. Twisting her around, he at last was able to remove her weapon from her grasp and throw it off into the woods. "There! Will you now listen to reason, lass?" he said soothingly.

She brought her foot down upon his, but it made little impact with the boots he wore. She swore, hopping up and down, holding her sore foot. "Now see what you made me do? I'll be limping for days," she screeched.

"Aiden!" Riorden called. "If you are done aggravating the Lady Emily, perhaps you can make your way back to camp. He means you no harm, my lady."

She quieted and pushed her way from Aiden's arms. "Nice to see you again, Lord de Deveraux," she purred smoothly, throwing a scathing look in Aiden's direction. "I just knew you'd find us sooner or later."

Riorden gave a slight bow and watched Aiden leap into his saddle.

"Come ride with me, Lady Emily," Aiden offered gallantly. He held out his hand for her to take, which was refused.

"No thanks. I'd rather walk," she fumed, and marched off in the direction of camp.

Riorden watched her go and looked up at Aiden, who had a look of admiration on his features.

"What a woman," he said, smiling, and sent his horse off into a gallop.

Riorden began his trek back through the forest and ran at a brisk pace. He could only imagine what awaited him when he re-turned back to camp. He gave a hearty laugh and quickened his pace. He would hate to miss anything that would surely prove entertaining if not baffle the mind.

CHAPTER 18

"Come on, you pansy. You're almost there," Emily called up to Katherine, who began to shimmy down the trunk of the tree, scraping her hands in the process.

"I hate you, Emily," Katherine fumed in righteous indignation.

"No you don't," Emily laughed knowingly. She turned to Patrick, who held out his hand for Katherine to take. "How in the world did he manage to get her up in a tree?"

The boy just shrugged. "He just told her to do as he bid, and up she went."

"I'm impressed," Emily declared.

"I do not understand what is so impressive about his orders," Patrick said in confusion. "If she is to be his lady, then 'tis her duty to obey the commands of her liege lord. Everyone knows this. Surely, where you come from, wives must needs obey their husbands. 'Tis the way of things."

Katherine at last stood on solid ground and turned to look at the young man before her. Since she was short, she wasn't surprised the boy was taller than she, most people were. Still, she needed to set the record straight that she had a mind of her own and she would use it.

"Do you have a sister, Patrick?" She smiled brightly when his face betrayed his answer.

"Aye, three of them."

"And they all do as they are commanded by their lord without question?"

Patrick sighed. "If you knew my sister Amiria, and even Lynet, you would not ask that of me and would know they do not. But 'tis an unusual circumstance, and not the normal custom."

Katherine's smile broadened, and she gave Patrick a slight hug. He was startled by the open display of affection. "I am not the norm either, my young friend. My lady friends and I are used to being independent and doing things on our own."

Patrick only crossed his arms in front of his chest and smirked with an inner knowledge he knew for certain. "That was afore you met Lord de Deveraux. Be prepared for change, milady."

She laughed out loud. "I will concede the point for the time being." She turned to Emily. "And you stop calling me a pansy! I would think you could come up with a different name that would be more pleasing to my ears."

Emily shrugged. "It fits," she proclaimed and went to sit next to Aiden on a log by the fire.

Katherine saw Emily pick up the stick she had used earlier and begin poking it in the fire. Aiden leaned over to whisper something in Emily's ear and received a shove that sent him soaring over the tree trunk with his feet flying up in the air. It was an amusing sight. Everyone laughed, despite Aiden's look of indignant anger thrown in their direction, once he regained his footing. He sat back down with a look that appeared as if he would behave. Emily, with good reason, kept her guard up.

Juliana stood next to Danior and both of them seemed completely tongue tied...a first for Juliana, at least to Katherine's recollection. To be honest, Danior appeared flustered, and she swore she heard Jewels break into a nervous giggle or two. Seeing the conversation didn't appear to be something to laugh about, Katherine assumed her friend was ill at ease.

That, of course, left Brianna. Katherine could only shake her head at her young friend, given she had Gavin's head lying comfortably in her lap. She told him to lie still as she applied a butterfly bandage to his chin. A chin she swore was damaged due to her own reckless nature while trying to defend herself. Katherine thought it strange that, just days before, Brie could barely stand the sight of blood when Katherine's own fingers were bleeding all over the place. Yet, for some peculiar reason, it didn't seem to now matter while she helped Gavin. She gave a muffled laugh, for what man wouldn't mind being the center of attention and being fussed over by a beautiful, young woman.

Where is he? Katherine searched the edges of the forest, pondering his absence. She peered into the darkness beyond the fire, yet saw nothing but dancing shadows cast in the tree limbs above their heads. She held her breath while she waited for Riorden's return. He couldn't have gone that far, could he?

A rustling of the bushes caught the attention of the group, and immediately, each man grabbed a woman, placing her in protection behind him, then each drew their swords. Even Patrick stood to protect Katherine, and she had the notion he would die on her behalf...a humbling thought, if there ever was one. She tried to peer around Patrick's shoulder to see if it was friend or foe and earned herself a warning glare from her young protector. It was a bit too reminiscent of Riorden. Then she heard the sound of the men's swords returning to the scabbards at their sides, and she was finally allowed to see what the commotion was all about.

Their eyes met, and Katherine again felt the pull of Riorden, as if only the two of them existed in this world. She waited breathlessly until he opened his arms wide. It was all the invitation she needed as she ran, closing the distance between them. She hurled herself into his arms and felt him embrace her, as if he never intended to let her go. She hugged him tighter and heard a small grunt from him, causing her to wonder where he was hurt. If he was like the men of the twenty-first century, he would only ask for medical attention if he was on his death bed. Thankfully, that didn't appear to be the case.

After several moments, she felt herself sliding down the length of his body until she stood on solid ground but inches from him. Solid being a relative word, seeing as her legs felt as though they were made of melted butter. He tore his gloves off, and she felt the warmth of his hands cup her face. His thumbs began to caress her cheeks in a slow, soothing motion. But oh those eyes! Even in the darkness, their blueness left her speechless as she stared at him. For one brief instant he began to lean down, and she thought he would kiss her. She watched him carefully, in anticipation of their lips touching, until his eyes widened, as if he realized what he was about to do. He suddenly pulled back, as he came to his senses, and straightened himself to his full height. *Damn! That special moment had been so close, and yet so far away!*

He turned her head and scowled when he saw the mark on her neck. "You are for the most part unharmed?"

"Yes, other than a few scratches."

The look he gave her told her to explain herself, so she showed him her damaged hands and the scrapes caused by her decent from the tree. It also appeared as if her already injured fingers were in need of some attention. His scowl proved he was not happy.

"I'll be okay…umm…fine. I have some ointment in my purse to help heal these," Katherine stated.

"I will aid you if you would allow it."

She smiled with a sudden feeling of being overly embarrassed. "If you insist."

"I do," Riorden exclaimed, and he followed her to where she had left her gear by the fire.

They sat down next to each other. Katherine picked up her purse and pondered its contents, not exactly certain of how she was going to explain the futuristic gadgets her leather bag held. Plastic containers, her spiral notebook and pens, her cell phone, for God sake, the first aid kit, and makeup, a travel size Kleenex packet, and if she dug down deep enough into this oversized bag she schlepped around, she was sure to find some chocolate and a granola bar or two. She could never remember what was to be found at the bottom of her purse, only that its weight told her she tended to carry too much.

She bit her bottom lip with indecision and peeked at him through lowered lashes. He waited patiently for her to come to some sort of conclusion, although it was clear he wanted to address her injuries quickly.

"I have to tell you that what I have inside this bag could be construed as witchlike in your time. I'd hate to be caught and burned at the stake," she whispered softly, knowing the truth of her words.

"I will protect you, Katherine, and no further harm shall befall you," Riorden vowed.

She could not be suspicious of the sincerity of his words as he once again reached up and caressed her cheek. "I thank you for your protection, but what I'll show you will no doubt leave you a little dazed, wondering at what marvels the future holds."

"Then perhaps we should proceed slowly and address the immediate needs of your care. The rest can wait 'til perhaps we are alone to discuss such wonders," he offered.

"Very well," she said and reached inside for the small travel first aid kit Jewels insisted she carry. The simple sound of the zipper caused Riorden to flinch, and actually stopped the conversation of the men gathered around the fire. "Sorry...We'll explain later."

Next, she took off the makeshift bandages and saw that her cuts weren't as bad as she had thought. They just needed a little cleaning and a new dressing. Opening up a disinfectant packet, she held it out to him. "It will burn, but just wipe the pad across the scratches and cuts."

His hands actually shook as he held something from the future. He continued to stare at it for several minutes.

"Riorden, you need to hurry or it'll dry up, and I don't have a lot of those in my kit."

He hesitated no longer but cursed when Katherine indeed flinched as he ran the soft cloth across her injuries. Next she held out a small tube of ointment and uncapped it. He held a look of such disbelief, peering at the plastic tube, that she was uncertain if he would be able to continue helping her.

"Riorden, it's okay. Just hold out your finger, and I'll squeeze some of this out. You can then smooth it over my hand, and we'll bandage everything up again," Katherine said confidently.

He looked at the ointment in wonder and began to do as she had instructed him. After several minutes, he began to bandage her hands with some gauze, another wonder from the future she was sure she would answer for at some point in their journey together. He finished quickly and gently took her hands in his own.

Clearing his throat, he once more gained his composure and gave her a mischievous grin. She could have sworn his eyes were sparkling from merriment at what he had accomplished.

"What about you? Where are you hurt?" she questioned softly.

"'Tis of no consequence, I assure you."

"Ha! I've heard that before. Really Riorden, I should see that your injuries are taken care of, as well."

"Nay, not this night, Katherine. Mayhap on the morrow you can see to it, when we are well rid of this place and closer to the village. I know of a warm spring that feeds itself into a small pond ideal for swimming if you are so inclined. 'Tis but a half days ride from here, if we do not stop often. It can be most refreshing after a long ride," he said firmly.

"I'm not much of a swimmer, even though I can hold my own...or a rider for that matter," she confided quietly.

"Then I will teach you. You must needs learn to ride, my lady."

"Easy for you to say. You've probably lived most of your life atop a horse," she replied and gave a very, unladylike yawn. "Sorry."

"There is not much left to the night, Katherine. You should rest, for we have a long ride ahead of us, come sun up," Riorden said light heartedly.

"But I'm not sleepy," Katherine exclaimed as she stifled another yawn. She looked at him, and he merely gave her an I-told-you-so look. "Well, maybe I am, just a little."

"Aiden will be standing guard. If you have no objections, I offer my shoulder as your pillow this night. I cannot vouch for the comfort of the mail beneath my tabard, however," Riorden stated as he opened his arm and clasped Katherine to his side. He began tucking his cloak around her as a blanket.

"You are a most chivalrous knight," she said in a hushed tone and heard him grunt some off handed reply. She reached up a hand and took hold of a length of his hair. She sighed contently and began to twirl it in her fingers.

"Be at ease, Katherine," he said quietly, and placed a chaste kiss on top of her head.

Katherine couldn't believe her good fortune that fate had led Riorden to find her. She began shifting around until she found the perfect place to rest her head as she snuggled into her knight. She would have been horrified and appalled to know that a short time later, a soft snore passed from her lips, causing Riorden to give a merry chuckle, while she continued, naively, to peacefully slumber the remainder of the night.

CHAPTER 19

Katherine stamped her foot, trying to make her point, and placed her hands on her hips, as if that would change his mind.

"Absolutely *not*!" she cried out.

"Kat…listen to reason," Riorden urged gently. He had a look set on his face as though he was trying to find patience with her, but she was so frustrated.

"No way!" she huffed pitifully, knowing he was right. She covered her smile, hearing the nickname that, apparently, caused him some amusement from her flight up the tree the night before.

"You shall be perfectly safe."

"Right! Not on that monster I won't," she declared, crossing her arms in front of her. He broke into one of those grins that was a half knowing smirk and half roguishly handsome devil. It about drove her crazy, and she felt her resolve weakening.

Riorden gave his horse an affectionate pat. "Do not insult my horse. He is most timid."

"He's huge, Riorden. I'm sure I'll meet my death when I fall off, which most assuredly will happen, knowing my luck," Katherine insisted awkwardly, trying to think of some other alternative than mounting that monstrosity of an animal. "I believe I've made it perfectly clear that I don't like heights."

"I will keep you safe, Katherine. Come, take my hand, and I shall hoist you up. You shall sit in front of me, just like my brother holds Lady Brianna."

She frowned in indecision. "You make me sound like a boat anchor," she mumbled half to herself. His laughter rang out, making light of the situation. She glanced backwards. Brie was indeed comfortably sitting on Gavin's lap, with his arms securely wrapped around her waist and his gloved hands holding the reins of his horse. Brie waved at her, wearing a smile that lit her serene countenance clear up to her eyes. Apparently, Katherine wasn't the only one who was finding love in the past. She couldn't be happier for her friend.

She looked up at Riorden and the hand he offered her. "You won't let me fall off this beast?" she asked, still uncertain of her fate with the animal.

"Nay, I will not. Now, come, the morn awaits us."

Katherine took his hand and before she could change her mind, she found herself deposited, much like a sack of grain, across his lap. She squirmed to right herself, cursing all humanity in her embarrassment. She was positive this wasn't the most ladylike way to get a man's attention. As she settled herself, he paid no mind to her reservations of sitting atop the horse. Instead, Riorden adjusted a small blanket on her lap to keep the chill from her legs. The morning was still nippy, and she could see her breath in the air.

"By the by...how did you know?" Riorden asked as he put on his gloves and took up the reins.

She felt the monster below her move. A fear of falling caused a startled gasp to escape her, and she made a quick grab for Riorden's waist. With a deathlike grip on the fabric of his tabard, she squeezed her eyes shut. Uncomfortable with the distance to the ground, she began to shake with the fear of falling beneath the massive hooves of the animal on top of which she was now precariously perched.

"Kat?"

She opened her eyes and looked up into his face, realizing she hadn't heard a single word he'd been saying. "What?"

He chuckled. "I asked, my lady, how did you know my horse's name?"

Her brows drew together in a frown of bewilderment. "I don't...do I?"

"His name, my dear, is Beast," he said, waiting for her reaction with a twinkle in his eye.

She rolled her eyes as she offered a silent prayer to the heavens to save her. "Wonderful!" she said under her breath, causing him to laugh heartily.

"'Tis all right, Katherine. Relax," he declared, and turned the animal to await the others.

Katherine observed the group in front of her and wondered if anyone else was panicking like she was, sitting on something that wasn't gasoline powered. But everyone appeared normal, or so she thought. Patrick was in the process of putting out the rest of their fire by scraping dirt into the pit with his boots. Brianna was chattering away with Gavin, who was laughing at her jokes. Juliana and Emily did seem slightly ill at ease, for obvious reasons. At least their feet were still on solid ground.

She drew her attention to the youngest of their group and watched intently as Brianna looked back and forth between two of the knights, as though she was assessing Gavin's features and those of his brother. Katherine could admit there was a slight resemblance, even though the shade of their hair coloring was different. She had the impression Gavin's brown hair would turn to lighter shades as the summer sun continued to grace its length. As if her friend couldn't help herself, and who could blame her, Brie hesitated only a moment before reaching out and touching a lock of his hair. Katherine saw Gavin smile at her friend, and she knew Brianna was completely lost.

"You don't look much like your brother," Brianna stated matter-of-factly. His expression changed slightly. "Did I say something wrong?"

"Nay," Gavin replied, somewhat solemnly. "I take after my mother."

"She must indeed be lovely, if you look like her," Brianna replied softly, and then blushed to the roots of her hair. Katherine held back her laughter, knowing Brie had, more or less, just called him beautiful.

"My thanks for the compliment, my lady," he said with a slight bow of his head. "I am afraid she has passed on, though."

"I'm so sorry, Gavin," she said, placing her hand on his arm. Then she reached out and tentatively touched the bandage on this chin. "Does it still hurt?"

Katherine could hear his chuckle from where she sat. "I would never admit it, even if it did, Lady Brianna. Besides," he said as his smile broadened whilst he gazed upon Brie, "'twas worth it."

Katherine hid her smile in her hand and turned her attention toward her other friends, who were still not on horses. Emily did not look happy with whom she would ride, and Juliana looked uncertain, as well.

She supposed if she were in Emily's shoes, she would be beside herself, gazing on such a handsome man. Katherine knew it would be Aiden's red hair that would have Emily flabbergasted. It had always been her downfall. Or maybe it would be his eyes, the color of violets. *Really? Violets? Who has eyes that color, anyway? Just look at him standing there with all the confidence of getting his way, surrounding his whole being.* He was tall, muscular, and in the prime of his life, although Katherine guessed he wasn't much older than Emily herself.

"You will ride with me," Aiden ordered Emily, who stood holding the fire poking stick as if it was, in truth, a blade made of the heaviest steel.

"And you'll keep your hands to yourself, or you'll draw back a nub! You got that buster?" Emily replied in kind.

"Why do you keep calling me *buster* or *mister*? You truly are the strangest lass I ever met."

"Yesterday, I was a wench, and now I'm strange?" Emily fumed, obviously insulted by his words. "Didn't you're mother ever teach you manners and how to treat a lady?"

Aiden marched to stand smack dab in front of her, almost eye to eye. His grin was one of pure cockiness, if Katherine ever saw one. "Start acting like a lady, and I shall treat you as such," he said quietly, through clenched teeth.

"Well...I never!"

"Mayhap, that is your problem," Aiden said, turning away. He placed his foot in the stirrup and swung his leg up over his horse. Emily stood there sputtering, trying to find words to say as a snide retort. He held out his hand for her to take. "Well? Will you stand there all day, or are you coming?"

"Only because I must." Emily conceded defeat finally, her words delivered sharply. Taking his hand, she allowed Aiden to assist her ascent. Katherine observed Aiden take special care to ensure Emily was safely established in his lap. His one last act was to wrench the stick from her hands and watch it sail off into the woods. With a satisfied smirk, he too waited for the last of their party to mount up.

Katherine could only imagine what was going on inside Juliana's head. From the amount of uncontrollable laughter that randomly escaped her friend's lips, she had the notion that Jewels probably felt Danior was the most handsome man she had ever laid eyes on. Juliana peeked at him through lowered lashes as she patted the neck of his horse to distract her. What amused Katherine was Danior appeared about as flustered as her friend. His mouth moved several times, as if to form some semblance of words he might say to Juliana, but only awkward silence remained between them.

Katherine saw how his sandy-brown hair blew in the breeze, causing it to become ruffled. He drew his hand through it, trying to make it behave, but it was a lost cause. Juliana must have been thinking the same thing, since a laugh escaped her. Danior scowled in return, showing off an old scar on his forehead. It was a striking combination along with his deep blue eyes. It gave him the dangerous appeal of that bad boy every woman just loves.

Danior finally found his voice although it croaked when he at last spoke. "Shall we?"

"Yes, of course," Juliana managed to squeak out.

He leapt into the saddle with ease, as if he had lived his life on a horse, which was most certainly the case. In no time at all, Juliana also found herself atop a horse with a manly arm wrapped around her waist. As he drew the hood of her cloak up over her head to protect her from the cold, Juliana blushed while gazing up at him. Danior, in turn, looked at her most intently.

"I have never seen that shade of green in someone's eyes," he said gently. "They are most lovely...as are you, Lady Juliana."

She sat nestled in his lap, with her mouth opened wide in surprise. Juliana wasn't used to compliments, so when she received one, she sometimes forgot how to react. A nervous, uncontrollable giggle burst from her lips. "Um...thank you." She whispered, so softly, Katherine barely heard her response.

Juliana must have been completely embarrassed as she all but hid herself beneath the hood of her cloak. But apparently, Danior had other ideas in mind, and Katherine was amused when he took her friend's chin and gently lifted her head so she gazed once more into his eyes. He smiled at her, and if Katherine knew her at all, Jewels just lost her breath.

"You are most welcome, my lady," Danior grinned sheepishly. He cleared his throat and looked at the others who were staring at him oddly. "What?" He huffed.

"Nothing. Nothing at all," Riorden replied, assuring him that everything was in order. Riorden chuckled and turned to gaze at Katherine where she resided comfortably in his lap. Then, to the men, he ordered, "Remember, we must now keep an eye out for the other who has slipped through our grasp."

"Is something wrong?" Katherine asked, and watched the men seemingly become uneasy at her question.

"'Tis nothing you must needs worry about, Katherine," Riorden answered honestly. "We are but looking for a missing prisoner from Bamburgh, in order that Danior remains in possession of his head."

This time it was the women of the group who cast glances from one to the other. For the time being, they kept their mouths shut and did not offer any advice.

"I see," Katherine said quietly.

"Let us be on our way," Riorden called to the group, and he pulled Katherine's hood over her head. "Hold tight, my love."

Any further chance of talk was lost to her as Beast moved beneath her. She held on to Riorden and the pommel of the saddle to help keep her balance. As she watched the scenery pass swiftly by, with the horse picking up speed, Riorden's term of endearment finally registered in her mind. He had called her *his love*. A most promising sign, for sure.

A sudden, uncontrollable shiver consumed her with the premonition she should be telling Riorden of Tiernan's aid. First, she needed to talk with her friends alone, and she promised herself she would do so at the first available opportunity. She tightened her grip around Riorden's waist and felt him lightly press her head to his shoulder with a gentle caress of his hand. She sighed contently and felt the gentle swaying of the animal beneath her. They rode for most of the day. In the late afternoon hours, Beast's steady and sure-footed gait began lulling her into a state of complete sleepiness. She dismissed the small voice nagging at her inside her mind and, instead of voicing her concerns, she closed her eyes and slept.

CHAPTER 20

The heavy mist that had surrounded them began to lift as Katherine cried out his name. Riorden stood there with his arms crossed against his chest. An angry expression was planted firmly on his face, and he looked as if he was so disappointed in her that it shook her to her very core. She began to tremble in fear that she couldn't make things right between them.

"You lied to me," he said briskly.

"I can explain," she pleaded as she tried to reach out to him. He drew back, as if he couldn't stand to have her place her hands anywhere near his body. "Please, Riorden..."

"I do not wish to hear your explanation, Katherine. You betrayed my trust and lied to me," he firmly voiced, yet again.

"I withheld information. There is a difference," she said shortly. "If you would listen to me, I can account for everything."

"I have had one lying, deceitful woman in my life," he began gruffly. "I will not have another, no matter how I feel for you."

"She was a fool to hurt you, but you can't punish me for something that happened in your past and before we met," she argued.

"Aye...I can."

It was a simple statement that spoke volumes. He turned from her, and she felt him slipping away. "Riorden," she cried out and saw him hesitate in *furthering the distance between them. He at last turned to stare at her, and she rushed across the space separating them.*

"*I love you,*" *she whispered, ever so softly, and reached up to tenderly cup his face with her hand. He held her hand, for just a moment, until he at last let go. The burning look he gave her made her feel as if she had been scorched. Since she was obviously given no choice, she dropped her arm. It hung limply at her side while tears streamed down her face. She had hoped that by telling him her heart's deepest desire, he would forgive her. His expression, however, didn't change with her confession, much to her dismay.*

"*Sometimes, that is not enough, Katherine,*" *he exclaimed, voicing his displeasure.*

She stood there, never taking her eyes from his. Her breath became caught in her throat with misery from the turmoil she was feeling inside. The mist returned and all but consumed his body until he disappeared in front of her eyes, much as he did when she had seen him as a ghost.

"*Riorden...come back to me, my love,*" *she called out, but silence was the only answer to her heartfelt plea.*

She stood there alone, shivering in the cold air, with the realization at what her omission had reaped. It had cost her everything. She had lost him.

∽

Katherine jolted awake and sat up, gasping for air. Her heart was hammering so hard, she felt as if it were about to be ripped from her chest. Disoriented, she looked at her surroundings. The mound of soft moss she had been lying on made for a comfortable bed. She had no clue how she had gotten there or for how long she had slept undisturbed.

She gathered Riorden's cloak around her. He must have given it to her, to keep her warm. She inhaled. The scent, which was all Riorden, reminded her of a rich, full-bodied, red wine and engulfed her as if he had wrapped his arms around her himself. For the most part, she was alone, with the exception of Patrick, who appeared as if he was anxious to be anywhere else than where he stood, guarding her.

She cleared her throat to gain his attention. Excitement leapt into his eyes at the prospect, she assumed, of leading her to the rest of their group, wherever that may be. She then heard the distinct sound of swords clashing. Her show of alarm and panic alerted Patrick, who came to her side to help her rise.

"Have no fear, Lady Katherine," he said. He gathered his sword and began to escort her through the trees.

"We're not at war?" she asked hesitantly.

He gave a boyish laugh and smiled broadly. "Nay, my lady. 'Tis but a bit of swordplay to keep us fit. I am glad you are awake so I may at last join the training."

She gave him a tiny smile, still feeling the effects of her nightmare. "Then lead on, Sir Patrick, so we don't delay. Far be it for me to keep you from your training."

Her comment seemed to have the desired effect on the young man as he ushered her to only a slight distance from where she awoke. They broke through a stand of trees, causing Katherine to stop dead in her tracks at the wondrous sight before her. She rubbed her eyes, speculating whether she still dreamed...but no. There before her was a sight she never thought she would ever behold, unless it was on a movie screen. It left her feeling numb.

He was absolutely magnificent. There were just no other words to describe him. Her knees had become weak, like melted butter. They began to buckle, and she plopped down to the ground right there where she had stood. She watched the display in front of her that was all Riorden...shirtless...his muscles bulging from his workout...glistening sweat gleaming on his smooth firm chest...swinging a blade with a grin of pure pleasure that seemed to radiate from every inch of his incredible body.

Surreptitiously, she reached her hand up to her mouth, just to ensure she wasn't embarrassing herself by having drool actually come from her lips. She was safe, at least for the moment. Still, she couldn't take her eyes off him. Good Lord above, what a sight he was! It was not as if she had never before seen nice eye candy, as they would say in the future, of good looking men with a six pack for a stomach. But as she continued drinking in the sight of her knight, she swore Riorden must have been working on eight. There wasn't one ounce of fat to be found on his sinewy body. She swallowed hard, just thinking of touching his skin.

Self-consciously, her hands went to her own body that was certainly on the side of curvy and not as lean as his. It made her feel insecure, and she began to wonder how she would ever be able to keep a man such as him. Katherine wasn't going to fool herself by calling herself beautiful. She was, in her own way, she supposed, but she certainly wasn't anywhere near model material. At least, she wasn't some high maintenance kind of a woman, but preferred the simpler things in life to make her happy.

She moistened her lips and returned her gaze to the spectacle in front of her. In reality, she had eyes only for one. Although she had to admit, the other men who stood before her training in the small glen were just as glorious as her Riorden. If she hadn't known better, she would have said four Greek Gods had come down to earth to tempt four young women to sin. From the look of her friends a short distance away, they were just as awestruck.

"My lady?" Patrick said, breaking the spell. "Are you unwell?"

Unwell? She was more than unwell! Unsettled, breathless, trembling with a need she hadn't felt in many years and wishing she could run her fingers down Riorden's resplendent body at her leisure. Or better yet, to take a dip in the pond, just the two of them, that now caught her attention. She could only imagine what Riorden would think of her if he could hear her thoughts. Lust rushed through her trembling body as she licked her lips. She was certain her face showed where her thoughts had wandered.

"Milady?"

"Huh?" she muttered and finally tore her glaze from her knight. "Sorry. What were you saying, Patrick?"

He chuckled, as if guessing what had befallen her. "Never mind," he said, offering his hand as he helped her rise. He took his liege's cloak from her, as if he thought it was too much of a burden for her to carry. "Lord Riorden has a fire burning, as you can see, for you and your ladies, once you are finished with your swim. They have been but waiting for you to awake from your slumber."

She nodded, not daring herself to express any form of a response.

She just knew it would come out as a jumbled mess. Instead, she made her way towards her friends, who sat in silence, watching the display that left them equally speechless.

Katherine sat down next to them and, finally, dared to look at Juliana. She reached for her hand, giving it a squeeze. "Wow," she exclaimed, since that was all she could manage.

"That's not the half of it as you can imagine," Juliana said. "We haven't even tried to form words. To do so would almost be unworthy of them."

"Can we go swimming now?" Brianna asked impatiently.

"I wouldn't mind a dip, either, although what I wouldn't give for a nice chlorine filled pool right about now. I guess I'll have to settle, since that's obviously not an option," Emily declared in a huff. "I feel as if I have all of nature clinging and attaching itself to my skin. I hate the great outdoors."

They all shared a laugh, but before they could rise, Katherine leaned in to speak to the ladies in a hushed tone. "I've had a horrible nightmare. So, I plan on telling Riorden about our aid from Tiernan's men. I have the feeling he may already have an idea of what's going on, from the dead men that were left behind."

"They can't take him back to the king," Emily announced shakily. "You know how they torture prisoners in this day and age, don't you? I won't have Tiernan subject to such a fate!"

"And I won't have Danior lose his head," Juliana said, just as nervously.

"Can't we think of something else to change their minds?" Brie suggested.

"We'll figure out some sort of alternative, but I won't keep such information from Riorden. I have this terrible feeling it wouldn't go well," Katherine proclaimed.

Katherine rose, and the others followed her lead. They went to the edge of the pond, which was cast in shadows from the trees above their heads. Drying cloths had been set aside for them with some kind of rough looking soap. It was a thoughtful gesture on one of the men's part, but Katherine could only imagine what the lye soap would do to their skin.

They all seemed to have the same idea at the same time and began digging in their respective purses. Between the four of them, they had travel size containers of shampoo and conditioner, lotion, and a nice rose scented bar of soap. It wouldn't go far, but it would be enough to see to their needs for now.

They looked at each other and again seemed to be on the same page.

"Do you think we should?" Brie asked, as if they were conspiring to come up with some deep secret operation to overthrow the government.

"It's relatively dark over here, and they are pretty busy," Emily added.

"Well, I'm not swimming with all my clothes on, that's for sure," Katherine said, pulling her shirt over her head. She watched as the other women started to do the same. Shoes were flipped off, socks unrolled, and jeans became unzipped then thrown into a dirty pile of clothes they had been living in for days.

Juliana giggled. "Katie's gone all commando. I don't know how you can go without undies, sis."

Katherine gave her a lopsided smirk and reached behind her to unclasp her bra. She twirled it around by the strap and flung it into the pile with the rest of her errant clothing. "At least I don't have a string up my ass, Jewels," she laughed, seeing her friend wearing a thong.

"They're comfortable," Juliana retorted.

Katherine laughed again. "I'll have to take your word for it."

She went to the edge of the pond, put her foot in to test the temperature, pinched her nose, and dove into the warm waters. She came up laughing. "Come on in! The water's fine!"

It was all the encouragement the other women needed. "When in Rome..." Emily declared pulling her camisole off and throwing it into the pile of dirty garments. With her bra and underwear still on, she jumped into the water. She was followed by the remaining two ladies who had decided to keep their bare necessities on, as well.

It seemed as if it had been so very long since they could just let go and do something playful. Soon they began to splash each other with water, and Brianna called out *Marco* to the response from the others of *Polo*.

The women were laughing so hard and having so much fun, they didn't realize there was no longer any sound of clashing swords ringing in the air. Instead, their merriment came to an abrupt halt, and all four women got extremely sheepish grins on their faces while they stood together waist deep in the water, stunned by what they saw on the shore.

It wasn't every day one looked up to see four grown men and a teenager with their mouths hanging open, apparently shocked to the very core of their very medieval minds. The women glanced at one another. They should have been blushing, especially since one of them was buck naked. The other three women might as well be, considering their soaking wet pretty lace bras clung to them in a way that left nothing to the imagination. But they were, in fact, modern women, thrown into the past yet used to showing skin in their own day and age. So, instead of being embarrassed, they did the most natural thing they could think of between them, given the circumstance. They began to laugh outrageously at the hilarity of it all.

CHAPTER 21

Riorden closed his mouth with a snap. For the life of him, he could not see what was so funny, causing the four naked women afore them to laugh so merrily. Well...not all of them were completely nude. Nay! It had to be his lovely Katherine, showing everyone her beautiful self with all that God had graced her. His beautiful Katherine, who was completely unembarrassed whilst he gaped at her, standing there with eyes focused only on him.

She began to blush a most becoming shade of red, even as he watched her tongue peek out of her mouth. A mouth surely just begging to be kissed. She licked her lips, and it was almost more than he could bear. Finally, she had the decency to duck down into the water to cover her breasts. Those perfectly full shaped breasts he swore his hands were just itching to feel. He felt a part of him stir and come to life.

"Patrick!" he called gruffly.

"Aye, my lord?" Patrick answered, grinning from ear to ear and obviously pleased by what was on display in front of his young eyes.

"Turn!" Riorden ordered harshly.

"B-but...my lord," the young man sputtered.

Riorden gave him a glance that brooked no disobedience, causing

Patrick to reluctantly turn from the vision he had been enjoying. He began muttering underneath his breath about life being unfair until Riorden held out his hand for his cloak. It was turned over to him without further comment from the lad.

"I think we have found us some mermaids, men. Shall we join them in their play?" Aiden teased and watched as the remaining women slowly sank down into the water at his remark.

"Do *not* even think it," Riorden ordered.

Danior appeared to be trying to find words to describe what little clothing Juliana was wearing. 'Twas obvious he was not pleased she displayed herself as she did.

"Really, Riorden, where did you say these four enchanting creatures came from?" Gavin questioned, although he was clearly in agreement with Aiden's suggestion.

Riorden sighed heavily. "'Tis apparent an explanation is in order. But first, I believe you three should offer your cloaks to the ladies, once I have rescued mine, who appears in more need of assistance than the others. I should add, you shall be gentlemen and aid them with your backs turned. Patrick, you go and tend the fire."

Riorden kept his eyes on his lady, unbuckled his belt, letting his sword fall to the edge of the pond and began to wade, hose, boots and all, into the warm water. He saw how Katherine began to move further into the shadows whilst he heard the other women making their way out of the water. A brief glance told him they were gathering their garments and going out of sight to change.

He continued his advance until he came but inches of her. His cape came to rest over her bare shoulders, not that it did a lot of good, for the garment all but floated behind her. He fastened the clasp about her neck with trembling fingers. He felt clumsy and wondered how one woman could affect him so. She was so very close that he felt heat radiate between them without so much as a single touch.

"You will not reveal yourself in front of my men again, Katherine. Do you understand me?" Riorden said through clenched teeth, trying to calm his irrational mood. She gazed back at him steadily, as if she had done no wrong.

"We call it skinny dipping in my time," she shrugged, trying to calm him with her words. "It's not a big deal." She reached up and began to caress his hair, as if to distract him. He felt her fingers gliding between its lengths. "It's so soft," she said, almost to herself.

"Call it what you will, but you will not be *dipping skinny* again, unless 'tis just the two of us. I will not share your beauty with any other."

She laughed whole heartedly at his words. "Well, when you put it in such a romantic fashion as that, how could a girl go against such a lovely request?"

The smile she gave him disarmed him to his very core. Afore common sense could prevail, he grabbed her about her waist and brought them chest to chest. She gasped as they made contact, skin to skin. She lovingly wound her arms around his neck. He swore she gave him the most seductive purr he had ever heard in his entire life. 'Twas most pleasing to his ears.

"Do you feel it, Riorden?" she asked huskily.

He gave a brief laugh, since he certainly felt all kinds of sensations, especially a part of him rising to the occasion. "What?" he asked. He easily held her with one arm whilst his free hand moved a stray lock of wet hair from her face.

"Your heartbeat next to mine," Katherine whispered, ever so softly.

He was momentarily startled at her words until the reality of them hit him full force. They were actually his own words spoken from his heart when they were both nothing more than shadows of what might have been. It humbled him whilst he did indeed feel her steady heartbeat next to his own. They were no longer ghosts, but flesh and blood. She had crossed *Time* for him, and he vowed he would keep her forever by his side.

"Aye, my dearest Katherine, I feel it, too," he replied profoundly, and watched in fascination whilst the pulse at her throat ticked rapidly. He was pleased to know he had such an effect on her, since the same held true of him. He felt her clasp her arms around his neck more fully as she molded her body to his own. It was almost his undoing.

"Isn't it wonderful when dreams come true," she added whilst she began to trace the planes of his face.

Riorden trembled beneath her gentle touch. "Aye, my lady, 'tis indeed most wondrous."

"Will you do me a favor?" Katherine asked timidly.

"Aye, my lady, anything you wish. I am yours to command."

"Anything?"

"Aye." He did not trust himself with an attempt at a longer response whilst she looked at him with those scorching aquamarine eyes.

"Then kiss me," she begged. Her words lingered in the air between them. "Please..."

His resolve to remain a gentleman vanished abruptly with her plea. His head swooped down and his mouth took possession of hers in a ravenous kiss. 'Twas as if he was starving, and only she could satisfy his hunger. His tongue plunged into her mouth and danced in tune with hers. He moaned at the contact. She moaned in response. His hands roamed down her backside and brought her closer, if that was at all humanly possible. He felt every glorious inch of her and knew in his heart he had found his soul mate. She was the other half of him, making him complete. She was what he had always been missing in his life. She was perfect for him, and she was his.

He deepened their kiss and felt as if time no longer had meaning to them. *Time*. He vowed *Time* would not steal her back and take her from his life. He broke their kiss. She took his lower lip and gave it a small nibble. *Merde!* Where did she learn to be such a seductress?

He reluctantly began to lower her back down the length of him, never taking his eyes from hers. He could tell by the look she gave him, she was disappointed. Wondering what she would do next, he had to remember to inhale when she surprised him by reaching out her hands to place them on his chest. He gave a sharp intake of breath as air rushed into his lungs whilst her fingers began to slowly explore his muscles, moving ever downward on his stomach.

"My God. You must be the most beautiful man I've ever seen," she murmured in awe, biting her lower lip.

'Twas taking everything within him not to smother that delicious mouth of hers in another searing kiss. "A man cannot be called beautiful, my lady," Riorden managed to choke out.

Katherine stopped her fingertips and laid her palms fully upon him. He sucked in his breath yet again, when she leveled her exquisite bluish-green eyes on him. "Oh, but you are…" Her words trailed off and hovered between them. She gave a tiny smile that could only be termed intimate before she continued touching him.

He could stand no more of her exquisite torture and made a grab for her hands, holding them playfully behind her back. A grin formed at the corners of his mouth, and he heard the sigh that escaped her.

Katherine's eyes reflected a teasing gleam as she licked her lips once more. Wiggling her arms, he released them, and she placed her hands upon his shoulders.

"Will you think me too bold if I speak my mind?" she asked hesitantly.

He chuckled. "Kat…you stand next to me, naked as the day you came into this world, and you are afraid to speak your mind else I think you too bold? What is it you wish to say to me?"

She did not wait long afore giving him her answer that sounded more like a soft caress. "I want you. Now…today…for all of our tomorrows…"

'Twas a simple heartfelt statement, and he did not doubt her words. "As I want you, Katherine. For all of ever."

"Then make love to me, Riorden, I beg of you," she purred with so much hope in her voice as she held her breath waiting for his answer.

"Katherine—" He knew she felt his hesitation. Disappointment and hurt flashed briefly in her features afore she hid her face from him. 'Twas as if he had broken her spirit.

She shook her head, as if she did not want to hear what he had to say. "I see. I certainly understand if you don't want to make love to me. I'm sure you're used to women who are far more beautiful than me, flinging themselves at you."

Riorden watched her arms drop from his shoulders in defeat until she gathered his cloak around her body, suddenly embarrassed at her lack of clothing. She started to back away from him, but he gathered her close again so her ear was now pushed to his chest.

"You are beautiful to me, and that is all that matters. Your loveliness even outshines the heavenly stars lit in the moonlit sky," he replied, caressing her hair.

She gave a startled gasp at his words and raised her head to stare at him, her eyes opened wide. "No one has ever said anything like that to me before."

"Then I am glad, I am the first." He leaned down and captured her lips in a fleeting kiss. *"Time* gave you to me. I have no intention of letting you return from whence you came."

She began to run her fingers along his cheek again. "I don't ever want to leave you."

He gently pushed her head back down onto his chest. "Do not think even for one moment, I do not wish to make you mine in every way, *ma cherie*. Listen to my heart and hear how it beats for you. Do not doubt your beauty in my eyes, for there is nothing I would change in you. You are all to me, just the way God made you to be. I will treasure every day we have together and will gladly give all I have that you may share my life."

"Then why not make love to me?"

He heard her teary whimper and tilted up her chin with his fingers until she looked on him again. He quickly placed a gentle kiss upon her lips. "When I make love to you, it shall be done properly, in a suitable setting when we are alone, and not with others in hearing distance. A man does so like to ensure his wife is well taken care of. I promise to devote myself entirely to the task that surely will require more than a few stolen moments in a pond."

"Wife?" Her voice trembled with uncertainty that she heard him make such a proclamation.

"Aye."

"Then you do find me attractive?"

A hearty laugh escaped him. "How could you doubt it, especially when all I saw whilst attempting to train was your very fetching backside diving into the water? I was so distracted, Danior almost lopped off my arm. You are lucky I still have a limb to hold you thusly, instead of a useless stump."

She smiled radiantly at his words. "Then you do want me?"

He grew serious again. "If I wanted you any more than I want you at this very moment, I would unman myself."

"That won't due."

"Nay, it will not," he said huskily and hoped his words appeased her hurt of a few moments afore. "Anymore afternoons like this one, and I will forever have to find a cold stream to plunge myself into, to put out the fire you kindle within me."

They walked from the water and began collecting her clothes, and yet she still hesitated to break the connection between them. 'Twas obvious she still doubted his affection for her, or that he could want her so completely, given her expression of disbelief crossing her face. She placed her small hand on his arm and rubbed her thumb against his skin. Goosebumps from her touch ran up his flesh. 'Twas a reminder that she was sent to him from heaven above.

"You're not just making fun of me, are you Riorden?" Katherine inquired apprehensively.

'Twas apparent, there was only one way to convince her. He took hold of her and inched her closer to his body until they could feel those strange currents radiating between them when they were together. Never breaking eye contact with her, he lowered his head and captured her lips. He bent her over his arm to more thoroughly dismantle whatever reservations she still might have that he did not care for her. He kissed her long, and he kissed her hard, until he finally let her come up for air. He took one look at her slightly swollen lips and knew he had done a suitable job. She steadied herself by reaching out to him for support.

He raised a brow at her. "Convinced?"

"Aye," she said, and the smile she gave him reached into her beautiful eyes this time with a confidence he was happy to see.

He nodded with her answer. "'Tis a good and proper response you give, for a woman who will now find herself residing in the twelfth century. Now go put on your garments and come meet me by the fire. There is much our group must needs discuss afore this night is at an end."

Intrigued when she crooked her finger at him, he leaned down to hear her words. Instead, he felt her hand reach behind his head and she gave him one last gentle kiss. He watched as her eyelids fluttered open and shyness finally overcame her. A giggle, much like those of her lady friend Juliana, escaped her lips. Riorden joined in her laughter as he sent her off a discrete distance to dress.

Riorden picked up his sword he had hastily thrown to the ground and buckled the belt that hung low on his hips. He brushed his mouth with his hand, still feeling Katherine's lips on his own. A devilish grin broke out on his face as he made his way to the fire to await his spectacular lady. He shook his head, thinking of what fate had graced him with, when it sent him a temptress for his future wife. He prayed Katherine was ready for all that being his lady would entail. For little did she know it, but she had awoken the lion in him. Given enough time together, he would see to it that she never doubted his affection for her...ever again.

CHAPTER 22

Katherine felt Riorden give her hand a reassuring squeeze. She returned it in kind and gave him a hesitant smile. She could feel the rough calluses on his palm and fingers from years of training and holding a sword. From time to time throughout the evening, she couldn't stop herself from glancing at its golden hilt where the blue, sapphire stone winked at her from the glow of the firelight. She could only imagine the continuous danger he had put himself in over the years that caused his need for constant training. To fight, to go to war, to kill without thought, or to survive. She shuddered at the peril he had endured and knew he surely thought nothing of it, since it was a part of his way of life. She would have to get used to it, as well, if it was to become a part of hers.

She supposed it spoke volumes he still sat next to her and hadn't bolted. She surmised that the fact the other four medieval men remained seated, as well, listening to the unfathomable tale of time and fate she imparted, said the same of them. From their expressions, however, she wasn't sure they weren't actually ready to get on their horses and ride as fast and far as the wind would carry them to any other destination than their current location. At least Riorden already understood, at least as much as was humanly possible, the unbelievable miracle that had brought four women eight hundred years into the past. He had, after all, had a conversation with a ghost several times, a ghost that had become flesh and blood, so what was there not to believe? And yet, it was a lot to take in over dinner and a campfire.

She thought of how the men had all grimaced when they learned to what lengths the women had gone to ensure Tiernan's escape. Aiden, in particular, had scowled at Emily ferociously, and it had appeared to take everything within his power to remain in control. Katherine wasn't exactly sure if Aiden wouldn't like to just grab a hold of her friend and turn her over his knee for a good old fashioned spanking. It was either that, or perhaps kiss her for her foolishness. Either one wouldn't have gone over well with Emily, given, it was Katherine's belief, that the only one Em wished to be kissing was Tiernan.

Telling Riorden of Tiernan's escape was almost easier than she thought it would be, especially with her last dream still haunting her. Attempting to tell them of how they had gotten here, which to be honest was still a huge stretch of the imagination, was, in fact, more difficult. The women could hardly believe it themselves. What they held in their purses would be even more startling.

"I know it's not easy to believe something like this can happen. I only know that it did. Call it fate. Call it God answering my prayers. Call it whatever you want...and yet, here we are, sitting with you fine gentlemen in a time not our own," Katherine said quietly to the group. She looked up into Riorden's handsome face and reached up to gently caress his cheek. He placed a kiss within her palm before clasping her hand again with his own. "I can't say that I'm sorry, for obvious reasons."

"Mayhap, 'twas faeries!" Patrick exclaimed excitedly. "I hear they can be most mischievous creatures, if they want to be."

Aiden laughed at his brother's words. "Maybe I shall go back to Bamburgh and see if these faeries will take me to your future. I can only imagine what wonders your modern times may hold!"

Riorden smirked at Aiden's enthusiasm for time travel. "Do not even think of tempting Fate, my young friend. Besides...your sister would kill you, *and* me, if you attempt such a phenomenon. I would not wish to answer to Dristan, either, truth be told, of your disappearance."

"Well...mayhap you have that aright," Aiden said glumly, turning his attention to Katherine. "Perchance you have something you can show us instead?"

"Is that a good idea?" Danior questioned. "Too much information is sometimes not a good thing."

The women exchanged knowing looks over the flames of the fire and laughed.

"It's good to know, that even through time, some beliefs don't change," Brianna chimed in. At Gavin's puzzled gaze, she continued. "We pretty much have the same thoughts in our day."

Gavin nodded and reached out for her hand. She took it without hesitation. "Do you wish to go home? Go back to *your* time, I mean?" he asked, as if afraid of her answer.

Katherine observed Brie's smile fade and could almost imagine her thoughts running amuck in her head as she gazed at Gavin. Handsome, strong, a living and breathing knight with chivalry ingrained into his very soul. He was someone Brianna could fall head over heels in love with, if the opportunity presented itself, or so Katherine thought. What was there not to like about the man who sat next to her friend, waiting with baited breath for Briana's response to his question?

"I don't know if that's even possible," Brianna whispered, with a small catch to her voice.

"But if it were, would you want to go back?"

Katherine's breath caught at the look that quickly passed between the couple, for it was almost as if she had eavesdropped on a private conversation between two souls.

"I think I'd rather stay here with you," Brianna declared, letting her answer linger between them. It apparently pleased him, since he placed a kiss on the back of her hand, and she sighed at such a lovely gesture of gallantry.

It appeared as if Danior and Juliana were having the exact same dilemma racing through their hearts, especially given the stolen glances they continually gave one another. Katherine watched as

Danior finally gave in to the battle within him and opened his arms to Jewels. She didn't hesitate and rushed into his embrace. Silence surrounded them. At least, Jewels wasn't embarrassing herself by laughing at something only she found amusing.

Juliana placed her hand over his heart and Danior covered it with his own. Katherine strained to hear her softly spoken words. "I'm so afraid for you, Danior."

"Have no fear, my lady. All will be well," he replied, placing a soft kiss on her forehead.

She lifted her gaze to his with tear filled eyes. "But, the king…"

He smiled and leaned forward. "Let me worry about the king, Lady Juliana." He kissed her. Juliana didn't seem to mind, her contented sigh told Katherine.

Emily, on the other hand, was looking around at all the happy couples with a frown on her face. Katherine knew Emily was feeling left out. But then she saw Em make the mistake of casting a quick look at Aiden, who gazed on her as if he too thought she might favor his attentions. His brow rose up in a silent question that anyone with common sense could understand perfectly well. Emily shook her head no. Aiden ignored her and did the unthinkable. Before Emily knew what Aiden intended, he leaned forward and placed his lips on hers.

The moment their mouths made contact, their eyes flew wide open in shock and they froze in place, lip-locked and staring at one another with dismay. Then they quickly drew apart. Emily's chest was heaving, and Katherine could tell, just by looking at her, that Em was not happy, at all. In fact, she looked completely grossed out. Her mouth formed a grim line and her eyes narrowed to meet his. He, too, had almost the same appalled expression.

"Yuck…that was disgusting! Don't ever do that again," Emily threatened, poking him in the chest with her finger at each word to ensure she got her point across.

His features showed the same amount of horror from their encounter. "My apologies, Lady Emily," Aiden replied awkwardly, with a small nod of his head. "I cannot explain it or even fathom the idea that as I kissed you…well…I felt as if…I fear as if…'twas, as if I kissed my own sister. Please, take no offense, but 'twas most unpleasant."

"None taken," she said shortly. "Maybe there's a reason why you and I come to blows and annoy each other so much. You remind me a little too much of my own older brother. My most obnoxious older brother, I should add."

"Then, I shall take over the duties of an older brother and watch over you, if you would grant me such an honor," Aiden said sincerely.

"I would like that," she replied and held out her hand for him to shake. He gave her another unusual expression, so she took a hold of his hand herself, began to shake it up and down, and they sealed their bargain between them. Both promptly began to laugh.

"Such a strange girl," Aiden muttered.

"Mister, you don't know the half of it!" Emily laughed and thumped him on the back like an old time friend, or now a long lost brother, until she threw herself into his arms. "Thank you, Aiden. I don't feel so alone now," she said softly.

Silence descended upon the group as each person seemed to be caught up with their own confused thoughts as to what the future would hold. Katherine fingered her jeans and could only think of the horror that would befall her, unless she found new clothing, and soon. Again, her hand was squeezed, and Riorden smiled at her. She had the feeling he knew where her thoughts were leading.

"We should reach the village on the morrow. Perhaps, 'twould be prudent that we procure the women a change of clothing suitable to our time, clothing that would be more in line with remaining unobtrusive," Riorden said calmly.

"What about our search?" Danior asked. "I must continue on, whether you aide me or not."

"It might be best if we split up in order that we cover more ground," Gavin suggested.

"'Tis not something I had not already considered. My main concern is for the safety of the women," Riorden replied carefully. "I will not take the chance of them being injured, if we must engage Irish rebels."

"We could divide and meet back at Berwyck. 'Tis not that great a distance, once we reach the next village," Aiden offered. "They would be safe with Amiria and Dristan."

"You can't split us apart!" Juliana and Briana called out in unison.

"Be at ease ladies. 'Twould not be for more than a few days, at most," Riorden said reassuringly.

Katherine protested. "There must be another way, Riorden. We have to stay together."

"We have already delayed longer than we should, and the trail grows colder with each passing moment," Riorden answered.

Brianna held back a sob, turning toward Gavin. "I can't lose you now that I just found you!"

"Time is of the essence, my lady," Gavin added, taking a hold of Brianna's hand.

"Aye, Danior replied. "I must needs return to Bamburgh bearing my wayward prisoner in irons with all due haste. Else, I sacrifice more than just my lands forfeited over to an angry king…much more than I care to part with."

Juliana sobbed. "I won't have Danior's life be at stake just because we don't want to be apart."

Emily huffed. "Just like Jewel's to be the voice of reason. Wouldn't we be stronger in numbers? Isn't that how stuff like this goes?"

Patrick tossed a stick into the fire. "We cannot ride as fast as we would like, if we have the women slowing us down. We could leave them at the inn and come back for them," he suggested.

"Enough, Patrick," Riorden said with blazing eyes. "I will hear no more of such talk. You do the ladies a disservice by suggesting such an idea."

"My apologies, my ladies and my lord," Patrick mumbled, clearly embarrassed he had spoken his thoughts aloud.

"Well, I, for one, go nowhere without the Lady Emily," Aiden said, putting a brotherly arm around her shoulder. "I did, after all, just now swear to protect her."

"Enough!" Riorden replied, holding his hand up to halt any further conversation. "We shall decide who goes with who once we have rested at the inn come the morrow."

"But, Riorden—" Katherine began.

"Nay, Katherine, I will hear no more of this discussion," Riorden interjected, taking her hand and giving it a quick kiss. "My mind is set. Trust me."

Katherine nodded, knowing Riorden would look out for their best interests, but she was still uncertain if splitting up was such a good idea. Gazing at her friends, each of them had a look of pure misery at the thought of not being together. She was sure her own reflection looked much the same. She was trying to figure out how to bring the group back to a more pleasant conversation, when Patrick edged slightly closer to her. She grinned as she looked into his youthful face.

"My lady?" he asked with all the curiosity of the young at heart.

"Yes, Patrick?" Katherine asked, trying not to broaden her smile. She just knew where this conversation was going.

"Could you not show us something in your satchel from this future of yours? Something to prove you are not from this time?"

She stole a glance at Riorden, who nodded his consent. There were so many options between the four of them, it was hard to know where to start. "We must be careful, Patrick, and keep this only between us. Do you understand?"

"Aye, milady!" Patrick replied eagerly.

"Well, ladies, what should it be?" Katherine asked her friends. "Shall we break it to them gently, or hit them...how did that song go? Hit me with your best shot, was it?" They all laughed.

"A magazine?" Emily supplied.

"Pens and Paper?" was Juliana's contribution.

"Music!" Brianna sighed.

"Music? From the lute, or did you have something electronic in mind?" Katherine smirked, causing Emily and Juliana to laugh aloud.

"Cell phones! Definitely get your phone out, Katherine" Brie said excitedly. "Wait until you hear this, Gavin. It's going to freak you out."

Gavin had a moment of doubt cross his face. "Do I wish to be...freaked out, Brianna?"

She laughed, again. "Sure! Why not?"

Five medieval heads drew slightly closer and watched intently as Katherine began digging around in her purse for her phone, which was buried at the bottom of everything she carried. She felt a candy wrapper and knew what she would bring out next. Pulling out the purple plastic, she saw she had their undivided attention as she placed it on her lap. She had been keeping the power turned off to conserve what energy she could.

She pushed the power button, and the white apple lit up on the screen. Patrick began to ooh and ah, much to Katherine's amusement.

"Is there a faerie living in the box, Lady Katherine?" Patrick asked in awe and began to cross himself.

Before Katherine could answer, she noticed Aiden fingering his dagger. She quickly reached out and grabbed her phone, bringing it up to her chest. The phone continued to power up, and now the men could see how a light was illuminated around the box and on her shirt.

"Maybe a couple of rules should be in order," Katherine said sternly as she saw Aiden now had a firm grasp on his dagger, holding it in front of him as if the phone would attack him. "First and foremost, this phone does not get jabbed, poked, stabbed, thrown, tossed into the fire, or anything else that may be your first gut reaction to what I'm about to show you. Understood?" She watched in satisfaction as Aiden returned his dirk to his boot and the other men nodded their acceptance of her terms.

"So, what'll it be Katie?" Emily asked smartly, trying really hard and failing to hide the grin that lit her face, knowing what was about to happen. "Hard rock and roll?"

Juliana swatted her friend. "Don't be an idiot, Em. They hear that, and Katie's rules will be broken within a matter of seconds."

Katherine gave a bit of a giggle. "Maybe some jazz. That wouldn't be too devious on our parts, would it?" She picked out a tune that was upbeat and pretty danceable then turned up the volume.

The men watched in earnest fascination, and they gathered closer around the small device Katherine had placed on the log. She hit the tiny arrow to play the music and stepped back to stand next to her friends. They all took a step backward and out of the way of the men investigating their first modern marvel.

The first notes of the horns sent all the men upright, and they instinctively drew their swords from their scabbards. Riorden was the first to remember her rules. As the electric keyboard and guitar began to join in on the melody, the men began to put away their weapons. The women roared with laughter at the looks on the men's faces and began to dance in time with the music. Katherine wasn't sure which amused her more...their shock at what was coming out of her phone, or their astonishment at the women dancing a very modern dance, which basically was move any way they wanted, with no particular pattern.

The song ended after a couple of minutes, and Patrick came and bowed low over Katherine's hand. She dropped into a formal curtsey, or at least her best effort of one. He bent down and whispered in her ear.

"A love song?" she asked merrily, wondering where he heard of Barbara Celine. "Oh...you ran into that lovely family we met, who offered to share their dinner. It's a song called *Tell Him*, sung by two of the most renowned singers in the twenty-first century. Brie, would you mind playing, and then we all can sing? We'll let you listen to the original version after we're done, if that's okay."

Brianna picked up the lute and strummed a few cords then nodded to the women who gathered around her. Two sang the parts of Celine Dion. The other two, of Barbara Streisand. Their voices sang in perfect accord. Katherine's full attention was focused only on the one man who had captured her heart. She poured out her very soul into each word until the melody at last came to a close. The men began to clap in appreciation, and from the pleasure expressed on their features, it was clear they had enjoyed the performance. They all took a seat, and Katherine played the song in its original format.

Riorden leaned over to whisper in her ear. "I must admit, I enjoyed your singing, my lady, but if you continue to gaze upon me as you just did during your presentation, I shall never make it to our wedding night."

Katherine giggled nervously and reached for her purse again to draw out a brightly colored orange wrapper. "I have dessert, but we'll have to share," she exclaimed enthusiastically.

She opened the wrapper and passed out three of the beloved chocolate peanut butter cups. Each of the women divided it in half to give a taste to the man sitting next to her. Katherine gave her share to Patrick, who looked on it as if it was poison. "Trust me...you're a kid, and you're gonna' love it!"

Patrick took a small nibble and then stuffed his half completely into his mouth, chewing in delight. The same could be said of the others around the fire.

"'Twas kind of you to give Patrick your share, Katherine," Riorden said as he held out a smaller portion of his treat. "Here, you may have part of mine."

She noticed a small piece of chocolate lingering in the corner of his mouth. Instead of taking the proffered chocolate, she sat up on her knees, placed her hands upon his shoulders and started kissing him. Her tongue flicked out of her mouth to capture what had originally captured her attention. He caught her about the waist and kissed her more fully.

"Feisty wench!" Riorden rasped when he at last was able to manage a conversation. He pulled her down into his lap, giving her a fierce hug. "Keep that up, and I shall need to go find that stream."

She placed her head on his chest. "Eat your candy, Riorden," she whispered with a sigh of contentment.

Katherine grabbed the edges of the blanket Riorden placed around her to keep her warm while he hummed a medieval melody softly in her ear. His deep baritone voice was beautiful, and she became completely absorbed listening to his song. She sighed, satisfied with how the evening had progressed. Riorden's arm tightened around her and caused her to smile...again...for what must have felt like the hundredth time since this crazy journey began. Life felt so very complete.

∽

Tiernan backed away from the edge of the trees, removing his clenched hand from the hilt of his sword. Emily was safe, but he swore jealousy consumed him when he witnessed her flinging herself into the arms of that redheaded knight. It had taken every bit of control not to hurl himself into their campsite and demand Emily come away with him. Who the devil was he anyway?

He began running to catch up with his group, although thoughts of envy coursed through every fiber of his being. He had beheld strange things going on this night and had no logical answer for the noise coming from the oddly colored box at their camp. Emily's voice, however, had been pure bliss.

At least he knew where they were headed. He quickened his pace, promising himself that he and his errant lady would have words when she got to her next destination. She had much to answer for.

CHAPTER 23

Katherine lost count of the hours in which she had endured the endless torture of bouncing atop Beast while their horses galloped north. The scenery had become but a blur as they flew like the wind across the countryside. From time to time, one of the men would scout the area ahead or on the ground, looking for clues as to the direction they should continue on in their journey. With every mile passing them by, Emily became more quiet and reserved. It was clear, she was indeed thankful Tiernan had evaded capture. Emily's happiness, however, became Juliana's nightmare, with visions of Danior's head sitting on a pike outside the king's gate. It seemed neither lady would win in this pursuit.

The small village of Tinsbury came into sight, and Katherine at last sighed with relief when Riorden pulled on the reins, causing Beast to slow his gait. She was beyond thankful, she would finally dismount off this animal that surely originated from the depths of hell. Everything hurt from the rigor of sitting on a horse for hours on end. Riorden had tried to see to her comfort as best he could by having her continually change her position, but it was no use. She just wasn't cut out for riding, at least not at this pace for a first go at it. There wasn't an inch of her body that wasn't tender in some way from the jostling she had endured. Along with her backside aching, and everything in between, she swore even her hair was bruised. Her only consolation, from the abuse she had received, was that Riorden had promised her a hot bath once they were settled at the inn.

Raising her head from her ever present placement on his shoulder, she spotted the first signs of civilization in the form of a small, thatch roofed dwelling on the outskirts of town. Katherine saw another and looked ahead in excitement at her first real glimpse of a thriving medieval village. Instead, she should have remembered her history and the conditions in which people at this level of a fiefdom lived. She could find no words to what she saw, and her own look of horror was mirrored in the eyes of her friends. Emily, for sure, looked as if she was about to pass out cold in Aiden's arms.

The road, if that is what it could be called, was little more than a mire full of muck, slime, and God only knew what else. She soon learned what the 'what else' was, when Riorden quickly maneuvered Beast to the left while the contents of a chamber pot were poured out of an upper floor window. If they hadn't moved, those contents would have splattered all over them. Katherine almost gagged at the stench engulfing her senses.

If the streets themselves weren't enough for her to take in, the conditions of the people were almost as horrible. Bad hygiene, bad clothing, and bad teeth were evident. One man, who smiled wide at her, had most of his teeth missing, and the few remaining were rotting away in his mouth. She could only pray that not all of medieval England was in the same condition, but she had the God awful feeling that wherever they traveled, conditions would be pretty much the same. It didn't seem to affect the men of their group as much as it did their modern ladies.

They slowed their pace as they neared what was most likely a market square. At least it appeared in slightly better condition than the outskirts of the village. Tinsbury was obviously a thriving place of commerce, and Katherine could see several small shops were set up in the heart of the town. Hawkers began calling out their wares and showing off their goods in proof that their merchandises were the best to be found in the area. It was clear to the merchants that nobles who had coin to spare were in their midst. They wasted no time in trying to get the group's attention to buy their goods.

Riorden halted in front of a seller where he examined a bolt of golden-yellow fabric. He flipped a coin to the merchant, who easily caught it, and instructed him to have the cloth delivered to the Black Bull Inn. They continued on while Katherine was amazed that he so easily spent his money, as if he had more than plenty.

She continued to study his features until he turned his gaze to her own, which conveyed her obvious, unspoken question as to what he had planned for such a costly fabric.

"The color would be most favorable on you," he said indifferently, as if he had read her thoughts. "You can fashion a garment from it."

"Me? Sew?" Katherine said stunned. "You must be joking?"

"Women of your time do not sew their garments?"

Katherine rolled her eyes at the thought of even sewing a button that had come loose, let alone a whole outfit. "I suppose some still do, but we buy everything that is already made. You just pick out your size off a rack."

"'Tis costly then," Riorden assumed.

"Yes, it can be, but I still wouldn't even know where to begin. I'd hate to ruin such lovely fabric."

"I will see then, whilst here in Tinsbury, if we can procure you and the ladies something suitable to wear for the short distance to Berwyck." Riorden suggested. "'Tis not much farther if we follow the shore. But I fear that if we continue our journey this day, the gates will be closed for the eve by the time we arrive. When we reach Berwyck on the morrow, Aiden's sister Amiria will see that a gown worthy of you is fashioned from the cloth."

They had reached the stable, and a boy ran to take the bridle of Riorden's steed. He dismounted easily and held up his hands to assist her, which she gladly accepted. Her legs wobbled beneath her, and she felt Riorden's arms go around her to steady her stance. She rested her forehead on his chest while her fingers grabbed at the fabric of his tabard.

"I fear you may need to support me, Riorden," Katherine said, between clenched teeth. "I'm not even sure I can walk."

She found herself ever so gently scooped up into his arms then he made his way, sure-footed, into the nearby inn. How he managed such a feat with the slippery mud beneath his boots was anyone's guess. He entered the relatively empty common room like a commanding general in the army and called for a bath for his lady then followed an older woman into one of the back rooms off the kitchen that was used, Katherine assumed, as a bathing chamber for guests.

Katherine was set down on her feet, but before Riorden left her side, she peered into the wooden tub. Her hand flew to her mouth in disgust.

"Please tell me, good woman, those aren't lice floating on top of the water," Katherine questioned repulsed.

The woman looked into the tub as if nothing was out of the ordinary. "Water's only been used three times, milady. 'Tis still good and clean enough for ye."

Katherine went to Riorden and begged him to lean down so she could whisper in his ear. "There's no way I'm putting myself in there. No offense, but even I have my standards of cleanliness. Jumping into a tub with floating lice isn't one of them."

Riorden smiled slightly at her effort to get her point across and placed a kiss on her forehead. He reached into his belt for another precious coin. Again it was flipped with amazing accuracy. "Bring a clean tub and fresh water to my chamber for my lady's needs."

The woman grinned, clearly pleased with the tender, then yelled to a man in the kitchen and ordered a tub and hot water be brought to the lord's chamber at once.

"Thank you, Riorden," Katherine said softly as he escorted her from the steamy room. "I'm sorry to be such a bother."

He harrumphed at her words. "You may bother me anytime it so pleases you, Katherine. I hope you will not mistake my motives, but I have asked for a room for your friends where the men will stand guard. For some unknown reason, I feel the need to keep you close. I will of course sleep on the floor," Riorden said, almost embarrassed he had asked such a thing of her.

Katherine smiled lovingly into his eyes. "Again, I offer my thanks for your thoughtfulness, my lord, and seeing that we are well cared for."

She found herself, once more, in his arms when it became clear her attempt at climbing the stairs was too much for her. They followed the old woman, who showed them to Riorden's room, and he set her down on a cushioned chair, ensuring her cloak covered her modern day clothing. She watched as several men managed to get a rather large tub into the room, and servants began filing in, carrying buckets of steaming hot water. Patrick followed in as one last bucket, for rinsing, was placed near the fire. He placed Riorden's leather bag on a nearby table and discreetly fled, without a backwards glance.

Tension filled the room as Riorden helped her rise. The heat from the water wasn't the only thing that suddenly became hot in the chamber, now that they were alone. Riorden remained a perfect gentleman given her current condition, and helped her walk to the tub where she mumbled she could manage on her own.

"You can stay, if you'd like," Katherine said, holding her cloak in front of her like a protective shield. "I won't mind. You have, after all, seen everything I have to offer."

He came to stand before her and placed a kiss on her parted lips. "There is a time and place for everything, Katherine, and we have a lifetime afore us," he said kindly. Then, he turned and headed towards the door, adding. "Besides, you have tempted me enough in the past two days. I do not think I could stand much more."

"I'm not sure how I managed that, with all the groaning I've been doing from the sorry state of my backside becoming bruised for all time," she complained roughly.

He came back to her quicker than she expected and took her in his arms, pressing himself against her. Her eyes widened in recognition of what she felt throbbing between them. Her breath left her, knowing she was the cause of his arousal. Still...nothing could tear her gaze from his until his mouth claimed hers in an alluring kiss. He would have most likely continued his assault on her mouth, if only a moan of pain had not escaped her, as the sound was not one born of passion.

Katherine opened her eyes only to see Riorden's smoldering blue-eyed stare. She wasn't sure what to say, given what had just passed between them. It was about perfect in her mind.

"Get in your bath afore it grows cold, Kat. I will be outside the door if you have need of me. We shall sup once you are done."

"You won't go far?" she asked in a hushed tone.

His eyes bore into hers, and she was again caught in the heat of his stare. "Nay, my lady," he said simply, and she watched him leave the room.

She slowly shimmied out of her clothes and lowered herself into the soothing water. The sting of its warmth began to have a calming effect on her bruised exterior. She closed her eyes to thoroughly enjoy the moment her gallant and thoughtful knight had provided her. He was most chivalrous. Katherine couldn't ask for anything more than what she had found in Riorden. She smiled with a contented sigh, thinking she was indeed blessed, as the warm water began to work its magic on her sore, abused body.

༄

The smoky tavern had grown quite rambunctious as the evening had progressed. The patrons of the Black Bull Inn had increased significantly as those in the crowded room called for more ale. Serving maids made the rounds with pitchers brimming with cool brew and avoided the grasping hands of those looking for something more than to merely quench their thirst.

Their small company had taken over one of the larger tables up against the wall where the men could keep a vigilant eye on the goings on of those around them. Only one drunken fool had dared to come forward with a proposition on his lips for one of the women. Danior quickly dispatched the man with his dirk landing sharply between the man's fingers, which the drunkard had brazenly placed on their table. He had mumbled an apology and fled while he still had his hand intact.

Emily fingered the wool of her dress beneath the table. She was fidgety and wished she was able to take out her pens and paper to write down a line or two of her latest story. It wasn't to be, however, for the women's purses had been confiscated by the men as a precaution against their contents falling into the wrong hands. It seemed they didn't wish to tempt fate any further than it had already been pushed by bringing four women to a time where they obviously didn't belong.

Perhaps that was not entirely true, Emily pondered, while she watched Katherine and Brianna emerge themselves into this whole experience of living in medieval times. They truly were meant for this time period, and Emily had the strange notion that, if given the choice, her dear friends would remain in the twelfth century. The same could not be said for herself or Juliana, if she were to hazard a guess into her other friend's thoughts. It did become a bit problematic, though, when even she could see that Jewels and Danior already had this unspoken connection between them. If a look could speak, it would have voiced in a thousand words they were falling madly in love with one another. Whoever said there was no such thing as love at first sight was a complete moron. It seemed to be happening all around her.

The evening wore on, the table was cleared of their meal, and the men began discussing their strategy to split up and meet back at Berwyck. By the time they finished arguing with the women of the group and at last appeased their worries, most of the patrons had left the inn for their own humble abodes, or so Emily assumed. She took a glance around the room, now that she felt more comfortable doing so, since most of the unruly crowd had disappeared. Her eyes were drawn to one lone stranger sitting in the corner with the hood of his cape pulled up over his head. For whatever reason, she couldn't look away, and at last, she saw him pull open his cloak, ever so slightly.

There, beneath the garment, was the sight of a familiar sash. Her eyes lit with excitement until she saw him cautiously raise his finger to his lips to gain her silence. With a slight nod of his head towards the door, he rose and left the tavern. Now her only thought was how she would make her escape to follow him. She must have news of Tiernan's whereabouts and find a way to warn him of the danger he was in.

Emily lingered behind as everyone rose to finally make their way up to their rooms. Was it just a stroke of dumb, blind luck, or karma giving her a little nudge, that she was the last to ascend the stairway?

Whatever the reason, she took the chance and carefully made her way out the front door without anyone noticing.

The night was dark, but the light from the open door of the stables lit her path as she made her way across the grounds. Opening the door, it creaked loudly, and the sound echoed harshly into the darkness surrounding her. Her arm was grabbed and she was hauled roughly into the stable. Emily gulped in a large breath in order to scream when she was pushed against the hard wooden door. Her mouth was covered, preventing her outcry. She began to struggle, all the while wondering why this continued to happen to her.

"Ye have led me on a merry chase, lass, following ye across the countryside," a voice whispered brusquely in her ear, as he lowered his hand slowly from her mouth. His voice, even though its harshness was evident, was like a sweet caress to her senses.

"Tiernan?" Emily asked softly.

Tiernan took the hood from his head, and she reached out her hands to feel his face beneath her fingertips. "Were ye expecting another?"

"No, but you have no idea what danger you're in of being captured."

"I have evaded worse and come out the better."

"You don't understand."

Tiernan captured her hands and held them roughly. "So, why do ye not enlighten me, Emily? Why is it ye ride with me enemy? Do I even now have cause to fear ye have already alerted them I am here?" he said gruffly.

"I wouldn't do that to you," Emily said shrilly.

"Bah! Why should I trust ye? Ye barely know me," he replied, just as hotly.

"I know you well enough to know you would never hurt me. Why are you so angry with me? I've done nothing but come to care for you."

He pressed himself against her as his eyes bore into hers. "Who is he?"

Emily looked at him in bewilderment as her heart accelerated with his nearness. He made her forget what they were talking about, but she quickly came back to her senses to answer him. "Who?"

"Ye know of whom I speak, woman. The redhead who has been all but mauling ye these many miles as I've watched ye come to favor him," Tiernan yelled.

A bitter laugh escaped her until she saw it only angered him more. He was jealous! "Trust me when I tell you, I feel nothing for Aiden other than that of a brother. Truly...He irritates the hell out of me."

"I repeat...why should I trust ye?" he whispered, releasing her hands, as if all the fight went rushing out of him.

Emily reached up and caressed his face, moving a lock of his hair that had fallen over his eye. "Because of this," she said softly and pressed her lips against his.

What started off as a tender kiss quickly turned to one completely out of her control. She was crushed against his solid body even while she attempted to clasp him to her more fully. Her heart sang with joy, knowing all this time he had been following her, despite his words he would have others do so. Surely, his kiss meant he had come to care for her.

Tiernan tore his lips from hers abruptly, as if he had come to realize his predicament of being captured. "Ye must go, Emily, afore they come looking for ye."

"I would rather stay here with you," she said, leaning in for another stolen kiss.

"Nay, lass, but ne'er fear. I willna be far from yer side," Tiernan said, and he placed another quick kiss on her lips.

Her name was being called from outside the stables with enough urgency that Tiernan reached for her hand and led her out the back.

"Tell them ye went to the garderobe," he insisted. He quickly ushered her out into the cool night and pulled her cloak around her to keep out the chilly evening air.

"Will I see you soon?" she asked, desperately wrapping her arms around him, not wanting him to leave.

"Soon enough, lass, soon enough."

With another quick kiss, he turned her away from him. Emily looked back over her shoulder and saw him disappear into the night.

Then she took flight at a fast pace. Rushing, she rounded the corner of the barn and ran smack dab into Aiden, who had an angry look plastered on his face.

"Where the hell have you been?" he admonished her with his hand still firmly planted on the hilt of his sword. He continued his assessment of the night to ensure there was no danger in sight.

Emily flipped her hair out of her face. "Taking care of business," she huffed.

"What business?"

She nodded towards the outhouse and her answer seemingly satisfied his curiosity.

"Next time, let me know. I will accompany you to ensure your safe return," Aiden ordered as he steered her back inside the inn.

"Can't I ever have a bit of privacy?" she asked bitterly as she began climbing the stairs.

"Nay! Not on my watch," Aiden declared and ushered her inside her room, closing the door behind him as he left.

The only light in the room came from the fire, and Emily saw Brie and Jewels were already in bed.

"Where have you been, Em?" Brianna whispered frantically, in concern for her friend.

"Just out catching some air," Emily replied with a smile. She took off her dress and, after carefully folding it, climbed into the bed. "Oh, my..." She let out a sigh of pure pleasure to feel the softness surround her being.

Juliana laughed softly from the middle of the bed. "I know how you feel. A feather bed! Have you ever felt anything more glorious than this?"

Emily turned on her side and watched the fire as it began to die out in the hearth. She had indeed felt something more glorious than what she would sleep on this night, and that very something had been found in Tiernan's sweet and memorable kiss.

CHAPTER 24

The low light of the fire cast glittering shadows on the walls surrounding them. He opened his eyes, and all he could see was the golden glow of her body as she lay atop him. She gave him a devilish smile, took his earlobe gently between her teeth, nibbling it, and began placing soft kisses down the length of his neck.

Her teasing did not stop there as she made a trail with her lips slowly down his chest. Her tongue flicked him here and there, causing him to gasp in the pleasure she sweetly gave him. Her fingers fanned out as she caressed his muscles, reaching ever lower down his taut stomach. She gave a seductive laugh and took special delight as she wrapped her hand around the hard pulsing length of him. She squeezed slightly and he felt as if he were about to crawl out of his skin if he did not make her his own in every way.

He flipped her over so she was at last beneath him. Taking hold of her hands, he brought them above her head afore she could extract any more of the exquisite torture she had in store for him. He looked his fill of her, marveling at the perfection beneath his gaze. Her tanned skin, kissed by the sun, was as smooth as porcelain. Her breasts were full and firm with their pink nipples, peaked from the coolness of the air, or was it from the passion and heat that seemed to radiate naturally between them? He leaned down and took one of those tempting buds gently into his mouth, teasing her now as much as she had him but moments afore.

Her moan reached his ears, and her back arched, begging him for more. He let go of her hands to cup both of her breasts in order to give each his undivided attention. She grasped at his hair until he at last looked up into her passion filled eyes, shining full of so much love. He never thought to ever see such an intense stare directed at him.

"I want you, Riorden," she whispered urgently as she reached down to once more take hold of him, "and I can tell you want me, too. Please don't make me wait any longer, my love."

"'Tis my turn, Kat. Be patient..." he said, a bit harshly, trying to hold back the urge to plunge into her softness and take this woman who meant all to him. He returned the favor of tormenting her to see just how easily he could make her writhe beneath him. It did not, in truth, take long as his lips tasted his way lower and lower down the curve of her waist and her stomach.

Riorden twirled a length of her hair between his fingers whilst he continued his assault on her senses. It gave him satisfaction to hear the tiny whimpers and catlike purrs now coming from his lovely lady. He raised his head and glanced at the tendril winding its way around his hand as if taking possession of him.

He frowned, astounded when the blondish-brown tresses began to transform into the color as black as midnight. The golden skin he had been caressing with his rough, calloused hands turned to the color of ivory and became much too lean for his taste. He jerked back in surprise, for no longer was it his sweet Katherine lovingly calling out his name in the heat of passion. Nay! 'Twas a face that had haunted him for most of his adult life. 'Twas his father's wife who now began to take command of his very soul.

"I knew you would come back to me, Riorden. You will always be mine," she declared knowingly with an evil laugh.

She wound her arms up and around his neck whilst her hair took on a life of its own. The black locks wrapped themselves around him in a binding grip, much like a spider that had trapped its prey in its silvery, sticky web. Her lips touched his, and he felt the air rush out of his lungs as her hair began to squeeze him tighter and tighter. She frantically whispered words of a sorceress, laying claim to his heart, even as he gave one last gasp for breath. Suffo-

cating him, she sucked the very life from his soul with her wicked and spiteful kiss of death.

∽

Riorden awoke, sitting up with a jolt. A cold sweat clung to his trembling body. He tore away the light blanket that had become entangled around his neck. His eyes scanned the room until his vision came into focus and he got his bearings straight. With shaking hands, he raked his fingers through his hair and took a deep, soothing breath. What had started out as a dream worth remembering had turned into his worst nightmare. He was not sure once he arrived at Warkworth that the reality of the situation would not still hold true.

He quickly donned his hose and boots then laid kindling onto the fire to take the chill from the chamber afore Katherine arose from her slumber. He made his way to the bed and watched her sleeping with a half-smile gracing her lovely face. She was having the most pleasant of dreams, it appeared. She was laying on her side with her hands drawn together beneath her cheek, almost as if in prayer. His gaze traveled the length of her body, noticing every luscious curve beneath the coverings. Coverings! She might as well not have anything atop her, since the blanket hid nothing from his imagination. It only caused him further frustration that he was not laying abed next to her.

The strap from the shift she had slept in hung loose from her shoulder, allowing him to view the outline of one of her breasts. 'Twas just scarcely visible, along with its peak, almost taunting him to reach out and cup it. Riorden's hand shuddered to feel the silkiness of her creamy smooth skin and the bared shoulder beneath his palm. He knew not how she could think herself undesirable to him, or doubt in any way that he wanted her. Aye! Want her he did, with every fiber of his being, and yet he still stood there, not giving into the temptation that was ripe for the taking.

His hands ached. His mouth became parched, desperately wishing to taste the sweetness of her kiss. His arousal was abundantly evident from the tightness of his hose. If he did not find some kind of release soon, he would be driven crazed from denying himself what he truly wanted. Katherine...in his arms...in his bed...but as his wife. Damn his code of chivalry to hell!

A groan escaped him, and her eyelids began to flutter open. She stretched herself, much like that of a feline cat upon rising from its slumber. 'Twas almost more than he could tolerate, seeing her completely uninhibited. Once recognition dawned on her that he stood hovering over her, she quickly threw the blanket from her body. Kneeling afore him, she hugged him with all her might. Every inch of her body seemed to mold itself to his own. He finally gave in to the pleasure of holding her and crushed her into his arms.

"Good morning, Riorden," she said shyly. "Did you sleep well?"

"Good morn to you, my lady, and nay, my slumber was not restful," he replied hoarsely, still feeling the effect of his dream. He inhaled deeply the scent of her hair. It smelled of flowers.

"I told you to get off the floor and sleep in the bed with me," she reminded him playfully.

"Ha! 'Tis not sleeping we would have done, I assure you, *mademoiselle*."

"I think that was the point, Riorden," Katherine purred sweetly. "I was having the most delicious dream." She began trailing a finger down his naked chest with a teasing gleam in her eye until she saw, he assumed, was his expression filled with remoteness.

"Is there something wrong?" she asked after several minutes of silence and perchance feeling the tension in the air surrounding them.

"Nay. Nothing that will not soon enough take care of itself, I suspect," he said briskly. His gaze devoured the sight of her since her chemise had fallen even further. Trying to get a hold on the sexual tension she unleashed in him, Riorden stepped back and began donning the rest of his clothing, along with his sword.

She reached over and clutched the blanket to her breasts, almost in embarrassment she had displayed herself so. She swung her legs off the edge of the bed and stood, taking the coverlet with her as a drape.

"Have I done something to upset you, Riorden?" Her voice trembled in her uncertainty of what she could have possibly done wrong. Worry was clearly etched upon her beautiful face.

Stupid fool! 'Tis not her fault you must deal with your past once you arrive at Warkworth. He knew trouble would be afoot afore he ever placed one boot upon his land. Riorden went to her and placed a kiss on her lips. She smiled, even though 'twas a weak effort, at best. He had not meant to hurt her feelings.

"We must away, Katherine. The sun is up, and we must ride," he announced as he strode towards the door. "You will want to say your farewells to Lady Juliana and Lady Brianna, will you not?"

"Yes, of course," she whispered softly.

"Then come and meet us downstairs. We shall have food to eat along the way."

Riorden watched her turn to dress, and he quietly closed the door. 'Twas either that, or break his vow to himself and go back inside, not letting her see the light of day until he ensured their passion for each other was completely sated.

∽

Several hours later, Katherine's eyes were still red rimmed from the amount of tears she had shed. She had tried to persuade Riorden and Danior to not go forward with their plan to split the women up, but they had been relentless. The four women had clung to one another in a teary farewell until Riorden said they must hasten their departure.

Determined to cover more ground, Danior and Gavin had taken Juliana and Brianna and headed further inland to scour the area to the west before turning back to Berwyck. This left the remaining party continuing northeast. It was likely they would make Berwyck by nightfall, if not sooner.

It was well into the late afternoon when Riorden had at last called a halt to their frantic galloping across the countryside. He left Aiden and Patrick to keep guard of the women while he went to scout the area around them. Katherine had never been more grateful to at last sit on something that wasn't moving beneath her. She now only waited patiently for Riorden's return. She was becoming concerned while she listened intently to the quietness of the forest. He had been gone quite a while.

Katherine had just stood to stretch her weary body when shouting reached her ears along with the distinct, loud sound of metal clanking against metal. There was no mistaking the sound of one sword smashing against another. She was on her feet, running in the direction of the raised, hostile voices before she even realized she had done so. Aiden's voice rang out calling her name as he, along with the rest of their company, rushed after her.

They came to an abrupt halt. Then Emily hurled herself forward into the scene before them. She was easily taken hold of in Aiden's steely grip. Tears began coursing down her cheeks.

Riorden stood next to Tiernan, his sword pointed at him. Tiernan's hands were raised in surrender. His sword lay just out of reach on the ground. Katherine watched as the man's gaze crossed the distance to Emily, who still struggled to get to him. His eyes flashed to the man beside him, and he gave a look of extreme disgust.

"'Tis not the first time we have met, is it Cavanaugh?" Riorden taunted, flicking a loose strand of Tiernan's hair with the tip of his sword.

"Cavanaugh?" Emily asked in confusion.

Katherine had never learned Tiernan's last name, but when Riorden said it, she realized who he was. As she recalled pieces of history, the reasons for these men's animosity towards one another began to fall into place. Tiernan was the leader of the Irish rebels. He was a famous soldier and fighter, celebrated by the Irish, who refused to yield to English rule. Standing tall and strong, he made an effort to quell his defiance as his gaze continually went to her friend. He had eyes only for Emily, who thrashed about to wriggle free of Aiden's grasp, without prevail.

"And now for your insolence, you shall suffer the consequences of not yielding to your king," Riorden announced.

"He is no king o' mine," Tiernan replied, distain dripping with each word.

Riorden pulled his sword back to strike, but was interrupted by Emily's plea.

"No!" she screamed. Pulling her elbow back, she forcefully jabbed it into Aiden's stomach, leaving him only able to exhale a loud "oaf." Free from his grip, she ran toward the clash of wills in front of her, using herself as a shield for Tiernan. She stood face to face with him, her lips trembling with fear.

"Back away, you foolish girl," Riorden spit out still in full battle mode. Emily only tightened her grip around Tiernan's neck and peeked at Katherine with frightened eyes.

"Do something," Emily mouthed to her. Emily turned back to Tiernan, who searched her face with a nervous smile and wrapped his arms securely around her.

"I love you," she said softly.

"And, I you," he said, just as tenderly.

Riorden's head jerked up upon hearing their declarations, and he swiveled in Katherine's direction. He looked almost as if she had struck him. A sense of *déjà vu* sadly overcame her. With a heavy sigh, she knew what was about to happen. She attempted to take a calm breath, but failed when it rushed out as she all but suffocated from remorse.

"You knew of her feelings for him?" he asked sternly, almost choking on his words. He did not lower his sword.

"I suspected, but didn't know for sure," she replied honestly, not taking her eyes from his.

"And you did not think it important enough to tell me?" he bellowed, standing there struggling, it seemed, with some inner demon.

"Riorden," Katherine said as steadily as possible, trying her best to defuse the situation. "Please, don't do this."

"Keep your distance, woman! Do not interfere in matters that do not concern you," Riorden roared.

She ignored him, coming close enough to place her hand upon his arm. She nudged it gently. His muscles were tense beneath her fingers. But he slowly lowered his sword while he listened intently to her soothing voice. "I am a firm believer that everything in our lives happens for a reason," Katherine declared gently, hoping her words would appease him. "We all have a purpose in this life. My purpose was to find you. You *were* and *are* my reason for being here, Riorden, just as surely as that man there is Emily's."

"You do not know what you ask of me, if I allow him to go free," he said, apparently stunned he had even voiced the words aloud. "'Twill mean Danior's life!"

"I understand what you're saying, but we'll find another solution. She loves him."

"Loves him?" he said annoyingly. "How can she love a man she has just barely met?"

"You can honestly ask that, knowing the same holds true for us?" Katherine questioned, with a hurtful expression crossing her brow. "You doubt that I love you?"

"Nay, Kat. I do not doubt your feelings for me."

Katherine nodded, but still knew his anger was simmering just below the façade he showed her. "Then, do not doubt Emily's feelings for Tiernan. I'm sure they run as deep and true as what we feel."

He mentally made a decision and motioned to Aiden. "Take him and return to the horses. We will follow shortly."

Aiden strode to the couple, who broke apart. His eyes raked Emily with a look of disappointment. Then he pulled out his dirk, heard her gasp, and began flipping the blade expertly in his hands.

He pointed its tip menacingly at Tiernan. "Harm one hair on her head, and you answer to me! If she sheds so much as one tear, I will be more than happy to personally slit your throat. Understood?"

Tiernan nodded his head in agreement, without saying a word. He took Emily's hand and headed back in the direction of where they had stopped to rest. Patrick followed along meekly, too stunned to even utter a sound.

Katherine waited breathlessly for what she realized was coming, and yet she didn't know how to stop the words she knew with all her heart he would voice.

"You lied to me," he snapped briskly.

"I withheld information. There's a difference," she said shortly. "If you'll listen to me, I can account for everything."

"I do not wish to hear your explanation, Katherine. You betrayed my trust and lied to me," he said again, more firmly this time.

Katherine understood his anger, but also realized there was some other, deeper emotion going on. "I can explain," she said, reaching out to touch him. He drew back, as if he couldn't stand to have her hands anywhere near his body. "Please, Riorden. Won't you listen to me?"

"I have had one lying, deceitful woman in my life," he began curtly, between clenched teeth. "I will not have another, no matter how I feel for you." His cloak whirled about his legs as he abruptly turned from her. His fury was more than evident with each and every step he took, distancing himself from her.

"I see," she said, standing her ground and trying to be the voice of reason. "So this isn't necessarily all about me not making some wild educated guess for what my friend felt for your escapee, as much as it is about your past coming back to haunt you."

"You do not understand," he retorted, turning to face her once more.

"Of course, I don't understand, Riorden. How could I, when we've barely had time to get to know one another? There is a lot we need to learn about each other's past, let alone our present. You're not the only one who has ever had his heart broken. I, too, know what it's like to be hurt by someone you love."

"And betrayed?" he questioned harshly. "Do you know what 'tis like to watch someone you care about turn to another, instead of you?"

She clearly saw in his eyes the pain that surely must have been mirrored in her own. "Yes, Riorden, I do. I know exactly what it's like. It's the ultimate sense of betrayal when someone you fall in love with cheats on you with another."

"'Tis far more complicated than that."

"Is it? Well, no matter the complication, it doesn't lessen the pain, or make the situation any easier, does it? It still feels as though you're dying a thousand deaths as each day progresses into the next. It still feels as if your heart is being ripped from your chest when you see them together and they're thrown into your face day after day, after day. Only time can heal that kind of suffering, Riorden. But it's also all about learning to let go of that pain so love, true and unconditional love, can find its way back into your heart."

"She married my father," Riorden yelled, as if years of pent up frustration finally burst free of his soul.

The proverbial light bulb finally lit in Katherine's head, and she staggered slightly at the thought of what lie ahead for her, if she was to stay in his life. "She's at Warkworth," she said slowly.

"Aye."

"Where you plan on returning to take over your title and lands? Where you plan on taking me?"

"Aye."

"Do you still have feelings for this woman?" Katherine heard herself asking and prayed he would say the words she longed to hear.

"I have not seen her since she wed, many years ago. I have just learned my sire has been dead these many months. I have no notion how I feel for her anymore," Riorden exclaimed, and she could tell he regretted his words the minute they left his mouth. He reached out to her. "Katherine, I–"

His words were, of course, the ones Katherine didn't want to hear. She shook off his hands, trying to collect her thoughts while jealousy, the like she had never felt before, coursed through her. All the insecurities she had ever felt with her failed relationships in her past came forward, piercing her heart like the sharpest of knives. Here, she had crossed time itself to be standing next to the man of her dreams, only to have some other woman from his own past standing between them and driving them apart. It was hard to compete with the memory of unrequited love.

"It seems to me, you still have issues to resolve with the lady. Before we get to Warkworth, you'd best decide which one of us you want," she murmured. Her voice quivered, as if she had already lost him to another. "I deserve much better than to come in only second best to some other woman."

"Katherine, this does not mean I do not care for you. I want you for my wife, for God's sake," he said, trying to persuade her of the truth in his words. He failed, at least for now, because her emotions where a jumbled mess, and so were his. There was so much anger surrounding him, she wasn't exactly sure how to deal with him.

"It really all comes down to choices, Riorden, so you'd best figure out what you want out of life," she whispered with a catch in her voice. "I won't spend mine paying for the mistakes she made with you."

"I know who I want in my life, Kat," he said smartly.

She was so hurt that his words sounded unconvincing. *So much for being the voice of reason*, she mused. There currently wasn't any hope for rational thoughts going on inside her head. All she felt was raw, angry, blinding pain.

"Do you?" A slight hysterical laugh escaped her.

"Aye, I do."

"Well, you can't have us both, that's for certain. So, let me make sure we perfectly understand one another." She looked him straight in the eye as she carefully enunciated her words with each poke of her finger firmly into his chest. "Never again, will I put up with, or stay with, a man who cheats on me, and I won't ever play the role of mistress, Riorden. Not for you, nor for anyone else!"

Katherine quickly turned away from him before he could see the tears threatening to fall down her face. She began to run, as fast as her feet could carry her, back to their group. She left him there in the forest, alone with his thoughts, calling out her name.

CHAPTER 25

Berwyck Castle

"They are from where?" Dristan inquired stiffly.

"'Tis more like when," Riorden replied sourly, leaning over the battlement wall. His gaze fled to the outer bailey where he would catch fleeting glimpses of Katherine whilst she ran the perimeter and length of the lists. He knew not how long she had been out there running, but it had been a while. He was impressed at her stamina and continued to watch her hair sway back and forth from the strap she had tied to hold it up in place atop her head.

"Well, wherever they are from, you best make things aright with your lady, Riorden," Fletcher commented wryly. "From what I have seen, you are not in her favor at the moment."

"Shut the hell up, Fletcher," Riorden threatened.

"Just a casual observation," Fletcher said mockingly.

"Do you not have the garrison to train or better things to do with your time, now that you are Dristan's captain of the guard?" Riorden huffed annoyingly.

"'Tis good to see you, too, Riorden," Fletcher laughed with cheerfulness then turned to Dristan. "I am off, my liege, to see what mayhem I can do to whip those men of yours into better shape, if you would care to join me. You too, Riorden, if you dare. I cannot think of a better excuse to be closer to your lady than to train in the lists. Mayhap, with a sword in your hand, she will see you in a better light than the one in which you currently reside."

Riorden made a swing at his longtime friend. It fell far short of the target, Fletcher's nose. Disgusted and thinking he must be getting soft, he watched whilst Dristan waved his captain away. Fletcher's laughter continued ringing in their ears, amplifying from the narrow parapet walkway.

The man is easily amused at the expense of others, thought Riorden. *Perchance he is right, though, and time in the lists is just what I stand in need of.*

For Riorden, the past several days had been unbearable, knowing how he had wounded Katherine's feelings. It had not been his intent, and yet he was unsure how to go about repairing the damage he had done with his foolish ranting. How could he make things aright when she would barely speak but two words to him?

Their arrival at Berwyck had been with mixed feelings, knowing their time alone together would be limited. Still...he had to smile as he remembered the look on her face when they had arrived in Berwyck's lists.

Dristan had been training, which was hardly surprising, with someone of smaller stature. He remembered Katherine reaching out to clutch his forearm, fearing for the smaller warrior's life, which had been evident by the gasps coming from her each time their swords had met. He could still feel his amusement at Katherine's reaction, when female laughter had bubbled forth from Dristan's adversary, and the helmet had been quickly whipped off to reveal Amiria's face.

Katherine could not have been more impressed than to find a woman had been beneath the armored helm. She had stood there with her mouth hanging open until she had finally voiced a very loud "wow", whatever that future word of hers meant. She then had let out a very loud "Brava" and had begun clapping her hands enthusiastically for the performance she had just witnessed. Considering that

Amiria must have practically just given birth, he too, had been impressed.

"What is it she wears on her face?" Dristan questioned, breaking the silence between them.

"She calls them 'sunglasses'."

"And their purpose?"

Riorden shrugged. "Something about protecting her vision from the rays of the sun."

Dristan raised his hand to shield his own eyes as he peered at the bright yellow orb residing high in the afternoon sky. Returning his attention to the lists, he gripped his chin in thought. "I did not know the sun could be so dangerous. What of her strange footwear?"

"She calls them 'tennis shoes'. She said they were made for running, and she would wear them if she saw fit to do so. The boots I provided her, apparently, hurt her feet too much."

"She should not be donning such strange gear. It calls attention to herself."

Riorden gave a small laugh of annoyance. "Believe me, I tried to tell her," he said angrily. "She merely flipped her middle finger up at me."

Dristan laughed uproariously. "She told you to sod off?" he finally managed to say, showing a flicker of appreciation in his eyes for Riorden's lady.

"I am glad to see you are as amused as she was," Riorden said irritably. "She saw my expression and told me in no uncertain terms she was glad to see…what did she call it? Oh, aye…that 'flipping the bird' meant the same thing eight hundred years in the past."

"You have found yourself a cheeky wench there, Riorden. If I were you, I would do everything in my power to keep her happily by my side."

"Ha! You do not know the half of it, Dristan," Riorden muttered, raking his hand through his hair. "I have come to the realization that not only is she compassionate, beautiful, and a seductress at heart, but when provoked, she is a bit of a spitfire, much like your own dear wife.

Dristan laughed again and slapped his friend heartily on the back. "I know I have told you this many times afore, but just remember, you shall never be bored with her, nor shall you ever regret taking her to wife."

"God help me."

"I believe he already has, Riorden," Dristan proclaimed seriously. "Your story is a hard one to believe, and yet the proof Lady Katherine is not of this time is clearly evident. We will meet in my solar later this eve so she can show us her future marvels. Do you think she will mind?"

"Nay. She will surely know you shall be discrete with the knowledge she shares with you."

Dristan clapped his hands together in delight. "Then come, and let us take Fletcher up on his invitation. It has been some time since I have taken you both on simultaneously. Mayhap, I shall even engage the Irishman you brought along to test his worth."

"God's Wounds, Dristan. I cannot, for the life of me, understand why you have welcomed him into your home as you have."

"The ladies pleaded his cause well enough that I felt Cavanaugh is a knight of honor and as such should be treated well rather than as a prisoner," Dristan answered.

"You may regret such an unwise decision if the king were to learn of such a treasonous act," Riorden said.

"You have that aright, but I still stand by my vow that he is welcome here. Now, let us away to the lists. I have the need to know how my knights are doing with their training under Fletcher's watch."

Riorden groaned at the prospect of what lay ahead for the afternoon. But then, a devilish smile played upon his face as he thought of how to at last get his lovely lady's attention. With that thought in mind, he began whistling a merry tune, took off his tunic, and made his way happily down to the lists.

∾

One step, two steps, three steps. Breathe in, breathe out. Don't think. Just look straight ahead. Keep putting one foot in front of the other. Another lap down, so let's do it again. Lungs are burning, calf muscles are tight from the strain of my run. Now I've gone and done it, for all I can focus on is his mouth-water-

ing, rigid, glorious muscles; the tight, washboard-like rippling of his stomach; the feel of his hot skin beneath my fingertips reaching ever lower; the sweetness of his kiss as our tongues dance together in unison. Ugh! Stop it Katherine! Don't think about that stubborn, idiotic man! Just keep running. One step, two steps, three steps. Breathe in, breathe out...

Katherine continued, ever onward, in her pursuit to free her mind of anything to do with Riorden. She kept her conversation going inside her head, repeating it over and over again. It was either that, or she'd be madder than a hornet. She had been so ticked off when Riorden had forbidden her to go for a run outside the castle walls. Was this how her life was going to be? Forever kept safe and sound behind the walls of a keep, never to feel the taste of freedom again? Well, she supposed that wouldn't be so bad as long as that arrogant man came to his senses soon. If he didn't, he'd lose the one person who would love him, unconditionally, for all time. Men!

Her thoughts were momentarily interrupted during her sprint around the lists when the lady of the keep joined her. She nodded to Amiria, who must have sensed Katherine's need to keep her own council. No words were necessary from the silent look they exchanged. She was glad for it. Her own thoughts were enough company for the time being, and she relished this time to herself where there was nothing to occupy her mind, except the dirt beneath her feet and her own inner demons she was struggling with. It seemed the emotions of her own troublesome past, at least where men were concerned, were also wreaking havoc with her weary mind, much like Riorden's past coming to bite him in his friggin' tight ass.

A movement caught her eye, and she tried, unsuccessfully, to avoid looking at the spectacle coming into her line of vision. Merciful heavens and good Lord above, but she would be hard pressed to ignore such a hunk of pure male ruggedness. She tripped slightly over her own two feet, and Amiria quickly reached out her hand to steady her. She'd be so pissed at herself to let him see how he had affected her. Luckily he did not see her falter...or so she thought.

He caught her gaze, flexed his bulging muscular arms, and grinned at her with an overconfident smile. One look across the lists into his startling vivid blue eyes, and she knew he'd seen her misstep. His smug expression, plastered upon his face, showed his awareness of how he had affected her. He knew exactly what he was doing, coming here without a shirt on, and what it would do to her. From the look he threw her while he began to swing his sword in front of him, he would enjoy every second of her discomfort.

"That damn son of a b–" Katherine's words were cut off by muffled laughter from Amiria.

"Let us not give in so easily and continue with another lap or two," Amiria suggested, "elsewise, you will never be able to live with him."

"I don't know if I'll be living with him at all, Lady Amiria."

"Do you love him?" she asked as they easily picked up their pace.

"With all my heart," Katherine replied without reservation and realized as she spoke the words aloud that they were, in fact, true.

"Then all will work out as it should," Amiria predicted. "'Twill not be easy at Warkworth, I assure you, until he dispatches that malicious wench to her dower house. Do not let her get under your skin, Katherine, for she will attempt to make your life miserable 'til he does so. I will not be surprised if she tries to win him back."

"Is this conversation supposed to make me feel better? Because, if it is, then I hate to tell you this, my lady, but you are failing," Katherine said with a grimace.

Amiria mumbled an apology. They began to slow down their pace and stopped when they came to the castle well. Amiria let go of the bucket hanging from a long rope, and upon hearing it splash into the water far below, she began to raise it inch by inch. Taking a dipper off a nearby hook, she offered it first to Katherine to drink her fill.

Amiria took Katherine by the arm to a nearby stone bench where they could watch the men train. If she had thought Riorden in the forest was a sight, it was nothing compared to watching Amiria's husband. He was clearly a master with a sword. He began calling out taunting words until he engaged both Riorden and the man she'd met, called Fletcher, at the same time. It was a very impressive sight, along with being quite overwhelming. There was a lot that could be said for such handsome medieval men with swords in their hands, enjoying their work out.

She felt Lady Amiria give her arm a gentle pat. Turning towards her, Katherine waited as the lady seemingly struggled to find the right words to say.

"Never doubt...he loves you, Katherine," she whispered confidently.

"How can you tell?"

"Oh, I have known Riorden de Deveraux for many a year now, so truly, he is not as hard to read as you might think," Amiria said with a gentle smile. "He has been watching you most intently when you are not looking. I have never seen him look at another as he looks on you."

"I can't imagine not having him in my life, now that I've found him," Katherine said sadly.

Amiria gave a sigh of understanding. "Men can be so pig headed sometimes, but they generally come around. Riorden will need your patience, Katherine, when he reaches Warkworth, and all your love. 'Tis not only the woman he thought he'd cared for he must deal with, but also the memory and ghost of his father. They did not part on good terms when Riorden left. Personally, I think, he regrets his harsh words he can never recant, now that his sire his gone."

"Warkworth is haunted?"

Amiria smiled again at Katherine's words. "Would that be so surprising, given that you yourself have come through time to be with the one you dreamed of all your life?"

"I suppose not, my lady."

"Call me Amiria, since we will be like family," she stated casually, squeezing Katherine's hand again. "'Tis a beautiful name, by the way."

"Excuse me, my lady?"

"Your name...Katherine. 'Tis a beautiful name. 'Twas my mother's, as well, which is why I felt a certain kinship with you when we first met."

They each became lost in thought, and Katherine, in particular, couldn't for the life of her take her eyes from Riorden's body as he trained. She sighed heavily.

Amiria finally broke through their silence as the first hint of a coming storm announced itself with the sound of distant thunder. "Trust him, Katherine, for he will never fail you."

"Never?" she whispered in awe.

"Nay, never," Amiria said confidently. "Normally, I would tell you Riorden will love you 'til his last dying breath, but in your case, my dear, I believe 'twill be more like until the end of time itself. We are truly lucky women, Katherine, since I also know how it feels to be so very blessed."

Amiria rose and left Katherine to her own troubled thoughts. The woman's words tumbled in her mind for the remainder of the afternoon. *To have him love me until his last, dying breath and until the end of time...how could I ask or want for anything more of him than that?*

CHAPTER 26

*T*orches lit the Great Hall, giving the room a hazy appearance whilst the castle inhabitants sat and ate their fill. The room was abuzz with lighthearted conversations and boisterous activity as the evening meal arrived at the already heavily laden tables. The smell of mouthwatering roasted venison and boar permeated the air, causing hungry knights to reach out eagerly for the succulent meat and fill the trenchers afore them. They cared not that their fingers burned whilst they tore at the tender meat, nor when the juices ran down their chins. They consumed the bounty of the meal with gusto, behaving as if they had not eaten in days.

A heady red wine was poured at the raised dais for those with a taste of something finer than the everyday drink of mead to accompany their food. Cool ale flowed from a keg that had been brought up from the cellars whilst serving maids skirted around outstretched hands of lusty knights looking for more than what would be poured into their tankards. Laughter abounded for those women who eagerly accepted the attention of their most favored knight with a promise of an evening of pleasure ahead of them. Occasional thunder, along with the raucous laughter, mixed with the sounds of musical chords as the castle's minstrels began to tune their instruments, plucking the strings of their lutes.

Occasionally, a bolt of lightning illuminated the room from the windows above, casting the occupants of the hall momentarily into a surreal display of eerie, flickering movements. 'Twas clear the storm outside was heightening in strength, if the sound of the howling wind and pelting rain was any indication of nature's turbulent fury.

Riorden drummed his fingers on the wooden table whilst his mood remained somber. He was not pleased he had been denied the pleasure of being seated next to Katherine at the high table. She was currently preoccupied in conversation with none other than Dristan and Lynet. Her bubbly laughter rang out, further irritating him, since he was unable to enjoy her company.

In truth, there was nothing out of the ordinary at his place of honor next to Dristan's wife and Aiden. Amiria chatted on amicably whilst she continually encouraged him to taste the food set afore the trencher they shared. Thus far, the only thing he had been able to swallow was the wine. Everything else might as well have been made of dirt, for it held no appeal.

His eyes darted to those who were noisily sliding tables out of the way so the dancing could begin. Even the sound of the wood as it scraped across the stone floor grated on his already stretched nerves. 'Twas not hard to notice Fletcher making his way to their table with a determined stride. Riorden shot a warning to the man, who blatantly ignored it with a loud, amused chuckle. When Fletcher made his formal bow to Katherine and extended his hand, Riorden about jumped out of his chair to protest until he felt a reassuring hand on his arm.

"He only bates you, Riorden," Amiria said softly. "If you do not wish for others to dance with Katherine, then I suggest you dance with her yourself."

"I am out of favor with the lady," Riorden muttered, under his breath.

"Only you can change that, old man," Aiden goaded with a knowing smirk and went back to his meal.

Riorden watched as Katherine rose with a warm smile, dropped into a curtsey, and quickly scooted around the table to take Fletcher's arm.

She glanced back over her shoulder at Riorden. Their eyes met and held. The space between them seemingly lessened by the intensity rushing between them. His thoughts shattered into a thousand pieces whilst his heart began to beat furiously with just one look from her. Was it only his imagination, or did she feel it too...those invisible ties branding their souls together as one? Did it appear as if her eyes were silently begging for him to rise and take Fletcher's place at her side, or was it just the lightning playing cruel tricks with his mind?

Riorden had just put his hands on the arms of his chair to rise and join her, when he saw her blink. The moment they had been sharing, however brief, rapidly disappeared, as if it had never occurred. Her face instantly showed her disappointment in him, as if he refused to feel the constant connection that pulled them together. She tore her gaze from him and searched out her lady friend.

"Come on and join us, Em," Katherine called out. "Think of it as line dancing."

Line dancing? What the bloody hell is line dancing? Riorden wondered. Apparently, Lady Emily thought the proposition of this line dancing had some merit as she all but ran around the table with Tiernan in tow.

"You'll have to show me the steps, Tiernan," Emily laughed brightly.

"'Twill be my pleasure, my lady," he replied enthusiastically.

At least someone was looking forward to the prospect of holding his lady, since 'twas obvious Katherine wanted nothing to do with him. Riorden fumed. He scowled watching the couple make their way to the middle of the floor. He was still unsure how he felt about a prisoner having free access to the castle when he should be residing in its pit. He put the fault with Katherine and Emily who had convincingly pleaded Tiernan's cause upon their arrival at Berwyck. Riorden would not gainsay Dristan's decision, since he was lord here, but that did not mean he had to agree with what he felt was an error in judgment.

The minstrels strummed their lutes, and lilting music commenced to fill the hall. Riorden viewed, with a frown, each step Katherine took as Fletcher maneuvered her through the difficult steps of the dance.

Her movements were awkward, at first, until she began to catch on to the pattern. Their hands touched. His mood soured. Fletcher lifted her high by the waist, circling sure-footed whilst he held her with her hands resting lightly on his shoulders. Riorden fingered his dirk that had somehow found its way from his boot to his hand. She threw her head back with a look of sheer pleasure and serenity etched upon her features. He had never seen her look more beautiful.

Riorden reached for his chalice, noticed 'twas empty, and motioned for more wine. Once filled, he took a long sip. He knew he was being unreasonable, yet had no idea how to stop the jealousy coursing through his head. The longer the music played, the fouler his mood became as he watched his woman being given to Nathaniel, another of Dristan's guards. His torture did not stop, when yet another took his place during the following song. *Merde!* Was the whole damn garrison going to take a turn about the floor with his lady?

'Twas not until he witnessed Fletcher cutting in for another dance that Riorden's patience came to an end. He stood, slamming his chalice onto the table. But 'twas Dristan's muffled laughter that had him sit his sorry arse back down and call for more wine. His eyes peered over the rim of his cup, never leaving his lady, who appeared to be the happiest he had ever seen her. His brow furrowed when, after another dance, Fletcher came to sit beside him now that Amiria had vacated the seat to see to her infant.

"A most remarkable woman, Riorden," he exclaimed cheerfully. "I wonder if she would favor my suit."

"You would be wise to forget such a notion," Riorden warned, placing his dagger on the table. Fletcher burst into laughter and slapped him on his back.

"'Tis about damn time you have become smitten with a fair lady. I never thought to see you, of all people, Riorden, besotted with jealousy over some maiden you just met. I must admit, 'tis quite comical."

"Glad I could amuse you so," Riorden mumbled. He continued his perusal of Katherine whilst it seemed his premonition would come to pass that Dristan's entire personal guard was to take a turn with his lady. 'Twas not until another knight escorted her about the floor that Riorden became concerned. He did not recognize the young man, and he scowled, watching the unfamiliar lad place his hands lower than Katherine's waist. "Who is that scoundrel?"

Fletcher's eyes scanned the room until his gaze landed on the spectacle causing Riorden's growing unease. "There are a few new knights here who have come begging to be trained by the Devil's Dragon. Dristan is still considering their worth or if he shall be wasting his time. From the look your lady is casting her newest partner, he would be wise to rethink his dancing techniques. I think your fair lady is about to take off his limb, if he reaches any lower."

"Excuse me," Riorden exclaimed briskly. His chair practically fell over in his eagerness to give aid to Katherine.

Afore he could reach her side, a scuffle arose between the untactful knight and another trying to lay claim to his lady. The two men began to push each other, and Katherine landed in an undignified heap upon the floor. Her skirts tangled about her legs whilst she tried unsuccessfully to move out of the way of the ensuing fight. Fury blazed in Riorden's eyes as he began pushing others from his path to reach her. She managed to finally rise as the two men now let fists fly. They tumbled to the floor amidst grunts of pain, from punches that met their marks.

Riorden crossed the distance between them, and Katherine flung herself into his arms. He felt her rapid breathing whilst he held her close and murmured words of comfort. Her body trembled, and he tightened his arms around her.

To add to the mayhem occurring in Dristan's hall, the keep's door unexpectedly flung wide with a resounding bang. With its opening, a flood of rain forced its way into the Great Hall, soaking the floor. Four drenched travelers stood in the portal, looking towards the warmth of the nearby fire. They began to make their way in that direction when one let out a fierce cry.

Danior pushed back his hood from his face, pulled free his sword from its scabbard, and stood there, in self-righteous anger. Then he made straight for Tiernan, as if possessed. The women in the hall screamed. Emily and Juliana shrieked the loudest. He had almost reached his destination when everyone came to a screeching halt at Dristan's loud, commanding bellow to cease and desist.

Dristan passed his son back to Amiria, who quickly ascended up the curved stairs of the tower. His fury-filled gaze swept the inhabitants of his hall, much like the storm inflicting itself upon the land outside his keep. Those with the most sense cleared away from the middle of the floor and the chaos that had erupted in but a matter of seconds.

"It appears that the festivities are over for the eve," Dristan's voice boomed as he crossed the floor to face the angry man afore him. "Danior, you and your company are of course welcome here at Berwyck. But Cavanaugh has proven his worth to me in the lists and we have come to an amicable accord. I will have you know that I have formally accepted his presence here as a guest. As such, he is under my protection and is not to be harmed," Dristan announced firmly.

"But, my lord—" Danior sputtered as his rain soaked cloak puddled beneath his feet. His gaze narrowed and thoughts of betrayal were clearly apparent on his visage when he saw Emily's hand clutched, with familiarity, in his enemy's.

Dristan held up his hand to cease Danior's words. "There is much to discuss, and discuss it we shall, but on the morrow, in my solar, after you and your party have rested." He held eye contact with Danior 'til the knight acquiesced, bowing his head.

Riorden continued to hold Katherine as her friends quickly came over to gather near her. Despite the tension in the room, 'twas clear to all present, by their joyful, yet concerned chatter, that the four ladies were happy to be reunited. They grasped each other's hands, looked at one another with relief, and hugged each other in gratitude.

"Your journey has been long and conditions harsh." Dristan addressed the two drenched, weary knights. "The women look exhausted. Rest now." He motioned to a servant, who led the way as Brianna and a shaken Juliana slowly followed up the stairs to rooms that would be prepared for them. Danior, though still exasperated, along with Gavin, reluctantly trailed close behind them.

The disturbance quelled, Dristan's eyes fell upon the shaking woman Riorden held tenderly in his arms. Dristan held out his hand. "Lady Katherine," he called out.

Riorden felt her heavy sigh against his chest and the gentle caress of her hand on his own, afore she reluctantly tore herself from his grasp.

"My lord?" Katherine whispered as she stood before the furious Devil's Dragon.

"It seems necessary for me to take matters into my own hands where you are concerned, my lady." He tucked her hand upon his elbow, as if taking possession of her. "You, too, shall be under my protection. Such a precious treasure should not be left alone where those unworthy of her may think she is available to their every whim," Dristan looked directly at the two men who had been fighting over her and watched in satisfaction as they lowered their eyes.

"You are too kind, my Lord Dristan," Katherine answered in a soft murmur.

Dristan patted her hand as though she was now a part of his family. His gaze then went to Riorden. "Hopefully, your knight over there will begin to realize the worth of having a woman such as yourself as his own. He would be wise to not allow past memories, along with petty differences that are of no worth at present, to cloud his better judgment and get the best of him."

Afore Riorden could form any sort of a response, he watched in disappointment as Katherine was led up the tower stairs. Lightning struck, and seconds later, thunder boomed across the land, as if God above was voicing his own form of displeasure at Riorden's foolishness. Come the morn, he vowed he would not make the same mistakes, ever again.

CHAPTER 27

*K*atherine sat before the fire, reaching down to add another log to the bright red flames in the hearth. The hours had seemingly passed by at a snail's pace tonight, and yet she was still sitting here, wide awake in Lynet's room. She supposed it was an honor to share the room with the beautiful young woman, who had confided her own heart's sorrow of lost love before she at last found her slumber. She understood Lynet's distress, because she had also been on the receiving end of feeling a bitter sense of betrayal when it came to someone she had given her heart to.

Funny, how she could now look back on it all and realize the love she had felt for those men, unworthy to have received such a gift, was nothing compared to what she had with Riorden. True...she hadn't known him long, but what she shared with him went far beyond some mere infatuation with his handsome face. Truthfully, if God was willing to send her such an earth shattering message by throwing her back more than eight hundred years into the past just so she could find her knight and a love worth keeping, who was she not to take advantage of such a miracle?

The slightest sound of tapping came from the door to the chamber, and Katherine pulled her robe closer around her shoulders, wondering who would be disturbing them at this hour. A quick glance at the bed only showed Lynet burrowing deeper beneath the covers. Katherine rushed, barefooted across the cold floor, when she heard yet another set of insistent rapping. She opened the door hesitantly and peeked out into the dimly lit passageway.

Riorden stood there with his arms folded against his chest and one booted foot propped up against the stone wall. He looked indecisive in his decision to disturb her and only stared at her with those incredible, sapphire blue eyes. She stepped into the cool corridor and closed the door quietly behind her so she didn't wake up Lynet.

A vision of a castle siege flashed in her mind, and she began to worry. Why else would he be here at this ungodly hour. "Are we at war?" Her hand shook at the prospect of a medieval battle outside of the keep's protective walls. She seemed to be asking that question a lot, lately.

"Nay."

Katherine relaxed, but wondered what was wrong that he stood looking so devilishly handsome in the darkened corridor. "Then what is it?" she asked in a hushed whisper.

"Nothing," he declared in a simple statement.

She waited for him to continue, but instead, his eyes slowly wandered up and down her body. She clutched her nightwear close against her throat. The intensity of his stare almost scorched her skin, making her feel as if she stood completely naked for his viewing pleasure.

"Nothing? You come knocking on our door in the middle of the night, and you have nothing to say?" she questioned with knitted brows. "Are you drunk?"

"Only from your beauty."

Her breath left her in a rush of emotions at his words. He pushed off the wall, advancing like the black lion he was until he stood but inches from her. *Good grief!* She could immediately feel the heat of passion radiate between them, and he hadn't even touched her yet. He came to stand behind her. Katherine held her breath in eagerness of what he planned to do next. Her senses came alive, as if her whole body screamed out for him. It was sheer agony waiting for the touch of his hands.

She felt his breath on her neck, and her reaction was instantaneous as tingling goose bumps of anticipation rushed down her spine. He inhaled the fragrance of her hair, and she hid a smile, knowing it smelled like her favorite scent of Japanese cherry blossoms. He reached out, taking her plaited pony tail in his hands and undid the tie holding it in place. His fingers gently laced through the length of her tresses as he unleashed locks that fell in a wave of curls down her back. She almost sighed aloud at the delight he gave her, performing such a simple act as unbraiding its length.

"I like your hair better when 'tis unbound, Katherine," he said, coming back around to stand in front of her with an alluring smile.

"You do?"

"Aye. 'Tis almost a sin to have such loveliness constrained so."

She looked up into his eyes and wondered at his words. "Are we talking just about my hair or our earlier argument of letting me jog outside the castle walls?"

"Perchance, 'tis a bit of both. I only thought of your safety, my lady. 'Tis a cruel world we live in, and I would not wish to lose you to another," Riorden professed in an honest attempt to apologize.

She reached up and traced his lips with her thumb until he took her hand and began kissing the inside of her wrist, sending tiny currents racing up her arm. "You won't lose me, Riorden. I belong only to you..." she swore with a wistful smile, "...for all of ever."

Apparently, satisfied at the reaffirmation of his own words of sharing an eternity together, he nodded. "Then come with me," he said, holding out his hand.

She took it with no hesitation and followed his lead as he guided her down to the second story of the keep. Two turns later, down the long torch lit hallway, he stopped before a door and pushed it open for her.

She entered and took quick note of her surroundings. There was no doubt in her mind this was his room, especially when she saw his belongings scattered about the chamber. The fire burned brightly, taking the chill from the air, and a light repast with a decanter of wine awaited them on a small table next to the hearth.

The room was sparsely furnished. A writing desk and chair sat in a corner by a small window, and two comfortable looking chairs were in front of the fireplace. A rather large trunk sat up against one wall with the lid open, and she could see his clean clothing neatly folded inside. His bed seemed to suddenly dominate her attention. For all her courage in the past several days, she unexpectedly felt nervous. Her shiver had nothing to do with being cold.

Katherine sensed when Riorden came up behind her, only this time, he pressed himself fully against her back, molding himself to her body. His hands slowly caressed their way down her numb arms until he clasped her shaking fingers with his own. He let go of one hand, placed his own on her belly then pulled her gently into his solid muscular form. She inhaled sharply at the sensation of his hard arousal intimately pressed against her body, a body crying out to be unleashed from the restriction of her damn clothing. All she wanted to do was reach out to at last touch the very essence of him.

Suddenly, she thought of the one precious gift she could not offer him, since she had foolishly given it away. She tore out of his grasp with a startled cry. "Riorden, I must speak with you," she spoke in alarm, worrying what reaction her words would bring.

He chuckled. "You tease me for days, then say you are mine, and now you wish to have speech?" he said in amusement. "Do you not think it can wait, *ma cherie*?"

She shook her head and moved to the window, not that she could see anything other than the lightning, illuminating the sky off in the distance. He came to her, as she knew he would, and turned her into his embrace.

Tilting up her chin, he gave her an encouraging smile. "Tell me, what troubles you so, Katherine. I did not mean this night to be anything other than one we would always remember with great fondness."

Her lip trembled. "I want the same, but you must first understand, times are so very different where I come from than they are here...so far into the past, Riorden," Katherine said with a quivering voice.

His laughter rumbled in his chest. "I cannot believe making love has changed that much in this future of yours, Kat."

She rolled her eyes with an exasperated sigh still hearing his amusement at her expense. "No, of course not. That hasn't changed in the least."

"It gives me great pleasure to hear it," he said while he nuzzled her ear with his lips.

She pulled away from him and tried again. "It's just that...I mean...the times being as they are...we as a civilization don't always adhere to the same standards as the nobility may in the twelfth century. You could say that our lack of morals make us a somewhat loose society."

"I really do not see where this conversation is going, Katherine."

She hung her head in embarrassment, trying to hold back the tears, which would surely give way at any moment. "It should have been yours," Katherine said, so softly he had to lean in to hear what she was saying. "If I could change things, I would Riorden. You have to believe me."

"Change what, Katherine?" he asked with a mixture of curiosity and concern.

"I wish I could...I wish I could give you..." she stammered with a crestfallen look and pleading eyes for him to understand what she was trying to say.

His eyes widened, as if at last he caught on to what she couldn't somehow manage to say. He pulled her close and held her again as his hand stroked down her hair.

"Are you, mayhap, trying to tell me you are not a virgin?"

"Yes."

"I see."

"I'm so sorry, Riorden," she said, and waited for the proverbial other shoe to fall. He said nothing and only continued to hold her. "I thought I was in lo—"

He silenced her by placing his warm fingertips on her lips. "I do not wish to hear how you felt for another, Kat."

"Please, don't be angry with me," she pleaded, trying to read his face.

"We all have a past we would like to forget, my sweet Katherine. What happened in yours cannot be changed and the same holds true for mine. We both need to learn to leave the past where it belongs and look forward to our future together."

"Nothing would make me happier."

"You are here with me now, and 'tis all that matters," he proclaimed honestly and then began to laugh. "Besides, this actually ends a dilemma I was trying to find a solution for."

She looked at him with confusion. "What was that?"

Her breath caught as she felt him lower the robe from her shoulders. He slid his hands down her back until he reached her bottom and pulled her completely up against his rigid body with another chuckle. "Virgins...I hear they are a bothersome lot, since they know nothing of what a man likes in his bed. 'Tis why I have never bothered being with them."

"And just how many women have you been in bed with, my lord?" she asked, raising her brow.

"Enough to know you shall have no complaints when I have thoroughly pleased you," he said huskily. "I had worried once I began making love to you, I would be hard pressed to pause, to give you time to rest. Now I do not need to concern myself with only having you once, but can satisfy my thirst for you until the dawn."

Katherine ran her hands up his tunic and began pulling it off his chest. The touch of his skin beneath her palms sent her pulse racing. "Only until the dawn?" she asked in a sultry voice.

He leaned down until his lips were but inches from her own. Their breath became as one. "All of eternity will not be long enough to show you how much I care for you. I love you, Katherine. I will love you until the dawn, until all of our morrows, until time ceases to exist."

She wound her arms around his neck and leaned into his muscled torso. "Then show me, my dearest Riorden," she breathed.

She laughed brightly as he suddenly scooped her up into his arms, as if she weighed nothing at all, and placed her on the bed. He sat on its edge in order to remove his boots, and Katherine wrapped her arms around his neck. "Hurry, Riorden," she whispered and began placing soft kisses on his ear and neck. She heard him groan and felt him shiver.

"You are distracting me, Kat," he said as the second boot finally thumped onto the floor. He stood, tearing off the remainder of his clothes.

Her eyes widened in startled amazement of what stood before her. There was certainly something to be said for her knight standing there with layered muscles and skin that had been kissed by the sun. Her gaze went lower, and she gasped. "Oh, my goodness."

Riorden chuckled at her discovery of what awaited her. "See what you have done to me?"

"Yes," she barely managed to say, and she licked her suddenly dry lips. "Is that all for me?"

He gave her a mischievous grin. "Aye, 'tis all for you, my love."

She began to fumble with the ties of her night clothes and found her fingers no longer seemed to be working properly.

Riorden took her hands in his and began to suck each of her fingertips. She moaned at the contact of his tongue. "May I," she heard him inquire as to assisting her. She somehow achieved a nod of assent. It was all she could manage, for she was already completely lost in the spell he had woven around her heart.

Again, he gave her that devilish smile she had come to love. As he took the gown in hand and pulled it off her, she heard it rip and watched as he threw the fabric carelessly behind him, and it floated to the floor in a puddle of silky linen.

The bed dipped as he joined her. When he lay atop her, she felt as if she had died and gone to heaven. She thought her body pressed up against his while they embraced each other in the pond had been like experiencing a small bit of paradise, but surely, this was beyond any words of description. It was perfect!

He kissed her and took whatever was left of her sense of reality away. Each kiss said a thousand words, awakening her soul. Each taste when their tongues met was as if they were pouring life into each other. Their hands explored one another until they knew every curve of their bodies intimately. Time stood still and held no meaning while they savored every second of this moment until they at last joined together.

Katherine opened her eyes as she felt Riorden move to enter the very core of her being. She could feel just the tip of him teasing her senses. Every nerve in her body was surely on fire while she waited with baited breath for him to continue. The blue of his eyes were filled with so much passion, she could tell it had taken everything in his power to have held out for as long as he had.

"Tell me what you want, my love," he said hoarsely as he strained not to enter her.

"I want you," she said hungrily as she caressed his back.

"You mean, this," he replied as he entered her just a fraction.

"More."

Still he teased her by not entering her completely. "How about now?"

She reached up and pulled his head down closer to her face. He kissed her again until she finally found her voice and could respond while staring up into his eyes. "I want you so deep inside me, Riorden, that I'll know you've forever touched my heart," she said, and cried out when she at last received, inch by glorious inch, what she had been begging him for.

"Then come with me, Katherine, and let us reach for the stars together."

He began to move in a rhythm known throughout all time. There was an urgency now between them as they were consumed with a sensation, almost like an addiction, which only the other could satisfy and fulfill. The tension began to build until Katherine could barely breathe as sweat glistened between their straining bodies.

Higher and higher they soared on their journey together. Just as Katherine felt on the brink of something so wonderful, and he could take her no further, he plunged deeper inside her one last time, and she felt it...that blissful release...like white hot lightning, radiating through every part of her being. She cried out his name, even as he called out hers, while she felt him pulsating his very soul into her own. Riorden had done what he had promised. He had taken her to the heavenly stars above.

Their rapid breathing as they gasped for air attested to the extent and power of what had inevitably passed between them. Katherine felt him move as if to leave her, and she wrapped her legs around him, clutching him firmly in place.

"No," she said in the softest of pleas, "please don't go as yet. Stay, Riorden, so I can feel your heartbeat next to mine, just a while longer..."

Their breathing at last returned to some sort of normalcy, as if she would ever know what normal was again after such an earth shattering experience. She wondered how long they stayed there, since time truly no longer meant a thing to her. Her fingers gently began moving their way down his back until she reached his firm buttocks. She couldn't resist giving both cheeks a squeeze. A deep chuckle escaped him, almost as if he was ready for more of what they had just shared.

"Are you trying to tempt me, my lady?" His voice practically dripped with enough passion to cause Katherine's pulse to once more increase.

"Perhaps..." She let her words linger in the air like an invitation to journey to the heavens, again.

He took her up on what she offered. His arms snaked around her until she now found herself on top of him. Her hair became like a veil around their heads and she wiggled her bottom, enjoying the sensation of being in control, or so she thought, as she felt him growing again beneath her.

Riorden growled and pulled her up by her hips until he slowly lowered her down so he filled her completely. She leaned her head back, relishing the feel of him and the exquisite pleasure she could now give him. He gave her a roguish grin, and she bent down, placing a kiss upon his parted lips.

"I love you," Katherine uttered with all the love she felt for this man she had crossed time for.

"Then show me, my Katherine," he said, kissing her again. Deeply. Fully. Until she had no doubt the lion within him had awoken, again. She laughed and took control, gladly setting the pace to their movements now.

The midnight hours waned, closer and closer to the morning's rising sun. Seemingly, the heavens themselves came shinning down upon the couple who at last fell asleep still wrapped securely within each other's embrace. For on this night, they had unknowingly sealed their earthly bonds to one another. God above was pleased, and their souls became united and would everlastingly transcend time itself. The sun rose high into the morning sky, and still they slumbered peacefully. They were as one. They were forever complete.

CHAPTER 28

Massive pounding penetrated Riorden's head and he woke as his chamber door crashed open. Wood splintered when it slammed against the wall. He automatically reached for his sword, or tried to, but found he was entangled with Katherine's hair hampering his movements. His bleary vision cleared enough to see the man standing at the foot of his bed was Dristan, whose anger was clearly registered on his stern visage.

"Riorden, my love, tell the idiot, making so much noise he disturbs our slumber, to go away," Katherine mumbled still half asleep. "You need your rest so you can love me again in the morning."

Riorden settled the covers over Katherine's shoulder and felt her snuggle into his chest with a heavy blissful sigh. He pulled her closer to him. "Kat...we have...unexpected company."

"Don't want any. Just want you," she muttered until Riorden gently shook her to fully wake her. "All right already, I'm getting up. But, it's best you learn now, I'm really not a morning person. Sheesh!" She finally opened her eyes and gasped upon seeing Dristan towering over them. She made a grab for the blanket and pulled it to her chin.

Riorden calmly waited for the storm brewing in Dristan's face to explode. He did not have a long delay.

"God's wound! What were you thinking, Riorden?" Dristan bellowed. "I said, I would give her my protection, and now I find you bedding her?"

Riorden shrugged. "'Twas only a matter of time afore the deed was done. Besides...she will be my wife."

"You damned well better make her your wife!"

"Really Dristan, there's no need to make such a fuss. Katherine and I will wed with all haste," Riorden snapped and then placed a kiss on Katherine's forehead as she laid her head back down upon his chest.

"Tell that to the three women who are in a complete state of panic, not knowing where their lady friend is. We were just about to send out a scouting party, thinking she slipped past the guards and was out running in her future gear!" Dristan roared. "The thought of someone finding her and burning her at the stake for being a witch would tend to make anyone edgy, especially if he had sworn to protect the lady. Is this not so?"

Riorden sobered at the thought. "My apologies, Dristan. I did not think–"

"Nay! You did not," he retorted.

Katherine sat up on her elbow. "Please, my lord, don't blame him for something I wanted just as much as he did."

"Did he force you?" Dristan inquired sternly.

She looked at him aghast. "Of course not!"

Dristan pointed the tip of his sword at Riorden. "You are lucky you have been my friend for as long as I can remember. I did not think you would ever do something like this to one who was under my care." He lowered his sword and took a deep breath.

"She is safe, Dristan, and no harm has come to her. I will watch over her always," Riorden vowed.

Dristan looked at the couple, wrapped up in each other's arms. "See that you do. Dress yourselves. I will gather everyone to meet in my solar, since the opportunity did not present itself last eve or this morn whilst we searched the castle for your lady."

Dristan strode through the doorway after unsuccessfully attempting to shut it to allow them some form of privacy. Unfortunately, the door now hung useless upon its hinges.

Katherine giggled nervously. "I guess the cat has been let out of the bag."

Riorden's brow drew together, since he had no idea of what she spoke. She must have felt amused at his look, since she laughed out loud and reached up to smooth the crease from his brow.

"You shouldn't frown so, my love. You'll get wrinkles," Katherine whispered softly and placed a kiss upon his lips.

He pulled her on top of him and ravished her mouth whilst he raked his fingers through her glorious silken hair. "I wish we had time to take up where we left off but hours ago. Mayhap, a door would help, as well. You have left me aching for you again. You are such a temptress."

"Later?" she asked breathlessly.

"You can count on it, my lady."

"I like the sound of that," she said as she rose from the bed, dragging one of the covers with her. "I've waited a lifetime to hear you call me your lady and only thought I would hear it in my dreams."

"Then 'tis something you must needs get used to, Katherine, for you shall be my lady for the rest of our days, and for always."

"I've died and gone to heaven then," she proclaimed and reached up bringing his head down so she could meet his lips.

"You have taken me there, as well, *ma cher*." He began donning his braies until he heard her laughter erupt. "What amuses you so, Kat?"

"Those are the craziest underwear I've ever seen!" She giggled again, covering her mouth with her hand.

"You can say such of my garments after what I have seen you wearing?" His brow lifted to mock her attempts to remain contrite and serious. It only made her mirth ring out louder.

"Sorry, but it's true."

"I have my doubts, Kat. I must admit, your undergarments do not leave much to the imagination, but I like them."

"Maybe, I should wear them more often," she suggested.

"Or just remain naked in my bed." He tossed her a wicked grin whilst drawing his hose over his legs and then sauntered to her side, holding out her robe to cover her. "Now off with you," he said, with a playful swat on her bottom. "I shall see you in Dristan's solar once you are properly clothed, although, I must say, I have enjoyed you naked in my bed. I am sure Dristan will continue to have a few choice words for me, so I might as well get it over with, else he make me pay for my insolence with an afternoon in the lists."

Riorden watched her wave goodbye and could hear the patter of her bare feet as she fled down the passageway. Her nightwear, half way under the bed, caught his eye, and he picked up the soft fabric from where he had tossed it the eve afore, when he tore the cloth hiding her from his gaze. He smiled and caught the faintest hint of her scent and breathed deeply. He would have to ask her what kind of flowers she smelled of.

Memories of their limbs entwined throughout the night assailed his senses until he felt himself harden. He carefully folded the ruined garment and placed it with his own clothing. He would keep it with him always, as a reminder of a night worth remembering.

He chuckled and thought on his previous conversation with Dristan. He hated to admit the man was right. Riorden was sure, if last eve was any indication on what the future held, he would never in truth be bored with Katherine by his side. Too bad the door was in ruins, else he would have satisfied his thirst for her this morn, afore she left.

He grabbed his sword and made his way from his chamber, already looking forward to the evening when he could take Katherine back into his arms. 'Tis where she belonged, and 'twas where she would forever stay.

~

Katherine made her way down the long third story passageway until she came to Dristan's solar. From the volume of raised angry voices she heard in the hallway, even though the heavy door was completely shut, she almost hesitated in announcing her presence. Knowing she couldn't put off the inevitable, she knocked only once before she heard Dristan's call to enter.

The room was filled with people, and the tension could be cut with a knife, it was so thick. Danior appeared as if he were about to erupt and take his frustration out on Gavin, who held him back from his desire to get his hands around Tiernan's neck. Aiden stood before Tiernan, as if guarding him, but everyone could see he was doing so reluctantly and as a favor to Emily.

Dristan and Riorden were also in a heated discussion. They both turned their eyes upon her as she entered then quickly returned to their conversation. Patrick stood by, waiting silently, as if he would like to be anywhere else than his present location. Dristan's son Royce seemed to be permanently attached to his father's leg. The boy's laughter rang out now and again as Dristan lifted his leg, as if giving the boy a ride.

The women were all sitting comfortably in one of the corners of the chamber where sunlight streamed in, brightening the room. Lynet sat at a loom, working on a tapestry, and Katherine was in awe of the splendid array of colors splashed across her work. It was a lovely piece of art. She envied the young girl her vision and craftsmanship, that she could create something so beautiful out of nothing but yarn.

Juliana was in her element and played with one of the tiny fingers of Amiria's infant daughter Liliana. The baby cooed in delight, and Katherine saw a bright thatch of vivid red hair escaping the small bonnet placed on her head. Knowing her parents, she had the feeling Dristan would have his hands full one day with a strong willed maiden and a line of suitors asking for the young lady's hand.

It was the look in Juliana's face, though, that gave away her friend's true feelings of concern. They were mirrored in Emily's while she and Brianna huddled together, holding hands as if they were afraid to let go. Katherine came and sat down, looking at each of her friends.

"Is it just me, or does it seem like ages since we've really sat and talked?" she asked them. Then Brie gave a muffled laughed. "What?"

"You've been naughty, sis," Brianna replied with a smirk that said they all knew what had happened with Riorden and her. "Well...what are you waiting for? Spill the beans. I'm dying to know how he was."

"Good grief, Brie, hush up, or you'll embarrass Katie in front of Lady Amiria and Lady Lynet," Juliana cautioned.

Amiria's mirth bubbled forth. "Do not hold back on my account. I am married, after all."

Lynet turned a lovely shade of pink and silently continued on with her task.

Their heads turned as one to Katherine and she regaled them with memories of her night with Riorden. She heard a collective sigh and could only imagine the dreamy expression her face held, since she felt as though she had laid her soul bare before them.

"It was that good, huh?" Emily asked, almost in envy, as she turned toward Brianna. "Maybe staying a virgin isn't as cracked up as we'd thought it'd be."

Brianna squeezed Emily's hand. "Don't be silly, Em. We both know, neither of us would dare what Katie has done before a ring was placed on our fingers."

"Ugh...you make me sound like some horrible person with no values," Katherine muttered in embarrassment.

Juliana passed the baby off to her mother and reached for Katherine's hand. "No one thinks of you like that, Katie. We've just had time to talk while you've been...umm...occupied and have come to the awful realization you'll want to stay here with Riorden, that's all."

Katherine stared into the faces of her dearest friends in the world, who all looked as if they were about to cry their eyes out. She opened her mouth to say something, anything that could change the situation, but before she could do so, the dam burst on whatever had been holding Danior's temper in check.

The women watched in horror when he leapt over Gavin to reach Tiernan. Bodies went flying in every direction as Dristan tried to haul the men apart. Aiden pulled Royce from the fray and pushed the boy into Emily's arms before turning to aid Dristan. And Katherine suddenly found her arms filled with a crying infant before Amiria pulled a dagger from her boot.

"Enough," Amiria cried out with an abundance of ferocity. The men ceased their foolishness as she thrust her dagger in front of those who had dared to disrupt the room.

"I will say this but once, so you had best listen to my words. This is my home, and my children are in this chamber. Try something like that again, and I will see to it myself you are dispatched from Berwyck. If you are missing a few vital parts whilst you leave, so be it. 'Twill make little difference to me. Do I make myself clear?"

Dristan came to her and she shoved her dirk back into her boot with a huff of righteous indignation. He kissed her lips before she returned to her chair and began quieting her child.

Dristan chuckled at her quick transformation. "My dragoness has a bit of fire in her when it comes to protecting our children. You would be wise to heed her words. Settle your grievances with one another in the lists, where things of this nature belong."

Danior and Tiernan both mumbled their apologies, but still kept a wary eye on one another.

The men came over to where the women now sat, and Katherine watched in amusement as each knight came to either sit or stand next to his lady. Obviously, much had occurred that she was not completely aware of, when it came to the affection evident with Juliana and Brianna towards the men who clasped their hands. Love was definitely in the air, and she saw she wasn't the only one who had found it.

She felt the warmth of Riorden's hands begin to knead her neck as if he already knew she was stiff from last evening's exertion. It had a soothing effect as she began to listen to the conversation surrounding her and the dilemma that continued to trouble the group.

"We have gone round and round in our ponderings for a solution and still end up in the same place," Riorden exclaimed in frustration. "I do not see how Danior can keep his head where it belongs, if Tiernan is allowed his freedom."

"I would really like to keep my pate attached to my shoulders, thank you very much," Danior muttered, clearly annoyed.

"You won't take Tiernan to the king," Emily protested.

"Easy now, lass," Tiernan said in a calming voice. "I willna see this upset ye."

"And I won't allow Danior's head to be severed and placed on some pike outside a keep! I'm rather fond of its current location," Juliana cried out and pushed herself into Danior's arms. Her sobs became muffled as Danior tried to soothe her, to no avail.

"Again," Dristan said, "back full circle."

Brianna stood up and began stretching after sitting so long. "Why don't they just go back to Bamburgh and travel back to the future," she suggested with a yawn as she sat back down in her chair. "That solves everyone's problem, including Juliana and Emily's, who really aren't all that cut out for such primitive living conditions. No offense intended, of course."

Katherine listened to Brie's words in amazement. A look of astonishment splashed across everyone's face, showing her they all wondered why no one had thought of the idea before.

Gavin leaned over and quickly kissed Brianna's lips. "You are brilliant, my lady."

"Well, it really doesn't take a rocket scientist to figure it out, you know," she declared with a smile.

"What is this 'rocket' you speak of?" he asked puzzled.

"I'll tell you about that, and more, later," she whispered, reaching up and touching his cheek.

Everyone began speaking at once until the chamber was a mass of confusing conversations that, once again, grew in volume. Those from the twelfth century began asking those from the twenty-first how exactly they had been thrown back in time. They wanted details in order to, hopefully, ensure such a miracle could be repeated, or perhaps reversed.

"You just ran down the passageway and stairs holding hands?" Patrick asked in awe.

Katherine nodded. "Riorden had just left his chamber, and I made to follow him," she began. "He looked so real that day. I still can feel the despair of my hand going through him, since he was just a ghost to my eyes. We were so close to each other, and yet more than eight hundred years kept us apart," she whispered, with a tear in her eye.

Riorden gently wiped away the moisture from her cheek. "I had gone to the chapel to pray for her soul. God heard my prayers and answered them in a way that will forever humble us," he said, in reverence.

"Remarkable," Dristan muttered and walked over to his desk where the women's future gear was displayed for his pleasure. "You will stay with him, Katherine?"

All eyes turned and waited for her answer. "Yes, my Lord Dristan, for you see, I love him."

"You would give all these modern wonders up just for him?" Aiden questioned as he came to stand next to his brother-in-law, gazing at the marvels before him.

"They're but things, Aiden, and sometimes, something so material is nothing compared to what matters the most in your heart," Katherine proclaimed, and her lips were brushed with Riorden's warm ones. Her heart flipped while she stared into his eyes. "I will never leave you," she whispered.

Riorden reached out and caressed her cheek. "Or I you," he replied.

"And what of you, Lady Brianna," Dristan asked, already knowing the answer. "Will you also stay, and make your home here in the past?"

"In the past or the present, I suppose time is irrelevant, and it's all a matter of how we now perceive things, isn't it? Besides, we've already talked about it, Gavin and I," she answered simply as she took his hand. "I'm staying, too."

Dristan clapped his hands. "Then a double wedding it shall be."

Katherine looked at him in surprise. "Excuse me, my lord?"

Dristan strode across the floor, clapped his hand down on Riorden's shoulder, and then took her arm, ushering her over to the table. "You have my protection, but I fear you must wed, and soon, afore I do my friend there some injury he cannot recover from for taking liberties with my ward. The same holds true for Brianna."

"I see," Katherine answered quietly.

"You have objections that I rush things afore you leave so I may ensure you are settled?"

"Of course not, my lord."

"Good. Lynet has agreed to work on your gowns, since Amiria is not so nimble with needle and thread," Dristan replied with a laugh at his wife's furious expression. He held up his hands, as if holding off her anger. "Well, 'tis true is it not?"

"Where is my sword?" Amiria threatened.

"Later, my love," Dristan ordered. He went back to his desk and lifted a pen to make markings on a piece of spiral note paper. "You realize, all this must be destroyed, so no one would ever come across something so damaging."

Katherine nodded and picked up her cellphone, feeling technology slipping easily through her fingers. No more driving her car, no more Saturday white chocolate mocha coffee, no more laptop to write her latest story, no more indoor plumbing.

"Lady Katherine..." Dristan prodded with a knowing smile.

"Huh?" She looked at him in puzzlement, since she had become lost in thought.

"I asked if 'twould be worth it."

Katherine immediately sought Riorden, and the same intense look passed between them that spoke more than any answer she could have given. Riorden came and took her hand, bringing it to his lips as if he had read her mind. She returned her attention back to the group and began to explain the modern wonders of the twenty-first century to those souls from the past who gathered around her.

At one point, she felt Riorden's hand upon the small of her back, and she looked at her devilishly handsome knight again from the corner of her sparkling, love filled eyes. Smiling, she knew without any doubt in her mind that Riorden would ensure she never regretted her decision to stay with him. She would gladly make any sacrifice, so long as she could remain forever by his side.

Yes, she thought. *He is, indeed, worth it.*

CHAPTER 29

A warm breeze blew in from the ocean, leaving a salty tang on the lips of the four women who sat on the sandy beach. Each lady was lost in her own troubled thoughts while they all held hands, savoring the feel of a sisterly bond that even time could not destroy. Although the sun was relatively warm, and Patrick's laughter rang out while he romped into the waves crashing onto the shore, the women remained somber and silent. It was a testament to the overwhelming feeling of sadness they knew was inevitable with their impending parting.

"Are you sure, Katie?" Juliana said in her softest voice that squeaked with unshed tears.

"I'm sure."

"But what if you change your mind?" Emily prompted, hope ringing in her voice that Katherine would come back with them.

"I won't. My place is now here with Riorden," Katherine stated with conviction.

"How will we know that you are, or were, happy?" Juliana asked.

Katherine finally turned her gaze from the ocean and looked upon her friends as tears fell down her cheeks. "You'll know," she said with the faintest hint of an elusive smile. "Somehow, I'll find a way to let you both know that Brie and I never regretted the choice we made."

Katherine wiped her face with the back of her sleeve and sighed heavily. One would have thought she'd be ecstatic, knowing by tomorrow she'd be married to Riorden. Inside, she was of course, but the thought of losing two of her closest friends certainly put a damper on the festivities.

"Do you really think it will work again, Katie? Are you sure they'll make it back to our future?" Brianna asked hesitantly.

Katherine closed her eyes and felt a peace settle around her heart. "They'll make it."

"How can you be so confident?" Emily demanded bitterly.

Katherine shrugged her shoulders, for how could she truly explain it. "I just am."

"Damn it, Katie! You're just full of short little answers today, aren't you?" Emily snapped. "I certainly hope you're right. I'd hate to get thrown back into a worse time period than the one we're in right now. You have no idea what I wouldn't give for a hot shower."

Juliana reached over and gave Emily a hug. "Calm down, Em. Everything will be alright, and we'll have Danior and Tiernan with us. How difficult can it be to give time a little nudge?"

"You're kidding, right? Going back to Bamburgh to try to slip forward into time, taking two medieval knights with us, is like asking karma to come and kick us in our asses," Emily retorted in a shout. "It's that whole damn fabric-of-time thing I always warn us about. We're changing history, for God sake! Does no one ever listen to me?"

"You need to chillax and enjoy the day, Em," Brianna said, trying to defuse Emily's anger. "Just think about all the firsthand knowledge you'll have when you get back to pour into your latest novel."

"Ugh! Easy for you to say, Brie. You're not the one traveling through time again."

Katherine shielded her eyes from the sun and saw Tiernan and Danior hacking away at each other as they practiced their sword technique. "Tiernan," she called out loudly, watching in satisfaction when he sheathed his weapon and came to stand before them.

"Aye, Lady Katherine?" Tiernan inquired. His sleeves were rolled up, displaying the strength of his arms, and he had a grin plastered on his face, showing how much he had been enjoying his training.

"Emily is freaking out and—"

"What?" he asked with furrowed brows.

"She's nervous," Katherine clarified. "Would you do me a favor?"

"Anything, milady."

"Go take my friend down the strand a ways and kiss her senseless. If she tries to give you any more grief, then kiss her again until she forgets what had her so upset," Katherine said, trying to hide her laugh.

"With pleasure, Lady Katherine," Tiernan said. He grasped Emily firmly in hand and towed her down the beach. They couldn't hear Emily's words, but they could tell they were obviously heated when her balled fist rose up and she began shaking it towards them. True to his promise, they watched in amusement as Tiernan grabbed Emily and kissed her. It placated her only a moment before she continued her tirade. He repeated the gesture. She looked as if she may have calmed slightly, but then threw up her hands. This time, Tiernan took her completely into his arms and began kissing her once more. Apparently, the third time was the charm, for the women saw Tiernan finally had their friend speechless.

Katherine returned her attention to the sea and felt the calming effect that always came over her whenever she watched its waves crash into the shoreline. Without taking her gaze from the ocean, she at last spoke to Brianna. "So, my dear little sister, are you sure you wish to postpone your own wedding and not get married tomorrow, as well?"

Brianna smiled brightly. "Tomorrow should be your special day, Katie. If it wasn't for you and Riorden seeing each other as ghosts, then none of this would have been possible. Besides, Gavin wishes to be married in Warkworth's chapel. Since he's not Lord Dristan's vassal, the lord really has no say on where we should marry."

"That couldn't have gone over well with the Devil's Dragon," Juliana replied, with a slight shudder. "Have you seen that man fight?"

Brianna shrugged. "Gavin assured him that nothing of an...umm...intimate nature would happen between us until we were wed. He made Gavin prove his worth out in the lists." She gave a short laugh. "I think Gavin is still hurting in places he didn't even know existed, since he told me he had never trained as hard as he did that afternoon."

"I guess that's settled, then," Katherine declared and saw the eagerness on her friends' faces. She laughed for the first time that day. "Oh go on, you two. Obviously my sparkling conversation is not quite up to par today, and I can see where you'd rather be."

Juliana leaned over and kissed Katherine's cheek, and the two women practically flew in the direction of their men. They took them by the arm and headed in different directions on the beach.

Katherine had a sense of *déjà vu* as she now sat there alone on the sand with her toes peeking out between the small white and tan granules beneath her feet. The past week had been hectic with fittings for her wedding dress, but more important was the need for speed. Riorden had been summoned back to Bamburgh at the request of an angry king, demanding why he wasn't at Warkworth. Their journey may have fit in with the long range plans of getting everyone back to Bamburgh, but it would have been nice to be able to enjoy this time while at Berwyck before they wed.

She looked up from ruminating about her concerns for the future, and this time, she knew she wasn't dreaming as her own knight came to stand before her with Dristan at his side.

"May we have speech with you, Katherine, and invade your musings?" inquired Dristan politely.

"Is it okay if we walk?" she asked.

Riorden held out his arm and she gladly took it, along with Dristan's, and the three of them causally strolled for several minutes. Katherine halted her steps and suddenly turned to look back in the direction of Berwyck Castle.

To say the castle was an impressive sight would be as if saying the Grand Canyon was nothing but a large hole in the ground. It sat high above on the mountaintop with the forest just far enough away that there would never be any question of an army invading Dristan's domain unseen. The curtain wall reached down to the seashore, but only a fool would try to navigate the rocky cliff it was perched upon.

Katherine closed her eyes, and a modern day image loomed before her eyes of the devastation awaiting, not only Berwyck, but Warkworth, as well.

Tears flooded her eyes as she turned back toward the two men. "It seems as though I do a lot of crying these days."

"What has upset you so, Katherine?" Riorden asked as he took her into his arms. She pulled away and pointed to the castle grounds.

"You must protect it, Dristan, with every fiber of your being. That goes for you, too, Riorden, where Warkworth is concerned," she said in a quivering voice.

Riorden leaned down and placed a kiss on her lips. "How did you know we were going to ask about Berwyck?"

Katherine gave a short little laugh. "That's a good question. I just had this feeling that, eventually, you would want to know what happens to your land in my day."

Dristan gazed at her as though she had lost her mind, or at least a small part of it, since it seemed as if she was predicting the future. In a way she was, truth be told.

"Berwyck is strongly enforced, Katherine, and made of stone. I have ensured every precaution has been taken in re-enforcing its foundations," Dristan interjected as he crossed his arms on his chest while he tried to appear as if the conversation was an easy one for him.

"Yes, I know, but—"

Riorden interrupted her. "Warkworth is just as strong, my love, and its walls will keep you well protected. True, 'tis not as large an estate as Berwyck, but 'twill meet our needs. If you desire to live elsewhere, I have a number of other holdings in England or France you may prefer."

"Riorden, it's not that," she said, her voice shaking.

"Then what is it?" he asked.

Katherine took both of them by their hands and looked upon their handsome faces. Here were two similar men who were the embodiment of all knightly virtues and would do anything within their means to protect their families. Any woman would most likely sell her soul in order to have someone of such conviction in her life. The fact that one had fallen in love with her was still a miracle in her eyes, and she was still trying to come to grips with the whole time travel concept. But how could she tell them of the destruction to come?

She took a deep breath. "Emily would say I'm messing with history. Perhaps I am, but I don't care. You have to know Dristan that, in my point in time, there is nothing left of Berwyck but a shell of the outer curtain wall. Everything is gone, right down to the very rocks of the keep's foundation," she said with a catch in her voice. "The place was completely ransacked for its stones over the years, in order to complete other foundations in the area."

She watched all color drain from his face and turned her attention to Riorden. "The same almost holds true for Warkworth. The keep was barely habitable when I saw it, and the rest had fallen into utter disrepair. You can't even begin to imagine how many millions of dollars or coin are necessary for the upkeep of medieval castles, especially those that haven't fallen under the protection of some historical society."

"I cannot believe it," Riorden said quietly. "All of it gone?"

Katherine nodded. "When my friends and I were traveling, we stopped at both locations. I felt a sadness overcome me at Berwyck I didn't comprehend. Although now I know, it had been your home. But Warkworth was to be mine in another place in time. It all makes sense now, and I can understand why I suddenly fell to the ground, when I saw the castle ruins. I could barely manage to make it back to the car.

"Maybe in some crazy distorted way and in the bigger scheme of things, I had already lived my life there with you. I assume it's why I had such a strong reaction upon seeing a place I had thought I'd never seen before. I am sure, Riorden, we had filled the hall with our children, watched them grow, from year to year, and loved each other for all of our days. I am just as certain, Dristan, that you and your beautiful lady did the same."

"Katherine, I–" Riorden interrupted while he raked his fingers through his hair.

She held up her hand. "Please. Let me finish this while I can. Neither of you can stop the hands of time that will claim the land, nor can you halt the centuries of war that will plague and ravage England. You may fight with swords and be masterful in your technique, but there are machines and equipment that are coming in the future that are horrifyingly effective in destroying all in their path. This may not happen within our lifetime, but it will come generations from now."

"We will teach our children to fight," Dristan said with his hand on the hilt of his sword.

Katherine looked upon them both with a grim expression. "A sword in your hand, no matter how well-trained you are, will not keep you, or them, alive, when the cannons and bombs explode and annihilate our homes. We must somehow prepare, not only ourselves, but our children, so in future generations from now, our people can look back and know we did all within our power to ensure our line and family heritage continued."

"'Tis much to take in, Kat," Riorden exclaimed, once more taking her hand and placing it in the crook of his elbow as they continued their walk.

"Yes, I know. Funny how time has a way of twisting people to its whim," Katherine said, in a hushed tone, and continued when she saw Riorden's questioning look. "It seems, I've become my own ancestor."

He looked startled as this realization struck him as somehow ironic, and yet Katherine could only manage a weak smile.

"You have given me much to think on, Katherine, and for this I am most grateful," Dristan proclaimed.

"Emily could most likely provide further details, my lord. She's a history buff, and we should pick her brain—"

"What!" Riorden and Dristan bellowed. The horror on their faces reminded her of movies with people running for their lives while in the middle of a zombie invasion as the creatures foraged for food.

Katherine laughed. "Not physically, guys! It means to ask her our questions. We should talk with her before we leave for Bamburgh."

Riorden halted, planted his feet apart, and crossed his arms on his chest. "You will remain here with Dristan, so I know you are safe."

"No," she said firmly.

"Aye, you shall," he exclaimed, just as sternly.

It was now Dristan's turn to laugh out loud. "A true battle of wills. This should prove most interesting."

Katherine threw him a look that must have reminded him of one his wife had given him on numerous occasions, since he continued to bellow at her expense.

"This is no battle of wills, my Lord Dristan, for I won't be left behind," Katherine said, placing her hands on her hips. "Furthermore, there is no way in hell I'm going to stay here without ensuring my friends have returned to their own time period. I'm going, and that's it."

Dristan clapped his hand roughly on Riorden's back. "You have your hands full with your *future woman*, my friend."

Riorden gazed down into her determined face. "You shall not always get your way, Kat, just so we understand one another."

She shook her finger at him. "Just don't leave me behind, if you know what's good for you. If you do, I swear to God, I'll follow you, if I have to walk there by foot."

He threw up his hands, knowing he had lost the battle. "Well, it certainly will not come to that. But that does remind me… How the devil are we going to get Danior and Tiernan into Bamburgh without either of them being recognized and captured by the king's men?"

Katherine knew an odd expression crossed her face that must have registered as mischievous. "I have an idea, although I don't think they'll like it," she said with a giggle.

Katherine began to tell the two knights of her plan to get everyone into Bamburgh, including two men who were wanted by the king. She hadn't progressed far in the details of her scheme before Dristan and Riorden's laughter rang out. Their merriment drew the attention of the others, who joined them in the hilarity of the possible subterfuge. Everyone was in agreement the plan had merit and could work, with the exception of the two men most deeply involved.

Danior and Tiernan scowled at one another over what would be demanded of them just to ensure they could live out their lives with their ladies by their sides. They gave Katherine a look, showing their displeasure. She muffled her laughter. Like it or not, their lives would be bound together. Hopefully, they wouldn't kill each other first.

CHAPTER 30

The golden sun began to peek over the ocean horizon, splashing the morning sky with a thousand shades of pink and orange. The further it rose, the more color splattered across the cloudless sky until all traces of the earlier shades vanished. 'Twas obvious, the perfect day was a gift from the heavens and a priceless tribute to the woman Riorden would call his wife for the rest of his life.

Riorden was in no rush to head down to the Great Hall. There was no need. Katherine and her ladies had insisted 'twas bad luck to see the bride afore the wedding. He had never heard of such a custom, but who was he to tempt fate? Nay, he dare not look upon her, if such an occurrence would displease God, and in His wrath, He would wrench Katherine back from whence she had come.

Patrick brought Riorden a small repast, along with water to wash and fresh garments Lynet had lovingly sewn for his wedding. He was not surprised when he saw the tunic. Gilded fabric had been embroidered and used as trim on the deep blue cloth Katherine herself had chosen, saying the color would match his eyes. He smiled, wondering how she would look in the golden material he had chosen for her. He supposed, he would find out soon enough.

A knock roused Riorden from his musings of his lovely lady.

Opening the door, he saw Aiden standing there, also dressed in his finest.

"What...no sword?" Riorden inquired in jest. He also was to leave his sword within his chamber, although he stowed a small, serviceable blade in his belt.

Aiden appeared completely ill at ease. "Nay! Amiria refused to allow such in the chapel. God's wounds, Riorden...I feel as if I am only but half dressed."

A chuckle rumbled inside Riorden. "Do not be so troubled, my friend. The mass and ceremony should be no longer than an hour or two. Surely, your sister will allow you your blade afterwards."

"Ha! Easy for you to say. She made it clear she does not trust me."

"Let me guess," Riorden mulled over. "She hid it from you, did she?"

"My twin knows me only too well, I am afraid," Aiden muttered miserably. "Dristan has hidden hers, as well. At least he managed to get her into a dress, instead of boots and hose."

"Knowing Amiria, I am sure she will in no uncertain terms let me know of the sacrifice she has made, on the behalf of my lady, to appear in such."

Aiden at last smiled knowingly. "You can count on it."

"Why are you here? It cannot be time, as yet, is it?"

"Damn, I almost forgot my purpose," Aiden cursed. "Dristan asked that you come to his solar. He will then accompany you to the chapel at the appointed hour."

"Then let us be on our way, since I am all but done here," Riorden said, and they made their way up to the third floor.

He had just taken the last step on the tower stairs, when he halted his progress to peer down the passageway toward Lynet's chamber. Intent on listening to the bubbly laughter of his soon to be wife and her friends, he began to hear a strange haunting melody, most likely coming from the machine Kat called a cellphone. She was so close, and he found he had missed her company this past eve, more than he would have thought possible.

He took a step in the direction towards where, in his heart, he wanted to be until he felt Aiden tugging at his arm.

"Come on, Riorden. You'll see her afore you know it."

They walked the short distance to Dristan's solar, and the door opened afore Riorden could even raise his knuckles to rap upon the wood.

"What took you so long?" Dristan muttered, ushering them inside the room and offering Riorden a chalice of wine.

Riorden saw Danior and Tiernan somehow managing a pleasant conversation for a change. 'Twas just as well as he would have nothing disrupt this day. Patrick was staring out the window. It seemed his preferred placement, whenever they were inside Dristan's solar.

"Is there aught amiss?" Riorden questioned, taking a small sip from his cup.

Dristan went to the desk and handed Riorden a small box. "The blacksmith just brought this up. I wanted you to see it afore we go below, in case you felt it would not do your lady justice."

"I am sure he followed my instructions." Riorden lifted the lid to view the golden band studded with small blue and green stones. He smiled, for 'twas perfect, just like Katherine herself.

"Will it suffice?" Dristan asked.

"Aye."

The door opened, and the familiar faces of Dristan's personal guard began to fill the empty spaces of the chamber; Fletcher and Nathaniel, Ulrick and Morgan, Drake and Rolf, Cederick and Bertram. They all came and slapped Riorden on the back. Filling their cups, they raised them high in a salute to their comrade-in-arms. The only two missing from their group were brothers Taegan and Turquine, who continued to journey with Ian. Riorden knew these men toasting him better than he knew himself and was pleased to know they would be with him to celebrate his marriage.

Just when he thought the room could not contain another soul, the door opened again, admitting Geoffrey, the last of Dristan's guard, along with his wife Kenna, Berwyck's healer. Amiria and Lynet followed close behind. But afore he could make his way to Amiria to ask how his lady fared, Kenna came to him and took him aside.

Riorden watched her as she stood silently with closed eyes, and waited for the inevitable moment when she would reveal whatever vision now possessed her. He had never gotten used to the knowledge this woman could reveal with but a single touch of her hand. A smile graced her face, and she opened haunting green eyes that could search into a person's very soul.

"She has come far to find you," Kenna whispered, taking his hand and holding it within her own.

"Aye," he said simply, wondering if she, in truth, really had any concept of exactly how far Katherine had actually traveled.

"'Tis more than just miles traveled by either foot or ship, I should think."

"Aye. 'Tis beyond the imagination on just how far she has come."

Kenna laughed. "There is no need to explain such to me, Riorden."

"Will she stay, Kenna," he dared to ask. "She will not be taken from me, will she, and be returned to from whence she came?"

She only closed her eyes for a moment afore she gazed upon him with a strained expression. "Be at ease Riorden. She will stay, but 'twill not be easy for either of you. Marguerite has already set in motion trouble, awaiting you upon your arrival at Warkworth."

"What does my father's widow have to do with us," he said in irritation.

Kenna only stared at him with a strange expression. "You have to ask? You bring home a wife, and you think 'twill be easy on you with Marguerite still residing at Warkworth? You know what a grasping woman she is, and why she married your sire in the first place. Why would you not think she will try to remain Warkworth's mistress and chatelaine?"

"She will be settled at her dower house," answered Riorden slowly. The matter was settled, as far as he was concerned.

Kenna continued, as if he had not spoken. "But until she is, beware of her. She will not be kind to Katherine and will do everything in her power to tear the two of you apart."

"My thanks for the warning. I will protect Katherine to my last dying breath."

She patted his arm. "I have no doubt of that, Riorden. You are a good man...as stubborn in some ways as my own Geoffrey, but still a good man. Do not let past memories ruin your chance for a happier future and remember always what you have been given. I do not have to tell you, miracles of this nature do not happen every day."

Riorden felt at a loss for words and watched whilst the room began to clear as everyone headed to mass, leaving only Dristan and Amiria, waiting by the opened door.

"My lady is well this morn?" Riorden asked quietly as he reached their side.

"She is more than well," Amiria said, smiling, and she tugged at his sleeve until he leaned down. She placed a kiss upon his check. "Be happy Riorden, for 'tis plain for all to see that Katherine loves you dearly."

The groom's wedding party made their way down the turret stairs and through the Great Hall, which was buzzing with activity as servants rushed to prepare a feast for the returning couple. Afore he knew it, Riorden was standing in the front row of the chapel, impatient to at last catch a glimpse of his beloved Katherine. He did not have long to wait, as her lady friends quickly took their places on the benches behind him.

Taking a deep breath, Riorden at last turned. His steady gaze swept to the rear of the chapel, and any breath he thought to take immediately left him in a sudden rush. He stood, humbly stunned by the vision afore his eyes.

The sun chose that exact moment to shower color from the stained glass windows above into the room as Katherine began moving through the chapel towards him. He stood completely still and watched in fascination as she walked from dimly lit shadows and then almost glimmered through each ray of colored light falling to the stone floor beneath her feet. He almost feared she was but a ghost, again, for she appeared so ethereal. Surely, no earthly being could appear so glorious in the sight of a mere mortal man.

She had left her hair unbound, and he realized, within his heart, she had done so just for him. A wreath of tiny flowers was placed upon her head with a sheer veil, which billowed behind her as she drew closer. Was it his imagination, or did her feet barely touch the ground as she all but floated towards him in a heavenly array of golden silk?

His hands actually shook whilst her enchanting eyes held him captivated and suspended, as if on the brink of heaven itself. Riorden could not, for the life of him, look away from her countenance as she drew ever nearer to his side. For in doing so, he was terrified he would awake and learn everything surrounding her had only been but a memory of a dream.

∼

Katherine took a deep, calming breath to steady her nerves while she continued her slow pace down the length of the chapel floor. There was really only one who held her gaze this morning, and he stood tall and proud, waiting for her to reach his side. The rest of the large room could have been empty, since her only thoughts were focused on the knight who would become her husband this day.

Husband! Her footing almost faltered with the realization she was really doing this. She was actually marrying her knight in shining armor from her dreams, and she'd be forever stuck in the past with no further contact with family and friends back in her own time. Dear God…was she perhaps making a mistake? She could run from here now, and everyone would surely understand her fears, wouldn't they?

Another moment of doubt clouded her thinking, and yet any further thoughts of bolting from the crowded chapel were taken from her as Riorden reached out his hand, firmly clasping her own. The warmth of his fingers soothed her second of panic, and she sighed when his lips gently touched the inside of her wrist. Good grief…what had she been thinking?

They sat down on the bench, side by side. It was a signal for the priest to begin his sermon. His voice droned on and on in a hypnotic, deep tone as he began the morning mass in Latin. *Latin!* She didn't comprehend one word of what he was saying and began to fidget, having nothing else to occupy her mind.

She gazed down at the gown Lynet had sewn together for her, which in itself was a creation of such beauty, she had been afraid to wear it. There was no doubt in her mind the girl was indeed talented. Katherine still couldn't believe Lynet had been able to assemble such quality work in the amount of time she had been given, including the dark blue embroidery matching Riorden's garments. It was quite detailed, for Lynet had stitched the blue flowery patterns on the hem, neckline, and at her wrists. Even the belt had been fashioned to match Riorden's colors in every way. They looked quite striking as they sat there together.

"Katherine, you are shaking, my love," Riorden whispered. "Be at ease and sit still."

"I can't," she responded and glanced at him beneath lowered lashes. "It's not helping that I haven't a clue what he's saying."

"If you do not at least attempt to pay attention, 'twill only make matters worse. Dristan and Amiria's priest is known to carry on 'til he is assured all have heard his message."

As if on cue, the good father halted his sermon, looked at Katherine and Riorden from beneath his bushy eyebrows with a frown, and then continued on, as if speaking louder would help aid those needing forgiveness of their sins.

"Now look what we have done," he muttered glumly. "He is sure to spout on for at least half the morn and delay when he finally pronounces us man and wife."

"That's just it, Riorden," she said frantically. "How will I know when to respond, if I don't even know what he's sputtering?"

She heard him quietly chuckle as he patted her hand. "You shall know."

She inwardly groaned at his short response. "Now, I know how Emily felt about my vague answers," she mumbled.

The priest cleared his throat, and from the sound of it, Katherine would almost bet her life he began again from the beginning of where they interrupted him the last time. She must have been right as it was Riorden's turn, doing the groaning next to her. They wisely held their silence and let the priest continue on...and on...and on...

After more time than Katherine thought could be possible, Riorden at last stood and took her elbow as he assisted her to rise.

Dristan came to stand beside them. "Scribe," he called out, and a man came forward bearing a small table and stool, which he quickly set down. Parchment and quill miraculously appeared in the scribe's hand, and he gave a short nod to Dristan.

"Proceed, Father Donovan." Dristan encouraged the priest.

The priest's attention focused on Riorden. "An accounting, if it pleases you, Lord de Deveraux, on what you bring to the marriage."

Katherine was relieved when he began speaking in a language she could at least understand.

"Take this down," Riorden ordered.

Katherine began to again panic while Riorden commenced listing off a number of properties in England and France. The list included acres of land, herds of cattle and sheep, ships docked in various ports, and enough coin to keep her and their children's children secure for many years to come. Titles, which had been bestowed upon him by his king or inherited from his father, came easily to his lips, and she could only shudder in misery that she brought nothing to the marriage other than herself.

"And what will you provide as a dower house in the event of your death?" Father Donovan asked.

Katherine immediately clutched at Riorden's hand. "Dear God, Riorden," she whispered to him as he leaned down to hear her words, "I can't imagine being here without you."

He caressed her cheek. "Have no fear, Katherine. You will most likely tire of me as an old man afore I meet my end."

She laughed slightly and saw the twinkle in his eyes. "Not likely, my lord."

The priest cleared his throat again and gave them an impatient stare." A dower house, Lord de Deveraux?"

Riorden thought before he finally answered. "Put in the contract a suitable property will be provided in which the Lady Katherine may choose from any of my holdings. The only exception to this is the estate of Warkworth, which will be given to the first born son we may sire."

"Any holding?" the priest said in shock. "'Tis highly unusual to bequeath such an offering, my lord. Surely, you could name a property of lesser worth that will be sufficient for her needs."

"*Any* holding of her choosing," Riorden reaffirmed and nodded his approval for the scribe to continue. Silence filled the chapel, with the exception of the scribe, whose quill was scratching furiously across the paper as he took down Riorden's commands.

"And what of the Lady Katherine?" the priest continued. "Who speaks on her behalf and of the dowry she brings to add to Lord de Deveraux's coffers?"

Katherine stood there in mute agony and complete embarrassment, knowing she had nothing to offer. Riorden held up his hand, and yet before he could speak a word, Dristan came forward and tossed a leather pouch of considerable weight onto the scribe's table. It landed with a solid thunk, and the numerous coins jiggled as they settled on the wood. A tear came to her eyes at such generosity until Aiden stepped forward and made the same gesture, followed closely by Fletcher. Speechless, she turned to gaze upon these men she barely even knew and realized, once again, that chivalry was clearly not dead.

Father Donovan nodded his approval as the scribe finished writing. At the priest's direction, Riorden and Katherine came before him and knelt down as they received the blessing of their union.

Katherine held out her hand at Riorden's gentle urging and a beautiful golden band studded with blue and green gems was placed on her finger. Father Donovan then took a silken cloth, tying it around both of their joined hands, and Katherine wondered at the tradition that surely must be Scottish, knowing they were so close to its border. Riorden only smiled at her as the priest spoke of how their souls would be bound together throughout all time as surely as this cloth bound their earthly bodies.

His words brought joy to her soul, and a peacefulness settled within her heart as she stared up into the blueness of her husband's eyes. He leaned down and gently kissed her trembling lips to forever seal their fate while the priest declared them married.

A cheer rose up like none Katherine had ever heard before, at least in a church. She was quickly led to the chapel's alter where their marriage contract was laid before them. She watched Riorden quickly sign his name, and she followed his lead on the place he pointed out for her. She was just happy she hadn't ruined the document with her tears of happiness, which coursed down her cheeks.

Riorden was pulled from her side and, as if on cue, her sisters of her heart surrounded her with hugs and their own tears of congratulations.

"Well, sis, how does it feel?" Brianna asked happily.

Katherine turned to her, not sure why she asked such a silly question. She just got married for heaven's sake. She was completely thrilled at the moment. "How does what feel, Brie?" she asked with curiosity.

Brie just laughed aloud then Juliana and Emily joined her, asking in unison, "How does it feel being a Countess?"

"What?" Katherine said baffled.

Juliana took her hand and gave it a reassuring squeeze. "I told you she hadn't even considered she would acquire a title."

"He's an Earl, for goodness sake, Katie, or did you forget that little fact while the two of you were making out with each other all the time?" Emily smiled knowingly. "You'd think she'd never done any of her homework while she was writing her manuscripts about English nobility."

"I'm a Countess," Katherine whispered in awe, much to the delight of her friends.

She stood silently for a moment until a faint smile lit her face, and her gaze traveled to her husband. She had been so wrapped up in her feelings for Riorden that possessing a title never crossed her mind, not that it mattered. A Countess! She was almost afraid to imagine what would surprise her next. Given the miracles that had already surrounded them, she supposed anything was possible.

CHAPTER 31

Riorden was impatient. Sitting at the raised dais in Berwyck's Great Hall, he sipped his wine whilst his gaze traveled to the entryway of the tower stairs, watching for his bride to return to his side. *How long could it take a woman to change from her finery,* he mulled over in his head for what must have been the hundredth time.

The wedding feast continued on as the revelers lingered to make merry. Voices were raised up in laughter and camaraderie. Tankards and chalices were continuously filled to overflowing of whatever beverage suited one's fancy. The dancers swayed in tune to the minstrel's music whilst the women's dresses swirled around them, filling the hall with a stunning display of color.

Katherine finally appeared at the bottom of the stairs, comfortably dressed in hose, tunic, and boots. She made her way to her lady friends, who gathered around her. They laughed, they cried, they hugged one another until Riorden thought they would never see each other again for years to come. Mayhap, this was, at the very least, true for two of the now solemn ladies who watched Katherine as she left their group. Time was quickly running out for Juliana and Emily, for they would head to Bamburgh within two days hence.

Riorden glimpsed Katherine wipe the few remaining tears from her eyes, afore she turned a bright smile upon him. When she reached his side, he enveloped her in his embrace until she lifted her head.

"So, will you tell me where we're headed, my lord?" she asked breathlessly, with a sense of excitement of the unknown.

He chuckled at her mischievous look. "'Tis a surprise, Kat. You must wait and see."

"You're not even going to give me a hint?" she asked him with a pout.

He kissed her lips until she smiled for him again. "Nay, although I hope you shall not be disappointed," he declared. "I would have preferred several days with you alone, but one shall have to suffice."

Riorden began ushering her from the hall but was stopped several times as well-wishers came to bid them adieu. At last, arriving outside in the inner bailey, he gave a nod of approval to the four men of Dristan's guard who would accompany them.

"Why are they coming with us?" Katherine asked quietly.

Riorden looked momentarily startled at such a question of what was a normal occurrence to his everyday life. "'Tis born out of necessity, Katherine. Better to have men guarding my back than to be caught unawares."

Afore he could hear her words of concern, Rolf led his horse forward and leapt into the saddle. "Too bad we must needs wait afore we can strip them down," Rolf laughed.

"Aye! We have not been witness to a proper standing up in some time, Riorden," Bertram called out from his horse, "especially since Dristan refused to allow us the privilege when he wed."

Ulrick laughed at the look his friends received and added his own jest. "Aye, 'tis just what the night will call for to ensure Riorden does a proper job of bedding his bride."

Drake began to chuckle, although he, at least, remained respectfully quiet.

Riorden watched as Katherine whirled on the men who made such crude remarks in front of her. He could almost feel the heat of her anger sparked by the blatant impertinence of their words.

"Sir Ulrick?" Katherine purred sweetly as she came to stand before the knight who had not as yet mounted his steed.

"Aye, my lady?' he inquired, somewhat nervously, for 'twas obvious he had not meant to offend her.

"Are you married, Sir Knight?" she asked, fingering the hilt of the dagger Riorden had gifted her with.

"Nay, my lady."

"I see," she began quietly. "Engaged?"

"Nay," he answered politely.

"And if you were about to be with your one true love on your wedding night, how do you think your bride would feel to be stripped down naked and ogled while you, as her husband, had your way with her in front of a bunch of witnesses?" she said bluntly. "Do you think this might not bother her? You wouldn't mind others saw her beauty that only should be a gift for you to see?"

"My lady, I meant no disrespect. 'Twas in jest, I assure you." Ulrick muttered.

Riorden watched, amused, as Katherine took her dirk and waved it menacingly in front of Ulrick's face, and laughed inwardly, for he had promised her he would teach her the proper use of the small weapon so she might defend herself. Her stance and mannerisms almost made him believe she would not need much instruction.

"I will hear no more of stripping me. Do I make myself clear?" Katherine inquired, tight lipped.

Ulrick nodded and put his foot into the stirrup of his saddle. Katherine was apparently satisfied as she returned to Riorden's side. "Must have been a man who invented such a stupid custom," she grumbled under her breath.

Riorden's mirth erupted at her words. He held his hand down for her to take and easily lifted her up into the saddle in front of him. "Ready, Kat?" he asked, taking the reins of Beast's bridal.

"As long as this monster has a steady gait, I suppose, I am," she said warily.

"I will ensure you are kept safe and will see to teaching you to ride, once we are settled at Warkworth."

"I can hardly wait," she uttered, although her tone held no joy at the prospect.

They rode north along the strand, much to his wife's delight, if her laughter, which mingled with the sound of the wind as it rushed by, was any indication of her mood. They entered the forest and slowed their pace. Riorden wished he could more readily see Katherine's expression. She had become quiet as they took in the beauty surrounding them once they at last halted their steeds.

Riorden had been here afore, and he looked over the glade where two knights awaited them. He swung his leg over Beast and lifted Katherine from the saddle.

"All is prepared?" he asked.

"Aye, my lord," one of the men replied.

"My thanks for seeing to the arrangements," Riorden said and watched as they took their leave. He turned to those whom he had trained and fought with for more years than he could remember. "Take turns to scout the perimeter. I do not have to warn you to keep your distance from the tent so Katherine and I may have our privacy."

Riorden did not wait for their reply and took Katherine by the hand. He led her through the tall blades of grass gently swaying in the afternoon's light breeze. They did not go far, and he heard his wife's intake of breath at the sight meeting her eyes.

A waterfall cascaded down from the mountainside, falling into a large pool. Flowers of every imaginable color bloomed in vivid shades, rivaling a rainbow. A large tent had been erected off to the side for their comfort this night. Katherine skipped in happiness to the edge of the water and leaned down to put in her fingers. With a wave of her hand, she smiled when a ripple formed at the water's edge.

"It's warm," she declared the obvious and ran back to his side, throwing her arms around his neck, "and it's perfect, Riorden. I love it!"

"Do you now?" Riorden said with a deep chuckle rumbling in his chest. "Perchance there is something else you love besides the scenery?"

"Hmm. I'll have to think about that before giving you an answer, I think," she laughed.

Riorden leaned forward and kissed her deeply. His tongue swirled with hers and he brought her close against his body. He broke off their kiss abruptly and gazed into her heavily lidded eyes.

"Do you suppose 'twill be long afore I have your reply?" he asked, and began nibbling at her lower lip.

She gave a breathless sigh. "I love you, Riorden, and will do so with all of my heart, forever and always."

He kissed her lips again. "Then, I am indeed most blessed to have such a devoted wife. I love you as well, my dearest Katherine."

Riorden noticed how her eyes began to twinkle as she backed away from him.

"Will they keep their word and stay away?" she inquired as she took off one boot, followed quickly by the other.

"Aye, if they wish to live to see yet another day, they shall," he said firmly. She gave him a beguiling smile and began removing her clothing, piece by piece, and letting them float to the grassy ground beneath her now bare feet. His mouth began to water in anticipation whilst his gaze devoured her perfect, naked body. She came back to him, as if stalking him like a lioness.

Katherine merely stood before him, not touching him, until Riorden thought he could bear it no longer. He watched as she bit her lip, and her stare went lower as a mischievous grin spread across her face. He stiffened and grew in size just from her heated gaze. She laughed, as if she came to the realization of the true power she had over him. Afore he knew her intent, she reached out her hand and caressed his manhood through his hose, causing a groan to escape his lips.

"I can feel you're ready for me, my lord, and yet you are sorely lagging behind, since, you can plainly see, I am already naked," she teased, her comment tossed over her shoulder. "Don't you want to go skinny dipping with me, Riorden?"

She ran to the edge of the pool and dove into its warm waters. Riorden watched her pert, little bottom disappear below the surface then tore at his own garments with an urgency and need to be inside his wife. She broke through the surface with a come hither look. Her heavy breasts glistened wet whilst she bobbed up and down in the water. He could not wait to take those taunt little buds into his mouth and suckle them to his heart's content.

Riorden never took his eyes from his lady and she opened her arms to him once he reached her side. Holding her naked, wet body next to his own, he walked with her towards the waterfall. Cooler water splashed down upon their heads as they neared the falls. He laughed when she began to sputter, for 'twas apparent she did not care for the spray in her face.

"You truly are a cat," he teased.

"Yes, I am," she spluttered, wiping the wetness from her eyes. "Please move, Riorden. I feel as if I'm going to drown."

His laughter rumbled in his chest as he slowly moved them behind the waterfall where a blanket on the small sandy beach awaited them. He did not even think she noticed it, since she was busily driving him crazy with those small, scintillating kisses she was trailing down his neck.

Once she had her feet beneath her on the sand, despite the fact she was still knee deep in water, she did not stop with the further torture she apparently had in store for him. Lower and lower, her tantalizing mouth and tongue went, making its way across his naked flesh. Shivers of desire coursed through his body. He had no idea of her intent until she took him in her mouth. He groaned, trembling in disbelief that she would dare to perform such a service. He leaned his head back in pure pleasure until he could stand no more.

Quickly, he lifted her until their bodies melded as one. She wasted no time in telling him of her aching need.

"Love me, Riorden," Katherine murmured softly, with eyes glazed over in passion.

"I do, Katherine," he replied with a sly grin.

"Now husband," she demanded.

"You mean, like this?" he asked and lifted her until he slowly entered the very essence of her womanhood. He heard her gasp at their contact whilst she wrapped her legs securely around his waist.

"Oh God...yes...just like that," she cried out hoarsely. "Make love to me, Riorden."

"I am yours to command."

"Then please don't make me wait any longer. I can hardly stand it. I'm dying, waiting for you to move deeply inside me."

"As you wish, my beautiful wife." He held her tightly to him and easily carried her to the blanket where he gently lowered her to the ground.

She may have been in a rush, yet Riorden took his time pleasuring his woman, ensuring she was fully satisfied to the best of his ability. They enjoyed the afternoon getting to know one another more intimately and were content with the knowledge they were now husband and wife. They had a lifetime of afternoons such as this ahead of them, and 'twould be a magnificent lifetime to look forward to. If today was any indication of what their marriage and future would be like, Riorden had no doubt in his mind that life with Katherine would, indeed, be grand.

CHAPTER 32

Soft laughter erupted from the couple, who sat on a bed of fur pelts facing one another. Flickering candles lit the interior of the tent, casting romantic shadows onto the canvas walls. Katherine leaned forward with a piece of fruit between her lips and watched her husband's roughish grin in anticipation. He came closer and kissed her lips, stealing the juicy tidbit from her mouth. He slowly munched on his prize then offered her a drink of wine. She declined with an elegant shake of her head. She was already feeling dizzy from the heady brew she'd been consuming all night.

"This is camping at its finest, you know," she declared, reaching for a piece of cheese and bread. She took a bite, hoping the bread would absorb the alcohol already in her stomach. Small wonder they generally watered down their wine in the twelfth century, or everyone would be walking around three sheets to the wind. "Do you always travel so lavishly?"

Riorden merely shrugged. "It depends. I only wished to see to your comfort this night, Kat. When 'tis for my personal enjoyment, I tend to partake in the finer accouterments available to me."

"So, you don't always journey with a tent and all these luxuries?"

He reached out and tucked a lock of her hair behind her ear. "Nay, my love, I do not. When in service to the king, one tends to grab what little gear one has, along with one's sword, in order to answer his summons. I have spent many a night with nothing but my cloak to cover me and the cold ground beneath my tired backside."

Katherine thought on his words with worry until she finally raised her troubled eyes to gaze upon his handsome face. "Must you travel often...in service of the king, Riorden?"

"'Tis a hard question to answer, Kat. Afore taking over ownership of Warkworth, I have been a vassal to Dristan and made my home at Berwyck, answering to Dristan as captain of his guard," he responded honestly, setting down his chalice and gathering his wife in his arms. "I have now inherited the responsibility of Warkworth, along with its people, and will answer directly to King Henry. 'Tis my duty as his knight, along with my oath of fealty, that I must answer his call when he should have need of me. You, too, shall have your place and duties, as Warkworth's chatelaine."

"But, I haven't a clue how to run a castle, Riorden. I had a hard enough time keeping my tiny apartment tidy, with all my research scattered everywhere." She observed his confused expression at her words before she continued. "My home was no more than four rooms, including the kitchen and bathroom...err...garderobe."

"So small? Warkworth's keep is much larger. But 'tis of no matter, Katherine, for I shall teach you what you must needs know."

"What happens if you must leave me for weeks at a time unless I go with you? I don't think I'd like court life very much with all its intrigues that I've read about in history books."

"We shall figure out a solution when the matter arises. 'Tis my hope, since I am commanded to return home and manage the estate, that I shall be allowed to remain there and only travel occasionally in order to appease King Henry. That should suffice to ensure my loyalty to him and the crown."

"Then I pray he'll allow us to live out our lives in peace," Katherine declared.

He leaned down and kissed her parted lips. It was almost as if he was trying to breathe new hope into her soul. "I have not even as yet ventured to my birthplace in many a year, my lady. There will be matters that must needs be resolved once we arrive," he said glumly.

"You mean with Marguerite," she whispered.

"Aye. She will not be pleasant. I wish there was some way to dispatch her without you ever having to lay eyes on her, but 'tis inevitable you shall meet."

Katherine rose up on her knees and slowly caressed the planes of Riorden's face. "Let's worry about her another day, Riorden. Tonight is just for us."

"Aye, you have that aright, my lovely wife," he said, kissing her fully again. She sighed and was about to pull his robe from his shoulders when he broke off their kiss abruptly. "*Merde!* You have me so distracted, I almost forgot the gift I brought for you."

She twirled her wedding band around her finger. "Surely, this is more than enough, Riorden. Truly, I love my ring and wouldn't ask for anything more."

"You will have to indulge me, my sweet," he said, reaching behind him and bringing forward a square velvet jewelry case. "Since I intend to spoil you for the rest of your life, I might as well begin today."

A giggle escaped her and she went to retrieve a fairly large sized box she had asked Amiria to have available here. "Then, I have something for you, as well. It's not much, but was the only thing I could think of to give you that you might treasure. I wanted it to be specifically from me and not purchased with coin belonging to another, since I didn't have any money of my own to spend."

"We shall remedy that when we get ourselves home. May I?" he inquired, holding out the box to her.

At her nod, he opened the lid, and Katherine was afraid to even reach out and touch the necklace resting on a bed of dark blue silk. Diamonds sparkled in the candlelight, along with a green square cut emerald of considerable worth. She attempted to form some kind of response to express the loveliness of his gift, but found herself unable to utter anything more than a startled gasp.

Riorden laughed at her expression. "I see I have made my wife speechless, so I assume it meets with your approval?"

"It's the most beautiful piece of jewelry I've ever seen, Riorden. It had to have cost a fortune."

"Let me worry about its cost. I assure you, I can afford it, and more, as you shall learn. Come now, turn for me so I may clasp it about your neck."

Katherine held up her hair and felt the warmth of his hands on her shoulders until the coolness of the gems came to rest on her chest. His lips caressed the back of her neck, causing her breath to catch and tingling goose bumps to race across her skin.

"You're distracting me, my lord."

"Aye."

She leaned back into him and he reached forward, cupping her breasts in his hands. Her back arched, giving him further access, while a moan escaped her parted lips. She turned her head. It seemed an invitation as his mouth took possession of hers, leaving her gasping for air.

Opening her eyes, she stared into his own and marveled again at the richness of their color. He gave her a devilish grin that conveyed his desires until she came to her senses and remembered her present for him.

Gazing down, she saw how the emerald pendant was poised just above her cleavage, as if drawing attention to the creamy orbs beneath her robe. She turned forward to him with a smile and noticed how his disappeared. "Well? How does it look?"

"Beautiful," he said huskily, "and the gems, as well." He reached out and slid his fingers across the tops of her breasts. "You may end up only wearing this for me, I am afraid. Otherwise, I will not let you out of my sight, my dear."

Katherine gave him a seductive look. "And should I wear anything else besides this necklace while I'm in your sight, by chance?"

"If I could, I would keep you in our bed and never let you leave."

"What a horrible thought!"

"You would have nothing to complain about whilst you were there, Katherine, I assure you."

Her laughter bubbled forth with a smile. "I have no doubt you'll have me pregnant in no time, my lord, if we continue as we have tonight."

He turned serious and placed his hand on her abdomen. "I look forward to having you carry my child within you."

"You'll make a wonderful father."

"As you will a mother. Mayhap, we should practice making love to ensure we are doing it right."

"Believe me, my lord, you are doing everything exactly right."

"Are you sure? Nothing you would wish for me to change?" he teased.

"Not a thing."

"We should still practice," he said, reaching for her hand and bringing it to his lips.

She leaned forward and kissed him. "Thank you, Riorden, for the gift."

"'Twas my pleasure."

"Okay, you're turn," Katherine said excitedly, remembering her purpose, and waited to see his reaction to his present.

He weighed the box in his hands. "'Tis heavy."

"Just open it, Riorden."

He did, and she watched his face. Was it her imagination, or did his eyes mist up as he lifted the frame out of the box and saw what she had given him?

"You wrote this?" he asked in awe.

"Yes," she whispered. "It's from my heart to yours."

He looked at her with eyes full of emotion. "I barely know what to say, my love. Will you read it to me, for I barely can see the words, I am so overcome by such a gift."

"If you insist," Katherine said softly and, at his nod, she began.

Eternal Promise of Love

When the sun slowly rises in the distant horizon
we shall join our hands on this, our wedding day,
beginning our new life together
that binds our love for all eternity.

For we have been given a rare gift, you and I, lovingly sent from the heavens above. We have discovered a love so deep and true, it fills our souls in a heartfelt song that lifts us high above the tallest mountain and unites us forever with unbreakable ties, which cannot be seen.

Having been brought together by an unbelievable miracle of fate, we have known, from our very first touch, we were destined for each other, for we have found the part of ourselves, which had been missing, and finally, heard the voice inside us saying, "This is the One."

*My vow to you this day is a solemn one,
coming from deep within my soul.
It is filled with all the love my heart can hold in a promise that shall belong to you alone, throughout all time.*

Into your keeping, I give you my heart, my soul, and my love. Cherish and treasure them always, keep them safe and protected well within you. Never forget that we are as one, and always a part of the other, especially when the seemingly endless miles may keep us at a distance.

I promise this day to love you in the only way I know, completely, honestly, and endlessly. To give you all that I am, or could ever hope to be, while at your side, placing my trust and respect for you, confidently, in your tender care, knowing you will never forsake the love between us, or ever let me down.

Our faith in each other shall also be placed within the other's care, to love, honor, and cherish until our last dying breaths. And when we are no longer tied to our earthly bonds, our souls shall continue their search until we are united again.

For, only when we once more meet in some other place in time, will we know for certain, what we have known from the start. That the deep and abiding love we constantly saw reflected in each other's eyes, was able to last beyond one lifetime and always endured, remaining, forever timeless, in an Eternal Promise of Love.

Silence filled the tent as Katherine finished and she raised her eyes to her husband. He only stared at her, as if he were searching deep inside her soul. Surely, he could see it was laid completely bare before him after such a reading, for she had poured out every emotion imaginable into her poem. It was the only gift she could give him, and she had wanted it to be perfect.

"I'm afraid it doesn't rhyme. I was never good at that kind of poetry," she said, slightly embarrassed when he remained silent. She continued on in a rush. "I wish I could have written the document myself, but I was making such a terrible mess of the parchment and had to ask Amiria to help me. It was the quill that was my downfall, you see, and somehow, I didn't think it would be right to write with a modern day pen."

Riorden at last shook his head and took the frame, resting it on the small table next to their bedding. He pulled her into his lap and began caressing her hair away from her face while she looked up at him.

"*Ma cher*, you have made me a most humble and thankful man this day. Forever will I cherish this rare gift you have given me," Riorden said, kissing her parted lips. "'Tis an offering of such value, I am unsure I am worthy. I speak not only of the beautiful words you have written, but of your proclamation of such undying love you have pledged this day."

She placed her hand over his heart, and he covered her hand with his own. "I know you have promised the same to me, Riorden. No matter how long I must search, my soul shall always find yours until we meet again in the heavens above."

"This is my vow to you, as well, my sweet Katherine. Forever and always will we be as one."

Riorden began to kiss her again, as if to seal their fate, and Katherine gave in to the passionate spell he wove around them. No further words were necessary this night, or even into the early morning hours. *Time* had brought them together. Forever would they so remain.

CHAPTER 33

The occupants of the elegantly appointed carriage could have cared less that every imaginable luxury had been prearranged to ensure they were comfortably settled. Nerves were stretched taut as the miles continued to roll by, bringing them closer to a destination they were not particularly looking forward to. Uncertainty loomed in the air, along with the unknown, making the silence between them almost unbearable.

The clip clopping of the horses' hooves continued onward and kept a steady pace, much like the counting-off of ticks from the second hand of a clock. It wouldn't be much longer before Bamburgh was in sight.

There hadn't been enough room in the conveyance for all eight of their original party, and Riorden had no issue when Katherine stated she would ride inside with her friends. Juliana and Danior shared the seat with her, leaving Tiernan, Emily, and Brianna riding backwards.

Riorden had his own group riding with him, for Dristan had been reluctant to let them travel without a proper guard. Gavin naturally rode next to his brother and they happily conversed, catching up on the years since they last met. Aiden had volunteered to accompany them, as well, most likely to ensure Emily arrived safely or had not changed her mind about staying. Nathaniel, Drake, and Ulrick had also joined their group. Although Ulrick seemed almost hesitant to do so, given his last conversation with Riorden's wife.

Danior and Tiernan remained aloof and ill at ease with good cause, considering they were hopefully traveling to the future, if all went according to plan. They'd made it perfectly clear they were uncomfortable with Katherine's idea of how to gain access to the interior of Bamburgh. They'd ended up taking out their frustration on one another in the lists the day before. At least, that had been the story Katherine had been told upon their return to Berwyck. From the look of things, Danior, in particular, appeared as if he were ready to voice his displeasure...again. It was only Juliana's hand, reaching out for his, that seemed to calm him.

The women could only stare at one another, as if impending doom was about to fall on top of their heads. In a way, this was true, so they took what time they had left to memorize each other's features, knowing their paths may never cross again. Their eyes were bloodshot from the amount of tears they had shed. There was no amount of comfort they could receive or give to one another that would make the moment of their separation any more bearable. It was inevitable their friendship would be torn apart.

Katherine took her gaze from the scenery that couldn't hold her interest and looked over to Juliana with a gloomy expression. "You have my phone to give to my mother?" Katherine asked, in a barely audible voice.

"Yes," Juliana replied, her voice cracked with emotion. "It's safely tucked away in my purse."

"I don't know why you don't keep it with you, Katie," Brianna stated solemnly. "I for one just wanted to hold on to something from the future."

Emily nodded her head. "We could always record something for your mother on one of our phones to give her."

Katherine only gave them a timid smile. "There's no point in me keeping it. I made the video while with Riorden and at our leisure. I can only pray it will give my mother and brother some comfort, knowing I am happy with my decision to remain here in the past. Besides, Riorden wanted to listen to music on our night together, so

I'm afraid I ran the battery down until it died. It's only a useless piece of electronics until it can be recharged."

"But you're so close to your mother, Katie," Juliana whispered. "She'll be devastated."

"She'll understand...in time," Katherine said tearfully. "You'll watch over her, won't you Jewels?"

Juliana reached over and took her hands. Her voice cracked with emotion. "You know I will."

"Then that's all I can ask of you."

"You know we'd do anything for you, Katie," Emily sniffled, trying her best not to cry.

Katherine looked around at these women who were most dear to her. "Just be happy, my friends and always keep in mind you, too, have been given a rare and special gift. Forever remember...love transcends time itself. Somehow, I have the feeling our paths may just cross again."

"At least Katie and I will have each other, just as you and Juliana will," Brianna added brightly, giving them hope.

Tiernan leaned over and gave Emily a kiss on the cheek. "I am most grateful to have found my Emily, but am still concerned on how I shall provide for ye in this future of yers."

Emily laughed and reached down beneath her feet for her purse. Digging around in the bottom, her face lit up when she finally showed him the handful of coins he had given her in the forest. "We'll live on these," she declared triumphantly.

Tiernan laughed. "Em...have ye lost yer senses, lass? Those willna last us but a se'nnight, if that."

The women laughed.

"What is so amusing, Juliana? I am just as mystified for my predicament, since I am no better off than he is," Danior asked with a frown, "and I will not have my wife become some washerwoman to support her husband."

Katherine squeezed Danior's arm. "Have no fear, gentlemen. The coins you possess may not seem like much here, but they're worth a small fortune where you're going. They are in mint condition, and, trust me when I tell you, the right buyer will pay a great deal for even one of those pieces."

"Yer future must be wealthy then to pay so much for a bit o' coin," Tiernan said and watched as Emily put away their future.

Danior nodded, but still seemed puzzled. "Coin shall only go so far. I will need to do something to bring in more wealth. I am not one to just sit idly by, doing nothing day after day."

"Aye! I will also go mad without something to occupy me," Tiernan joined in and, for once, the two men seemed to have a common bond.

"Well, you're both fantastic with a sword, you could teach the techniques of that," Brianna suggested. "Or, you might try lecturing on medieval studies. You do have firsthand knowledge of the time period, not that anyone would know such information, other than us."

Danior laughed aloud. "Someone will pay us to speak of such things? They must be daft."

Katherine smiled, thinking of how these men would see their time period. "Get a hold of Simon when you return to present day Bamburgh, ladies. I have the feeling he'll know exactly how he can help you."

"You think so, Katie?" Emily asked, somewhat hesitantly.

"I have the feeling he's looking for us even as we speak and will most likely be able to solve the issues of passports, identification, and even a buyer for some of those coins, if he's not interested himself. I wouldn't be surprised if he bought the whole lot."

"We'll find him," Juliana promised.

The carriage began to slow, and Katherine saw the walls of Bamburgh rising up in the distance. "We're almost there," she whispered softly, and took her two friends by their hands.

"Oh God, I can barely stand it, knowing Em and I will never see you both again," Juliana cried out.

"Never? I think fate will be in our favor, someday," Brianna answered as she waved out the window to Gavin when he passed by.

Emily squeezed her friend's hand. "Of course it will. I can't go through the rest of my life not calling Katie a pansy now and then, can I? How could I do that, if we never see each other again?"

"By the way," Katherine said with a smirk towards Brianna, who winked at her, knowing her thoughts. "Brie and I, or maybe I should say our significant others, have added to your wealth. I'm sure you'll find it enough to ensure you live comfortably for the rest of your lives."

"That was very generous of them," Juliana answered breathlessly.

"Purely selfish reasons on our part, I assure you. Who knows...maybe someday you'll both decide to buy a castle somewhere here in England, knowing that, perhaps, Brie and I rode over the same land as you now own."

"I like that idea," Emily ventured to say.

"Sounds like you thought of everything, Katie," Juliana said, managing a meager smile.

Katherine leaned forward and placed a kiss on both Juliana and Emily's cheeks. "Anything for the cause, my dearest sisters...anything for the cause."

~

Riorden swept the inner bailey with a practiced eye as the carriage carrying his wife rolled in behind his small procession. The king's guards took notice of his entourage, but since he wore the colors of Warkworth and carried its standard, he was not questioned as to his business with the king. He was an Earl, after all. He might as well take advantage of the privilege the title afforded him.

Dismounting Beast, he motioned with his hand, and lads from the stables quickly came to lead the horses towards shelter. He waved away another, who made his way in the direction of the carriage to open its door.

"No need. I shall see to my wife and her ladies myself," Riorden commanded as he let down the stair. "See you to a second chamber for my wife's attendants. She will want them close at hand, if she has need of them during the night."

"As you wish, my lord," the young squire answered respectfully then scurried off to see to the rooms.

Riorden's men surrounded the carriage, waiting for the women to alight. He opened the door, and the delicate hand of his wife was held forth. He took it gently into his own as he helped her down from the step, and she carefully held her dress so she did not trip.

She dipped down into a deep curtsey afore him, once she was on solid ground. "My lord," she said meekly. When she stood again, she looked at him through lowered lashes.

"Wife," he said loud enough for those nearby to hear. "I hope you have managed well enough during our journey."

"Aye, husband, but I am most weary. Perchance, my ladies and I may rest afore we sup this eve?"

Riorden tucked her hand in the crook of his arm. "Arrangements are already being secured, my dear. Shall we?" he asked, pointing towards the main entrance of the keep.

"Of course," she answered and looked over her shoulder. "Come, ladies."

Riorden suppressed a grin as five cloaked women exited the carriage. None seemingly noticed two were more heavily built than the other three who were delicately framed. To the casual observer, the women were just taller than the others and none could see their features. Their hoods over their heads concealed all, and their cloaks hid their garb, with the exception of the hem of their gowns peeking through their capes as they walked. For all intended purposes, there was nothing out of the ordinary about the women, who were elegantly dressed, following their lady.

"'Tis most embarrassing," Danior quietly complained.

"Shh!" Juliana whispered, with a quick glance around them. "Do you want to be heard?"

The door to the keep was opened for them by a richly appointed servant wearing the king's colors. As Riorden's eyes adjusted to the darker interior, he saw the Great Hall was filled to capacity with elegantly dressed courtiers. Noblemen and women quickly cast their gaze at those who entered, and Riorden had to firmly take Katherine's elbow to steady her step when she faltered, ever so slightly.

"Easy now, my love," Riorden whispered softly.

"There's so many of them, Riorden," she said frantically in a hushed tone, "and they're all staring at us."

"'Tis not every day I bring a wife to court, Kat. Besides, we need not have speech with any of them, my sweet. Just remember, we but have to make it to the other side of the room without our ruse being discovered."

"That's what I'm afraid of," she muttered.

He watched her gaze take in the women who began to step forward and noticed one, in particular, who cast a menacing glare at Katherine, as if she wished she could take his wife's place at his side. It did not go unnoticed by Katherine, who appeared to make a point of glaring directly at the woman as they passed her. If anything, the woman's look only seemed to deepen in its intensity.

"Are they all so grasping and eager to stab one another in the back in order to gain a title or more wealth?" Katherine asked under her breath.

Riorden brought her hand up to his lips and kissed its back. There was a collective sigh from some of the women who had witnessed such openly displayed affection. They continued forward afore he spoke quietly for her hearing alone. "What? People do not wish for the same in your time, my love?"

She gave him an annoyed sideways look and then rolled her eyes, causing laughter to rumble in his chest. "It seems different here, somehow, if that makes sense," she said softly as she remained cautious of those who continued to gawk at them.

He shrugged his shoulders. "People are people no matter the time, Kat. There shall always be those who will do all in their power to take what is not rightfully theirs. Sometimes, the cost is more than most can bear."

Katherine did not reply and perhaps no further words were needed. Riorden felt her nervousness radiate from the forced smile she plastered on her lovely face. Her friends were in no better shape and clearly were not used to playing their part in the intrigue they must resort to in order to save the lives of two men.

Several acquaintances hailed Riorden from across the crowded room, and yet he only gave the briefest of nods and continued his way through the hall. He was thankful His Majesty was not sitting in the chair placed on a raised dais. He was not sure if he was as yet ready to have his ears scorched from the wrath of an angry king. He would think about his part in the deception to King Henry another day and beg forgiveness from God above. If the king found out of his role in Danior and Tiernan's escape, that is, if Katherine's plan actually were to work, he knew his head would be hacked off and rotting in the hot sun come the morn. 'Twas not a pleasant thought he cared to consider today or any other day in his near future.

CHAPTER 34

The ground shook violently beneath her feet while dancing, iridescent lights flashed brilliantly before her eyes. The fear of falling through time consumed her while a heavy mist began to surround her entire being. Desperately, she reached out her hands in a hopeless attempt at grabbing the comforting strength always surrounding Riorden. She encountered nothing but air. Closing her eyes, she could still see the stunned expression on his face as he lost his grip on her hand. He had been her life line, her reason for existing. Her breath left her. Her heart actually felt as if it had stopped its beating. Panic set in until she lost all hope.

"Riorden!" she screamed, and then listened as her voice echoed all around her until even the sound of her own words faded into nothingness.

Only the stillness of silence met her ears. All was quiet now and, as she opened her eyes, she found herself alone, casually sitting on the heavily worn steps of a circular turret in one of Bamburgh's towers. She raised her eyes to the walls, and she looked forever upward at the spiraling structure above her. Smoke no longer emitted from the torches set in the sconces, hanging on the stones above her head. Such devices were now long since gone. They had been replaced ages ago by the modern marvels of electricity and light bulbs.

"Oh God," she cried out, "how could you take him from me so completely!"

Sobs of agony wracked her body and consumed her until she could barely breathe. Her heart was actually hammering inside her chest. She wrapped her arms around herself, rocking back and forth, trying to keep what little sanity she had left. Completely bereft, she continued to sit on the cold stone stair, wondering how she would ever possibly manage, even one day, without Riorden in her life. He had come to mean everything to her, and she had lost him.

She felt it then...that tingling sensation, knowing he was somewhere near. Raising her tear streaked face in a last ditch effort of hope, she wiped the moisture from her eyes while she looked around, trying to locate the source of where she would espy her knight. And then, she knew with every fiber of her being just where she would find him.

She practically flew up the stairs until she fell scraping her knees. But she didn't care if they pained her. Getting back up in a frantic need to see the only man who would ever possess her heart, she dashed down the passageway until she reached his chamber door. It hung open like a welcoming invitation for her to enter. It was as if he had been waiting for her. He stood there, watching her step into his chamber with the sun glistening on his body, as if he, in truth, stood before her. And yet, this was not to be, nor would it ever be so again. Clearly, they were merely vague shadows of ghosts to each other, once more.

"Oh, Riorden," *she whispered miserably,* "I'm so very sorry."

He gave her a sad sort of smile and held out his hand for her. He had done this once before...this man, who she had come to love with all her heart. She slowly made her way to stand next to him until she too held her numb and lifeless limb but inches from his own. It was still there...that rare and special connection between them that Time *could not separate. She felt the sensation of electric currents racing up her arm that she could only feel with his nearness. He made her senses come alive.*

"Live your life to its fullest, my dearest love, and know, I shall always be a part of you," *Riorden whispered to her soul.*

"How can I possibly hope to accomplish this, when I've lost you?" *she said as tears of regret escaped her eyes.*

He gave her a radiant smile. "Lost me? Nay you have not lost me, **ma cherie**. I shall live inside your heart for always," *he said, pointing to her chest.*

"Yes," *she said softly,* "forever will you remain in my heart, Riorden."

"Besides...I have given you the best part of me, Katherine. You, even now, carry it tenderly and protected well within you," he exclaimed, with his own sense of loss shining in the depths of his vivid blue eyes. "See you to my son, my sweet, and raise him well."

She placed her hand on her stomach. "A child?"

He chuckled. "Aye. He will be a strong healthy lad and of much comfort to you."

"How can you know I'm pregnant?"

"You must needs ask, wife?" he queried with a raised brow, knowing she doubted his words. "Suffice to say, you, too, shall know soon enough."

"I'll never see you again," she whispered quietly, and watched his image begin to fade.

"Aye, my dearest Katherine, you will. When you gaze into the eyes of our son, you shall see me for all of your days until we meet again."

"It's a long time to wait, Riorden."

His roguish grin about dropped her to her knees. "'Twill be worth it Kat, I promise."

"I'll hold you to your vow, Riorden," she said, trying to memorize every inch of his beloved face.

"My soul will find yours, Katherine. If it takes until the end of time itself, I will find you once more," he swore.

She reached out her hand as if to touch him, but stopped inches from his cheek. He gave her that smile she so adored and sadly watched him disappear, knowing he was now only but a memory in her mind.

Slowly, she walked to the window to stare with sightless eyes at the view he had been gazing upon but moments before. She quickly realized she had awoken to her worst nightmare and, in her utter sorrow, could only now wonder if she had, perhaps, dreamed and imagined the whole damn thing...

~

The earth began moving forcefully beneath her as she cried out in terror with her fear of falling through space.

"Katherine, awake my love. You are but dreaming."

She heard his voice, as if from afar, and almost refused to answer his calling. If she could stay in her dream, knowing he was still with her just a few minutes longer, she would have done so. But it wasn't to be, if the insistent shaking of her shoulders was any indication. Someone was, annoyingly, demanding her attention.

Her eyes flickered open to the darkness of their chamber, and her immediate recognition of who was gently attempting to wake her caused a gasp of delight to rush from her lips. She quickly flung her arms around Riorden's neck and held on, as if her survival depended on him to save her. She was sure she heard him groan from the force of her embrace as he wrapped her in the comfort of his arms. She was safe.

"What is this you do, Kat?" he asked with concern. "You act as if you have not seen me in some time."

"It's not that, Riorden," she said still trembling from the nightmare that had plagued her dreams.

"Then tell me you enjoyed our lovemaking afore you decided to sleep the eve away. Did I bore you so much, *ma cher*, that sleep was the better alternative than my clever conversation?" he teased.

She took his face between her palms and tenderly caressed the planes of his cheeks with her thumbs, as if this might be the last time she saw him. Trying to find the words to express what she was feeling seemed an improbability at the moment, so she merely continued to look intently into his eyes. She gently stroked the lids of his eyes, ran her fingers through his hair, touched the stubble on his chin, and felt the silkiness of his lips.

Nothing in her life had ever prepared her for the deep and abiding love coursing through her veins for this man she had taken as her husband. To call it only love was almost a sin. Surely, what she felt for Riorden was more than just some small, four-letter-word term of affection.

"Why so serious, my lovely Katherine?" he pondered aloud and kissed her lips.

"I thought, I had lost you," she answered in a simple declaration of the sorrow consuming her.

"Never," he vowed.

"Tell that to what's going on inside my head, Riorden. Look..." She held out her hands to him. Her fingers shook until he took them in his hand and brought them to his lips. "I can't make them stop. I had a dream I went back, or forward, to the future and—"

"Hush now. *Time* would not be so cruel as to tear us apart now that we have found one another," he said with a stern voice of disapproval. "Do not even think I would allow you to be taken from me in such a manner."

"You'll keep me safe then? You won't let me fall through the time gate when the others are leaving us?" she said frantically.

He laughed at her foolishness. "Stay here in our chamber if I cannot convince you I will keep you safe. We shall then have no worries about such a happening."

"I have to see them leave with my own eyes. I have to know—" she quickly halted midsentence and sat there waiting. One look at Riorden's face and Katherine knew he had felt the same sense of urgency. "Riorden! They have to go and now!"

"We must make haste." He leapt toward the door with her following closely in his footsteps.

They made their way to the chamber next to their own and rapped on the wooden door. It opened slowly, and once Gavin saw who stood there, he opened the door wider to admit them.

Gazing around the room, Katherine confirmed that Juliana and Emily were already impatiently waiting. It was when her eyes fell upon Danior and Tiernan that she became angered.

"Are you two out of your minds?" she admonished, noticing the two men had donned their normal everyday garments. "Where are the dresses we had made for you?"

Danior went to Juliana and tucked her hand within the crook of his arm while Tiernan did the same with Emily. They stood together in a united front of determination, and perhaps this was a good sign the men would become friends someday.

"I shall not be going to the future, or anywhere else, for that matter, dressed as a woman," Danior exclaimed.

"Damn your pride to hell, Danior! Do you want to get yourself killed?" Katherine exclaimed.

"Aye!" Tiernan chimed in. "'Twas unmanly enough the first time to have to use such a ruse to gain entrance to the castle. I willna be making a fool o' myself again, showing up in Emily's future world dressed as a lass."

Riorden laughed, although from Katherine's perspective it wasn't anything to laugh over.

"Leave it be, Katie," Emily urged.

"We've already tried a million times, and they won't budge," Juliana exclaimed, rolling her eyes.

Riorden came forward, breaking off any further conversation. "We must away, and now. Katherine and I know the time is right for your traveling this eve. You must go, and you must make haste, afore the portal closes," he declared, ushering the group toward the door. He held up his hand to Gavin and Brianna. "Keep your lady here, brother, where there is no chance she may fall from your side where you may not wish to follow."

"But I have to go see them off, too," Brianna cried out and flung herself into the arms of the three women, who already had their arms wrapped tightly around each other.

Katherine turned to her young friend. "Please Brie, do this for me. Quickly, say your goodbye's and stay here where I know Gavin will keep you safe until I return."

Brianna nodded mutely and gave Juliana and Emily a brief hug before she threw herself into Gavin's arms and sobbed out her misery.

Katherine stood there also, in mute silence, holding on to her sisters' hands. "I'm really not sure what else to say that we haven't already said before."

Juliana and Emily both smiled at her, and perhaps this was the way she would like to remember her friends' faces, knowing they would find a lifetime of happiness.

"We'll see each other again, my dear sister. Perhaps not in this lifetime, but surely when we meet back again in the heavens above," Juliana promised.

Katherine smiled and gave them each a kiss on their cheeks. "Well, you know what I've always said about us...I like to think we were together there once before, waiting to come down to this earthly planet. I can see us all just sitting around on a lovely bench, chatting away in a beautiful garden created by our Heavenly Father.

It's why I think we always felt so close from the very first time we met."

"You know, we've felt the same way, too, Katie," Juliana replied honestly.

Katherine gave them one last hug before she whispered in their ears. "Brianna and I will be waiting for the both of you. You'll just take a wee bit longer to join us again, that's all."

"Ah, damn it, Katie," Emily sniffled, "you're gonna make me cry. Anyway, I just may pop back here, from time to time. You know, just to check in and make sure you haven't gotten tired of that handsome devil you married."

"Not a chance, Em."

"Ya never know," Emily said, with a wink toward Riorden.

"Ladies..." Riorden urged, opening the door.

Riorden and Katherine led the way as they raced down the passageway towards the tower where they had traveled more than eight hundred years before. She could feel the necessity to hurry, since they had taken longer rounding up their group than they should have. At last, they finally reached the entrance where they could see the eerie glow, confirming they were right in their assumption that the portal was active.

The two couples took each other's hands and Juliana was about to step forward when a gut wrenching feeling assaulted Katherine. She quickly took hold of Juliana's arm and jerked hard, practically wrenching it from its socket.

"Ouch! What the hell's the matter with you Katie?" she grumbled irritably, rubbing her abused limb.

Katherine watched Riorden intently and waited to see if he came to the same conclusion as she of the premonition she had felt just seconds before. "Well...what do you think?"

He looked down upon her and nodded. "Aye, Kat, you have it aright. 'Tis the wrong way."

"What the heck do you mean, it's the wrong way?" Emily gasped. "We went down these same set of stairs when we traveled through time, remember? I knew this was a bad idea."

She was silenced when Tiernan placed a quick kiss upon her lips.

"Aye, you went down the stairs to travel back in time," Riorden explained and began rushing them through the passageways and toward another tower so they could back track and arrive on the correct side of the portal. "You must go up the stairs to return to your time, or so Katherine and I think."

"It's just a hunch, but it would make sense," Katherine added as she ran to keep up with her husband.

"Just a hunch? You people are all friggin' nuts," Emily yelled. "Do you actually mean to say we would have been hurdled back even further in time just now?" Emily said in a state of panic, and Tiernan's lips met hers again in a hasty kiss to, obviously, shut her up.

"God help us," Juliana prayed.

Katherine was attempting to calm her friends, when Riorden came to a screeching halt as his boots slid across the smooth stones. She could see the tower stairs, and how the future awaited her friends to return back to their own time period. They had but one obstacle to get through that rapidly turned into two, and then three.

Riorden drew his sword as shouting from the corridor brought another into their sight. A total of four obstacles now stood in their path. From the look of things, the king's guards were just as surprised to see the man who they considered an enemy to the crown. The sound of steel being released from the scabbards of Danior and Tiernan echoed in the air as they looked to Riorden for their orders.

"Do not kill them," Riorden commanded. "I will not have their blood on my hands when I must needs answer to my king."

He pushed Katherine behind him, and stumbling, she grabbed Juliana and Emily's hands as they huddled near the entryway to the tower. She could almost feel the pull of the future, trying to urge her into the stairwell in order for her to return to her proper time. But she ignored the prompting and further distanced herself from the steps.

Her gaze traveled to her husband and she swore she held her breath while he engaged first one guard and then another. The three men fought valiantly as the sound of steel clanging against steel resounded loudly in their ears. True to his words, one by one, the guards were knocked senseless and landed in a heap on the floor. Then a fifth guard began running down the passageway, coming to aid his fallen comrades. Riorden again brought up his blade.

"Go," he yelled at Danior and Tiernan, and they grabbed their ladies.

Katherine was torn between watching after her lady friends and keeping an eye on her husband. She saw Riorden stumble and land on one knee upon the floor. Sounds of the footsteps of yet another guard were heard, fast approaching. With her decision made, she gave a quick glance of goodbye to her friends before hurling herself forward. She began pounding her fists on the sixth guard's back, despite the pain she felt from his chainmail underneath his tabard. He stood and began moving backwards, trying to disengage Katherine from around his neck.

"Katherine! Nay!" Riorden yelled as he engaged the newcomer with his blade of steel.

All at once, everything seemed to Katherine as if it occurred in slow motion. She saw how her friends, along with their men, stood in a glowing haze on the steps of the tower, as if they were between two worlds. She could actually see the electric lamps shining brightly on the walls of twenty-first century Bamburgh.

She heard Juliana and Emily, as if they were in a tunnel, call out her name in warning at the same time the guard at last gained his freedom by pushing Katherine off his shoulders. She lost her footing and began toppling backwards to fall inside the turret.

"Riorden!" she screamed out his name with an anguish born of desperation, knowing *Time* was pulling her forward and away from him. She saw his fists swinging at his two adversaries, pelting them until he knocked the guards out, one at a time. He turned and immediately leapt towards the portal.

Reaching out her hand, she felt him firmly grasp it, and yet his face strained with all his might to pull her back to his side. Those unwelcoming tiny lights that originally brought her happily back into the past began to brighten before her eyes. The floor beneath her feet began to tremble. And then she knew without a doubt, while she stared for the last time into her husband's beautiful eyes, what she had dreaded all along would happen. Only another miracle could save them.

CHAPTER 35

Riorden watched the horrified look on his wife's visage and felt a force beyond his ken attempting to rip Katherine from his life. He continued to hold tightly to her hand, even whilst he felt her slipping from his grasp. *Merde!* No one or thing would wrench this woman from his side. She belonged to him, and he would be damned if *Time* would take her. He tugged harder, hoping to bring her back to him, once more.

He watched her mouth moving and was frightened for the first time in his life when her words whispered inside his head, as if she was a ghost, yet again. *Bloody Hell!*

"I love you, Riorden. Throughout all time will I love you..."

"Nay, Katherine. Do not leave me," he bellowed and reached out with his other hand to take a firmer hold upon his wife. "God, I pray, do not take her from me. I beg of You!"

Struggling to maintain his grip, he watched in alarmed fascination as Tiernan and Danior disappeared afore his very eyes while Juliana and Emily stared in shock at their now empty hands. They were at least still with his Katherine, and yet they seemed not of this world whilst they earnestly attempted to reach their friend.

Suddenly, the two women frantically dove forward and gave

Katherine a mighty push, causing his wife to momentarily teeter on the edge, between the present and the future. And then… miracle of all miracles, *Time* released her, as if against its will, and Katherine violently slammed forward into his arms. He crushed her to him as they stumbled onto the floor from the sheer force of power that had held her captive.

"Thank you, God," Riorden whispered whilst he held on to his wife as if he would never let her go.

Katherine swiftly regained her senses and turned, staring for the last time at her friends. The two women became more and more transparent afore her eyes until they were but shadows. Together, they blew her a kiss in a final farewell, took each other by the hand, and vanished into thin air.

Just as quickly, the time gate rapidly diminished with fading, glowing lights. Abruptly, they were cast back into the dimness of the castle and life in the twelfth century. The torches began to sputter, giving off smoke, and all appeared as it should, as if nothing out of the ordinary had just occurred.

There was not much in this life that could cause Riorden to lose his composure, and yet holding his wife as she turned and cried on his shoulder was almost more than he could bear. He swore he was shaking almost as much as Katherine whilst she began to mutter incoherent sentences of what he assumed was gratitude to a higher being. They had much to be thankful for, and he could spend the rest of his days humbly praying and still 'twould not be long enough to show his undying love for this woman God had given back to him.

The guards roused from their stupor upon the floor, quickly rose brandishing their blades, and looked for the threat that was surely surrounding them. In a daze of confusion and seeing nothing unacceptable, they put their swords away and turned to stare at the couple, who stood there, silently waiting to be put under arrest.

"Is the lady not well, my lord?" one of the guards questioned.

"Excuse me?" Katherine whispered as her gaze flew to Riorden, who only shrugged his shoulders.

"Did you perchance fall?" the guard asked again, looking more befuddled than afore.

Riorden watched in surprise whilst the king's men turned as one and began to leave the passageway. The only knight remaining was still looking around, as if some form of trouble was about to sneak up on him.

"There is nothing amiss," Riorden proclaimed whilst tucking Katherine under his arm and holding her as she wiped away her tears. "'Tis just a minor misunderstanding that has been resolved."

The knight nodded, as if at last understanding why the lady had been in tears. "'Tis best they know their place early on in the marriage, my lord. Made the mistake of letting my wife have her way from the start, and now I have a most vile mother-in-law meddling in my affairs, day and night!"

They watched as he nonchalantly turned and strode after the other knights, calling for them to wait up. Stunned, they could only stand in numb silence, wondering what had just occurred and why they were not being led away in chains. 'Twas difficult to comprehend the significance of such a matter and what the outcome would mean to their future.

"I don't get it," Katherine said as her breath left her in a swift rush.

"I am most bemused, as well, Kat," Riorden agreed with a shake of his head. Reaching down, he pulled his wife back into his arms. He felt her shudder until she took another calming breath and raised her face to his. 'Twas the most beautiful sight he had ever beheld in his entire existence.

Her eyes widened, suddenly, and she turned slightly to glance down the corridor where the knights had just left. It was empty now, with no one in sight.

"We changed history," she whispered breathlessly.

"Impossible!" Riorden gasped as he, too, followed her gaze. "There must be another explanation."

"Didn't you see their faces, Riorden? They had no idea they had been chasing Danior and Tiernan before the time gate swallowed them up, or even fighting with us, for that matter."

"An interesting concept and one we can discuss behind the privacy of our locked door," he declared and began ushering her away from the turret he never wished to step into again. "I swear, you shall be lucky if I ever let you out of my bed after the scare you just gave me."

"An interesting proposition and one, I think, deserves further consideration," she said quietly.

Riorden was at a loss for words, so he said nothing, even when she inquired where they were going when they walked past their chamber door. When they came abreast of Aiden's room, the door squeaked open and Patrick poked his head out.

"All went well, my lord?" he asked sheepishly.

"Aye, Patrick. Our friends are where they belong," Riorden answered, bringing Katherine closer to his side.

Patrick looked up and down the passageway, uncertain of its safety. "And are there any more ghosties about, my lord?" he asked, in a shaky voice.

Katherine laughed and reached out to rumple the boy's hair. "None this night you need to worry about, my young friend," she said happily. "Go get some sleep."

Riorden continued onward until they began to climb upwards through another stairwell leading to the battlement walls of the keep. He pulled his wife to his side as they reached the stone wall to gaze out over the ocean as its waves crashed harshly onto the shore. Its sound gave him the soothing relief he had been in need of.

Whilst they stood there, side by side, a feeling of complete peacefulness and contentment filled Riorden's soul and he leaned down to take possession of Katherine's lips. He cupped her face with his hands until she at last gave him a timid smile.

"Why did you bring us here?" she whispered breathlessly.

Riorden smoothed the hair from her face and tucked a strand behind her ear. "Somehow, I thought it appropriate, my love."

Katherine's gaze traveled along the stones and she reached out to feel their surface beneath her fingers. "It does have a special meaning, doesn't it?" She smiled.

"Aye. 'Tis the place where I was first able to touch you. Now that *Time* has given you to me again, I plan on keeping you nearby, Kat," he vowed.

"That was way too close to my liking," she said simply, since no further explanation was necessary.

"Aye, and I pray, never again shall we have a time gate try to steal you away from me."

"I believe we've tempted fate enough for the rest of our lives, don't you?" she asked, with a fleeting look of insecurity as she held tightly to his arm. "Can we do our best to stay away from Bamburgh in the future please?"

He gazed down at his woman and kissed her lips to silence her. If he had his way, they would never step one foot on the grounds for the rest of their lifetime. He would not take the chance of losing her, ever again.

∽

Katherine lay naked, curled up against her husband's side, while she ran her fingers lightly across his chest. Sighing contently from the pleasure he had given her, she moved closer to him and was in high spirits while blissfully listening to his heart beat beneath her ear. It was sure and steady whereas she was positive, just a short while ago, it had been pounding as fiercely as her own. Riorden had taken her to new heights in his love making this night as if to make a point that she belonged to him. She could have sworn they had touched the heavens, and was sure, her feet would never touch the ground again. She felt his rumbling laughter within his chest.

"With such a heavy sigh, should I assume, my sweet, you have no complaints?" he teased while he lifted her so they faced one another, side by side, on their pillows.

She touched his cheek and shivered when he placed a kiss on the inside of her palm. "If I were any happier, I'd...well...to be honest, I don't know how I could be happier than I am at this moment."

"I see I shall have to strive to prove to you throughout our years that each day can only get better, as long as you are by my side, sharing my life."

"I know we'll have many happy years together, my dearest Riorden."

"Aye, that we shall, for somewhere in time, I have found you, and I plan on never giving you back," he vowed, kissing her lips.

"I'll be loving you throughout all eternity," she said with all her heart.

"As I will love you, my dearest wife," he declared, rolling her beneath him, and he magically began to show her just what the future would hold for her as his wife.

Hours later, as Katherine watched her husband sleeping, she could only wonder what the future held in store for them, once they reached Warkworth Castle. She could almost hear *Scarlett O'Hara's* voice saying how she'd worry later about all her troubles another day. Perhaps, tomorrow would take care of itself.

Katherine curled up once more on her husband's chest and felt the warmth of his arm wrap around her, bringing her closer. Reaching up, she began to twirl a piece of his hair between her fingers while still pondering the mysteries of life.

She had learned at least one lesson from her journey across time. For in between the past, present, and future, there seemingly lays a finite line where time has no meaning, and the courage to follow one's dreams resides. Only she can know when, in the course of her own life, the right time to take those first crucial steps of making those ideas a reality will come. She smiled, thinking it was never too late to go after her deepest desires.

For Katherine had indeed followed her heart, even if *Time* had to give her a little push towards having those dreams come true. Against the most improbable odds, she had found her knight in shining armor, and he was everything she could have asked for in a husband, and more.

Riorden...even his name sweetly thought of in her mind brought a feeling of confidence, knowing forever across time, their souls would somehow manage to find one another. Only within his arms had she found the one thing she had been in search of all her life. Katherine had at last found true love, for Riorden had given her the gift of tomorrow. She was home.

EPILOGUE

San Francisco, Present Day
Six Months Later

The dimly lit coffee shop was filled to the brim with people complaining about the long line, along with other noisy conversations, as the customers waited impatiently for their turn at the counter. For two, the clamoring voices didn't make one bit of difference as their nimble fingers practically flew across the keyboards of their laptops. They had been inspired during the past several months and had almost completed their latest manuscripts. Their "babies" were almost ready to take the next vital step toward publication.

Emily grabbed her backpack, withdrew a packet of tissues, and dabbed at her eyes. "Damn...that is just so friggin' awesome, if I do say so myself," she announced as she shut the cover and reached for her strawberries and cream Frappuccino.

Juliana hit the save button, and she also closed her laptop and put it away with a laugh. "I'm almost done, too. I hope we don't have to do much time traveling in our future to get some form of inspiration for our next endeavors, though," she said, taking a sip of her coffee. "I don't think I could handle it twice in one lifetime, thank you very much."

Emily gazed around the shop sadly. "It still feels like such a bizarre and crazy dream, doesn't it, Jewel's? I mean, who would have thought we'd travel back to the twelfth century, let alone get the opportunity to come back home."

"I sometimes have to pinch myself to make sure I'm not dreaming," Juliana confessed, "and yet I know we were there, seeing as we're missing a couple of sisters here at our table."

Emily sniffled again. "Ah, please Jewel's, don't remind me of that again, will ya? I swear, all I've done is cry my eye's out for the past six months. I thought, I was made of sterner stuff than to become some pansy, like Katie."

Juliana laughed. "Now wouldn't *that* be something she'd just love to hear. I can almost hear her cheery voice, right now, ringing out in laughter as you call *yourself* a pansy for a change."

"She would've loved that, wouldn't she?" Emily said as a sob tore at her heart.

Juliana reached out a comforting hand. "What is it, Em?"

Tears filled Emily's eyes, once more. "We've just lost so much, Jewels, and I hate talking about Katie and Brie in the past tense. It was only months ago that we were all sitting here together, planning our vacation."

"Yes, dear, I know, but look what we've gained..." Juliana replied in a reassuring tone.

"But they should all be here, too," Emily grumbled, reaching for another tissue. "It's just not fair. I feel so empty without them and–"

"Oh, for heaven's sake," Juliana huffed as the door to the coffee shop opened to admit another pair of patrons.

Was it Emily's imagination, or did the place seem to quiet down when the two newcomers entered. She looked up from the tissue she held over her eyes to see who could cause such a ruckus. She wasn't surprised to see two of the most handsome men she had ever laid eyes on scan the room. Admiring their physique while she could, she noticed how their jeans fit their legs just right while their shirts hung open at the collar and fit their chests snuggly. Their laughter rang out in merriment, causing many female eyes to rake their forms, as if they were stripping them naked and enjoying the view in the process.

"Tiernan!" Juliana called out and the two men advanced toward their corner booth.

Emily felt him slide in next to her and, before she could voice any words, he kissed her most soundly.

"Tiernan…really…we're in public," Emily said in a snit, although it was hard to stay mad at the man when he looked at her as he did.

"Aye, that we are my beautiful wife. I must admit, I like the tradition o' how Lady Katherine asked me to get yer mind off yer troubles," he responded, and kissed her even deeper this time. "Has she been at it long, Juliana?"

Juliana's short snort of laughter, which she covered quickly with her hand, escaped her before she could stop it then she glanced sidelong at Danior. "Long enough, I'd say."

"Stop yer crying, Em. We're about to embark on another grand adventure," Tiernan declared, with a wide grin of pleasure.

Juliana turned to Danior. "You've been to the post office? You have the package we've been waiting for from Simon?" she asked anxiously.

"Aye, Jewel's, that we do, and the Lady Katherine was right," Danior said, wrapping his arm around his lady and giving her a hug. "Simon took almost the whole lot of coins with the exception of what Tiernan and I kept for…how do you say this? Ah, yes…for a rainy day. We are bloody rich, I tell you! I cannot wait until we return to English soil so I can see firsthand what some of our money has bought us."

"I'll miss living here," Juliana said softly. "I never thought I'd live anywhere else but in my own country."

Danior pulled her closer to his side and tilted her chin up so he could stare into her mesmerizing green eyes. "Second thoughts, my lovely wife?"

"Oh no…never Danior. It's just a big adjustment, that's all," she said, with a timid smile.

Tiernan's laughter rang out. "'Twill not be as hard as the one *we've* had o'er the past few months. The cruise ship that brought us here was indeed most splendid as was our drive across yer glorious country. Who would have thought a place could be so grand? Truly amazing!"

He leaned forward and their group drew their heads closer so they could hear his whispered words. "I canna wait 'til I get on that..." his brow furrowed thoughtfully. "What did you call it, Em?"

"An airplane, babe," Emily replied, with a short laugh as she clasped his hand in her own.

"Can ye imagine a machine made o' metal able to fly us high up into the heavens?" Tiernan said in wonder.

Danior shook his head. "Nay, I cannot, and yet these modern time machines can supposedly also fly a man to the moon," he retorted with a shake of his head, "although I still do not believe such rubbish."

"'Tis almost as wonderful as those horseless carriages I canna wait to get my hands on," Tiernan exclaimed with a roguish smile, rubbing his hands together in anticipation.

Emily groaned at the prospect of her husband behind the wheel of a car, and yet her heart gave a small leap, watching his gorgeous, smiling face light up in excitement.

Juliana leaned forward, placing a kiss upon her husband's cheek. "You have a lot to learn about our time, Danior, but I'll be with you every step of the way."

He quickly kissed her lips. "You had better be, Juliana. I do not relish being stranded in this strange time of yours without you by my side."

"I promise, you'll never have to worry about that," she said breathlessly.

"I shall endeavor to hold you to your word, my love, but here," he said handing her a rather large manila envelope. "Surely, your curiosity must be driving you mad, wondering what our friend from across the pond, as you say, has sent us."

Juliana reached for the envelope with shaking fingers and handed it to Emily. "Here Em, you do the honors. I'm trembling so badly, I'm afraid I might spill coffee all over it."

Emily took the envelope and began carefully opening the package. Peeking inside, she saw a smaller envelope, which she opened first. With tears in her eyes, she took out a couple of brochures and laid them on the table for her friends to see.

"Look!" she said, amazed at what she was actually seeing. "It's

Warkworth and Berwyck Castles, and they're in pristine condition. How the hell did that happen?"

Juliana passed on one of the pamphlets to Danior, who whistled, while Tiernan opened the other.

"Looks to me like they changed their past," Juliana explained, "or their future."

"Maybe, in the long scheme of things, it's all just one and the same," Emily said in wonder.

Tiernan picked up another sheet of paper. "Here Emily, read this. 'Tis a letter from Simon."

Emily took the document from her husband. She took a deep breath before unfolding the letter and then began to read.

My Dear Friends:
I am sure you will be just as surprised to see, from the contents of this envelope, that a recent change of events has radically altered the course of history. I have made discreet inquiries to several of my colleagues, but I can find nothing in any of my research over the past several months to prove beyond any shadow of doubt that Berwyck and Warkworth Castles are not anything but what you see in the brochures I have sent you.

When you asked me to do a bit of studying on the matter, I had thought you were both daft, and yet my curiosity was piqued at the prospect of what I might uncover. For some reason, I alone seem to be the only person who remembers history for what was a fact but a few short months ago. I had been to both estates numerous times in the past and saw with my own eyes the crumbling and decaying walls of the two castles. Yet today, they stand in meticulous condition, owned by the same families for several generations.

I am sure you will be amazed by the photograph I have had reprinted for you. Although I was unable to get the original painting, I did, however, obtain larger framed copies, which I will have for you both at your new place of residences, once you reach England. I think, you will be most pleased by what your eyes will behold.
I look forward to further conversations with you all.

Cordially Yours,
Simon Armstrong

Emily took the picture out of the envelope and laid it on the table so everyone could see it at the same time. Carefully, she peeled back the protective paper to reveal the treasure beneath. Immediately, she sat back in her seat and could only stare in wonder at what was before her eyes.

It was a rather large family portrait, with Warkworth Castle as a backdrop. Katherine and Brianna sat together on a stone bench, clasping each other's hands, with Riorden and Gavin, standing tall behind them. They were older, and their children sitting with them gave an indication as to their age.

Brianna looked radiantly happy, with her four children of various ages sitting around her. Emily could only surmise what a handful the two boys had been, as they appeared close in age. The girls, on the other hand, looked like two, demure, young ladies of breeding, and Emily could only wonder how far off the mark she was in her assumption.

Her gaze fell to Katherine and the serene look within the depths of her blue-green eyes. She appeared to be about in her mid-forties. Riorden had his right hand resting on one of her shoulders. The other was on the hilt of his sword. His jet-black hair was worn shorter with a hint of grey residing at his temples. But it was his eyes that remained the same spectacular color, drawing one in to wonder what he was thinking. No matter his age, he still had that commanding presence that always seemed to surround him.

Their son stood next to his father. There was no mistaking who his sire was as he was an exact replica with the exception of his hair, which was the same color as Katherine's. His eyes looked steel-grey. Emily thought he was, maybe, twenty years old, give or take a couple of years.

The second child, a daughter, sat next to her mother with a book open on her lap and appeared to be, perhaps, three years or so younger than the older boy. Her long, blondish-brown hair had been pulled back and was braided with flowers. She had an innocence about her that even a picture clearly showed, and Emily had some unknown feeling within her that this girl loved to write and sing.

The last family member was a little girl of maybe eight years of age, with hair as black as midnight, just like her father's, and clear blue eyes. She sat at Katherine's feet, although one could almost tell it was done reluctantly. She had a bright smile on her pixie like features, which could be due to the antics of a black puppy with a curly tail, lying next to her. Or maybe her expression was from being young at heart. In either case, Emily just knew this one had kept her parents constantly on their toes.

Emily reached over and firmly grasped Juliana's hand. The two women turned as one to look upon each other, with tears in their eyes until, in unison, they began to stare once more with loving fondness at the picture of their dearest friends.

At last, they had the answer they had been searching for, and yet, perhaps, they had known it in their hearts all along. Just as Emily and Juliana had found love and never regretted their decisions to return to the present, the same held true for their twelfth century sisters. They, too, had found true happiness, for it was as if the pinkish cherry blossoms depicted along the edges of the picture were a sign made just for them.

The faintest smell of their floral essence reached Emily's nose just as surely as she watched Katherine's smile broaden, ever so slightly. She turned to Juliana and they both broke out in laughter as they hugged one another.

Time truly was endless. Their friendship had and would always endure...

AUTHOR'S NOTE & ACKNOWLEDGEMENT

Author's Note & Acknowledgement

There are several matters I would like to clarify as to the historical accuracy of this novel. First and foremost, *For All of Ever* is a work of fiction.

Bamburgh Castle does date back to 547 A.D. when its history was first recorded. It's been called the home to the Kings of Northumbria. The keep is the oldest surviving part of the castle and its construction began in 1164. Any references to the armory, tunnels, and a room of artifacts or collections in the castle's lower levels are entirely from my imagination. For purposes of my story, King Henry II arrives at Bamburgh to reside.

Lord William George Armstrong bought Bamburgh from his distant relative in 1894 in the hope of restoring the buildings and grounds so the place would be made available for retired gentlemen. He died before he could see the project completed. Since he had no children, his nephew and only heir, William Watson Armstrong, completed his great Uncle's dream in 1903 by making Bamburgh a private home for retirees. The Armstrong's continue to own Bamburgh castle today. However, Simon Armstrong and Tiernan Cavanaugh are both fictional characters.

The ghost story of a knight haunting Bamburgh is also a work of fiction although the storyline is similar to the castle's most famous ghost, *The Pink Lady*. You can find more information on several ghost sightings, Bamburgh's history, and visiting the castle on Bamburgh's official webpage. If you have a love of castles, you will enjoy perusing this extensive and informative site.

Berwyck Castle is an imaginary castle although, as I mentioned in the author notes in *If My Heart Could See You*, there was a castle at Berwick-upon-Tweed at one time. The majority of its stones have been reused for other foundations nearby.

Warkworth Castle is still standing as it has over the centuries and was passed back and forth by the Percy family and the Royal family since 1332 when Edward III granted Warkworth and its castle to Henry de Percy II. Enormously expensive to maintain, the Duke of Northumberland passed Warkworth Castle to the nation in 1922. Having both Berwyck and Warkworth in pristine condition at the end of *For All of Ever* is fictional on my part, as the author of this story.

Second, I would again like to thank several people for all their support while I completed this novel.

To my mother and daughter Jessica – yes, I know…there's not a whole lot of conversation going on with me when I'm absorbed in my writing or editing. Thank you both for all your understanding, encouragement, and patience, especially when I freak out about marketing my already published first novel *If My Heart Could See You*. You two are my voice of sanity helping me to keep all this together and I love you both very much.

To Tricia Linden – the best critique partner a woman could ever have. You continue to keep me motivated and excited about my writing. I'm very thankful and grateful for our friendship.

To Barbara Millman Cole – I'm so happy you were recommended to me as an editor. You continue to make my work shine. Thank you!

To Evangeline Gaff, Mimi Madsen, and Jessica Makens – Thank you ladies for breathing life into Brianna, Emily, Juliana, and, of course, their significant medieval knights. Without your inspiration, this story wouldn't have been half the fun it was to compose. This novel is for all of you!

Last, but not least, I would like to express my sincere thanks to you, dear reader, for choosing my second novel, *For All of Ever*. You may be wondering what happens next for Katherine and Riorden. The sequel, *Only For You*, will be out soon. *Only For You* continues Riorden and Katherine's story as they journey to Warkworth where they will meet with devious, scheming and ambivalent trials that test their wills to remain together.

I hope you enjoyed reading *For All of Ever* as much as I enjoyed writing about the adventures, fortunes, and loves of my characters. If you found my book a fun read, nothing would make me happier than for you to go to the retailers and write a nice review. It's the best way you can help support me as an Indie Author trying to make a name for myself. I appreciate each and every kind word that has been given to my debut historical romance, *If My Heart Could See You*. My readers are the reason my first published novel became an eBook bestseller. Thank you again for all your support!

With Warm Regards, Sherry Ewing

OTHER BOOKS BY SHERRY EWING

Medieval & Time Travel Series

Knight of Darkness: The Knights of the Anarchy (Book One)

Sometimes finding love can become our biggest weakness…

Knight of Chaos: The Knights of the Anarchy (Book Two)

In the chaos of war, can one knight defy the odds to find peace with the woman warrior he loves?

Knight of Havoc: The Knights of the Anarchy (Book Three)

One lone knight. One strongminded maiden. When duty wars with love at first sight, which will win?

To Love A Scottish Laird: De Wolfe Pack Connected World

Sometimes you really can fall in love at first sight…

To Love An English Knight: De Wolfe Pack Connected World

Can a chance encounter lead to love?

If My Heart Could See You: The MacLarens, A Medieval Romance (Book One)

When you're enemies, does love have a fighting chance?

For All of Ever: The Knights of Berwyck, A Quest Through Time (Book One)

Sometimes to find your future, you must look to the past…

Only For You: The Knights of Berwyck, A Quest Through Time (Book Two)

Sometimes it's hard to remember that true love conquers all, only after the battle is over…

Hearts Across Time: The Knights of Berwyck (Books One & Two)

Sometimes all you need is to just believe… Hearts Across Time is a special edition box set that combines Katherine and Riorden's stories together from *For All of Ever* and *Only For You.*

A Knight To Call My Own: The MacLarens, A Medieval Romance (Book Two)

When your heart is broken, is love still worth the risk?

To Follow My Heart: The Knights of Berwyck, A Quest Through Time (Book Three)

Love is a leap. Sometimes you need to jump…

The Piper's Lady: The MacLaren's, A Medieval Romance (Book Three)

True love binds them. Deceit divides them. Will they choose love?

Love Will Find You: The Knights of Berwyck, A Quest Through Time (Book Four)

Sometimes a moment is all we have…

One Last Kiss: The Knights of Berwyck, A Quest Through Time (Book Five)

Sometimes it takes a miracle to find your heart's desire…

Promises Made At Midnight: The Knights of Berwyck, A Quest Through Time (Book Six)

Make a wish…

It Began With A Kiss: The MacLarens, A Medieval Romance (Book Four)

Sometimes you need to listen when your heart begins to sing…

Regency

A Kiss For Charity: A de Courtenay Novella (Book One)

Love heals all wounds but will their pride keep them apart?

The Earl Takes A Wife: A de Courtenay Novella (Book Two)

It began with a memory, etched in the heart.

Before I Found You: A de Courtenay Novella (Book Three)

A quest for a title. An encounter with a stranger. Will she choose love?

Nothing But Time: A Family of Worth (Book One)

They will risk everything for their forbidden love…

One Moment In Time: A Family of Worth (Book Two)

One moment in time may be enough, if it lasts forever…

A Love Beyond Time: A Family of Worth (Book Three) in the Bluestocking Belles' boxset *Under the Harvest Moon*

Can love at first sight be reborn after heartbreak, proving a second chance is all you need?

Under the Mistletoe

A new suitor seeks her hand. An old flame holds her heart. Which one will she meet under the kissing bough?

A Mistletoe Kiss in the Bluestocking Belles boxset *Belles & Beaux* (2022)

All she wants for Christmas is a mistletoe kiss…

A Second Chance At Love

Can the bittersweet frost of lost love be rekindled into a burning flame?

A Countess to Remember

Sometimes love finds you when you least expect it…

To Claim A Lyon's Heart: Lyon's Den Connected World

A gambler's bet. A widow's burden. Will one game of chance change their lives?

The Lyon and His Promise

A gentleman's lifetime regret. A widow's tarnished reputation. Can they repair the past to create a bright future together?

You can find out more about Sherry's work on her website at www.SherryEwing.com and at online retailers.

SOCIAL MEDIA FOR SHERRY EWING

You can learn more about Sherry Ewing at these social media links:

Amazon Author Page: http://amzn.to/1TrWtoy
Bluestocking Belles: http://bluestockingbelles.net/
Bookbub: www.bookbub.com/authors/sherry-ewing
Dragonblade Publishing: https://www.dragonbladepublishing.com/team/sherry-ewing/
Facebook: www.Facebook.com/SherryEwingAuthor
Goodreads: www.Goodreads.com/author/show/8382315.Sherry_Ewing
Instagram: https://instagram.com/sherry.ewing
Pinterest: www.Pinterest.com/SherryLEwing
TikTok: https://www.tiktok.com/@sherryewingauthor
X: www.x.com/Sherry_Ewing
YouTube: http://www.youtube.com/SherryEwingauthor
Newsletter Sign Up: http://bit.ly/2vGrqQM
Facebook Street Team:
www.facebook.com/groups/799623313455472/
Facebook Official Fan page: https://www.facebook.com/groups/356905935241836/

ABOUT SHERRY EWING

Sherry Ewing picked up her first historical romance when she was a teenager and has been hooked ever since. An award-winning and best-selling author, she writes historical and time travel romances to awaken the soul one heart at a time. When not writing, she can be found in the San Francisco area at her day job as an Information Technology Specialist.

Learn more about Sherry where a new adventure awaits you on ever page:

Website: www.SherryEwing.com
Email: Sherry@SherryEwing.com

Printed in Dunstable, United Kingdom